The Somewhere Aching Series

A DAUGHTER TO DIE FOR

book one

Tanya Madsen

Published by
Aching Hearts Press*
Stories that bruise beautifully™

Roy, Utah, United States
www.tanyamadsen.com

ISBN: 978-1-970593-00-6
Cover design by Tanya Madsen
Interior formatting by Tanya Madsen

To Rich, who gave me the courage.

The course of true love never did run smooth.

William Shakespeare,

A Midsummer Night's Dream

Table of Contents

Friday ~ Day 1

Chapter 1

Judith

Judith Monroe was an angry girl, and she wouldn't deny it. She despised her pathetic mother, her dirtbag father, her bratty sister, and all nine of her ex-boyfriends and nineteen hookups ranging from reasons like excessive nerdiness to excessive drugginess. She even hated the smart one. What was his name, Lance? For being too damn smart.

Everyone had the same effect on her. They tried to make her feel like the losers they were. She wasn't a loser. She was a victim. A survivor of a future wrecked by parents who put themselves first and left her to come in last for the rest of her life. At almost twenty years old, she had plenty of life left in her. What was she supposed to do now that her whole purpose for existing was gone?

"Judith" was another reason she hated her mother. Seriously? Judith? What a terrible name to curse a beautiful girl with, regardless of whether it once belonged to some war heroine way up in the branches of her family tree or not. It was damn ugly! And a constant embarrassment for her at all the beauty pageants her parents thrust her into for years, then abruptly cut her off when the divorce drained all their resources.

Judith used to be a perennial queen. No one could match her allure. Now, thanks to her parents, her attributes were all going to waste. Growing up, there were dancing and acting classes, voice lessons and martial arts—the works. Judith was their prize, and she loved that it was she and not her stupid sister who kept her parents together. When the world could see, they were about as compatible as pickles and ice cream, her dad being the ice cream. Who was she stuck living with? The pickle.

Judith glared at her gorgeous reflection. Time to slip on her bridesmaid's dress and look stunning. Too bad she couldn't wear it to a competition and take home a trophy instead of to this bullshit wedding.

Her new stepmom was like gooey chocolate syrup. She drowned out all the best parts of ice-cream dad with her loud voice and lewd jokes, to which he replied by turning red and playing dumb.

While Judith appreciated his need to rebound as far as possible from her mother in personality and appearance, she couldn't understand why he had to marry the hag. Lori wasn't worth the hassle and spent all her time smothering any hopes of an inheritance for his daughters with her insatiable lust for shopping.

After high school, her dad refused to pay for her modeling career. He suggested that she get a job instead. Now she worked as a server in a restaurant and it sucked. Mom was trying to relive her twenties by returning to college, and there was no money anywhere. She sighed in despair. Life was so unfair. She stared at the long shelf covered in beauty pageant trophies and feared they meant nothing now. Which meant she meant nothing now.

Judith watched the curtains start to blow wildly at her window. It smelled like rain, which was good for her current mood and bad for her gown. This whole thing was a farce. Dad had been shacking up with Lori ever since he left Mom. Why the marriage facade? To appease the guilt for what they did to his family? And then there was her mom. Still hung up on a guy who treated her like shit. It was embarrassing.

"Judith? Do you need help with your hair?"

Her mom knocked, then shook the handle. Was there no end to the irritation? She still pretended she was a pageant mom, waiting with the curling iron and hairspray.

"No, Mom. Of course, I don't!"

"What about the dress? Does it still fit?"

"Yes!" What was she trying to insinuate? Bitch.

"Okay, we need to leave in less than ten minutes."

"Fine, Mom. I still don't know why we are doing this."

"I know. It seems ridiculous, even to me. Now hurry. Lizzy and I are waiting."

Perfect little Lizzy. A straight-A student who graduated from high school a year early and was now a college girl, mom's bestie, so sweet and good, got everything she wanted and everyone loved her best—little brat.

Life was hell with her mom and sister. Her only hope was that her dad would relent and take her to live with him once the honeymoon ended with psycho-shopping Lori, or she'd move into a homeless shelter. At this point, anything was better than this.

Judith listened to her mom walk away, then plopped down on her bed and considered her place in life. She was beautiful, but that was useless these days. Sure, people stared at her and guys lusted after her, but that meant nothing. Secretly, she wanted to find someone who could rescue her from her stagnant life. That seemed impossible. All the guys she had met sucked. A bunch of losers partying it up on their daddy's dime looking for a free whore. Not their soulmate.

She had a ton of unresolved pain from her childhood. Being a perennial trophy winner wasn't all rainbows and sunshine. Too many maelstroms were eager to cast their shadows on innocent things, such as pretty young girls. Worse, it wasn't she who enjoyed the accolades but her parents. Mainly her dad. The same one who dumped her for Hag-Lori.

It was all too much. She couldn't cry. She wouldn't cry. She hadn't seen her dad in months and didn't want to witness him marry that bitch. It would kill her. Her eyes burned as she tried not to think of all her dad memories. He was such a wonderful dad before Lori. Why had he changed? If only she could read his mind.

One thing was clear. It would take a perfect man to incite her to fall in love. She would never let a man do to her what Dad did to Mom. She would bring down all her considerable pent-up wrath on any man who hurt her. Burn him into dead meat. She'd turn into Black Widow or even Harley Quinn and make him regret it.

To make herself feel better, Judith mentally relived all the many competitions where she heard those words "And the winner is!" Why was life so cruel? It wasn't for all her friends who were now partying it up at out-of-state schools or making wedding plans. Judith had no idea where she was going in life. She had always focused on beauty pageants instead of academics, convinced that it was her looks that would take her places. It turned out that beauty wasn't enough. You also needed money—lots of it.

Judith wanted to curse, scream, and throw one of her usual fits, but contained herself. Now wasn't the time to vent but to pretend. Time for competition mode. Smile prettily and prance down the aisle in front of the sleaze her dad chose over his favorite daughter, who was once affectionately known as his *one and only weakness.*

Presently, she had even more pressing matters—a matching sandal to find and her cell phone to charge and not forget. She had fistfuls of lustrous waves to scorch into bridesmaid curls and layers of carbon-black mascara to apply. Followed by dozens of tears to blink back from leaking past her rigid barriers and ruining her dry-clean-only pale-pink satin.

Chapter 2

Martha

Every relationship has a moment where a couple must decide if their devotion can last forever. After deliberation and sleepless nights, sometimes the result of passion, at other times the aftermath of a quarrel, they must weigh their emotions against their memories and decide. Is the fighting worth the making up? Are the debts worth the purchase? Does the laughter cancel the tears? At that moment, the lovers commit no matter the cost or call it quits.

For Martha, that call-it-quits moment came twenty years and two months into her marriage. It was an unremarkable winter day, and she was on her way to school when the text from Craig popped up.

> I'm sorry, love. We're done. I'm leaving you. I met someone else. Let's talk more about it over dinner tonight. Meet me at the Bongo Lounge at six.

Martha pulled into a gas station and reread the text. She should have seen it coming. Two months earlier, on their twentieth anniversary, she pledged her heart and soul in a lengthy addition to a soppy card that he was her one and only. She should have taken his apology for losing the card as a sign. He probably threw it out, as she later learned that he had been sleeping with Lori for a year. Why had her heart deceived her? Convinced her that, despite appearances and a history of incompatibility and loneliness, they were meant for each other? So much for gut instinct.

Martha had struggled for years to become a psychologist. Then, three years ago, she decided to return to school to pursue her doctorate and aspire to a professorship. Now, she was a broke post-grad student living on loans and spending all her spare time drafting a one-hundred-thousand-word thesis. Ironically, marriage counseling was her specialty.

Her colleagues thought she was insane for attending the wedding ceremony of the man who cheated on her. She tried to explain to them that it wasn't to provide moral support to Craig or vainly try to win him back, but to prove to everyone she was stronger than she was. She needed to appear over it and moving on. Whatever that looked like, that's how she wanted to seem.

He left her for Lori, but it had little to do with her, she told herself a dozen times a day. At least that's what everyone said. Her therapist, her mother, and even Craig swore she was the picturesque wife and perfect mom, just not for him.

Martha dug around in her small jewelry case for her rhinestone bracelet and earring set and slipped on heels. She tried not to study her reflection in the mirror as she applied eyeliner and a dash of mascara to accentuate her hazel eyes. She chose classic colors to blend with her olive skin, which was once flawless but was now starting to wrinkle like crêpe paper. Pretty like a wilting rose—one you pressed into a book. She was an antique. No wonder Craig replaced her. She left the best of herself behind in her twenties.

Martha re-spritzed her chignon, which lopped to one side, tucked her curls and secured them with bobby pins. Her dark hair was a hopeless wavy mop. She compared it to Lori's straightened blonde mane and laughed. Other than helping him build his concrete-pouring empire in the community, what did Craig ever see in her?

She exited her cluttered bedroom and, in the hallway, gathered her thoughts. Why was she doing this again? Oh yes, to prove to herself that she was strong. Because the girls needed closure, which Craig's marriage would provide. He left them as much as he did her, and they were equally devastated. So why did the right thing feel like the wrong thing to do?

There were so many combustible moments before making it to the car that it was like maneuvering through a minefield. Judith was wearing too much makeup, but when Martha tried blending the smudges from her mascara, Judith swore under her breath. Lizzy had gained a few pounds since the dress fitting, and the seams were so close to bursting that Martha had her slip into sweats for the ride at the last moment. Lizzy's change led to a fight in which Judith begged to change. Martha refused. She couldn't handle getting both daughters dressed and ready at the venue, and they were out of time. If they didn't leave now they'd be late. Only two years apart in age, the sisters weren't enemies but they weren't friends either. Lizzy was laid-back and needed her mom to stick up for her, and Judith was chronically antagonistic.

While waiting at the light to enter the freeway, Martha suddenly sensed the gravity of her decision. Sometimes it was impossible to live up to her own sweet nature. How could Craig demand this? He offered to compensate her for the gas but she declined. Too proud to let the only man she ever loved know how deep it hurt to be thrown a few twenties as he rode off into the sunset with Lori.

When Lori asked to have the girls be her bridesmaid and flower girl, Craig wouldn't stop begging, probably because she had no relatives willing to walk down the aisle with her for the fourth time. Martha didn't relent for Lori. She did it for Craig. He still had that effect on her. That lopsided grin and wild energy had always won her heart, and he knew it. Lori had stolen everything from her, and the last thing she wanted to do was make her wedding dreams come true, but here she was.

The girls were thirsty, so Martha pulled off the freeway to gas up and please her darling brats. Martha gave them cash for fountain drinks and smiled as they scampered across the parking lot. It brought back memories of road trips to Judith's beauty pageants and the occasional vacation.

Judith wasn't in the least bit embarrassed to be traipsing around in her skimpy formal. Martha watched her preen and prance, basking in the attention of every human in the parking lot, always the beauty queen.

The girls returned with ICEEs instead.

"Isn't it a little too cold for those?"

Martha noted the goose bumps popping up on their forearms as they sipped greedily in the cooling late-March afternoon. It had rained all day, and although there was a break in the downpour, it would start up again at any moment.

"You cold, Mom?" Lizzy asked.

"No, but I will be hitting this place on the way back for a coffee. Come on. We're gonna be late."

"Hey, Mom, will you make Lizzy let me use her phone since you refused to return and get mine?"

Martha sighed and rolled her eyes.

"Can we just let it go? You can't survive one night?"

"How am I supposed to survive a sixty-minute drive to the middle of nowhere, a long boring ceremony, a corny reception and a tiresome ride home without my goddamn phone? You know how I hate doing this wedding thing. Without a distraction, it will be unbearable."

"I'll let you borrow mine. Good enough?"

Martha watched Judith decide. It wasn't quite the triumph of watching Lizzy surrender her phone, but a close second.

"Sure, I guess."

Martha smiled like a super mom—a genius at compromise.

"Can I use it now?"

Martha reached into her purse and handed Judith her phone.

"Here are my AirPods, too."

"Thanks!"

Judith grabbed them and flounced into the back seat.

Back on the freeway, Martha glanced in the rearview mirror. Judith found a blanket and cuddled up despite her heels and curls, making her look like the spoiled little girl her father had once been so proud of.

Martha loved her daughters. They were her life. Her reason for getting up and going to work, cleaning, cooking, and holding on. If it weren't for them, she would have crumbled when Craig left. She would be worse than alone, more like the people she helped and the patients she read studies on. Quite likely, she'd be traumatized for life.

Chapter 3

Nicolas

What am I looking for?

A woman who will love me, who I can make happy, who will never leave me.

What's it gonna take?

Seducing her with my mad Casanova skills.

Who's it gonna be?

A perfect replica of the one who abandoned me.

You can do this, Nicolas!

Nicolas recited this to himself in the bathroom mirror.

This is what it took to make your dreams come true. Constant self-talk.

He dressed and groomed himself carefully for another grueling night of working as a server for Lazique Catering. His beauty was his secret weapon, and he never knew when lightning would strike. He had to remain vigilant.

His soulmate was out there, and she was the reason he was still hanging on, trying to survive this lonely life. Maybe he'd meet her tonight. He certainly hoped so.

Nicolas was sick of sleeping around. Seducing women was expensive, time-consuming and heartbreaking. But he had no choice. He needed to find the Replacement, fix the past or die trying. Why was his quest for love so difficult? He was a near-perfect guy. A little crazy but mostly perfect. Where the hell was she hiding, this girl of his dreams? Every time Nicolas seduced a lady, he felt like he was betting on the roulette wheel, watching it spin and spin and land on every number but his.

Nicolas swallowed all his pills with disgust. Why couldn't he be a normal person? Why did he have to be mentally ill? Why couldn't his good looks and excessive charm win him his soulmate? He was desperate and lonely and obsessive was his middle name. At this point, he'd settle for anyone as long as they were even a bit like the one who abandoned him.

He returned to invoking The Secret. He had read the inspirational book *The Secret* when he was twelve years old and knew instantly that it was the answer to all his prayers. He believed in self-talk and knew it was his only option because, so far, no one in his twenty-five years had stepped up and shown him even a glimmer of love. Still, he was determined to get some love, and all it took was making a single woman fall for his ample charms.

I am irresistible, I am sweet, I am loved.

Not "I will be loved." That suggested something that would happen in the future.

No. "I am loved." He had to psych himself out into believing he deserved it right now. That was invoking The Secret.

He tucked in his white shirt and coiffed his thick, dark hair. Applied cologne and stared at his beautiful reflection. There wasn't a single reason he wouldn't find love. Over seven billion people out there, half of them women! Someone had to have a heart compatible with his.

Nicolas wandered through his dad's house and wondered if he should stop by to say hello. Na. Later. Then he headed out to his dad's car. Time for work. Game on. Hopefully, tonight was the night. His soulmate would walk right out of his dreams and into his arms. Where he eagerly waited to carry her away to his own private universe.

Chapter 4

Martha

Martha rolled down Highway 189 following the navigation directions to Heber and headed east on Lake Creek Road, where the Timber Moose Lodge sat tucked away in a forest next to a small lake. The marriage ceremony would be followed by a catered dinner, a stocked bar, and a live band. Craig and Lori rented the whole lodge for the night and booked many guests into the luxury rooms.

They joined a long line of cars until a valet knocked on Martha's window. Martha got out and handed him the key and Judith yelled,

"Remember not to lock the doors, please? My sister and I plan to hang out in the car tonight. So, thank you."

Cowed by her beauty and nodding, he climbed into the driver's seat. Martha grabbed Lizzy's dress off the door grip in the back seat and herded her girls towards a beautiful lodge surrounded by aspen and pine.

Martha avoided the front entrance, a massive set of stairs leading through huge doors. She dragged them around the back, looking for another way to the dressing room. She weaved through a flock of servers taking a break from the kitchen.

"Excuse me." She waved to no one in particular, "Can you show me a secret way to the dressing room, please? We have a member of the wedding party unfit to be seen." She laughed, and everyone stared at Lizzy.

A heavy-set woman with remarkable dreadlocks smiled and said, "I got you. Follow me."

Martha followed, accidentally bumping into a server. He turned around, and they locked eyes. She gasped. He was the best-looking guy she had ever laid eyes on in her life. She touched his shoulder apologetically.

"I'm sorry. I'm a klutz. Nerves, I guess."

Martha felt his gaze on her as she hurried through the door, reminding herself that male attention was the last thing she wanted tonight.

To her chagrin, Craig was waiting, looking fabulous in a tux, his red hair styled and a surprising tan to his ruddy complexion that made his green eyes pop. Gorgeous as ever.

"What took you so long? Why isn't she dressed?" He pointed to Lizzy. "And what in God's name did you do to your face?" Gawking at Judith's darkened rouge and black-circled eyes. "You know, we have a professional photographer here, right? Why can't you follow through when it matters most?" He glowered at Martha.

Typical that Craig would blame it all on her. Martha didn't bother defending herself.

"Point us to the dressing room and we'll get everything worked out." She smiled thinly.

"It's through those doors. Be quick. Don't let Lori see you looking like this or she'll freak."

Martha herded the girls towards the dressing room. After making perfect out of fifteen minutes, they rushed to find the photographer, where the wedding party lined up outside against a massive arbor decorated with vines, pink peonies and spring daisies among a whole plethora of hothouse foliage. The result was stunning. Judith and Lizzy shone like starlets in their pale pink gowns, and as an outdated model of her younger self, Martha didn't look too shabby either.

Judith relented, letting Martha fix her hair and touch up her makeup like old times. Judith looked so much like she had at that age that it could make a skeptic believe in conspiracy theories about cloning. Lizzy somehow managed to improve her posture in the dressing room and squeeze into her dress.

The pictures were awkward and stressful as everyone played a game of standing musical chairs. Martha gazed at her beautiful daughters and ignored the man who had shared her bed for twenty years and the woman now clinging to his arm.

Soon, it was over, and they migrated towards the lawn where the ceremony was about to take place. Martha found a place to sit facing a platform overlooking a lake. They had a pastor to officiate. Martha wondered what church he belonged to. Craig wasn't religious, so this had to be Lori's doing.

Martha swore she wouldn't compare herself to the woman who replaced her. But as she watched her lovely daughters float down the aisle to "Canon in D" followed by one of the most beautiful women she had ever seen, it was impossible not to. Lori was five-nine compared to Martha's five-two. Bleached teeth, straight blonde hair compared to Martha's unruly brown mop, perfect boobs, although surgically enhanced, were three times the size of her own and a body that had never endured the travails of childbirth.

Lori was radiant in a tight-fitting white gown, and everything about her sparkled—her misty eye shadow and pearly lip gloss, her brilliant pink manicure, and her diamonds, which Martha was inclined to believe were genuine and a gift from Craig. He had never bought her so much as a watch. She felt like shit.

They exchanged wedding vows and sealed the deal with a touch-too-intimate kiss followed by rounds of applause from the guests. She turned to follow the flock into the lodge when a hand rested on her shoulder. It was the pastor.

"Mrs. Monroe?"

"No longer. You can call me Miss Diaz."

"Miss Diaz, you are a benevolent woman. Supporting your ex-husband like this?"

He smiled with a shadow of concern.

"Why, thank you."

Overcome by emotion, although Martha didn't understand why.

"I see that you've been walking in darkness but after that comes the light. Things will get better. Don't give up. And always remember, you have the greatest blessing of all—you have a daughter to die for." He gestured at Lizzy as Judith stepped forward. "Oh, you have two daughters." He blushed with embarrassment, as if his admonition no longer made sense.

Judith had returned to their side, much to Martha's surprise, and she caught her glaring at the pastor. Martha gushed.

"Pastor, you're right. Children are the greatest blessing."

He nodded and walked away. Confused by his odd outburst, Martha stood there trying to digest his meaning.

"What did he mean, Mom? A daughter to die for?" Lizzy asked, cuddling up to her arm for warmth.

"He meant that my girls are awesome superstars worth dying for. And he's right."

She gave Lizzy a peck on the cheek and took Judith's hand in hers.

"How nice of him to comfort you after that humiliation," Judith said acidly.

"He must sense my distress. I'm trying, but it's hard."

"Mom, you're insane. Are you sure we can't leave right now?" Judith pleaded. "We gave them their stupid pictures and pranced up the aisle like the minions they wanted us to be. Now they can go off into the sunset convinced they're not complete assholes. What more do they want? I'm tired and I hate this place."

"Judith's right. We don't have to go and hang out with those hateful people. They're here for Dad and Lori. They all suck."

Martha didn't want to go into the lodge. Instead, forget all about tonight, go home and stream a movie with a bowl of popcorn. But it was too late to turn back now. They would all know it bothered her if she didn't attend the reception. The only way to keep face was to finish out the night. It was only one night. It would be over soon, and then she would never think about him again. She would pack up the rest of Craig's crap that she hadn't yet dumped in the trash, and she would start planning her future. It was now an issue of pride. She refused to let Lori think she was hurting. Although she would have to be inhuman not to.

"Girls, I know this is rough, but please help me get through it. We won't stay long. We'll eat, chat for a bit and then leave. I know what you're feeling, and I'm right with you. I can't bear for them to think this bothers me."

"It does bother you!" Lizzy cried. "You don't deserve this!"

"Whatever. Do what you want. Lizzy and I will chill in the car. I hate everyone here, including Dad, and I want no part of their stupid party. And if anyone tries dancing with me, they're gonna get it," Judith warned and stalked off.

Martha understood her girls so well and envied Judith's ability to be as bratty as she wanted. If only she could be like that. If only anyone gave a shit about how she felt.

Chapter 5

Judith

Judith gritted her teeth and smiled through all the pictures, only for the camera's sake. She hadn't taken a bad picture once and wasn't about to start now. But standing next to Lori, her perfume as pungent as bathroom spray, Judith wanted to pick up her skirt and run for the woods.

The photo shoot took forever, as if the only reason they were having the wedding was for the coffee table scrapbooks Lori would have professionally done up. It wasn't love that was for sure. Her dad acted as though caught in a bear trap. He winced every time he smiled.

It was so easy to manipulate her dad; she should know. She was the master of the house growing up, and he gave in to her every whim. So, it came as no surprise that Lori figured it out. Judith wondered if her dad stuck with Lori to prove to the world that, no, he wasn't a total jerk. He only cheated once. This was love, right? Dad was Lori's fourth marriage, and she was his second. Not too difficult to see who wore the pants.

After the pictures, they had to walk up the aisle. Judith was excited for only one reason: it gave her a chance to shine the way she used to at pageants. Surely, every eye would be on her, not the bride.

There had to be at least two hundred people here. Many were unfamiliar, but Judith recognized a few faces from her dad's company. A string quartet stroked out a rendition of "Canon in D" as she followed behind flower girl Lizzy. Judith was shocked at how lovely her sister looked tonight. Her mom had the magical touch. And she was secretly relieved when Mom gave her the last-minute do-over. It made sense. She was as beautiful as any princess and deserved royal treatment.

Judith stood next to the woman she hated most in her young adult life so far and watched as her daddy sold his soul to her. When she shed a tear, it was for this sad fact and not for joy at their nuptials.

A sharp breeze rolled off the lake until her bare arms were freezing. The ceremony seemed to take hours. She had already compared herself to all the females on the lawn, and satisfied with being the prettiest, she moved on to judge who had the most money based on their clothes. The results arrived quickly. Lori's grandmother looked positively loaded.

Judith scanned for cute guys, found none, and felt cheated. What was the point of dressing up and going anywhere without a new guy to wrap around your little finger? And she still had a whole night watching boring old people dance and get drunk. Yuk.

Lori's dress was scandalous, and its youthful charm only made her look like an aged woman pretending to be a virginal bride. It was ridiculously revealing and expensive. So that was why Dad couldn't pay for a spring break trip to France with her besties from high school. She trembled, hating him even more, then glanced at her mom, who looked sad like a cat without her kittens and lost like a captain without his ship.

What was wrong with her mom? She was still pretty, had a kick-ass education, and a job that didn't stink. Someday she'd make professor and take home major bank. Why was she hung up on her dad? Why didn't she reinvent herself like in the movies? Or join a dating app and hook up with a hot, rich guy?

Judith thought the divorce was her mom's fault because she refused to read the signs that he was losing interest and win him back. Now that it was all over, at least she could stop blaming her forgiving attitude on "just doing it for the kids." The last thing she wanted was her mom sucking it up for her.

The pastor's speech was unbearable. He kept ranting about the sanctity of marriage until Judith wanted to puke. Did he realize who he was marrying? Somebody who cheated on his wife, then left her for this hag, and abandoned his children?

Judith spent the rest of the time planning her own wedding. There would be no long boring speeches, and no one over the age of fifty would appear in the pictures. Everyone would show up color-coordinated, and an adorable Boston Terrier would be the ring bearer. Her husband would be perfect, and she would put him through a lie detector test to determine whether he was the cheating type before sharing vows with him.

Her mom would stop being a people pleaser, and her dad would promise to leave Hag-Lori at the door and pretend to be the father she remembered him to be for an entire day. She would have the loveliest dress and breathtaking photos in a garden under a lattice arbor covered in climbing roses. It would be like the movies, but better, because she was better looking than most actresses, and beauty was the secret to all success.

After the ceremony, Judith tried not to notice her mom pretending hard that it didn't hurt. What kind of person was that pathetic? Her mom smiled as her ex-husband married another woman, then hugged them both, ignoring her dad's searching eyes. Was he betraying a hint of remorse right now? Nope. Judith concluded bitterly as her dad shrugged her mom off and squeezed Lori's hand as if she needed reassurance. There wasn't a shred left of the man she once threw her arms around and colored pictures of butterflies for.

They headed to the reception hall. The sky sparkled with dusky shadows, and the air was freezing. Judith pleaded with her mom to leave. This night was only going to get worse. But her mom was like Joan of Arc, determined to burn at the stake for her beliefs. Helplessly furious, she stomped into the reception hall and vowed to be angry for the rest of the night.

Tanya Madsen

Chapter 6

Nicolas

Nicolas knew Martha was the Replacement at first sight. When she bumped into him outside the back door, it was as if an avalanche had unleashed itself from the nearby mountain and swept him away. She touched his shoulder, he turned and he knew her instantly. Tonight, he would get his game on and give her the royal treatment.

Nicolas fervently prepared the dishes for the guests while the ceremony dragged on. He hated weddings. All this pretense just so a couple could rub it in everyone's face that they were in love and you weren't. There was so much food and so many drinks and he had to treat every guest like goddamn royalty. He hated this job too, but kept it for one reason only. It gave him access to sexy older women.

Watching her now that the reception was in full swing, he claimed her table as his to serve. She hovered in her chair like an angel, and he devoured her with his eyes as she sat unnervingly still, trying not to show her humiliation. Even the old ladies murmured their astonishment that the groom dared to invite the ex.

From ten feet away, she kept trying to prop up her crooked chignon. Chignons were for women with thin, dull hair, not for her thick, wavy, almost auburn tresses. He wanted to remove those curls from that lump and brush them back into a halo around her face. Then he imagined searching the rest of her body to see if all her hair was as delicious.

From a distance of three feet, he counted the fine lines around her eyes. She had to be over forty, he prayed to himself. *Please, God, let her be over forty.* He wanted to kiss every one of those lines and proceed to kiss every single square inch of her.

He imagined her naked and bringing her such joy as she had never experienced. It was challenging to keep focused on his job, she distracted him so, especially because her emotions assailed him like punches to his gut. She was unhappy, and Nicolas knew immediately that his purpose in life was to make her happy.

Trying not to cry and barely holding her liquor after only three drinks, she used up her napkin and then grabbed an unused one from a nearby table to dab at her eyes. He served each cocktail himself, saving her the tedious wait in line. He was that sort of guy.

Why did she come? He wondered. Was it true what the gossiping bitches were saying just out of earshot. She wanted to make the groom look bad, and in so doing, only turned the knife on herself?

No. She was innocent, wronged and oblivious to the snobbish criticism she riled among the disgusting Craig Monroe co-conspirators. Nicolas loved her even more for their hatred of her, and he understood why she braved the reception when he glimpsed her daughters.

The older one was a breathtaking beauty close to his age. A beauty queen he discovered, after experiencing a massive and somewhat embarrassing hard-on from checking her out, which incited him to ask around to learn her name, then initiate a dire Google stalking session. She emanated an enchanting aura of rage and discontent while the younger daughter sat, nail-biting between nervous smiles.

Nicolas stared at the angry girl, her fury stirring something profound inside his soul. He knew her from somewhere and felt like he had always known her. He tried desperately to catch her eye, lingered far too long at their table, and ogled her until he was nearly crazy with lust. Finally, he got himself under control, tore his eyes away and returned them to her mother.

Tempting. So very tempting. But he needed more than sexual attraction. He was on a mission to replace the one he lost. He couldn't allow girls his age to distract him from satisfying this unquenchable thirst for love by the one who abandoned him.

She didn't touch her food, but he knew it wasn't to gain approval from the snobs. She simply wasn't hungry. Besides, the food gave her something to stare at while she pretended not to cry into the napkins. Understandably, he didn't clear her plate until last for that reason.

When the dancing stepped into full swing, she avoided eye contact with all men, and to his annoyance, he wasn't the only male with eyes on her. She was an easy target. Recently divorced, still licking her wounds. Perfect fodder for a man who liked a wronged woman to make himself look better, or worse, a pig with secret eyes for her daughters.

Nicolas longed to throw down the porcelain dishes, toss the fine-stemmed goblets aside, reach out his hand and lure her into his arms. Convince her that these people are nothing! He wanted to whisk her away from her life and take her to his secret place where she belonged. He wanted to and he would.

His only concern was that once he followed through and they were together, he might want to kill her, too. And there was nothing he could do to want something else. His love was like a beautiful storm—intense and unforgettable, but potentially deadly—and he didn't know why. He was obsessed with finding love so why did he also want to screw it all up?

Martha—a biblical name, proper and sweet—he loved it. Now, he had to talk to her and listen to the nuances of her voice to understand her nature better and determine their soul compatibility. It was vital that she loved him in return.

What should he call her, ma'am? No.

Miss? Not after referring to her daughters as Miss when he served them. The daughter. His eyes were back on her. She was boiling with rage, glaring at her father. He loved her for her unpretentious fury, and he shared her hatred. The man was an asshole. To dump his family and replace the lovely Martha with a sleazy trophy wife? His heart pounded as she stood, yelled at her mother then flounced off. He wanted to follow. Ask for her phone number. Stand before her, smile his most seductive smile and watch her respond to his charms. No. Nope. The mother. Remember the plan!

Madam. That's the title he would use.

Yes. With her delicate features and thin frame, he envisioned her on a dreamy Paris boulevard, lounging in front of a quaint pâtisserie, eager for his passionate kisses. Then his hands around her neck, pushing her under the mirrored surface. Drowning was his most erotic fantasy, and he didn't know why.

He saw her face—or was it his face—bloated with water. Drowning slowly until her heart went silent and her skin grew cold. He blinked away the horrifying image and rewound, back to his damsel in distress on a dreamy Paris boulevard, waiting for him to swoop her off her feet and save her from her loneliness.

"Madam, would you like another glass of champagne?"

He touched her hand as he removed her plate.

"No, thank you. Listen, do you know when they plan to cut the cake?" She laughed nervously, staring at the table. "I feel like a fly on the wall. I'm no good at these sorts of things."

Was she itching to leave? His chest tightened. He'd never forgive himself if he let her slip out of his life like a haunted shadow. He slowed his movements as he cleared her table.

"Soon, I imagine. Long day at work?" He focused on projecting an aura of concern, which worked even without making eye contact.

"No, just a long ride home to look forward to. Another reason why I can't indulge." She drained the last of her champagne and handed him the glass, still without looking at him. "Thank you, though." She turned away, dismissing him politely and sighed.

Bitch. What a bitch! He was so nice, far nicer than most servers, her only supporter in this den of vipers, and she had the audacity to dismiss him? But then she looked up and her smile widened in surprise as they locked eyes.

"Oh. You. I am so sorry for bumping into you earlier."

"It was my honor." He gave a dazzling smile, which seemed to instill confidence in her.

"Hi, I'm Martha."

She offered her fine-shaped hand.

"Nicolas." He took it, overwhelmed with a desire to kiss it.

Martha blushed, removed her hand from his grasp, and stroked her neck. So demure. Exactly like her! Had she forgotten how handsome he was? His attention flattered most women. Now he understood. It wasn't rejection. She simply hadn't gazed into his dark eyes and ogled his perfect features and hard body. But now that she had smiled like women always did when they saw the whole package, he felt a thousand percent better.

Martha sensed his agitation and placed a hand on his arm, the firm tips of her manicure pressing through his dress shirt. He was trembling, his body shaking. And she was touching him. Touching him, sending chills through him, sending an electric current straight to his dick, forcing him behind the serving caddy to hide his growing excitement.

"Are you okay? They working you too hard back there?" She laughed lightly.

"Oh, I'm fine. I apologize. It's so hot in here, or is it just me?"

"No, you're right. I'm positively roasting. These dancers put off so much heat. Here, let's step outside. I could use the company. You need a breath of fresh air, and so do I. Actually, I need more than fresh air. I need a fresh new start."

And I am the one who can give it to you.

Nicolas watched her blink back tears as he deliberated. Oh, how he wanted to wipe those tears away! Ached to take her down the lantern-lit pathways and show her the best haunts at this overpriced mecca for the rich. But if he did, he'd be sorely tempted to drag her off and make love to her behind a large ponderosa. At that moment, he made a crucial decision. She was coming home with him. Tonight. There could be no ties between them whatsoever at this event.

Where were her daughters? Did they notice him speaking with their mother? Out of the corner of his eye, he chased the crowd wildly, trying not to think of the gorgeous daughter who threatened all his plans. They were nowhere in sight.

"I appreciate the gesture, but I'll be fine. Enjoy the rest of your evening, and please enjoy the cake. It appears they're about to cut it."

"Oh, okay then." She smiled blandly. "I should go and try to find my girls." She replied, giving him the up-and-down stare followed by a tiny wave as she walked off.

Nicolas sensed her eyes undressing him, and it made him want to strip naked for her pleasure. He had no self-control and didn't care. His wild nature was part of his allure. Imagining what she felt as she checked him out filled him with indescribable ecstasy. He was born with these stunning looks to lure her into his life. And soon she would know it.

Nicolas held her damp napkin to his nose, trying to inhale a whiff of her fragrance. She was a near-perfect replica! Sure, there had been dozens of other women, but no one like her. It wasn't just her beauty and delicate build but her strength. She faced this humiliating event with more grace than he could ever possess. She was a goddess, and he was now obsessed with one thing only: making her his goddess.

What to do? She probably lived in the valley. He would have to cut out early and follow her. However, this venue was out in the sticks. He had an idea. Tossing her napkin on the plate, he removed his apron, hurried to his car and unlocked the trunk. He grabbed a wrench and looked around in the parking lot. Which was her car?

Nicolas caught sight of the two girls sitting on the hood of an older Ford Focus. He heard Martha call them, and they sauntered after the sound of her voice like a couple of lion cubs. Darting between cars, Nicolas found his way to hers, removed four of the five lug nuts holding the front left tire and loosened the last one.

He returned to his car, tossed the wrench into the trunk, and the lug nuts into the trees, then returned to the lodge. Time to wash a million dishes at light speed and beg to leave early. If this didn't work, he would follow her home and plan to take her tomorrow. Of course, he didn't think he could wait that long. Didn't think he could wait fifteen minutes—time for a quick pleasure session in the bathroom stall.

Ten minutes later, after washing his hands thoroughly in the sink and feeling more composed, Nicolas stared at his reflection in delight. He was a homme fatale, a handsome devil with a heavy dose of boyish charm. Black, dreamy, deep-set eyes betrayed a bit of his inner psycho. Thick dark hair kept perfectly tussled as if rising from a fantastic romp in the sack. He thought of everything.

He projected an erotic bad-boy vibe that made women pant and plenty of men, too. People might wonder if he was a movie star or fantasize about him as disenfranchised Russian royalty. He'd admit to either.

Six feet tall and slim yet muscular, he ensured his clothes fit in all the right places. Nicolas was more than eye candy—he was eye cocaine. He stared at his perfect features and brilliant smile. He was witty without being a smartass and a class-A flirt. Some found his looks too much to handle; he was keenly aware of this and loved rubbing it in.

Nicolas kissed his biceps and posed from side to side. He looked delicious. This was it. It was time to follow through. His plan would work. It had to. He believed in fate and how it changed on a whim. Martha was the one he had waited years to find, the Replacement he so desperately needed. Soon, she would know it and him as intimately as humanly possible.

Chapter 7

Martha

Martha and her daughters walked up a flagstone pathway circling the lodge. The air was chilly and wet, so she was glad the bride and groom had opted for an inside reception. It was near twilight, and lanterns now lit the path ahead. The whole experience was like a fairy-tale fantasy except for the part where it sucked.

Guests flocked around her through the doors, making her think of a ball game at a stadium. When did Craig make so many friends or were they all Lori's? As Martha entered the lodge, she gawked. The place was phenomenal. A vast timber frame with massive windows poised to exploit the gorgeous surroundings: the most enormous chandeliers she had ever seen hovered, illuminating fat armchairs upholstered in rich leather.

The floral arrangements and decorations alone probably cost a year of her meager salary. She peered into a kitchen where dishes were being prepared and set on caddies, then rolled out to the tables. She noted a bar set up where a line was already forming. She found their table and they sat down. A full band played swanky jazz numbers. Martha wanted to laugh out loud. Craig liked heavy metal and old-country tunes. What the hell had Lori done to him?

The plates of food began to arrive, and Martha laughed again. Contrary to Craig's incessant bragging that the wedding feast would be the crème de la crème, the food was the same old mediocre catering fare—sliced ham, green beans, and potatoes, a plethora of salads and a spread of little appetizers. The bar was exceptional, true, but the line was ridiculous. The crowd spent the night in a line wrapped around the room.

Her daughters sat next to her, making fun of what people were wearing and how they were dancing. Dancing was in full swing almost at once. No one seemed to like the food. The drunker the guests got, the worse their dance moves became. Martha recalled her own wedding reception held at Craig's parents' house. The party lasted an hour, then Craig and his friends got drunk, and Martha had to help him to bed. She spent the night working on a research paper and editing his—no fancy honeymoon for them.

After picking at their food, the girls took off. Martha sat all alone, ignored by everyone. The server kept plying her with drinks until she finally waved him off. When he persisted, she looked up, struck by the gorgeous guy she had bumped into when she arrived. He was sensitive to the fact that she was a pariah, which gave her a thrill of relief. At least someone cared, even if it was a stranger.

Such a good-looking boy, Martha thought. Why was he stuck in catering? Martha was grateful for the smattering of attention he gave her. It didn't imbue her with the confidence to flirt with the male guests or even dance merrily with friends who also attended her wedding. Now they avoided her and kept their eyes on Craig as if to say: *We are here to support him, and it has nothing to do with you.*

Eventually, the happy couple cut the cake, and a handful of people clapped. Martha didn't even stand. When the band began to play decent renditions of pop tunes from her era, Martha tuned out everything inside her head. Suddenly, it was nine thirty, and her daughters were shaking her shoulders.

"Earth to Mom. Are you drunk?" Judith was annoyed. "Mom, can you hear me?" She snapped her fingers in front of her face.

"I thought you girls were taking a walk," Martha murmured.

"We've circled this awful place twenty times, then sat in the car for a while. There's not a single thing to do here," Judith snapped.

What had she been hoping for? This was as good as it was going to get. Not one person, apart from the server, acknowledged her presence. Was she a martyr? Did she crave emotional abuse? Or was she just tired? Lizzy tucked an escaped lock of hair behind her ear and whispered.

"It's not you, Mom. It's them. Remember what you always say? Don't care what they think."

"Yeah, Mom, I actually agree with her. These people suck, including Dad. Let's go home."

"Have you been crying?" Lizzy picked up a wet napkin from the pile. "Let's get you out of here." Lizzy looked close to tears herself. "We shouldn't have come. They're treating us like we're the reason he left or something."

Martha caught Judith glaring at the excited newlyweds, who were trying to make up for lost years and a superbly dull reception.

"For the record, this is the biggest bunch of losers I have ever seen clumped into one spot at a single time. It's like watching a nature show about rodents or snakes crawling all over a log." Judith declared loudly.

Martha stood and let her daughters pull her out the front door and down a flight of steps worthy of Cinderella. She flagged the valet who went to retrieve her car.

"Sorry, girls. I left my purse. Tell the valet I'll be right back."

Martha rushed up the stairs and back into the reception hall. She knew why she had left her purse. Nicolas kept staring at her from across the room, making her feel awkward in her skin. To her utter embarrassment, he was waiting at the door, her purse slung over his shoulder.

"Missing this? Think you left it deliberately?" He grinned, and her insides tingled.

"Subconsciously, perhaps, not intentionally."

"You speak like a shrink," He flirted as he tucked it onto her shoulder, stroking her bare arm.

"I am, in fact."

"Serious and sexy. Love it."

Wow, this guy was hitting on her. Never in her life had she even talked to a man this hot. It was almost painful.

"You know how to flatter a woman." She smiled at him shyly.

"Listen, I'm out of here in less than an hour. I would love to hook up and take you out. Erase this awful night from your memory. I've heard them talking, and they aren't treating you fairly." He leaned over her, his dark eyes consuming her like a bug in a Venus flytrap. "Martha, you are special. I don't think you realize it."

Her heart began to race. She would love nothing better than to run off with this gorgeous man, even if he did look half her age. But her girls were waiting in the car, and she needed to be there for them. Tonight turned out to be far more traumatic than she expected. It was time to lick each other's wounds.

"I appreciate that, but it has been a rough night for my girls and me. Your consideration of my feelings has been the highlight of the evening, and I thank you for that." She gave him a small peck on the cheek.

"You have no idea how much you are missing out." He chastised her with a gleam in his eye.

Should she give him her number? Should she? Was she even capable of having a hookup? Martha thought of having sex with this guy and was thrilled beyond belief. She heard a voice screaming inside her to take her chance and try something new. Staring at this handsome male who was interested in her for some reason, she felt her heart pound with hunger. She yearned for something to fill her emptiness, and after two years of celibacy, sex sounded terrific. But she deliberated too long, and he decided for them both.

"Sometimes we have these moments of serendipity. I'm happy I was able to make the evening more bearable. You take care, Martha." He squeezed her arm and walked away.

As much as she would love to be the kind of girl who'd run off and bed a perfect stranger, she had never done so before and wasn't about to start now. She was a different kind of woman. A woman who didn't know how to be loved. Didn't even know when she wasn't being loved. She had no idea how to change. It would likely take the rest of her life to heal from Craig's betrayal and trust another man. By the time she was eighty, she'd be ready to date again. Martha sighed with disappointment and glanced back for one last glimpse at Nicolas, but he was already gone.

Chapter 8

Judith

"Mom? Can we go yet? This sucks! Please. Let's leave," Judith pleaded.

The food sucked, the music sucked and the people sucked. Good Lord. How much more did she have to endure?

Her mom sighed but retained her glazed expression and didn't respond. She was ignoring her. A scream welled inside Judith's throat—such frustration and anger. Judith didn't know where to put it. Sometimes she was unsure how to form sentences without exploding in rage.

Why was she so crazy? Why did the slightest glimpse of her mom's sad eyes send her into a tizzy? Was she destined to be one of those women-turned-serial killers, and one day, she'd lose her mind and murder someone? She hoped not. At least not tonight. As a final attempt to force her stupid mom to leave right now, Judith slapped her hips in frustration and muttered.

"Well, I'm done. I'll be in the car whenever you decide not to be pathetic. Are you coming, Lizzy?"

She hesitated expectantly, putting her sister in the middle and forcing the dumb brat to choose sides. To her surprise, Lizzy followed.

"Sorry, Mom, she's right. We'll be waiting."

Slightly relieved for the backup, Judith let Lizzy trail behind until they were well out the door and away from Mom.

"Do you think she'll grow a brain soon?"

"Doubt it," Lizzy said slowly, never comfortable talking shit about their mom.

"She'd better. I'm dead tired and starving. Could you believe that food? Gross."

"I think there's a bag of chips stashed under the passenger seat."

"Race you there!" Judith cried as she hiked up her skirt and pounded down the dirt pathway through the trees to the parked cars. One thing pageant training gave her was plenty of practice balancing on heels. She ran like a movie star, beating Lizzy by a long shot. She knew Lizzy didn't mind, understanding her big sister well enough to know the easiest way to force her into a better mood was to let her win at something.

The valet wasn't a complete idiot. He unlocked the doors as she demanded. Inside the car, Judith forgot about her mom-rage moment and even shared the bag of chips without thinking. They munched down the Lays and scored a baggie of Now and Laters. In the back seat, their backs to the doors and feet crossed on each other's laps, Lizzy asked.

"Do you think Mom will ever remarry?"

"Are you crazy? She'll be stuck on Dad until she dies. Did you see the way she stared at him? He dumped her, and she still swoons. Plus, mom dating? Get real. She's stuck with us. I for one ain't letting another man near our house."

"Don't you think she'd be happier? I hate seeing her so sad. It's not fair."

"Nothing's fair, especially love."

"Why doesn't Dad want us with him?"

"Too many memories. He hates being the bad guy, and putting up with mom's moping face keeps him light-years away from the house."

"You blame Mom for everything," Lizzy said quietly.

Judith wasn't sure why she hadn't learned to shut her mouth. She kicked her legs off her lap.

"Stupid brat. You don't understand anything."

"Someday you'll love Mom again."

Lizzy replied, rubbing her sore shins, and began to crawl into the front seat for safety.

"Whatever. Who said you get shotgun?" Judith snapped.

"I need protection from my jerk sister. You're a sociopath, you know."

"Hey, take that back!" She smacked Lizzy hard on the crown.

"Stop! I'll tell Mom!"

"Crybaby. You called me a sociopath."

"Well, you kicked my legs."

"You laid your fat stumps on my gown. Your feet are dirty."

"You aren't the queen you think you are," Lizzy pouted. "You think we all need to bow down to you. My whole life, I've lived in your shadow. I am so done with it."

Judith calmed down. She hated it when Lizzy got all mopey about not being like her. Sometimes she felt bad about being the prettier sister. But most of the time it pissed her off that Lizzy was such a crybaby. Lizzy was pretty, too, just shy. And she didn't care about doing anything to accentuate her looks.

"Sitting in the car sucks. Let's walk around. We can use this blanket."

"We'll walk around for a bit, but then let's go and try to convince Mom to leave again."

"She's too busy burning herself at the stake."

They crawled out of the car and sat on the hood, cuddling under the blanket.

"It's too cold." Lizzy was shivering after a minute.

"We need to move our feet. Come on."

Judith saw her mom outside. She waved at them, and they sauntered up to her.

"Isn't this place beautiful?" she asked wistfully, seeming a bit drunk.

"Yeah, if you think you're a king but still like camping. I think it's bullshit. If you're gonna be out in the woods, you need to be in a tent, not in a lodge fit for royalty with five-hundred-inch flat-screen TVs." Judith retorted.

"You're probably right." Her mom agreed.

"Go back inside, Mom. When we're almost frozen to death, we'll come and yell at you to take us home."

Judith had so many mixed emotions right now that trying to walk them off was a good thing. Her mom nodded and turned, then walked away. Judith grabbed Lizzy's arm and synchronized their steps, the blanket wrapped around them like they were Jewish refugees in *Fiddler on the Roof*. Judith loved that movie. Especially the Jewish daughter who fell in love with the Christian boy. She wanted to be that girl and piss everyone off. Judith clung to her sister for warmth and decided that the first thing she needed to do with her life was move to a city where it never got this goddamn cold.

Chapter 9

Martha

The sky was pitch dark when they headed home. They were barely out of the parking lot, and the girls were already half asleep in the back seat. Martha peeked in the rearview mirror. They looked like the babies they once were. Lying on top of each other, curls awry and mascara smeared. They were her beauties, and she loved them to death. The pastor was right. She had daughters to die for. Even with Judith's raging temper, she understood. What Craig had done to them ruined their lives. If only she could fix it.

After slowly driving out to what she remembered as the main road, she turned and, after a minute, was confused. This was a dirt road, not the way she had come. Slowing down, she rechecked the map and realized she had made a right when she should have taken a left. Martha was awful with directions. Craig had done all the driving over the years; she hated figuring it out on her own.

Martha reflected on the night. It was awful, except for the server. Nicolas was so considerate and gorgeous, too! She would have considered his offer if she were fifteen years younger and a hundred times prettier. But Martha knew to stay in her lane. The way he stared at her sent chills down her spine. Some indescribable feeling—not lust really, more of a longing for something not quite real. A fantasy, she thought.

His eyes. Martha shuddered. There was something wrong with him. Nicolas was dangerous, and when he gazed at her, she felt consumed. Anyhow, he was delicious beyond belief but too damn young. Wasted as a server, though. As a marriage and family counselor, Martha had counseled many people who sold themselves short. This dissatisfaction bled into their closest relationships, poisoning everyone around them. If only people could be their best selves and knew what that even looked like.

As she continued down the dirt road, she found a place wide enough and turned around, returning the way she came. A minute later, the car lurched to the left side, and she heard a dragging sound as she ground to a halt. Shit. Her tire must be flat. And, of course, she canceled the roadside assistance on her car insurance policy to save money. Sighing, she turned off the car and unfastened her seatbelt, leaving the headlights on.

"Mom?" Lizzy asked. "Where are we?"

"Go back to sleep. I gotta check something out. Be right back."

Martha exited her car and closed the door. Using her phone as a flashlight, she stepped over to the wheel, and her jaw dropped. The tire was missing. What the hell? She turned around, looking for it. How did it fall off? How did something like that happen? The lug nuts must have come loose. Good grief. What should she do?

Typically, she would have called Craig, but that was no longer possible. She walked ahead of the car, scanning the darkness for the outline of a tire. How would she put it back on? The lug nuts would be long gone.

It would start raining again at any time. The sky was so dark, and this road was utterly desolate. She racked her brain for anyone who might be able to help her. She debated waking up Judith and asking her to help pull this tire out of the ditch. Martha wanted to sit in the dirt and weep. She deserved this. Her foolish bravado in the face of unrelenting humiliation and pain demanded a punishment, and this was it.

Her nipples hardened painfully in the chilly night air. She should have brought a sweater for the drive home. She frowned at her heels. This was going to be an impossible task. But first, she needed to retrieve that damn tire.

Oncoming bright head beams suddenly blinded her on the opposite side of the road about thirty feet ahead. A door opened, but it did not shut. She squinted into the blinding light and waited for a form to show. Someone approached her on the far side of the road, walking along the ditch. A man with shirt sleeves rolled up, wearing dress clothes. Was he also from the wedding reception? And then she recognized him, and her heart took a deep dive. It was Nicolas. She waved, overjoyed.

"Hey, beautiful." His smile sent a thrill through her. "Need some help?"

"Yes, oh, thank you. You're a godsend! My tire fell off and rolled away. I think it's down there in the ditch. I can't pull it up by myself."

"Show me."

He took her by the arm and walked down the road with her, turned to her and said, "I must know. Would you have hooked up with me if your daughters weren't with you tonight?"

His gaze was piercing, inches from her face.

"I would like to say yes. But I'm not that sort of girl." She laughed apologetically.

"Maybe this might change your mind."

Nicolas leaned forward and kissed her. Martha had never experienced a kiss like this. Craig hadn't kissed her in years. You could have sex without kissing, and that had been the fate for most of her unhappy marriage. Trapped against his lips, she surrendered. This was like a scene out of a movie, not something that should be happening to her. Finally, he pulled away.

"Please come home with me." His dark eyes filled with longing. Martha sensed his desperation. He needed her. Why? Why her?

"I'm sorry. I can't. My girls."

"But you're the one. I have to."

"I can't just leave," she explained helplessly. "Why me?"

"Let me show you. If you only knew how special you are."

"How am I special?" Martha was feeling her therapist's voice kick in. She wondered why. Because she sensed there was something wrong with this boy. Something very wrong indeed.

"Please, I promise you will never regret it if you leave with me right now. I'll make sure of that."

She stroked his clean-shaven jaw, and he kissed her again—this time with greater urgency.

"I wish I could," she murmured, falling under his spell. "But no. I have my girls. I have a life."

What life was there? She had lost her husband. She had given up her counseling career in pursuit of a greater dream. Her daughters were now adults. She was facing a future of nothing more than mounting debt and loneliness.

Nicolas nodded sadly. Rubbing his hands together, he sighed and whispered.

"I'm so sorry to have to do this, Martha, but I must. Please forgive me."

It happened so fast, she didn't have time to react. Nicolas punched her on the side of her head, and she fell to the ground. Lying on her back, that frightening emotional disturbance flashed in his dark eyes as his fist made contact again, and she passed out.

Chapter 10

Nicolas

Quickly, Nicolas gathered Martha in his arms, raced to his car, and then placed her in the back seat. Her hair was falling out of that grotesque chignon. He removed the jeweled comb. All her curls fell in a halo around her face. Tossing the comb into the ditch, he closed the door, climbed into the front seat, backed up, turned his car around and zipped away.

Nicolas lived less than thirty minutes from the lodge. It was taking a risk leaving her unrestrained. She might wake up and try to escape, but he had no choice. This was all a bit impromptu. More than impromptu, it was insane. Then again, according to several shrinks who treated him over the years, so was he.

His heart was racing like that of a long-distance runner. He had never done anything this reckless in his life. What was he doing? He glanced in the rearview mirror for the hundredth time. She stirred but did not wake. How would he get away with this? He just abducted a woman on the side of the road like some highway serial killer. What was he thinking? But he had to. There were times in life when you had to go for it. This was more than a compulsion. It was fate.

Nicolas was sure Martha was the one for him. If he could prove this fact to her, she would thank him for abducting her. And Nicolas did not doubt that he would prove it to her between her legs within a day. He was that good. Like a map in his head, he planned it all out, deciding where he would keep her, how he would explain why he took her and what he would do with her. He was sparkling with erotic energy. He had no idea how he would ever sleep again.

Nicolas drove down the dark country roads. His father's house was in the middle of nowhere, like a classic fortress on the cliffs of Cornwall, but instead, it was surrounded by miles of desert.

Even if she could get out, which she couldn't, she would never make it back to civilization before he learned of her escape. She was his now, and that's how it had to be. He pulled onto the last long stretch of his journey, until a mansion with massive windows, illuminating an impressive view of the mountains to the east, loomed ahead.

Turning off the car, he exited, opened the back door, and stared at his sleeping beauty. Relieved she was still sleeping, he lifted her into his arms and carried her to the front door.

It took a bit of coordination to unlock the door with his phone, but once inside, he carried her up the stairs. In the guest bedroom, he placed her on the bed. He took a breather in the desk chair and stared at her immobile form. What if she hated him? What if she wouldn't respond the way he wanted?

Martha was so beautiful it was almost painful. Gently, so as not to wake her, he rolled her over on her side and unzipped her dress. Once unzipped, he pulled it down over her feet. Undressing her was unbearably erotic, and he wanted to touch himself, but he needed to save it all so he could savor it with her.

Nicolas stroked her cream lace panties and matching bra. Carefully removed those as well. He left and entered his bedroom, grabbing the handcuffs off his nightstand. Returning to her side, he cuffed her hands to the white wrought-iron headboard and positioned her just so. He was an expert in the art of sex, having been forced to make it his life's work. He fingered her manicured nails, which drove him crazy at the reception earlier. Then forced himself to stop touching her and sat down to wait.

Nicolas planned how he would first gain her consent. Sure, he took her, but it was his calling, and she needed it. She needed love, and he was the one who had been sent to love her. He had to explain this to her. He didn't want her to be scared. God forbid that she reject him in any way.

To kill time while he waited for her to awaken, he tried to relax, and his mind immediately went to Martha's daughter. Flouncing around in that sexy dress. Haughty and hot. Thinking of her made his cheeks flush and his heart ache. She would never like him. No girl his age would like him because he was a mess, and he knew it. That's why he needed the Replacement to love him. Pulling out his phone, Nicolas messaged his dad.

> Hey, I picked up a new lady friend tonight.
> She's a keeper.

He waited. A few minutes later, he received a reply.

> Really? Good for you!

> She's the one who will help me. She's a psychologist.

> Awesome. Enjoy yourself. Someone has to.

> Maybe you can meet her sometime.

> I'd like that. You know where to find me.

> Talk later. I have to get my game on.

> Make it a home run!

Nicolas hated his dad. He really did. But in moments like this, when he could shove his face into his successes, Nicolas was glad he hadn't yet killed the asshole.

Martha moaned and moved her head from side to side. He was shaking and had no idea how to calm himself. Once he was seducing her, he'd chill out, but until then, he was going to be a mess. After another five minutes of torturous waiting, Nicolas moved things forward a bit. He turned on the lamp. Finally, she opened her eyes.

Tanya Madsen

Chapter 11

Judith

Silence woke Judith. It was so quiet that she could hear Lizzy breathing. She pushed her sister off her and sat up. She rubbed her eyes, then swore. Now her mascara was everywhere.

"Mom?" she called out. Nothing.

Where did she go? She wasn't in the driver's seat. The car was off, and the headlights were on. What the hell? Judith opened the door and stepped out. Her feet were bare. The ground was wet and cold. The rain had stopped, but her feet were now muddy. She tiptoed forward and gasped. The front tire was missing!

"Mom!" she cried out, looking around frantically.

Turning back to the car, she grabbed Lizzy's foot.

"Lizzy, wake up! Mom's gone!"

Her sister sat up, rubbing her eyes. Now they both looked like ringtail raccoons.

"Huh?" Lizzy crawled out of the car and stared around.

"Mom!" she screamed.

They took turns screaming for their mom, their cries echoing the sound of crickets. Lizzy began to cry.

"What is happening?"

"I don't know," Judith answered. She was scared. Something terrible had happened, and she had slept right through it. "Go find the tire," she ordered Lizzy, who then walked down the road.

"Judith! Mom's phone!"

Judith raced to her side. The phone lay face up near the edge of the ditch, the flashlight blazing. Lizzy picked it up, shined the light forward, and continued down the road.

"I think I see the tire down in this ditch. But there's a lot of tangly brush. I'm afraid I'll fall in and die!"

"You won't die, for heaven's sake. You have your shoes on. I don't." Thankful to have an excuse.

"Put your shoes on, then. I can't do this alone. And it's too dark to pull it out." After a minute, Lizzy returned to her side. "I can't do it. Judith, we need help."

"Who's gonna help us? Dad? He's probably so far up Lori's vagina right now that he can't crawl out. He won't care that Mom disappeared."

"Someone took her. Right out from under our noses. While we were sleeping! Who would do that?"

Lizzy kept wiping her nose, which irritated Judith. She wanted to cry too, but now was not the time for tears. It was time to kick someone's ass.

"Most likely a psychopath. Give me the phone."

Lizzy handed it to her. Judith stared at the screen, deliberating, then entered the pass code, annoyed even further because it was still her dad's birthday. *What the hell, Mom?* She stared at the screen, afraid to make the call. She had never called 911 before, and it seemed terrifying. Everyone was mortally afraid of the cops and the last thing she wanted right now was to have to be nice to some asshole in a uniform. But she had no choice. She called 911 and hit speakerphone.

"911, what's your emergency?" A woman with a flat voice answered. She sounded put out, which made Judith even angrier.

"Um, hi. My sister and I are stranded. Our car broke down, and my mom went to fix it. The next thing we know, she's disappeared, and we are all alone."

"Are you in any danger?"

"I don't think so. There's no one here now. But my mom is missing. And our tire fell off, and we need help."

"What is your current location?"

"We were leaving a wedding at the Timber Moose Lodge. I have no idea where we are, but I see plenty of trees, so I don't think we are far from the lodge."

"What is the last building or street you drove by?"

Judith racked her brain. She had fallen asleep as soon as they had left. She had no idea how long they were on the road!

"I'm not sure! I'm sorry. Let me figure it out."

Lizzy was shivering by the time they got back to the car.

"Turn on the car and crank up the heat," she directed. Then she picked her way over the rocky road to the passenger's side and got in. Bathed in warmth, Judith pushed her seat back and placed her freezing toes on the vent.

"Ma'am? Are you still there?"

"Yes!" Judith cried.

"Have you been able to locate your position?"

"The map shows we are on a road called Blue Spruce Drive. It's a dirt road."

"I'm sending a patrol car now. They should arrive within a few minutes. Stay in the car. You say your car broke down?"

"Yes. The tire. It's gone. It rolled off and fell into a ditch somewhere. Even if we could find it, we couldn't put it back on without those tire thingies."

Lizzy was still crying, and she wanted to smack her. The last thing she needed was tears right now.

"Okay. I'll stay on the line until they arrive."

"Thank you!" Judith cried.

"Are you safe?"

"My sister and I are now locked in the car."

"Are you warm?"

"We turned the heater on and are starting to thaw out."

"You say your mom has disappeared."

"Yes! She has!"

"Did you see or hear anything?"

"No, like I said. We were asleep. My sister remembers our car jolting and hearing mom pull over, turn off the car and get out. She also remembers bright headlights, but she didn't hear a thing. This is so awful. Who would do this to my mom?"

Judith counted the minutes as they ticked by, mentally replaying everything that had happened since they left. But there was a massive hole where, like the selfish brat she was, she fell asleep.

After ten minutes, lights flickered in the distance.

"Someone is coming!" she cried.

"A vehicle?"

"Yes! Is it the police?"

"I believe so." The woman sounded relieved, and that gave Judith such confidence that she opened the car door and raced in front of the hood, waving her arms like an air traffic controller.

"Here! We are here," she screamed.

The lights crawled closer—finally. Thank God. She had never been so relieved to see a police car in her life. She waited for the officers to exit their vehicle, barely holding back from racing into their arms.

"Miss?" An officer held a flashlight pointed directly at her eyes. She squinted and cried.

"Thank you, oh, thank you!"

"Are you and your sister alright?"

The second officer stepped forward, and she stared in disbelief. Her cheeks went crimson as the flashing lights illuminated his tall form. He was young, not much older than her. He smiled as though he recognized her, which made her body flush red like her cheeks.

"Miss, we understand you've had quite the scare tonight. Can you tell us what happened?"

"Um." For the first time in her life, Judith had stage fright. Flustered and nervous, her teeth had started to chatter.

"Miss?" He held out a hand to steady her.

"I'm sorry." Shivering uncontrollably, she pitched forward and threw up the chips and candy from earlier right in front of his shoes.

"It's okay. You're in shock. Here, let me help you."

She let him guide her to the back of her car and open the door. He sat her down.

"I'm so sorry., she muttered through chattering teeth, wishing she were dead. He handed her a wet wipe.

"No worries. I've seen it all. You've been through something horrible. Feeling freaked out is normal. But we're here now, and we'll make sure you and your sister are safe."

Judith stared up into the policeman's eyes. They were a warm brown and reminded her of her favorite dog, Curry, who died when she was thirteen. Those loving eyes begged her to let him climb on her bed and cuddle. She could never say no—not once.

He leaned against the open door and put a hand on his hip.

"I'm Officer Salviati, and my partner is Officer Jones. We'll take your statements, gather any evidence, and get your car in order or set up a tow truck."

"Will you find my mom?" she asked, trying to control the tremor rising in her voice.

"We'll do everything we can. Of course, it's the detective who does that. Trust me, you are in good hands now."

She stared up at him in amazement. Everything about Officer Salviati reminded her of Captain America. Except he wasn't on the big screen. He was right in front of her.

"Sit tight. We have an ambulance on its way. It's mighty cold, and we want to ensure you're okay. Do you have a jacket?"

"A blanket."

She grabbed the blanket from behind her and pulled it around her shoulders. Judith had the wild impulse to reach out and throw her arms around his neck. This was ridiculous. She hated cops. All her friends hated cops. Cops were the worst thing about America, right? But for this one, well, she had to make an exception.

"No coat on a night like this?" he joked, looking up at the sky as it started to drizzle.

"We left home in a hurry to arrive at the wedding on time. I even forgot my phone."

Such a trivial thing, she considered. And she had acted like such a baby about it.

"You stay here."

Judith watched him walk away. Salviati was tall and well-built, with powerful shoulders and a slim waist. He was stunning in his uniform, like somebody modeling as a cop instead of an actual cop. She didn't make a habit of checking men out, usually too absorbed with herself. It was unnerving to feel her eyes pulled in his direction, like he was the center of gravity. He conferred with his partner, then returned to stand in front of her, opened a notepad, and procured a pen.

"Miss, I need to get some information. Are you well enough to make a statement?"

"Um, yes," she managed, but her voice sounded like that of a little kid. She was still so embarrassed by her barfing in front of this guy.

"Can you tell me your name?"

"Judith Monroe."

"Birth date?"

"March thirtieth two-thousand and three."

Salviati gazed down at her, and she caught a hint of a smile. Judith smoothed her hair and wiped under her eyes, surreptitiously checking him out from boot to forehead. He was no longer looking at his notepad. He was staring at her, staring at him as he asked for her home address. She recited her address, and when he asked for her phone number, a thrill of excitement coursed through her, but realized that it was for the case report.

"Can you take me through what happened?"

Judith locked eyes with those steady brown orbs and felt dizzy.

"We had just left the reception. I was so tired already, half asleep. I heard a thumping sound. My mom pulled over and told us to stay in the car. I drifted off." Her face went red with shame. "Lizzy says she noticed headlights. I didn't see or hear a thing. Finally, I woke up. Mom was missing, and the car was off, but the headlights were on. I got out and walked down the road. Eventually, I found her phone lying on the ground. Flashlight on, pointing up. But no mom."

"Can you show me where you found the phone?"

She pointed down the road, and he nodded. She stood, picked her way down the dirt road, and stepped on a sharp stone.

"Ouch." Judith pitched forward, and he caught her. He laid a warm hand on her bare arm and another on her upper back. She tingled all over as her heart began to race.

"I'm sorry," he apologized. "I didn't realize you weren't wearing shoes. It's fine. You can point to the location."

"No. You need all the facts. It's just ahead." He kept her steady as she tiptoed forward, then pointed over to the shoulder of the road.

"I see a little impression where it landed because the dirt's soft. And oh." She pointed. "Footprints."

"You're right. Okay. Let's get you back to your car. It's gonna start pouring any second."

Judith's pulse beat like a tribal drum as she walked beside him. He was so tall and emanated confidence and security. She wondered how old he was and what his name was. She wanted to know everything! She tried to scheme a way to make further physical contact, but to no avail. Seated back in the car, she watched as he pulled his notepad out again.

"So, you heard nothing?"

"Crickets," she giggled, and the corners of his mouth turned ever so slightly. Then he shook his head in disbelief.

"Is it possible she got a ride from a friend? Plans on coming right back?"

"Then why drop her phone?"

"You have me there."

"And even if Mom did leave, she would have told us first. She's that sort of mom."

"Anything else you remember?"

Judith racked her brain, willing some clue to reveal itself.

"I feel so awful. I should have helped her. This is my fault."

Her eyes welled up, and tears sprouted. He stared at her with surprisingly genuine empathy.

"It's not your fault. These things never are."

This was so humiliating. She was tough. She had skin like the Incredible Hulk. So why couldn't she hold it together in front of this guy? No. Police officer. Not a guy. He was a cop, and he was doing his job. She looked up and bravely locked eyes with his. Mesmerized, lost in a staring contest, hopelessly drawn like bugs to a night light, neither could look away until Judith recognized this feeling from all her girlhood dreams and smiled, which made him smile. It was like they both knew at that moment.

They had found the one they wanted.

Chapter 12

Judith

After taking her statement, Salviati said,

"I'll have to get your sister's statement too. Wait here," he cautioned, then joined his partner, who was pointing out the tire in the ditch.

She studied Salviati in the flashing lights as they conversed. He looked intelligent and serious about his job. It was raining again as he ran a hand through his hair. Those large, steady hands and, better yet, no wedding ring. He folded his arms, and his biceps were huge. Judith had always lusted after slim guys with deep-set eyes, wispy goatees and wild hair. This cop was muscular, with soulful eyes, clean-shaven and short hair. Probably straitlaced too. Keeper of the peace. A regular Boy Scout. She figured he was her worst nightmare—someone who wouldn't condone underage drinking or smoking pot and who lived with his mother. And still, she couldn't stop staring.

Salviati broke into laughter as his partner relayed a witty anecdote, and she nearly swooned. So damn gorgeous. How could this guy be hiding out in the sticks? How did he end up being a cop? Salviati followed his partner down into the ditch.

Judith felt suddenly irritated. They didn't seem to be taking her situation seriously. She needed to do something about that. Holding up her damp gown, she picked her bare feet over the stones and frozen wet dirt, water pooling into her cleavage.

"I think we were sabotaged," Judith yelled, and they both turned.

Salviati shook his head, and she caught his partner's smirk as Salviati sprang out of the ditch and took her by the arm to lead her back to the car.

"Miss, let us do our job. Wait for the ambulance, okay? You don't need to be walking around like this." Pointing to her bare feet. "It's freezing and wet."

"You don't understand. Someone at the wedding did this. It might have even been someone my dad paid to get rid of her! Who knows? He's an asshole, and we were at his wedding to the woman he cheated on my mom with. He's guilty as hell. Please! Listen! Find those tire thingies. I bet they will show signs of being damaged. No wheel falls off like that! Someone planned to take my mother!" she was shrieking now.

"Miss, you need to calm down." Salviati tried to drag her towards the car, but she dug her feet in and refused to move.

"You aren't going to find her, are you? My mom will be just another missing person's report! Like all those people on TV documentaries. You've got to do something now!" she screamed and grabbed the front of his shirt frantically. Murderous rage slid through her. She wanted to fight, to break someone's head open. She wanted to kill the man who did this.

Salviati removed her hands, holding them firmly in his. He was like a radiator generating serious heat. He sternly replied, "I said calm down."

Another wave of dizziness hit her, but for an entirely different reason. Her soul went sideways as the hands of fate steadied her.

"Miss Monroe," Salviati addressed her like the father she once had. "Don't make me take you down to the station. You don't seem like someone who would enjoy a night in a jail cell for assaulting a police officer. Please, I realize you're distressed but also in shock. And shock makes people do crazy things."

Judith gazed up at him, and a hunger so acute devoured her from the inside out. She was ripped apart by her mom's abduction as much as consumed by her sudden feelings for this guy. It was all too much. Judith wrenched out of his grasp and rolled towards the ditch, sobbing. A bush tangled against her gown. She didn't care.

Wordlessly, Salviati scooped her up as if she were a pillow. Judith had never been picked up by a guy before. She was way too independent for that. But she wanted this cop. And even more, she wanted him to save her. She wrapped her arms around his neck and buried her face in his collar.

"You don't understand. I'm a horrible daughter. I treat my mom like shit and I know it. Now she's gone, and it's my fault. I'll never see her again. I'll never be able to apologize!"

Judith watched the lights from the ambulance approaching.

"We all do horrible stuff from time to time. Now is not the time to think about that. Will you please be patient? We have a crime scene to deal with here and don't need you contaminating it. If the perpetrator left even a shred of evidence, we'll find it. He won't get away with this. Got it?"

Judith inhaled his scent. A heavenly mix of woodsy and mechanical, very masculine. She wanted to kiss him so badly. Salviati was generating such an intense magnetic attraction, spinning her crazy in love after knowing him for less than twenty minutes.

Salviati set her down in her car as the ambulance pulled up, then took off. The EMTs rushed to care for her and Lizzy. They gave them emergency blankets and checked their vitals. Judith's blood pressure was high, so they escorted her to the back of the ambulance and had her lie on a gurney while they treated her for shock. Gave her water to drink and put socks on her frozen feet.

A cop, introducing himself as Detective Finley, arrived. He came over and asked her the same questions as Salviati. Once again, she felt mortified for admitting she had fallen asleep instead of helping her mom. His eyes judged her, and she wanted to scream in her defense. The wedding was awful and exhausting. Of course, she immediately crashed out!

"Have you found anything? Any evidence?" Judith demanded.

"We're gathering it as we speak. It's muddy, and they left clean shoe prints and tire tread, so we're taking photos now. Looks like they backed up and turned around."

"How are tires going to tell you anything? Every car has tires," she replied flippantly, then added, "are you going to go and question the guests? They're all getting drunk at the reception. Soon they won't be able to stand. Someone must have seen something."

"What makes you so sure it was someone from the wedding?"

"Don't you guys all go off of motive? What stranger would have it in for my mom?"

"You'd be surprised. There are tons of cases of people getting abducted when their car breaks down, likely by a stranger."

"You can bet it was one of those assholes," she fumed, pointing in the direction she thought the lodge might be located.

"Honestly, I'm not sure we are dealing with an abduction. Your mom might have hitched a ride. And tires can fall off on their own, you know."

Finley walked away. Judith was irate. Why weren't there more cops? Why weren't they out arresting possible suspects? This was taking forever!

Salviati walked up to the back of the ambulance, his arms folded in front of him and his legs spread as if trying to put distance between them, looking every bit like a cop.

"I found a lug nut."

"That's what they are called!" She laughed, smacking her forehead. Tire thingies? He must think she was an idiot.

"An ill-fitting tool stripped it. And there's only one. Where are the other four? Good job, detective," he added shyly. Sunshine ripped through her. This attractive police man was flirting with her!

"Will you please do something for me?" Judith tried to sound as demure as possible. "Will you keep me informed of any developments regarding this case?"

"Ah, Detective Finley will be your best bet. I just take down reports. He does the actual investigating."

"But I want you to do it." She didn't try to be coy. She desperately wanted to talk to this cop again.

"I'll see what I can do." He nodded and walked off.

Judith hopped down from the ambulance. A tow truck arrived, and they decided the car was drivable as they put the tire back on her mom's car. They removed one lug nut from the other three tires, secured the tire that had fallen off, and recommended that she have the car serviced first thing.

She nodded distractedly and tasted her breath. Yuk. Reached into the cup holder, grabbed a container of Tic Tacs, and crunched a few down. She was starving and had the urge to swallow the whole container of minty candies.

Standing next to the car, she surveyed the scene. The damp soaked through her socks, but she needed to search. That detective wasn't gonna do anything! There had to be evidence they missed proving her mom would never leave them like this, and she would find it. She slipped past the patrol cars and continued into the darkness, scanning the ground for anything. Maybe he dropped something, or her mom left a clue. Something!

Thirty feet away, she glanced back at the vehicles with their flashing lights, reminding her of parades. One in particular, where she rode the float as the beauty queen for some contest or another. It had been the highlight of her life for years, but now it seemed stupid and pointless. She saw Salviati glance her way, and she stepped down into the ditch to hide. If the cops could search for clues, well, so could she.

The slope was gentle, but the ground was soft and unstable. She sank into the dirt at the bottom of the ditch. Completely hidden from the road, now she peered around. On top of a nearby bush, she caught a sparkle of something and gasped. Turning around to rush back up the hill, she ran smack into Officer Salviati, who looked very annoyed.

"Miss, you need to return to your car and stay there." He pointed down the road and snapped his finger.

"I want to search too!" she cried, hands on her hips, pouting.

He ran his hands through his hair and made a sound of frustration.

"Please. Do as I say. I don't want to have to—"

"What? Arrest me? That detective doesn't even think someone abducted her. I have to find some evidence, or he won't look for her!"

"Get back to the car. Now." He flushed angrily, and Judith fluttered with delight at his emotional outburst.

"Fine. I'll go. But first, you need to tell me your name." Judith sucked at flirting. Brusque and direct, when she wanted something, she went for it.

Salviati stood above her, staring down, his eyes roving all over her. He couldn't hide it.

"Uh." Taken off guard and flustered, he stammered, "it's Justin. Justin Salviati."

"Well, Justin, thank you for being so kind to me." She smiled at him adoringly.

"Of course. It's my job." He was definitely nervous now.

Judith wobbled as she tried to step up the incline, and he held out a hand to help her. He was so close. Practically begging her to do the most daring thing she had ever tried in her almost twenty years. More thrilling than all her beauty pageants combined. Grabbing him by those impressive shoulders, she pulled him down to her as she stood on tiptoes and kissed him. She didn't care if he was a cop and this was breaking the law. He was the most beautiful man she had ever seen, and she wasn't about to let him go without him knowing it.

To her shock and amazement, he didn't shove her away. Sugar to her spice, he melted against her mouth like milk chocolate. Judith had kissed a fair number of guys. Nothing like this. His arms balanced her, holding her to him. Lips soft and unhurried, her whole body melted into Zen. Usually, make-out sessions with her quickly evolved into speed sex. This could last forever. He tasted like warm sunny days in the back of a pickup truck, although she didn't know what that felt like.

The rain fell steadily, trickling down their faces, and she pulled away, trembling. Even in the dark, she could see that he was so red-faced that she wanted to kiss him again. Salviati grinned at her sheepishly.

"Don't tell my partner, or I'm finished," he replied in a low voice.

"You're not going to arrest me for assaulting a police officer?"

"If I arrest you, it won't be to take you down to the station, that's for sure. I've gotta get. I shouldn't have followed you down here, but wow, that was some thank you."

"More than a thank you, it's an invitation."

"I can't accept any invitations." He was firm but betrayed himself with an iceberg-melting smile.

"You have to. I won't take no for an answer," she demanded. "And promise to call me."

"After this, you may not be able to get rid of me." He whispered, and his words rolled through her like a hot body massage.

Judith placed her hands on his chest and frankly confessed.

"You are gorgeous, Salviati, like some real-life Captain America. I have never met a guy like you in all my life."

She held his gaze, slid her hands apart, wrapped her arms around his waist, and hugged him. He hesitated, then leaned down and kissed her again. Passion ignited in a frenzy, and Judith moaned with delight, which led to touching, faster kissing, and more touching until he pulled away.

"I gotta go. Jones will wonder what the hell is going on."

"Wait. I found something." She took his hand so naturally that she couldn't imagine a world now in which she was unable to touch him. "Here." She pointed to the comb lying on top of the bush. "My mom was wearing it tonight. Someone must have tossed it when they took her. It's proof, isn't it?"

He gasped, "go back to your car and we'll take care of this."

Judith trudged up the hill and rushed back into the light to find Detective Finley.

"I found my mom's hair comb lying in the ditch. It's proof! Someone threw it there! Probably one of my dad's creepy friends who obsessed over her for years. My mom is gorgeous and sad, and like every guy at the wedding, was checking her out. Please! Go up to the lodge and investigate the guests. They are all spending the night, but someone left early. I know it! Maybe they have cameras and you can catch whoever followed us!"

He nodded distractedly and headed in the direction from which Salviati was coming. The wheel was reattached to her car, and their vehicle was now fit to drive. The tow truck was leaving. Judith plopped into the driver's seat, reliving every microsecond of their kiss. And then the second kiss, which quickly included his tongue and how his hands eagerly cupped her breasts, followed the contour of her hourglass figure to circle her slim waist. How she stroked his biceps down to his hips, then around back to cradle his butt. Every second was priceless. She was never going to sleep again until his body was lying next to hers. In the horror of this nightmare, she met someone she knew would change her life forever.

Fifteen minutes later, Salviati walked up to her. Judith had the engine running and the heat blasting. She looked up at him eagerly.

"We've gathered all the evidence we're likely to find. Great job finding the comb. Are you lucky or what?"

"Tonight, I lost everything and immediately struck gold." She said it with meaning. "Now I just go home? Leave? How do I do this? It's like I'm giving up." Choking back a sob, she covered her face, unwilling to drive away without her mom.

"This has got to be brutal. I can't imagine."

"I have to find her." Judith's lips tightened with determination.

"Miss Monroe—"

"Judith." She smiled at him. "Call me Judith."

He glanced from side to side to see if anyone was standing within earshot.

"Judith. Let us do our jobs. We will find her."

His eyes, oh man, were blazing with interest. In her! Judith realized she had thrown a match on a field covered in gasoline, and there was nothing but fire between them now. Why did she kiss him? Judith never chased any guy. They all chased her! She had her pick and grew bored with them quickly because they were all the same: vain, entitled, lazy, horny little brats like her. This cop wouldn't care about her history of beauty pageants or future modeling plans. He lived in the real world, and for the first time in her life, Judith was eager to join him there.

"Listen," he said under his breath, "I shouldn't. God, I hope they don't fire me for this. I'll call you tomorrow. Hopefully, I'll have an update on the case."

"If you don't, I'm gonna come down to your station and stalk you."

"And make me file another report?" His smile shot through her like a dozen of Cupid's arrows. "Good night. Drive safe." He shut her car door.

Judith entered home into the navigation system. She paused and watched Salviati speak to the detective, starving for something she couldn't define but knew he had in spades. She slowly pulled forward then headed home.

Her mind was racing. Lizzy was in a stupor. She barely spoke ten words for a statement. Judith had no idea what to do. Lizzy was a mama's girl. How would she wake up tomorrow without mom or return to school on Monday? This was a living hell. Instead of reliving the nightmare, Judith replayed their kiss all the way home and imagined so many delicious fantasies about this cop that she was sure she'd never fall asleep.

At the condo, she dragged Lizzy inside and up to her bed. She rushed to her room, grabbed her phone and opened her Facebook app. She searched until she found the right Justin Salviati, the cop with that gorgeous smile, and fired off a friend request. Was she being too forward? Of course she was! There were times in life when being passive would not get you what you wanted. She remembered his warm eyes and even warmer body, and felt like she was growing wings.

Disappointed that he didn't accept it immediately, Judith flew into the bathroom, removed her torn and filthy dress, and cleaned and moisturized her face. She brushed her hair and her teeth. Years of being beautiful taught her never to shirk her routine. As she crawled into bed, she checked again. To her delight, Justin was now listed as one of her friends.

As she drifted off, she took a long stroll down fantasy lane. How their first time would go, what she would be wearing, where they would be— every detail. Finding her mom and saving the day. Murdering the person who took her. Maybe she wasn't supposed to be just a beautiful girl after all. Perhaps she could be what the pastor said she was.

A daughter to die for.

Chapter 13

Justin

Justin climbed into the passenger's seat of his patrol car, his heart thumping madly. Nothing like this had ever happened to him. He was a country boy with country plans. This—what the hell was this? It felt like the aftermath of an earthquake. An hour after that kiss, he was still shaking.

Once they were both seated, Jones turned to him.

"Are you alright?"

"Yeah." Justin forced a laugh. "Why do you ask?"

"Well, the older daughter was giving you googly eyes. And she was gorgeous too. That can mess with any guy, especially a young buck like yourself."

"Really? I hadn't noticed," Justin replied nervously.

Jones stared a hole through Justin.

"Bullshit. I'm old enough to know when I'm caught in a sexual tension traffic jam. I was walking through soup around you two. Drawn to each other from the second you met. Couldn't stop touching each other if your lives depended on it. You, holding her, picking her up and chasing after her. I caught it all, Salviati."

Justin gave in.

"Was it that obvious?"

Jones slapped him on the shoulder.

"Did she hit on you?"

Justin nodded, and Jones slapped him again.

"So, angel boy is falling from grace. Don't worry, we've all been there. Saving a pretty girl on a dark and stormy night? I loved it when she started beating on your chest and you had to warn her about assaulting a police officer. Did you see her face? I wish my wife looked at me that way. Pure sweet desire. Then she collapsed, hoping you'd pick her up, and you fell for it big time. Judith is super-hot for you. You'd be a fool not to notice."

"I was trying hard to keep professional, you know, maintain my distance. I'm not sure what happened."

"What happened? They call it instant attraction. Takes over the body completely until you ain't in control anymore. It's rare. Don't meet too many people who can push those buttons, so consider yourself lucky."

Justin didn't reply. He lay back and replayed it all in his head. Life had been boring for some time. Hadn't left town in nearly a year; he just worked and saved his money. He had his hobbies, sure, but he wasn't heading anywhere. Didn't regret his decision to go into law enforcement. It was either that or the military, and he was a homebody, so deployment would prove difficult.

Now wow. Why would a girl like Judith kiss him? He was about as far from her type as you could get. Old-fashioned and boring, lived in the country and loved living in the country. She was in for a huge disappointment. But still, that kiss. No one and nothing had ever made him feel so damn good.

"What do you think of this case?" Justin asked.

"Think I'm glad I didn't go for detective when I had the opportunity. There ain't a chance in hell of finding this guy."

"I disagree. We have the tire tread. Might find a print on the hair comb. You can't pull off an abduction these days without leaving some evidence behind."

"I'm sure they'll vet the entire sex offender registry in the state."

"I hate to say it, no matter how much frou-frou implicit bias training they give us, it doesn't change a thing. There's a reason stereotypes exist. They always end up being spot on. Gangbangers, prostitutes, junkies and their dealers, thieves, child molesters—we've seen it all, and they always fall in line with their profile. Criminals are seriously unoriginal."

"Makes it hard not to make snap judgments, that's for sure." Jones agreed.

"This guy? I'd say he's a psycho with mommy issues."

"Or someone passing through, jonesing for a new squeeze to keep him company in the back of his rape van."

"The daughter might be right, and the perp is someone from the wedding."

"I see." Jones grinned knowingly. "You have an impetus now. Not only got to save the girl, you now need to save the mom."

"It's not like that."

"Need those plaudits, huh? She was undressing you with her eyes. Don't think it's gonna take much to win her over. We just won't tell the boss."

As much as he could be engaged in that line of thinking, it was more than that. When Judith confessed that she was a bad daughter, it brought back the way he acted the last time he saw his dad. He told him he never wanted to see him again. Then he never did. He wanted to spare her from such remorse.

And yeah, she had him hanging on cloud nine about now. He did want to help find the mom and make this girl like him even more. How did you get a girl like Judith to want you? She seemed the type to have her pick. Was there a way to get inside her head? It would take a high-level head game, and he had no idea how to do that. His experience with women was minimal.

"Let me give you one piece of advice. You just saved Judith from a nightmare, and she's looking at you like you're her hero. You don't wanna get all hung up on someone who's in a post-traumatic state, and when they snap out of it, you're done for."

Jones was right. Judith couldn't possibly like him. Sure, he worked out and had a great body. At least everyone said he did. He was the gentlemanly guy his mama brought him up to be. Didn't party or sleep around, never spent money on frivolous shit, drove an old car, had no interest in cruises, casinos or traveling the world, and had never indulged in expensive hobbies like extreme sports and off-roading. Justin cared for his mama and brothers, went to work, and fixed cars in his spare time. This girl. He had to know. He opened his phone and googled her name.

"You doing the search?" Jones looked at his bright phone.

"Yeah." Justin's heart fell. "She's some sort of beauty queen. Has won a ton of contests."

"I can agree with that. Damn, what a looker. At least she's not jailbait."

Justin scrolled down, feeling worse and worse. This girl would never like him. He stared at a photo of her smiling as she was handed a trophy. Then he saw her in his head tonight, so scared and devastated. He wanted to throw his arms around her against the cold desert night air, tuck her to his chest and warm her to the bone.

He couldn't push her out of his head. Shivering in that revealing party dress, all that cleavage and nipples popping through the thin fabric, he couldn't stop staring. Did she notice? Smooth tan skin. Flashing green bedroom eyes and long, dark reddish-gold waves rippling over her shoulders like a mermaid. Full lips encapsulating a seductive smile. She was gorgeous.

He was never going to sleep come morning. Maybe never again. How could he forget that kiss? No girl had ever hit on him like this. She even called him Captain America. It was more than a kiss. She called it an invitation. He shouldn't have kissed her again. A straight-up violation of his duties, but worth every second. He thought of how his hands went straight to her perfect breasts and nearly groaned out loud.

A notification popped up with a friend request from Judith Monroe, and his heart flip-flopped. Nervous, like he was in school, about to give a presentation. Riled up with surprising confidence, he clicked accept. Wow, as in wow. He couldn't stop smiling. He had to pull himself together and not stare at her photos all night. Not think about how his body responded to touching her or how long it took his dick to settle back down.

Back to work. Get back to work. Justin closed his app and pushed all thoughts of Judith from his mind. He then remembered, opened the statement he had taken, and entered her phone number into his contacts without Jones noticing.

Something awoke in him tonight. Justin had been living in a daze for the last three years. Since becoming a cop, life had been just work-sleep-work. Those days were over. He realized now how badly he wanted to be in love. And that meant getting out there and making it happen.

Tanya Madsen

Chapter 14

Martha

Martha flickered her eyes open to the pain as it pulsated in her head and around her wrists. A cool breeze blew across her bare skin. She was naked, her hands cuffed above her head. What happened?

Racking her brain, she tried to remember. They were driving home from the wedding—the car. Something was wrong. She pulled over. The tire. She had lost the tire. Someone stopped in front of them. She turned into the bright headlights. That hot server, Nicolas. What was he doing there? His kiss, his plea for her to leave with him, his fist, and nothing.

The girls. Oh God, they were still in the car sleeping! Martha tried to sit up, and there he was. Seated in a chair next to the bed, his face was a gorgeous mask. He looked pleasant and pleased, having made the choice for her. The fact that she was naked meant only one thing.

"Where am I?" Martha asked.

"With me. Here." He gestured to the room.

"Why?" The question came out like an accusation.

"Why not?" He shrugged. "You are the woman I've been searching so long for."

He proceeded to unbutton his white shirt.

"Surely, a young guy like you doesn't need to abduct a middle-aged woman to get laid. Please, it's not too late. I have no idea where I am. Just let me go. Drop me off on a street corner somewhere. I promise I will never say a word of this to anyone."

"Is that what you want?"

"I just said so, didn't I?"

"After tonight, you won't. What I'm about to do to you will change you forever. You will never be content with another man after me. I plan to become your one and only. For life."

He stepped out of his slacks and boxers, folded them up and placed them on the back of the chair with his shirt. Nicolas was perfect in every regard, like he just walked out of a fantasy. Aroused beyond belief, she hadn't had sex in so long and wondered if she was even able to climax with a man anymore.

"I am going to give you the absolute best sex you've ever had. You will never want another man inside you again."

"That's pretty arrogant." She couldn't help but argue. "It doesn't matter what you do. I'm shackled to this bed, so I doubt it will be enjoyable. Which ruins all your hard work." She tried to sound like a stern mom, but he grinned like a naughty boy.

"Are you giving me a challenge? Challenge accepted." He licked his lips.

"I'm just saying I don't like being restrained."

"Have you ever been restrained?"

"No."

"Then you have no idea what you're in for. Your orgasms are going to blow your mind."

Orgasms? As in, more than one?

"I haven't had an orgasm in years. Not a real one," she confessed.

"I know. That's why you're here. And the restraints are for me, too. Knowing I'm in complete control, making your hottest dreams come true. It's so sexy."

"I see." Excitement whirled around in her stomach. This was nuts. She should be screaming for her life. Not getting wet at the thought of having sex with this man.

"Martha, I've slept with dozens of women. I'm what they call a Casanova. Trust me, I'm taking you to heaven. But first, I need to ask your permission."

"Isn't it too late for that?"

"I've never raped a woman, and I have no plans to start now. Please trust me. I know I was supposed to do this. It's like a calling from God. You are unhappy and lonely when you deserve to feel loved and desired. Your ex never loved you, and no one at the wedding showed you the slightest bit of attention. It was horrible. I want to make it all up to you and make you feel better than you have ever felt in your life. You were begging me to take you."

Martha was speechless. No one had ever shown interest in her feelings. Why did Nicolas care? She thought of her first time with Craig, the only guy she had ever slept with. It was always so much work to have sex with him. Now she understood why. He was never that attracted to her. She had often wondered what it would be like with someone else, but was too shy to initiate an illicit relationship. This was her chance. Staring up at this gorgeous guy, she couldn't believe a man this hot even wanted to have sex with her.

"Okay, you have my permission. But nothing painful. I don't like pain."

He crawled on top of her and lowered his face to hers.

"Of course. I'm here for your consummate pleasure. When I'm done with you, you'll never want to leave my side again."

He smelled delicious—some musky cologne with light tones of something erotic. His breath was sweet like he sucked down a dozen mints. Martha decided that Nicolas cared far too much about being perfect. It seemed pathological.

Nicolas kissed her, and she responded like she had earlier when looking for the tire. She remembered how she had checked him out with open lust at the reception. He nibbled along her neck, and sparks of ecstasy erupted in her pelvis. She was already moaning, and he hadn't even gotten started.

"I'm ready now," she whispered. "Go for it."

"It's been ten seconds. My, you are horny."

"Nicolas, please."

He sat back and smiled. "Oh, Martha. You poor angel. I bet Craig never spent more than a few minutes dedicated to your pleasure. Let me wipe those memories away for good. You haven't come once yet. You've gotta come at least twice before it's my turn."

He rolled her nipples around his tongue until she gasped, groaned, and wished her hands were free so she could run her fingers through his luscious hair. He worked his way down her stomach, kissing along her c-section scar, which embarrassed her for some reason. Like he was calling her out for bearing children. He nibbled and sucked her inner thighs and along her pubic line, slowly moving towards the center where she itched and throbbed.

By the time Nicolas spread her legs wide, she was begging for it. God, oh God, she should have tried to get laid after Craig left. Nicolas must have seen it. Her sexual frustration, her loneliness, and her wanton desire for someone to touch her. She was an open map and he navigated her effortlessly. Easily won the challenge and gave her the best orgasm ever.

Martha couldn't help but psychoanalyze the whole experience. Nicolas knew what he was doing and enjoyed doing it. Into domination and clearly obsessed with older women. You didn't choose to be this way. Probably in early development, something had formed him to prefer mother figures. He believed himself to be her sexual savior.

It felt like hours had passed. Martha had never trembled or moaned this much in her life. Nicolas was relentless. His mouth and hands were everywhere in places she didn't even know could arouse her until he had her nearly screaming with delight. It was unreal, something out of a fantasy, just not hers.

Although she was aware of her bodily responses, her mind was still very rooted in the present. Her wrists hurt, her mouth was dry, and her body was growing exhausted from the stimulation. His skills were off the charts, but he wanted validation. Kept asking if she liked it and how intense her orgasms were, like she was a part of a case study.

Finally, he entered her and took his sweet time. He was mechanical. His face looked as though he were performing or taking an exam, trying not to screw up or forget the correct answers. She was silent now as their bodies moved together. It was a long time before he climaxed. His beautiful face contorted, and he shuddered violently as he lay against her.

"Your heart is in overdrive. I did that to you." He sounded terribly satisfied with himself.

"Yes, you did." She answered automatically.

Nicolas pulled out and stood, grinning like an errant schoolboy.

"Was I big enough? I felt enormous inside you, but you can never tell. When I saw how petite you were, I hoped you'd love it. I do everything possible to enhance my size. Pills—you name it. I'm not sure how big your ex was, and obviously I can't compare, but I really would like to know."

Was he talking about his dick? How old was he, sixteen?

"You are bigger than he was by far." She gave him the answer he expected, and he smiled with relief.

"That's so good to hear. So, it was the best you've ever had, right?"

Nicolas sat beside her, his hands folded in his lap, and kissed her chastely. His mannerisms were those of a little boy, which was disconcerting.

What was the point of lying? He already knew the answer.

"Yes, Nicolas, it was."

"I am going to do this to you every night. Soon you'll be screaming my name and begging for me every second I'm not here. And if you don't, I'll make sure that you do."

What was wrong with him? Nicolas was desperate for approval and accolades. This made her sad, and his vulnerability made her uncomfortable. What possessed a young man to become a Casanova who preyed on older women?

"Will you let me out of these cuffs?"

"Of course. I'm not an animal. I just wanted our first time to be unforgettably hot. To give you a damn good reason to be happy about me taking you. You belong with me, to be pleasured by the best lover this world has ever known. I'd go again. I would go all night, but I'm sure you're tired, and I am a gentleman."

He left the room, returned wearing a silk robe, and bent over to unlock the cuffs.

"The bathroom is through that door with towels, soap, lotion, razors, everything you need. There's also a mini fridge by the bed with plenty of snacks and drinks, and I'll cook you a delectable supper every night. I will lock your door for now. Eventually, I'll let you out of your room. But you'll need to prove yourself to me first."

"What will that take?" She rubbed her sore wrists.

"You seemed excited, and I doubt you were faking your orgasms, but I want more. I want you to beg and scream like you mean it. I want your complete and undying adoration. Finally, I want you to promise to love me and never leave me. Then you'll earn a bit of freedom."

"Nicolas, why me? I'm old. I have kids and the stretch marks to prove it. You're so gorgeous, you could score a supermodel."

"I am obsessed with finding a woman I lost years ago. Plus, girls my age never like me anyway. You are perfect. Your ex never tried to satisfy you. Your daughters don't respect you. Everyone in your life underestimates you. You can't give yourself a break. Well, I'm your break, Martha. In this castle, you are my goddess."

"How long have you been doing this, trying to find this woman?"

"A while now. I am searching for the one who will love me, who I can make happy, who will never leave me."

"That's a tall order."

"I know she's out there. And you should thank me. I've been an avid disciple of the female body since childhood, and you get to reap the rewards."

"That's disturbing, Nicolas. Since childhood?"

Nicolas flushed deeply at this admission but didn't answer.

"I'll return with plenty of sexy lingerie tomorrow. I'll use your dress and bra size to make sure they fit. I won't let you wear much else, I'm afraid. This house has a ton of cameras, and I want to be able to fantasize about you whenever I want. Tease me insatiably, so I'm eager to take you to heaven when I get home from work. You are an exquisite dessert, and I intend on devouring you until you want me more than you wanna breathe."

He blew her a kiss as he shut the door. She heard a lock engage. The house was silent. She was afraid that if she cried, he would hear her. So she went into the bathroom, turned on the shower, sat in the corner and let the tears flow.

Saturday ~ Day 2

Chapter 15

Judith

Judith woke up at seven and stalked Justin Salviati online for the next two hours. He was not a social media junkie, but he had posted occasionally, going back to his first year of high school. Had a lot less friends than her and she was relieved. It sucked when a guy was more popular than she was.

Twenty-four years old with a degree in criminology, he had two younger brothers, liked to work on cars and loved his mama by the looks of all the hugging photos of the two of them. He lost his dad when he was thirteen, and she was dying to know how. Had only one long-term girlfriend from nineteen to twenty-one—a sweet-looking red-headed girl, but they held each other in their photos like siblings. Judith didn't feel the slightest bit jealous.

The more she read about Justin, the more she decided she liked the things he liked, the music he liked, and his Instagram was cool. He liked a few tame sexy lady pics, but mostly he liked retro muscle cars, and weirdly, pictures of exotic birds. Was he a bird watcher? Maybe. Even that sounded hot to her.

Wasn't on any dating apps unless he used a pseudonym. Started at the police force when he turned twenty-one and seemed married to his career. His birthday was in June. A Gemini. Such a challenge, Geminis. They drove her crazy. Justin had big professional plans. Awesome. Although she intended on totally derailing his life. He had no idea what was coming.

Judith gaped at his workout pics, shocked by the depths of her lust. She wasn't into buff guys who were oddly intimidating and very much in love with themselves. Besides, they were difficult to wrap around her finger, so she usually didn't bother. So why Justin? Why was she breaking all her rules for him?

Judith screenshotted one of his pics where he was under the hood of a car with his shirt off, dog tags hanging around his neck and down his bare chest. She was dying to read what they said and blew up the pic by five hundred percent to no avail. Staring up under the hood's shadow, Justin smiled at whoever was taking the pic. That smile, like a hair removal laser zapping at her soul. It hurt somehow because those smiles weren't for her, but she was determined to make them be.

It looked like he lived in the country, though. She wondered where. He'd better call her today or she'd make good on her promise and stalk him tonight. She had already picked which of her sexy pics to sext him with when he got in touch, and she was feeling positive despite everything.

Finally, she tore her eyes away from Justin's amazing abs and called her dad at nine a.m. It went to voicemail as usual. Fuming, she hung up and texted him instead.

Dad! Call me! It's an emergency!

Half an hour later, her phone buzzed.

Stop being such a drama queen. What is it?

A psychopath last night abducted Mom, and we have no idea where she is. Call me!!!

Thirty seconds later, her phone rang.

"Judith, we are ready to board our plane to Brazil. What the hell is going on?"

"I said, Mom was abducted last night!"

"What do you mean, abducted? That's absurd!"

"Of course it is! Someone, I believe, from the wedding, sabotaged our car. We were on this dirt road when our tire fell off. Mom went to investigate. Lizzy remembers seeing headlights, so we figured someone had pulled over to help her. The next minute, she's gone!"

"This is unreal."

"Totally insane!"

"What do you want me to do? Did you call the police?"

"Of course we did! Please send me the guest list of everyone invited to the wedding. I think it's one of your pervy friends that's had the hots for mom all these years and decided to take their chance."

"None of my or Lori's friends would ever do this." He protested.

"Dad, I'm begging you. I don't care if you leave on a plane with her and do whatever. I'm over your complete betrayal of our family."

"Honey, it's not like that."

"Yes, it is, and you know it. Just send me the goddamn list so I can investigate it. It might be nothing. But if you ever cared about mom, you'll do this."

"I am sure the police will conduct a thorough investigation."

"They have nothing, Dad. They're not even convinced someone took her! I will never forgive you if you don't do this for me. Ever." She threatened.

He sighed.

"Fine. I'm looking for the list now. I'll email it to you. But you're not going to find anything."

"We'll see about that."

"Are we good here?"

"Sure. Fine. I hope you and Lori get eaten by piranhas."

Judith finished nastily and hung up, refusing to let him have the last word. She waited for the email, but a text came through instead. All she read was,

That was rude. Lori and I—

She hit delete. What an asshole! He wouldn't think of delaying his precious plans. Judith had one prayer in her heart. Her mom would replace her jerk of a dad and move on, pronto. If she did, then they all could.

Judith waited for another half hour. The email still did not arrive. He lied. He wasn't going to follow through. She wanted to rip out all her hair in fury. How dare he trick her? What a bastard!

Enough was enough. She would call this detective, have him issue a warrant, and force her dad to hand over the list!

She searched until she found Detective Finley's number on the paperwork and called. Voicemail. Of course. Not a single person cared about the way she felt. They all deserved to die. She left an acidic message requesting a call back, threw her phone down on the bed, and crashed out on top of it.

Sometime later, her phone rang. She sat up and searched for it in a daze.

"Hello?"

"It's Detective Finley, returning your call."

"Yes, detective. Thank you!"

"How can I help you?"

"I wanted an update on the case."

"It's only been sixteen hours," he cautioned.

"I think I have a lead for you. I am convinced someone from the wedding took her. We need to get our hands on the guest list. I asked, but my dad won't send it to me. Could you issue a warrant and make him? Then investigate the guests."

Silence filled the line.

"What makes you so sure we are looking for a guest?"

"There is no other explanation. Our car was sitting in a parking lot for four hours. My mom was crying and sad, and a ton of guys were checking her out."

"I'll consider what you're saying. We'll look into it. We are now awaiting lab results on the tire tread and hair comb. I'll keep you posted."

That was all they were willing to do? She was right. She knew she was right! She caved in, which was very unlike her.

"Okay, thanks." And she hung up.

Judith searched for her dad's address. He wasn't going to help her. Which meant she would have to help herself. Lori was like an eighty-year-old and wrote everything down on paper. She would surely find the guest list tucked away in a drawer somewhere.

She grabbed her mom's car keys and headed out. Had no idea where Lizzy was, but she didn't care. No one was on her side in this. Every so often, you had to step up to the plate and hit your own home run, and that's what she intended to do.

She pulled up in front of her dad's house, rage boiling over once again. They lived in a giant mansion up in Cottonwood Canyon. Why didn't karma work the way it was supposed to? She went to exit the car when her phone buzzed. She scanned the number. Unknown. A thrill started in her chest, crawling down to her toes as she read the message.

Hey, Judith, it's Justin.

She kissed her phone and messaged right back.

You remembered me!

Did you think I'd forget?

Hoping you wouldn't, but I'm sure you save damsels in distress all the time.

Not damsels as hot as her, though.

You think? Last night was one of a kind. Are you doing okay?

Not really.

What's up?

My dad is an ass, so I have to break into his house and steal something.

Twenty seconds later, her phone rang. She debated, then answered.

"You won't talk me out of it," she warned.

"Breaking and entering is a crime carrying a sentence from one to, I don't know, a lot more years in jail. Maybe even prison."

"He wouldn't turn me in, she insisted.

"You wanna take that chance? What's so urgent that you can't just ask him?"

"He's on his honeymoon, and he doesn't care."

"Wait for him to return."

"Justin, whoever took my mom was at that wedding. I need the guest list. I begged him. He said he would send it, but he never did. I'm going crazy here!"

"Can't you let Detective Finley do his job?"

"He isn't going to find anything. I called Finley, and he blew me off."

"Finley's an excellent detective. He wouldn't do that."

"When I insisted that he issue a search warrant and make my dad give him the list, he told me it wouldn't happen."

Justin laughed. Of course, it was a sexy laugh, like everything else about him.

"Do you have any idea how law enforcement works?"

She paused, feeling chastised. Growing defensive, she retorted.

"When my mom turns up dead, I'm gonna blame you guys."

"Don't break into his house. I'll talk to Finley myself. See if he will consider interviewing the guests. Please, Judith. You're a sweet girl. I don't want you to end up in the system for something stupid."

"Me, sweet?" she scoffed, "not a chance."

"Well, parts of you are sweet."

"Which parts?" she asked coyly.

"It's difficult to decide."

"I have something that might help you."

Judith opened her selfie collection and selected a picture an ex-boyfriend had taken of her lying on the bed, propped up on her elbow, with her other hand beckoning with a finger. The sexy pose accentuated her splendid curves, as did the red bra and panties. She hit send.

A moment later, he replied.

"Wow. No one has ever done that to me before."

"What?" she asked in alarm.

"Sent me a pic like this. I'm not the sort of guy girls like you ever consider."

That was bullshit.

"You're wrong. What do you mean, girls like me?"

"You know, hot girls. And I'm not wrong. I'm an old soul into old dude shit and seriously not cool."

He called her a hot girl! She felt giddy with joy.

"We could argue about that for the next five hours, or you can tell me. You like? Or too much?"

Suddenly shy and concerned that he did prefer sweet redheads who hugged him like a sister.

"You are sweet and red-hot."

"I don't send those to just anybody," she cautioned.

"You don't have to. You have like a million pics online, just about as hot."

"You stalked me, too!" She was delighted.

"You really were some beauty queen. Blew away all your competition, didn't you?"

"Those days are long gone. I haven't won a single thing in years. Now I'm a boring, almost twenty-year-old with a stupid day job like everyone else."

"So old! Judith, you can send me all your sexy pics. I'll keep them to myself. Set up a shrine on my phone for you."

She blushed down to her blood vessels.

"And, Mister Old Soul, you are mistaken. As far as men go, you are top shelf. Like the booze that's five hundred dollars a shot or something."

"What a compliment. Even though I'm a cop? Girls find that out and they're long gone."

"I think outrageously sexy pics of you working on muscle cars more than make up for your dubious profession. But you must tell me. Why the dog tags?"

"You noticed those? They were my dad's; he died in Afghanistan."

"Oh. I'm sorry." She was such a dunce. Of course, they were his dad's.

"It's fine. He left us when I was twelve. A year later, he died. We were devastated, but we moved on."

"Who took the pic?" She had to know.

"My mom."

Judith wanted to bend over and kiss the earth. The gods had brought into her orbit the sweetest man in existence. What did they want in return, she wondered?

"One more question. Sorry, I'm a super stalker. Why birds? Do you like watching them?"

He laughed heartily.

"Think I'm a weirdo? No, I just love birds. They're so funny. Especially birds of paradise. Have you ever seen the dances the males do to attract females? YouTube it. It's crazy how hard they work for it. They're so beautiful and, you know, birds are the last living relatives of the dinosaurs. So yeah, I'm a bird guy."

Judith might melt out of her skin. This guy was scary perfect.

"I'll check them out online."

There was a long pause.

"Are you still at his house?"

"Yeah, well. You're right," she conceded. "No one can ever tell me what to do or change my mind about anything, but somehow, I'm not sure how, you just did. I won't break in. Talk to the detective and we'll do things the right way."

"That's my girl," he said warmly.

"I'm your girl now?"

"After last night, I guess we'll see."

She was so happy that she thought she might not be able to respond.

"A girl can dream."

"Listen, I'm working twelves for the next three nights, helping to cover a shift for a coworker. After that, I want to take you out and repeat that kiss you gave me. Meanwhile, keep your pics coming. I might find the courage to send you something, too. I gotta say, my body is excited to see more of yours."

"Well, mister policeman, I'm pleased to hear it. And don't be ashamed of being a cop. I have never seen any cop rock their uniform like you do."

"You think so?" Justin chuckled.

"Yum yum is all I will say. You take care for the next twelve hours, and don't you be making out with any other damsels in distress."

"I think I just rescued the hottest damsel I'm ever likely to meet. Talk to you soon."

They said goodbye, and she lay back in her seat, stars twinkling in her eyes. Scrolling through her sexy pics, she debated. A little too much skin. This guy was soft, almost naïve. He needed a gentler approach. This was a time to tease, not torment. Seduce him straight into her arms. Time to take more photos, suggestive but not overt, and drive him crazy. Judith was a winner. She loved competition, but she especially loved the prizes. Justin was the ultimate prize, and she was now determined to have him no matter the cost.

Chapter 16

Justin

Oh. My. God. Justin lay back, staring at the photo of Judith. Was he still dreaming? Was this happening? He hadn't felt so deliciously aroused, maybe ever. He got up and went to grab something to eat.

Mom kissed him on the cheek.

"Hi, sweetheart. Have a good night last night?"

She donned her apron and bustled around the kitchen, her long skirt swishing as she moved. She was already putting a pan on the stove to cook him eggs. He was a mama's boy, and he let her spoil him rotten. But she needed it. After his dad left, she was devastated, but when he died, she nearly lost her mind. Justin knew his mom yearned for someone to love, so she turned all that affection onto her sons, especially her oldest.

"I had a rough night."

"What happened?"

Justin told her about Martha and her daughters.

"My word! How awful! Those girls must be in pieces about now."

"Yeah. They're shaken up." He paused. He had always confided everything in his mom and didn't think this was something he could hide from her. "Um, something happened, though."

"What?" She froze in alarm.

"The oldest daughter. Well, she hit on me. Kissed me, actually."

"Oh, honey!" His mom gave him a peck on the cheek. "Tell me all about her."

"That's the thing. I was thrilled when we met, and even more so after the kiss. We even talked on the phone just now. She's dead set on finding out who took her mom, and I'm afraid she's gonna start breaking into people's houses looking for clues."

"Why don't you join her?"

"Mom, I can't break the law."

"Love is worth sacrificing for."

"Don't know if it could ever be anything like that. Here. See for yourself."

Justin opened his phone and brought up a slew of pictures of Judith on her Facebook page wearing gowns and bikinis, smiling and performing—all of it.

After scrolling through, she handed the phone back to him.

"What's the problem? That she's gorgeous?"

"Look at her! She's like some beauty queen."

"She was a kid when she did this stuff, years ago, and she's a woman now. I see an insecure girl who no longer gets her worth from winning trophies. Tread carefully, son. Judith needs someone to love her for who she is. Bet she's had a dozen crummy boyfriends and never one single guy friend. You, my dear boy, are precisely what she needs."

"You think?" he asked incredulously.

"I know. Now you had better bring her here. I wanna meet her. I'll tell you if she's worth your time in less than five minutes."

Of course, his mom radar. He needed to deploy that weapon at once. She could tell a cheater, a gold digger, or a nag from a mile away.

"We'll see."

"You already called her?"

"I had to," he stammered. "She was about to break into her dad's house and steal something."

"Sounds like a spitfire."

"You could say that again."

"Justin, you need a life. Not just taking care of your family. Something for you to live for. You have your cars and the million chores around the house, and I'm so grateful for you. But I want you to find your heart's desire and ride off into the sunset with her. You play this through to the end. Who knows? She might end up being the girl for you."

Justin ate his eggs and went to get ready for work. He had three long nights ahead of him and a lot to think about. The phone containing Judith's pic was burning a hole in his pocket. He told her he'd send her a pic. God, of what? He thought about it and smiled.

Filled with ideas and possibilities, he headed off to another night of holding the peace and made a promise to himself. He would give this his all. If Judith were the kind of girl who needed stability, he would take it slow and convince her he didn't want to screw her and leave her. She seemed to like the fact that he was a cop. A good guy. He needed to work with that. Be her hero. He had to play his own game to capture her interest, and, like a bird of paradise, he needed to get ready to dance.

Chapter 17

Nicolas

Nicolas replayed his newly minted memory with Martha. How her thighs trembled against his cheeks as she came, how he held her to his lips, prolonging her ecstasy. She needed some work, but this was much better than any other woman. Critiquing his skill, he wondered if he should have teased her more or asked if she preferred another position. For their first time, though, it was epic. The best part was that he didn't feel the urge to kill her. At least not yet. Which was an excellent sign. To him, it was a sign of fate.

Nicolas made two perfect omelets and then sat down to read the news. To his relief, there was nothing about Martha's disappearance, so he stalked the daughter online again. He wished he could friend her on Facebook so he could get access to her entire life, but Nicolas didn't use social media anymore. He tried, but deleted all his accounts when he felt awkward and weird about it. He didn't have any friends in real life, so it was ridiculous to pretend he had fake friends, either. Plus, seducing was something that worked only face-to-face. And he couldn't tell if someone was a suitable replacement from their online photos. People were full of shit.

But for the daughter, he'd make an exception. He might even make a new fake account or something just to talk to her. Of course, that was ridiculous. He had abducted her mom and was now engaged in a mission to turn Martha into the Replacement. The daughter would never love him anyway. Still, he dreamed about her last night and woke locked in a deep mental quagmire with her soul. Was this torment his punishment for stealing Martha—that he would become obsessed with her daughter? He hoped to hell not. His phone vibrated. It was his dad.

Everything went well with your lady friend?

She's remarkable. I want you to meet her.

Any time. Have you told her about me?

No. I'll let it be a surprise.

Are you making plans to move back to your place?
Let me have my house back?

Not so fast.

You said this arrangement was temporary. I've
been more than patient.

Let me settle things with my soulmate first. I
promise. It won't be much longer.

Well, okay then.

I'll have to send you the footage of our first
romp. It will give you a boner that lasts for days.

I've told you before. I'm not interested.

I'm sending it anyway.

Nicolas felt positively malicious. His dad couldn't have sex presently, so it was a singular kind of torture. When he let him meet Martha dressed up the way he planned, he was sure it would drive him up the wall. He couldn't wait.

He shoved the rest of his eggs in his mouth like he did when he was ten, then carried Martha's plate to her room. He sat in the chair and stared at her. Tears welled up in his eyes. She was an angel. He was sure of it. Soothing his madness in a way no one ever had before, like a drug. So much more effective that he stopped taking all his pills. He wanted her now, but he had to leave for work. He had to keep up pretenses in case the police started nosing around and asking about the staff at the wedding.

At work, Nicolas was in such high spirits that his boss Dina badgered him about which of the hotties he took home with him. He refused to say, but she wouldn't relent, so he lied and made up a guest, and she socked him in the arm, pleased. Happy to know this grueling job came with a few perks. He rushed through his shift and drove into the valley to stop at the adult store, picking out various lingerie and thinking of Martha's skin and what would cling to her perfect little curves the best. She was petite but had a delightful rump and perky breasts, and God, he had to get out of this store.

Back in the car, he opened his phone and clicked on the security app to select the camera for her room. She was lying in bed, staring up at the ceiling. He wished she would touch herself and imagined her fantasizing about him the way he was about her. Nicolas stopped at his apartment in town and picked up clean clothes. He kept the place for hookups in the city, but now that he had found Martha, he could let it go. Nicolas knew she was afraid. He had abducted her from under her daughters' noses, so he had to do everything possible to make her happy and convince her she belonged with him.

Now his mind turned back to the daughter. She was so gorgeous. And angry. Her anger matched the tempo of some internal rhythm deep inside him, and he didn't know what to do now that the beat had commenced. Pulsating and erotic, he knew it would drive him insane, but he had no idea how to stop it.

The daughter was in his head, blazing in color. He had never experienced this. Women were all blank canvases, and he sought to write the narrative of the Replacement on their faces and bodies. He didn't know what to do with this. Was it lust? Yeah. But deeper too. He kept having images of her invading his thoughts, forcing him to stare at her photos constantly. It was out of his control and really frustrating.

The daughters surely called the police, and they were all looking for Martha right now. But they would never find her. If things got desperate, he would use up all his dad's fortune, hire a private jet and whisk her away to a deserted island—whatever it took to stay together.

Nicolas thought about tonight and stopped at the grocery store to buy food for a delectable meal. There was more than one way to crawl into a woman's panties. On the long drive back out to the sticks, Nicolas thought of everything that had led up to this moment in his life. He had suffered a lot, but the result was finding Martha. She was better than all the women combined. Catrina, minus the heartbreak. He thought about her for a second, then wiped his face, erasing her from his mind. There would never be another Catrina, thank God. Martha would make sure of that.

Chapter 18

Martha

Martha lay in bed, waiting. She couldn't get up because she had no clothes. How could Nicolas do this? How could anyone be so selfish and cruel? He wanted to please her, but at the expense of her entire existence. Last night, Martha realized that Nicolas was eye candy but nothing more. He was too vain, self-conscious, and needed to be committed for further evaluation. She sensed deep-rooted emotional instability in him, and it scared her.

Nicolas unlocked the door late afternoon and entered with a bag on one arm.

"Here you go, my lady. Get dolled up. I'm going to make us dinner."

"I feel ridiculous walking around in my underwear," Martha admitted. Just the thought of it made her blush.

"I could have you walk around in nothing whatsoever," he warned, "but the titillating coverage is preferable. I want to be panting for you by the end of the night. And I hope you will oblige me by being the best goddamn tease possible."

She rummaged through the bags. The lingerie was beautiful and very sexy. She held up a red teddie.

"Do you have a preference?"

His eyes lit up with approval. "That's what I'm talking about. You want me to decide. I like it. Wear the red one. It will enhance your olive skin."

He went to shut the door, stopped, and asked.

"Are you a picky eater? I'm a great cook, but I can't stand people who are gluten-free, meat-free, chemical-free—all that shit."

"No, I'm not picky. Just not too many calories. I try to watch my weight."

Martha laid everything out on the bed. He also bought her perfume and makeup. She took a long shower in preparation for this man's one-woman harem, applied makeup and lotion to her skin until it was buttery soft, stared at the new manicure she had gotten for the wedding, and wondered how long she would be a prisoner. The tips would grow out in a few weeks and need refills or removal.

An hour later, he came for her. He rushed forward with a smile of approval, grabbed her waist, and bowed backwards like they were in a black-and-white romance.

"I have waited so long for you," he murmured, "come, let's eat and talk. There's plenty of time for the fun stuff later."

Nicolas escorted her downstairs. The house was incredible. The stairs were Carrara marble. Genuine silk Persian rugs covered the hardwood floors. The furniture was expensive and well-appointed. How did he afford all this on a server's salary?

"Whose house is this?" She wondered out loud.

"It was my dad's. I inherited it."

Pulling a chair out for her, he handed her a heavy cloth napkin. Served her a plate of salmon on a bed of kale, along with a hasselback potato and poached plums with cream for dessert. Poured her a glass of red wine and turned on a lilting female folk band she had never heard before.

Martha was ravenous, but she maintained her ladylike manners.

"You like it?" He waited expectantly.

"My God, Nicolas, it's delicious. Where did you learn to cook like this?"

"I do work for a catering company. My boss has taught me a lot. I found it handy. According to the Internet, the thing women like right after a superb lover is a man who can cook." He smiled, pleased.

In this one instance, Martha conceded he was right.

"So, tell me all about yourself." Martha wasn't a flirt, and she didn't bother trying.

He gazed back, starry-eyed. Evidently, her eyes on him were enough.

"Well, I was born into a wealthy family. I spent five years at Berkeley working on a degree in anthropology."

"I'm impressed. I'm always attracted to smart men."

"I am smart," he bragged then confessed, "but not really focused. I don't want to go to graduate school. Don't know what I want to do, actually. All I ever wanted was to find the right woman. I've had some problems in that area until I met you."

Which happened less than twenty-four hours ago. Nicolas was nuts.

"Love is difficult to find," Martha admitted.

"Why do you say that?" Nicolas asked as he cleared their plates.

"I was a therapist for thirteen years before I returned to school to earn my doctorate. So many couples are not in love. It's a heartbreaking business. Counseling, I mean."

"Were you any good?"

"I thought so. I saved a few marriages. The constant theme with every couple was the lack of basic compatibility. They came together because of the sex, but after the dust settled, there wasn't enough in common."

"That won't be the case with us."

Was he really planning on keeping her long-term?

"If it is well—"

"What?"

"I hope you can help me, Martha. The truth is, I have a problem. When a woman lets me down, I get too heartbroken. That makes me feel vindictive. I hope I don't hurt you. I don't want to. I'm just saying it could happen, and if it does, it's not my fault."

Was she dealing with a psychopath here? Had he murdered any of his ex-girlfriends?

"I can help you, but I'm no criminal psychologist."

"I didn't say I was a criminal," he snapped, "I'm guarded and defensive, and yeah, I can be pretty cruel."

He held his hand out to her and tucked her into his body.

"How old are you, if I might ask?"

"Thirty-three."

Whew. At least they were born within the same decade.

"And how old are you?" He kissed her cheeks.

"Forty-two," she admitted.

"Don't be ashamed of your age. I'd have never picked you if you were less than forty."

They slid back and forth, and Martha looked into his eyes. There was no way he was thirty-three. He barely looked twenty. She felt like a child molester.

"Why do you think you go for older women?"

"I could tell you why, but it would ruin the whole evening. Let's save that topic for another night." He kissed her again, then pulled her onto the couch for a make-out session. And of course, like with everything else, he was supremely talented.

"Let's go upstairs. I want you to dance for me, then I'm gonna take you to heaven."

"Dance! Whatever for? I can't dance," Martha protested.

"Because the one who abandoned me used to dance for me, and sometimes I'd join her. I don't know, it will be nostalgic, I guess." He reddened, and Martha saw that he was embarrassed by this admission.

This was proving to be more challenging than writing her goddamn thesis. She had no rhythm whatsoever. This was ridiculous. There were plenty of sexy women in the world. Why had he picked the least sexy woman he had likely ever met? She had minimal experience with men and almost zero self-confidence in bed.

"Nicolas?"

"Hmm?"

"Are you going to keep me locked up in my room all day, every day? Because I'm gonna go crazy."

"Um, well, I guess I can let you out. I wanted to make sure you liked me first. But okay. I'll let you out tomorrow and see how you do. Then we'll go from there."

"Thank you."

"You get upstairs. I'm right behind you."

He went to the kitchen, and she went to her bedroom.

Five minutes later, he was at her door, acting like a giddy schoolboy. The more Martha was around Nicolas, the more she was aware of his childlike behavior. It was seriously alarming.

"Tonight, we'll be in my room. I have a big bed and it's all set up for what I'm planning."

She followed him meekly into his room. To her shock and confusion, he turned on the Spice Girls' "Wannabe" and started chugging his shoulders and swaying his hips like a tween.

"Now dance for me. When I can't take your sexy moves anymore, you'll know."

"Why the Spice Girls? Aren't they a little before your time?"

"They were her favorite band. Since you're like her, the same age and looks, I figured you would like them too."

"Do you have anything strong to drink? I don't think I can manage this sober." She confessed.

"Alcohol inhibits the sexual experience. There's no judgment here. I get off on the fact that you are this sweet lady trying to be erotic. That's how it was with her. And the clumsier you are, the hotter it gets me, if that makes any sense."

Martha's body burned with embarrassment. Nicolas was a complete freak. Who did this? What kind of attractive young man chose to be this way?

She stood at the foot of his bed and thought back to high school when she loved the Spice Girls and Posh Spice was her favorite. Posh made her believe she could be smart and sexy too, until she hooked up with Craig, and he unraveled all her Spice Girl mojo.

Remembering dancing with her friends, Martha put herself back into her fifteen-year-old body, forced herself to see this gorgeous male sprawled in front of her as her bestie Jenny, and began to sway.

She moved her hips, stroked her body and waved her arms above her head. Captured his eyes and refused to let go. Legs spread, she sang along because, yeah, she still remembered all the words. It was easier than she expected. She swung her curly mop around, dorky and sexy at the same time. Finally, he crawled forward and took her hands in his.

"You get an A, Miss Diaz."

How did he know her maiden name?

"I googled you, of course," Nicolas answered the question running through her mind. He hopped off the bed and twirled her around singing the words—so he knew the lyrics too, cute—laughing like a kid jumping on a trampoline as he bounced her around the room. They danced like lunatics, yelling the lyrics to the following three songs. She hadn't had this much fun in years. Finally, flushed and winded, they plopped down onto the bed.

"Time to get this party started," he declared with a kiss, and she let him carry her away.

Two hours later, he was finally asleep. Martha regarded the young man next to her and felt strangely maternal. She had read so many studies on damaged people. Now, she was living it like an anthropologist in the backwoods of a third-world country.

Nicolas was such a beautiful guy. It made no sense for him to be this messed up. Somehow, she had to uncover his issues, then maybe he would set her free. She would never tell a soul. They wouldn't believe someone this hot would abduct her anyway.

He didn't put her in handcuffs, which was a relief. And it was a repeat of last night. Tons of orgasms, and he came three times, which was an impressive show of fortitude.

Martha was tired and scared for her daughters, and she missed her comfy sweats. But she was still alive, and as horrible as it sounded, a part of her was enjoying this. The pleasure was exquisite. Never in her life had her body felt so desirable. Feeling sexy for the first time was thrilling, and her confidence was at an all-time high. Nicolas was sexy and fun to be with, even if he was a psycho who abducted her. But it couldn't last. He would hurt her eventually, whether he wanted to or not. Sooner or later, Martha knew this would all end in tears.

Sunday ~ Day 3

Chapter 19

Judith

Judith had stayed up way too late taking pics of her body up close. It was up to Justin to figure out what they were. She also took a couple of sexy selfies. One from behind, bending over in her thong, and looking back over her shoulder. Another one of her naked boobs while standing next to an open window to make her nipples pop. She would hold off on those for now. Wondered if he'd send her a dick pic, then decided he wasn't that kind of guy and felt relieved. She had received those pics since she was fourteen. Why couldn't guys learn the art of the tease?

Her phone pinged. Her hands shook so hard that she couldn't unlock her phone. He had already sent her a pic! She fell back into bed and kissed his face. He was sitting up in bed, shirt off, blowing a kiss at the camera. She was so in love with this man.

Oh, Justin!

Judith replied with the pic of her eyes.

Gorgeous.

Floating now, Judith cast her mind to the critical problem at hand. How to get a hold of that damn guest list. She needed to exercise and center herself, and then the answer would come.

Judith went for a four-mile run and cooled down on her front step. She noticed a dark Mercedes parked with someone sitting in it and sensed they were watching her. She frowned. A Mercedes in this complex? Walking over to the car, she banged on the tinted window. The driver lurched forward and took off.

Justin was right. Breaking into her dad's house would be foolish, but she might be able to break into her dad's Facebook account. After a shower and lunch, she opened her laptop.

Before the divorce, she worked for her dad as an administrative assistant, and once, her dad used her computer for an entire day. He logged into all his accounts, and she never wiped the history. So, unless he changed his password, which was unlikely because he was old and old people never thought about internet security, she would be able to log in, no problem.

Sure enough, it worked. He hadn't logged on in a while, but she could see his feed and determine which of his friends attended the wedding based on their posts. One of them had to be the perp. She scrolled through his photos, mostly taken before the divorce. He hadn't deleted any of them.

A photo he posted four years ago caught her eye. It was during one of her beauty pageant trips to Houston. Mom was lounging in a red bikini in a chair beside the hotel pool, smiling at the camera. Dad had taken this photo. Her heart thudded with misery as she stared at her mom's face. Everyone was right. They did look alike. Her mom glowed in the photo, probably because her dad spent time with her that day. And he was only happy because his darling daughter took home first prize yet again.

Judith lay back and cried as she scrolled through his photos of the family he once loved, mostly of her mom. She was such a horrible person. Why had she mistreated her mom? Why did she hate her so much? She had to find her. It had to be she who saved her!

Judith thought about how her dad had betrayed her mom and how she had kept holding on, hoping that he might come back to her. It was pathetic but understandable. If Justin had done to her what Dad did to Mom, she would have never let him ditch her either. But that would never happen. Justin was perfect.

Scrolling through the comments on her mom's bikini pic, one hit her in the face.

> Hot. If you ever walk out, buddy, she's mine.
>
> You can have her, lol.
>
> Don't tempt me, man. Martha is a goddess.
>
> No, this is a goddess.

She clicked on the link her dad provided to a stupid wannabe playboy model. Even back then he was an asshole. Clicked back to the profile of the horny friend. Scanned his recent feed, and sure enough, he was at the wedding.

He posted pics of himself with two ladies on the front steps as he left early. Judith remembered seeing him checking her mom out from across the room. Yeah. This guy was a definite suspect. Quickly, she searched online. In less than a minute, she had his address. Draper. Not too far. She had an appointment to have her mom's car serviced at the tire shop. After that, she stopped at the mall to buy some new panties in case she got anywhere with Justin the next time she saw him. Then she went to a coffee shop to pass the time. She had already called in sick to work and was afraid they might fire her, but she didn't care. All that mattered was finding her mom.

Late in the afternoon, she drove out to Draper. Found the guy's house, parked across the street, and waited. Stared at the sleepy-eyed Justin pic for a while and imagined lying in bed beside him. Impulsively, she sent him a text.

> I know you have a long night ahead of you.
> Hope it goes well!

> Thanks. Whatcha doing?

> Not much.

> Where are you?

Judith didn't reply.

> ???????

What was wrong with her? Why couldn't she lie to this guy?

> I hacked my dad's Facebook and I found—

> What?

> Some guy was creepy about the pics my dad
> posted of my mom, and he was at the
> wedding. So, yeah, I'm outside his house.
> What's this called? Surveillance?

Her phone rang and she answered.

"Yeah?" she replied meekly.

"What the hell is wrong with you?"

"No one believes me. I know I'm right. What if she's a prisoner in his house right now?"

"And what if he calls the cops because there's a strange car parked outside? Or worse, what if he is our guy? He'll murder you."

"I'm not stupid. I'm across the street," she retorted.

"It doesn't matter. It's considered loitering if you're sitting in a parked car for hours. And if there's an HOA, you're in trouble."

Was there an HOA? She looked around. In this neighborhood, yeah, there definitely was.

"Justin! Please!"

"Hear me out," he begged, "you can be arrested for obstruction of justice if you interfere with a police investigation. Nothing you are doing right now is helping your mom."

"Oh shit. He just pulled up."

"What? Don't you dare do anything stupid."

"If he has nothing to hide, he won't mind me breaking into his house." She insisted.

"If you do, I'll call the cops on you myself."

"I'm pretty sure I could flirt my way out of getting arrested."

"Goddamn it. Well, now I won't be able to concentrate at all tonight."

"I'm sorry! I shouldn't have told you. You have this crazy power over me. I can't lie to you. It's horrible! No one has ever done this to me before. It's like you are a truth serum."

"I'm happy to know I have some power for good. Judith, for the love of God, turn on your car and go home."

"What the hell? He's already leaving again. Why? He has a gigantic house. She could be anywhere in there! Why can't the police check his house out?"

"Because it's breaking the law to do unlawful searches."

"I wanna peek in his windows. Is that breaking the law?"

"If he finds you on his property, he's within his rights to shoot you for trespassing."

"I hate everything!" she screamed.

"I know, and I'm sorry this has happened. Losing your mom like this is the worst thing I can imagine."

"What if your mom was taken and you thought you could find her?" She was crying in earnest now.

"That's a hard one. Okay. Listen, do your online research. I get it. You might be right. It may have been someone from the wedding. But please don't break into any houses."

"Okay," she sniffed. "This would all be different if that detective would listen to me."

"I talked to Finley. They are currently looking at it from two angles. First, whoever took your mom walked along the ditch, leaving deep shoe prints in the wet soil. We have a man's dress shoe size ten. The second thing is the tire tread. These tires are only found on high-end luxury cars. One telltale sign is that the rear tires are wider than the front. They are custom-made and expensive. Shops keep detailed records when someone buys them. It shouldn't be too difficult to track down the owner."

"That narrows it down to about half the guests," she retorted. Then she added, "That car lot was stuffed with luxury cars. It's no wonder crimes are never solved."

"At my station, they are," he snapped.

"Sorry. That was rude."

"It was."

"Speaking of luxury cars, a Mercedes was parked outside my condo today when I got back from my run."

"You run?" He sounded excited.

"Yeah, I keep a rigorous workout routine."

"I love it. So do I."

"I couldn't help but notice," she said sarcastically, "you're so ripped, you could be a model."

"Except I don't care about shit like that."

"Yeah. You're perfect," she sighed. "Do you think the Mercedes outside earlier was a coincidence? I'm positive the driver was watching me."

"Not to sound too pervy, but I'd stop and watch you run, too. If you see it hanging around again, it could be a cause for concern. Like I'm telling you now, loitering in your car can get you into trouble."

"Fine. I'll go home."

"Are you sure? You won't ghost me and run after this guy?"

"He's ugly. I'm sure if he took my mom and went to rape her, she'd drop dead from horror and he'd be trying to bury her somewhere right now."

"I don't know who did this, but he's one hell of a psychopath. Abductions like this rarely happen."

"Psychopaths. Is there any way to tell if someone is one?"

"Sadly, no."

"Oh, he's back again."

"Okay?"

"He's got a woman with him. Damn it! I was so sure!" Judith cried.

"You don't know what you're doing. There's a right way to conduct an investigation, but this is not it."

"I may not know all the rules, mister policeman, but I believe in my heart that I'm right. That's gotta count for something."

"It's called gut instinct, and yes, you can solve a case on that alone. But right now we need to examine the evidence."

"Please don't let Finley drop this case. I'm afraid he will, since he wasn't even convinced she was taken!"

"Finding her hair comb tossed into the ditch was a game-changer. He won't drop this."

"That's a relief."

"Now, my lady, get on home and send me another of your delicious photos. I have a long night ahead of me, and I want something to waste my time fantasizing about."

"Okay. And Justin?"

"Yeah?"

"Thanks for being my Jiminy Cricket. You know? From Pinocchio?"

"You are so adorable." He laughed.

Judith rang off and drove home, obscenely disappointed. Every cell in her body screamed with sorrow. She was sure—so sure—but dead wrong. No, not dead wrong. Just wrong. She needed to go back to Facebook and dig deeper. As she pulled into her parking space, she had another call. It was her dad. Without preamble, he growled.

"Did you hack my Facebook account? I got a message that someone else signed in!"

"Yes?" she replied in a tiny voice.

"Judith, what the hell?"

"Dad, please! Send me that list! I'm going out of my mind. I need to know who was there. The police have narrowed it down to someone wearing size ten dress shoes and driving a luxury car, which describes half the guests!"

"Are you shitting me?"

"No, I'm not!"

He sighed.

"I can't believe this is happening. Your mom and I didn't always get along, but I would be devastated if anything happened to her."

"Then please!"

"Fine. Although Lori will have my head. There. I sent it. Now get out of my Facebook account, delete my password and leave us in peace!" He hung up.

To her astonishment, the guest list popped up in her inbox..

> He came through for me! Here's the guest list.

> I'll send it to Finley. Promise NO MORE DETECTIVE WORK!

She didn't reply as she devoured the guest list.

> Not hearing you!

What was he thinking? That she was going to give up now?

> Won't do anything stupid.

> Not good enough!

She sent him the pic of her lips puckered up for a kiss.

> Still mad!

Judith had the list now. She was going to vet each one of these assholes that went to support her father and shun her mother. And somehow, solve this mystery and save her mom.

Chapter 20

Justin

Justin had lost control and spiraled into infatuation. It was so embarrassing. He had never been a fool for any woman, not even in the depths of his teenage years. Since he met Judith, he hardly slept at all. He just kept pulling out his phone to stare at her. He lost all appetite for food, even his mom's superb cooking, and he hadn't worked out since last Thursday. He hated working overtime if it meant getting no sleep. A man of routine now raging on pent-up testosterone and years of unrequited lust, he found himself so captivated by this sexy woman that he barely knew himself. It was as if once caged, now set free, and Judith was the first woman he encountered in his cage-free life.

He needed a cold shower every ten minutes to wake him up, cool him down and lower his libido. Could people tell? Was pretty sure Jones noticed. Justin was used to being the reliable one. His whole life, people said things like, "He's so mature for his age," or "Look how he stepped up as the head of the family, what a little man!" Justin liked being that guy and didn't like being this guy. Why was he attracted to Judith? She wasn't concerned about the law and had no guilt over breaking it!

The worst part was that the more he tried to talk himself out of seeing her again, the more he wanted to. He had never experienced desire like this. He thought of every girl he had ever kissed—a total of five—and how they made him feel like a good guy, a gentleman. From their first moment, Judith riled him up. Turned him into a caveman. He wanted to drag her into his mountain and roll a boulder in front of the entrance. And when he came home, he wanted to ravish her on a floor covered in skins. The feelings she awoke in him were insane in their intensity and utterly alien to him. Justin thought he was a good guy, but he realized now that he was just a regular guy who had finally met the girl who could push all his buttons.

Last night was boring, and he rehashed everything they said to each other in his head. She said he was top shelf. She said he rocked his uniform. How did she know exactly what to say to make him feel amazing? But now he had to stress about her going off half-cocked and breaking into strangers' houses! How had he let himself get hung up on this girl? One kiss. Was he that pathetic? One kiss and he was a goner.

Justin smiled. She liked his relatively chaste photo. He sensed that pushing her away and playing hard to get would drive her crazy, and that's what he needed her to feel. Crazy for him. Refused to let this be a fling while she pined away for her mom. Then the moment they rescued her, he'd be yesterday's news.

Justin was obsessed with what it took to make someone want you in their life. You had to show them you were indispensable, but you also had to have some power over them. What could he give her that she couldn't live without? It was great that she thought he was her Jiminy Cricket, and it was adorable that she had seen Pinocchio. But he couldn't end up being a fling. Which meant he had to put the brakes on this and slow things down until he figured out a way to get inside her head. Sighing at this realization, he finished getting ready for work.

At the station before his shift started, he asked for updates on the case. They dusted the hair comb for prints and found nothing. The shoe print was also a dead end—a flat tread. Size ten was the most common for a man. The tires were key. Custom and expensive, they were now looking at cars that ran these tires and compiled a list of registered owners of Camaros, Corvettes, BMWs, and Mercedes in the nearby area. What kind of guy driving a two-hundred-thousand-dollar car needed to go and abduct a woman? With two witnesses right there!

Later that night, he got another text from Judith. Elated, she sent him the guest list. He opened it, forwarded it to himself, and then emailed it to Detective Finley. One thing he was sure of was that this abductor had a record for unlawful behavior, which meant he left a trail. Now, all they needed to do was find it.

Chapter 21

Martha

In the morning, Nicolas was gone, and a note was lying on the bedside table. The writing was tight, straight, uniform and neat. Where did he learn to have such flawless handwriting? Martha profiled her psychopathic lover.

Nicolas was a controlling person with a need for perfection. He probably never had a lover for whom he didn't control the narrative. Restraints made sure of this. Methodical, his role-play never deviated, as if he were in a film, critiquing himself the whole time. Self-conscious and obsessive. It was uncomfortable, his pathology.

Martha wondered if seducing older women was even enjoyable for Nicolas since he seemed to treat it like a job. His pretend relationship with her was a fantasy where she played a role. She was determined to discover the root of his bizarre obsession.

Martha, you're exceeding my expectations, so you get to leave the bedroom. There's a surprise waiting for you in the basement. Remember, you are mine now. This is just something to keep you entertained while I'm away. Your ardent lover, Nicolas.

Martha waited until she heard the delightful click as the lock disengaged. It was disconcerting that he was watching her somewhere, but she was so happy to be set free that she put it out of her mind. She raced to her room to shower, dress and eat.

Wandering through the house, Martha peered out the windows and checked the doors. This place was a fortress. The windows were all casement-style and had electric locks, just like the doors. The desert landscape stretched for miles in all directions. She really was in the middle of nowhere. She heard a click and turned. The basement door was ajar. She stepped through the doorway and tiptoed down the stairs.

At the bottom of the stairs was another entryway, and she slipped through. Recessed lighting flooded a modern basement apartment, and plush carpeting hid the sounds of her steps as she entered a combined kitchen and living area. She noticed a flat screen TV and shelves of books covering one wall. A cup of coffee sat next to an iPad on a kitchen island. Lights from a camera blinked in the corner of the ceiling. Someone was living here.

A sound startled her. Martha turned, and standing in a bedroom doorway was a naked man, towel-drying his wet hair. She gasped and he looked up, staring at her barely clad body in disbelief. Martha focused on his face with difficulty. He was attractive in all the right places. Imagined running her hands through his chest hair. She liked a man with hair. This waxing and shaving were just weird. He wrapped the towel around his waist and put up his finger.

"One moment, be right back."

She heard a drawer open and clothes pulled from hangers. Three minutes later, the man re-entered the living room dressed.

"You must be the new girlfriend? I can tell from the delightful apparel."

Martha folded her arms across her chest feeling mortified.

"Nicolas told you about me?"

"He tells me everything whether I want to know or not."

Martha shook her head, confused.

"Who am I?" He grinned.

She nodded. Why the hell was this man down here?

"I have the sad misfortune of being Nicolas's father."

It made sense: his gorgeous physique and handsome features, a few decades older and much more to her liking.

"He told me you were dead and he inherited all of this."

"I'm sure he would love that. Then all of this would be his. I'm alive and well."

"What are you doing down here?"

"This is my house. I designed it, and my company built it. Hi. I'm Erik."

He leaned forward and offered his hand.

Martha shook it, and the warmth from his fingertips tingled up her arm.

"I'm so confused. I have been ever since I arrived."

"I can imagine. My son is not well, not emotionally at least."

"I figured that much. I'm a psychologist."

"Ah, I see. It makes so much sense."

"Why?"

"He told me you were the one."

"Okay?"

What the hell did that mean?

"What's your name? Coffee?"

"Martha. And yes, coffee would be great. I miss coffee."

"Not surprised you have been left wanting. Nicholas would never think of providing anything so mundane. If it's not about your sexual pleasure, it doesn't quite meet his deliberations."

"I'm sorry. I have no idea what's going on here."

"Start from the beginning. Tell me how he found you. But I have to tell you, he sees everything. This whole house is under surveillance, which he can access with his phone."

"Will he be angry that I'm down here?"

"He wants you to. Otherwise, he wouldn't have lifted the locks."

"Erik, you said?"

He nodded.

"Why are you down here?" she probed.

"It's a complicated story. Why don't you tell me yours first?"

Martha sighed. Where to start? She wanted to tell him everything, which was uncharacteristic of her.

"I met Nicholas at a wedding."

"Your wedding?"

"No. My ex was getting remarried to the woman he left me for."

"And you went?" He looked incredulous.

"I didn't want it to seem as though it bothered me. I have a problem trying to come off tougher than I am," she admitted.

"I understand that. I'm the same way. I come off solid, but usually I'm like a disaster zone." He handed her a cup of coffee. "I should have asked. Milk? Sugar?"

"I take it black." She smiled and took a sip. For drip coffee, it was pretty damn good.

"Nicolas gives in to my whims on a few things. One of those is providing me with locally roasted coffee beans, which I prefer. I try to support small businesses whenever I can."

The hot liquid slipped down her throat and warmed her for the first time since she had arrived here.

"So was Nicolas a guest?"

"No. He was a server. Worked with the catering company."

"That's what a two-hundred-thousand-dollar education gets you these days." Erik rolled his eyes. "Did he hit on you? I mean, why the hell did you move in with my son?"

He was implying why a woman her age would shack up with a younger guy.

"He's not that young," she replied defensively.

"How old did he say he was?"

"Thirty-three?"

He laughed and downed the rest of his coffee.

"Try twenty-five, just last month. How old are you?"

"Forty-two." Martha was horribly embarrassed.

"He told me he goes for older ladies, but I had no idea he was lying about his age. What an idiot."

"Nicolas flirted with me a bit while serving my table, but I thought nothing of it."

"Oh, he has a way with the opposite sex. The same sex, too. He gets that from his mother. I've always been shit at dating."

"I doubt that." Martha wished she could take the words right back. She flushed even more.

Erik smiled, and she tried to figure out his age. If Nicolas were twenty-five, he would have to be close to fifty. He had a fine net of crow's feet around his eyes, but his body was in great shape. He couldn't be much older than her.

"So he flirts with you and you decide, screw it? If my ex gets to be happy, so can I."

"No. Nothing like that." She shook her head nervously.

"How did he convince you then? I am struggling to see what that kid, good looks aside, has to attract a diva like you."

He called her a diva. Nothing could be further from the truth.

"You won't believe me if I tell you."

"Try me."

"We left the reception—"

"We?"

"My daughters and I."

"Kids too? He hit the jackpot."

"One is almost twenty and the other just turned eighteen."

"You leave with your girls. Then what? I'm having a hard time seeing how you two came together."

"The reception was out of town, up in the mountains. It was late, around ten when we left. Suddenly, my car lurched to a grinding halt. I got out, and you wouldn't believe it. My front left tire had fallen off and rolled away. Someone must have loosened the lug nuts. Now I know who, of course."

He frowned. "I don't like where this is going."

"I turn around and there he is. Nicolas. My girls are sleeping in the back seat. He punches me in the face, and the next thing I know, I'm naked. Handcuffed to his bed. And he's getting ready to have sex with me."

Erik ran a hand through his shaggy dark hair.

"I can't believe this, not even of Nicolas. My God, Martha. I'm so sorry."

"All I can think of is how scared my girls are right now. And their father won't care. Won't even notice I'm gone."

"I doubt that. He must be an idiot to have replaced you. I'm sure the cops have opened an investigation."

"They will find nothing. Nicolas took me on a pitch-black road. No witnesses. I might as well have been abducted by aliens."

"Did he tell you why he chose you?"

"We don't talk much, if you get my meaning." She replied, embarrassed by this whole situation.

"You are his type." He looked her up and down.

"How do you know that?"

"He shows me the footage of him with his girlfriends. He likes to rub it in my face. He's getting laid and I'm not. You know. Typical son-to-father angst."

"You said he told you I'm the one who will help him?"

"Well, yeah. Bragged that his new girlfriend was a shrink and would help him understand why he is the way he is. Whatever that means."

"I didn't specialize in criminal psychology," she professed.

"Is he a good lover? He swears he's the best," he asked bluntly.

Martha flushed, marveling at the absurdity of this situation.

"First off, although he asked for my consent to have sex, he took me here against my will," she replied acidly.

"Of course. I can't wrap my head around it. I always believed he took women home who fell in love with him."

"And second, um, not really." She lied without understanding why. Didn't want this man to know it was the best sex she had ever experienced. "I should have guessed his age by how quickly he comes." She lied again. "And the handcuffs suck." What was wrong with her?

"He tells me he's the best lover in the world. Sees himself as some Casanova."

Why didn't she tell him the truth? This was far worse! Nicolas was giving her the most erotic experience of her life. It was embarrassing to admit. She was a modern, independent woman. She shouldn't be enjoying her abduction.

"Can you help me?" she asked, her voice wavering.

"Believe me, if I could, I would. I am as much a prisoner as you are. I guess it's time for my story, huh?"

She nodded, disappointed that he wasn't her saving grace.

"About six months ago, Nicolas dropped by. Finished with school, he had no idea what to do with his life. Of course, I warned him about majoring in anthropology, but he had decided never to listen to his father from birth. He visits and says he wants to stay with me for a while. He says he's trying to find his soulmate, which I thought was sweet. This apartment was my office, but I offered that he could crash down here. About a week after he arrived, he asked me to come down. I did, and he told me he was taking over the house. If I tried to leave, he'd kill me. If I did leave, he'd kill her. I didn't believe he would, but I decided to go along with it and keep the peace."

"Who?"

"His mother. She's now in a home for the disabled. Had a severe stroke."

"What happened?"

Now Erik flushed. "Nicolas tried to kill her. She went to the hospital. After the police questioned him at length, he attempted suicide. I was the one who found him. It was traumatizing. He ended up in the psych ward, and due to several extenuating factors, he received treatment and was in and out of the mental hospital, followed by a care center for a few years. Nicolas thinks I was the one who initially got him institutionalized, but I didn't. He did that to himself."

"Good Lord," she replied in astonishment.

"When he was eighteen, he earned his GED. Then, he took his SATs and got a high enough score to land him at Berkeley. I've paid for his tuition and living expenses every step of the way since he left the hospital. Hell, I even added him to my cell phone plan. After graduation, I paid for his apartment in the city. He did whatever until he decided to move in with me."

"How did he attempt to kill his mom?"

"Slipped something into her iced tea. She passed out and fell into the swimming pool. He called 911 and tried to pull her out, but I believe he pushed her in to begin with."

"Are you sure?"

"Nicolas told the cops and the shrinks that his mother had Munchausen syndrome by proxy, and he gave her some of his pills out of self-defense. It was true that the woman took him to doctors repeatedly. I know because I had to pay all the bills. But I'm not sure he's being honest. You can't believe anything with Nicolas. I mean, he tells me he has all these fantasies of drowning women. Is it because he watched his mother nearly drown?"

"Drowning fantasies can mean a lot of things."

"But none of them are good."

"What's with all the electric locks?" Martha asked.

"You noticed?" Erik replied dryly. "This house was a commission from a polygamist family. Some super-rich guy with multiple wives and a bunch of kids. Only in Utah, right? Oddly, he requested electric locks on all the doors that can only be engaged via Wi-Fi or code, and as you have seen, the handles won't engage unless the door is unlocked. And surveillance in all the rooms, even the bedrooms. I mentioned it to a contractor, and I guess he ratted them out. Next thing I know, the cops arrested this guy, and the sale fell through. After trying endlessly to find another buyer, I gave up and have used it as a getaway ever since."

"Why do you stay here now? Surely, you could talk to Nicolas. Convince him to let you go."

"I can't leave, Martha. I haven't even tried. He changed the Wi-Fi password and then installed a mesh messenger on my iPad so that we can keep in touch via Bluetooth. I told my company I was taking some time off. When there's an emergency, I write up emails and save them as drafts, and he sends them without me knowing when. Am I happy about the arrangement? No. I have allowed myself to become a prisoner. But I was a shit father. I was never there for him. When I reacquainted myself with Nicolas as an adult, I realized how damaged he was, and I've let him get away with this as some form of penance."

"You hide out down here while he abducts women and woos them into falling in love with him?" She was incredulous.

"I never thought he would abduct anyone. I thought he was just your typical desperate, horny kid. I never see him except when he visits occasionally to brag about his soulmate quest and how obsessed he is with finding someone to love him, which means I don't love him, and no one ever has. It's a horrible feeling, seeing someone who looks a lot like you, but they are broken into pieces on the inside."

Martha shook her head in disbelief.

"Nicolas has it in for me. I'm not even listed as his father on his birth certificate. His mom was a baby mama from a one-night stand. As a result, I didn't have much to do with him growing up. She kept me away, although she welcomed my money with open arms. He resents me and would like nothing better than an excuse to bash my head in. I'm going along with this, whatever it is, hoping that he gets sick of being here in the middle of nowhere and lets me go."

"That's a passive approach," she replied with disapproval.

"I was burned out around the time this happened. Being stuck down here in peace and quiet has somehow replenished me. But after six months, I am sick of it."

"Is there any way to call for help? Any way at all?"

"I built this isolated mansion as requested. We are miles from the nearest town and have no neighbors. If he received a notification that the front door opened, he would be dragging you back across the desert long before you reached safety."

"Nicolas could seduce any woman. What does he want with a middle-aged divorcee?"

"I don't know. He never dates girls his age, and I'm not sure why. Maybe older women are more of a challenge."

"I think you have that backward. He preys on older women because they are easy targets. It's the younger women who challenge him. My daughter Judith puts guys through hell to date her. Nicolas is very insecure. He couldn't handle their criticism."

"He took you, which is terrifying. How does he think this will end? You'll fall in love and run away together?"

"That about sums it up. I am part of a fantasy where he is a savior, making all my dreams come true. He is recreating a relationship that ended badly in his past. It's uncomfortable and very sad. I think someone hurt your son when he was young."

"Oh." Erik fidgeted awkwardly. No one ever liked to talk about child abuse.

"And letting me down here, I think he's setting me up. Unlocking those doors to see how I'll act around you."

"It's possible," Erik admitted.

"He warned me that he was vindictive, and I know he's possessive. I'd rather not push it."

"If he is setting you up, he's doing it to punish me. Knows it would drive me mad to be around a woman like you. He's right."

Martha smiled shyly. She had no idea how to respond.

"I'm so happy I met you. I was going crazy, locked in my room all day yesterday," she confessed.

"I'm delighted beyond words to have met you. I don't know what he's playing at but I don't care. Forgive me. I've lost my social skills from all these months of isolation. But I have to say, you are the most beautiful woman I have ever met."

Erik was so genuine that she almost believed him. He took her hand and kissed it. She flushed, remembering that she was standing here in her underwear.

"I can't pretend to be happy down here. It sucks to be a prisoner in your own home. I'm used to traveling, meeting people, fine dining, overcoming professional challenges, and I need a decent haircut. I worked hard for the better part of two decades to establish my business. Nicolas has taken all of that from me. But I don't know what to do. Like you, I would rather not cross him. Spoiled as a kid, he had a doting nanny and a mother who coddled him. I was never there, so I'm guilt-ridden. He chases older women because he has mother issues. He denies trying to kill his mom, but something is seriously wrong with him. I guess I'm afraid of him, and I know I've let him push me around in the hopes of trying to mend our relationship. The fact is, Nicolas is unstable, and I don't want to trigger the end of the world."

"I am going to dig for clues upstairs to see if he has abducted any other women. And I'll ask him about the drowning fantasies. But this has to end. I don't like restraints, and I miss my girls." She said it with a sob in her throat.

"I don't want you to go back up there. I can't bear to think of what he's doing to you. I can't believe even he is capable of this."

"I don't want to either. But I have no choice."

"Please come again." Erik looked at her, pleading. "Let me know you're safe."

"The last thing I feel is safe," Martha whispered. She turned to go. Erik grabbed her arm and pulled her into a hug.

"You poor, lovely woman. I could kill him for what he's doing to you."

She nodded again, pulled away from his arms, and left the way she came.

Chapter 22

Nicolas

Nicolas had thought of nothing else all night. He had to see that daughter again and figure out why he was so drawn to her. Then he had to get hold of Martha's passport. Hoping to resolve both issues together, he headed into the valley before work.

Perfect timing. Judith left her condo and sat on the front step, stretching and preparing for a run. He stared and stared. What was it about her? She was gorgeous, but it was more. She looked angry as she scrolled through her phone, slipped it into the pocket of her running tights and took off. Everything about Judith reminded him of a wildcat—sleek and graceful. He watched her until she disappeared then got out of the car. Hopefully, she was stupid enough to keep her door unlocked. To his relief, she was. Which meant she didn't intend to be gone long. He needed to move fast.

Quickly, he searched through the clutter for a filing cabinet, a box or anything else that might hold significant papers. Being a control freak, he wanted to tidy things up. He again decided that he was doing Martha a great service by saving her from her messy life. Ten minutes of searching did not yield any results. He headed upstairs, telling himself he was checking in Martha's bedroom, but he knew what he was really here for.

In Judith's room, he inhaled her essence and felt like he was experiencing an alien abduction. Thinking of her took him to another world and made him want to be someone else entirely. Why was he drawn to the daughter? This was going to drive him mad. She wasn't part of the plan. Martha was the plan! He stared at her trophies, all coming in first place, and ogled her pageant-winning photos. Went through her closet and drawers. He wished she had a journal lying around so that he could read and discover her secrets. He knew it was creepy but he couldn't stop himself.

Nicolas lay in her unmade bed and imagined her on top of him and him wearing the cuffs. He fantasized about all the heavenly things she would do to him, which was taboo—not allowed because he needed to remain in control. He pretended he was a regular guy who wasn't forced into this obsession with chasing older women. Judith represented a different life, a normal life, one that he would never have.

He wanted to lie here until she returned. What would she do if she found him? Could he dazzle her with his charms? To his shock, he mentally played out a scenario where he seduced her. He had never considered doing that to a girl his age. Even though it was hot, this was ludicrous!

Forcing himself up, he wandered around her room one last time, wishing he could take something of hers but not wanting to give in and be a complete pervert. He had to screw his head on straight. Finding Martha was bringing his obsession to a close. What was to follow? He didn't know and was afraid to find out.

Nicolas slipped downstairs and out the front door, then waited in his car. Less than ten minutes later, Judith returned. He was so aroused that he could barely contain himself. Wished he could be a psycho and film her. Her body was unbelievably gorgeous. Covered in sweat and breathing hard, she stretched languorously on the step. He followed her movements, made powerless by the weight of his desire.

No. The mother. Martha was the Replacement. Not the daughter. What was he doing? Then she noticed him. Stared right at him through the tinted window and stalked towards his car. Terrified, he turned the ignition as she banged on his window. Attuned to her like he was with Martha, but a thousand times more acute. Judith was angry and afraid, and she knew he was the one who had taken her mother. She wanted to kill him. He could feel it. Nicolas rammed the car into drive and roared away.

Heart pounding, he looked back, terrified she would take down his license plate. He wondered if it was too late to let Martha go and take the daughter instead. What the hell was he doing? Martha was the one. The One! Screw this daughter shit. Forcing his mind back into its old pattern, he headed to work and futilely tried to erase those blazing green eyes from his mind.

Chapter 23

Martha

"You met him today? My dad?" Nicolas asked over dinner.

He served lamb chops with rice pilaf, a mixed greens salad with a homemade dressing and raspberry sorbet for dessert.

"You told me he was dead," Martha replied sharply.

"He practically is. He was barely a part of my life. Did you like him?"

"Are you testing me?"

"A little." He gave her a facetious grin. "See how you respond to other men. But part of me feels bad too. I mean, I keep him down there and you up here. I'm gone a lot. Imagined you could both use the company. Plus, if we get married, he'll have to get to know you anyway."

Good God. Nicolas was already hearing wedding bells.

"He told me you just turned twenty-five."

He scowled. "I wish he hadn't told you that."

"Why?" Martha probed. She was using her therapist's voice now.

"Because now you'll see me as a dumb kid. I want to be so much more, and I can! But you must give me a chance."

"Nicolas, there is so much more to a relationship than sex. You realize that, right?"

"What else is there?"

Martha noted the arrested development in his mannerisms. Now that his actual age was known, he was sulking, biting his lip, and defiantly holding his arms across his chest.

She laughed. "You poor boy. I'm sorry if I call you that. It's clear you've suffered, and it makes me feel for you despite what you've done to me."

"Done to you? This is an outrage. I saved you, Martha! Your life was shitty and you were all alone. That bastard threw you over for some hag-whore. I saw how they all treated you at the wedding, how they talked behind your back. And I knew right then I had to fix it, fix you."

"Nicolas, come here." She gestured with her arms. He stubbornly stood where he was, five feet away, like a petulant child. "Fine." She threw her arms up. He raced forward and pushed her back on the couch.

"Is this better?" He rubbed his groin on top of hers and began to kiss her neck.

"Let's talk for a while, shall we?"

"I'm sick of talking."

She pushed him off her and sat back up.

"You've been telling your dad that you fantasize about drowning women. Is this true?"

He looked at his hands for a long time.

"Yeah."

"But they're just fantasies, right?"

"So far, yeah. But they're vivid. I mean, it feels like they're happening or have happened. It's weird. And usually, it's my face in the water when I drown them, so that's weird."

Someone had tried to drown him, she was sure of it. Martha decided then and there that she would help this kid if it was the last thing she did. Should she suggest it?

"I don't think they're fantasies." She took his hand in hers. "I think they're memories." She kissed his brow. A chaste kiss, but he shoved her down, ripped down his slacks and sucked her into a sexual frenzy.

Afterward, lying on the floor staring past her at the full moon shining in the window, he confessed.

"The lightest touch from you takes me to the moon. It was that way when you touched my arm at the wedding reception. I got so hard that I nearly dropped the plate in my hand."

"I'm sorry I have that effect on you. I'm sure I've never had it on anyone else."

"I'm not sorry. I knew instantly that you were the woman I was looking for. Lightning never strikes in the same place twice, right? Well, I was thunderstruck by you."

Martha was quiet. She was stroking his face, so confused. Here she was sleeping with this kid, almost twenty years her junior, and all she could think about was helping him with his emotional issues. She needed some goddamn therapy.

"Do you really think these are memories?" His eyes radiated fear.

"I'm afraid so."

"If they are memories, then I am sick. I thought I was just a pervert with a drowning fetish."

"And you might be. But people can repress awful things that they witnessed or experienced, yet they find a way of resurfacing over time."

"I don't remember anyone trying to drown me."

Martha thought of what Erik had told her about his mom, but said nothing.

"When do you have these fantasies?"

"Usually, I wake up feeling stuck in them, or when stressed or super busy at work. It's annoying. Let me tell you."

"In the aftermath of dreams or when stressed."

"I hope it doesn't make you hate me." He pulled her into his arms.

"Of course not. If anyone can understand, it's me. Please, though. No matter what happens between us, try to restrain yourself. Lock yourself in the bathroom or something. I don't want to die."

"I would rather not think of it right now. The best part is, I haven't had the urge since you came home with me."

You mean, since you abducted me, she wanted to correct him, but refrained.

"That's encouraging."

"I want you to tell me about your family. Actually, I want to know about your daughters. The older one."

He sat up, knees to his chest, and looked at her with interest.

"Judith?"

He nodded.

"How old is she?"

"Almost twenty." She studied him closely. Nicolas was like a child. He couldn't hide his feelings or desires. "What do you want to know?"

"Um, anything. Does she have a boyfriend?"

Martha smiled inwardly. This poor guy. Attracted to Judith like every other boy his age. If it weren't for his dysfunctional pathology, he would have flirted with Judith instead of her at the wedding.

"Judith has had a ton of boyfriends. They don't stick around for long. I'm not sure who breaks up with whom, but I'd venture to say she dumps them."

"She's a beauty queen?"

He looked her up online, too? Wow, this was serious.

"Judith took home first place in nearly every contest she's ever entered. She's competitive, that one. Daddy's prize winner."

"Until he abandoned you." He looked sad. "That's why she's so angry, huh? I felt her rage at the wedding."

"Judith is a hellcat, my dear girl. She hates me. I failed her by losing Craig, and I don't know how to make it up to her. You like her, don't you?" Martha nodded encouragingly and took his hand in hers. He flushed with chagrin as if caught red-handed.

"I don't know. I was just curious."

Nicolas said he didn't go for girls his age. Now she understood why. He had this compulsion for older women that was outside his control. He was a prisoner to some trauma hidden in his past. Caught behind bars, looking out at girls like Judith, wishing he could be someone else. It was heartbreaking.

"I can see you two together, you know. You're both insanely beautiful and desperate for love."

"She's desperate for love?" His eyes popped with surprise.

"Well, her dad meant everything to her and then he left us. From what I've observed, she dumps all her boyfriends because none of them love her. They just want the prestige of sleeping with a beauty queen. It's painful to see my daughter treated so horribly. These guys are a bunch of losers, let me tell you. Where are all the gentlemen, the lovers, the heroes? What has happened to this world?"

"I wanna be that sort of guy. The lover. The hero." Nicolas offered.

"You are." Martha stroked his cheek, and he looked elated.

Nicolas lay back and stared up at the ceiling.

"It's crazy to think someone out there might understand me." He replied cryptically.

She wanted to say, *Nicolas, let me go. You deserve to be with a girl your age who can understand you. It's not me, dear boy. Whatever I represent to you is dangerous and unhealthy.*

"Martha, let's go upstairs. I want to hear you scream my name. I intend to get as hard as humanly possible and drive you insane. Is that too much to ask?"

"Did we not just have sex?"

"That was a quickie. A tantalizing taste. I am thirsty, my lady."

What should she do? She thought of how she lied to his dad about how Nicolas treated her in bed. Then she thought about how he wished he could be with her daughter, and she wished she could be with his father. Unfulfilled dreams haunted them both. She was a replacement for someone in his life who had abandoned him. She shouldn't be playing along with this, but she had no choice.

"Yes, I will." She took his head in her hands. "But you must promise me to consider what I've said. About trying to resurface your trauma. It will only help you in the end."

"I will. But first, we have some urgent business to attend to." He picked her up and ran up the stairs.

Oh, the glories of youth, she thought. Then considered his interest in Judith and wondered if that was where his heart truly belonged.

Monday ~ Day 4

Chapter 24

Judith

Judith woke up late. Lizzy was at school, and the house was dead quiet—one more reminder that her mom was gone. Usually, she would be listening to her music, humming as she cleaned. It used to irritate her. Now, she would do anything to hear her mom's sweet voice again.

She had stayed up until after four a.m., cross-referencing guests using social media. Nearly all the guests had private accounts, but many were friends with those who had made their accounts public, so she could easily piece together clues. She searched for evidence of anyone who might be creepy, perverted, or a danger to society. So far, apart from the one pervert, she hadn't found any other potential suspects. This was so depressing. She called Detective Finley and left a message asking for an update. She wondered if they were now looking at the guest list.

Judith considered whether there was a way to find a criminal by their shoe size and realized it was impossible. She was tempted to send Justin another sexy pic, but didn't want to disrupt his sleep. Plus, she felt bad that she was lying to him after all. She had every intention of stalking the next possible suspect.

Around noon, she got another pic from Justin and about died. He had his hand in his boxers, staring at her with those sultry, dark eyes. He had his hand right on top—right this minute! Oh, sweet Jesus. She was so excited that she quickly fired off the pic of her juicy ass.

Enjoy, hot shot.

God, Judith.

You started it.

More. I want more.

Video call? I'll let you see everything!

She spent the next four hours researching online guests who knew her mom or had met her mom. Around five, her phone rang. It was Justin.

"Get any more sleep, my sexy man?"

"Yeah, but filled with sex dreams, so I'm not rested."

"How are you still single? You're so gorgeous it's unreal."

"Because I'm picky and old-fashioned and, I don't know, never found what turned me on."

"I'd better turn you on," she insisted.

"To say the least. That pic was just what I needed."

"No. What you need is me in your bed, tiring you out completely," she corrected.

"Don't go there. I'm already horny enough. Listen, I have to head to work soon. I wanted to tell you that I did give Detective Finley the guest list. He reminded me that if we are looking at guests, we must also look at staff. And that's a hell of a lot of people."

"Figures."

"Finley has given the green light to cross-reference owners of cars that run these fancy tires with your guest list. We've also contacted the staff and asked anyone to come forward if they noticed anything suspicious."

"That's wonderful. So, he believes me now?"

"Well, you were persuasive and pushy, and you might be right. Other than the tire tread, we don't have any leads. But it will be hard to track these rich car owners down. They're all impossible to reach. Are you done investigating now? Do you believe me when I say we've got this?"

"Sort of?"

"You're still looking into possible leads, aren't you? Anything so far? Knowing you, you stayed up half the night searching."

Judith sensed his eyes blazing in her head. Why was it so hard to lie to this man?

"I did, and nothing so far. But there were a ton of guests."

"I don't like it, but I guess if you restrict it to online research, nothing more. But that's it. No stupid shit. And if you find anything remotely odd or see a red flag, please let me know."

"Of course," she laughed nervously.

"I have to head to work now. I'm so tired. One more night of misery. Are you doing alright?"

"Apart from being all alone and missing my mom like crazy? This silence is killing me. She would always be singing, and that's how I knew she was at home. Now I hear nothing."

"I wish I were with you."

"Me too."

"Are we still on for tomorrow?"

"You kidding me? I wish I were a nerd so I could build a time machine and get there sooner."

"You're so cute. Did you like the pic I sent?"

"You're gonna drive me insane. The next time, it better be my hand in your boxers."

"Please don't put those thoughts in my head. I'm gonna spend the next twelve hours tormented out of my mind."

"Torment is right. I have never wanted anything as badly as I want you. Not even all those trophies."

"Now you're making me feel special."

"You are special. You have no idea how special."

"Ah, Judith. What have you done to me?"

She giggled.

"You mean, what am I going to do to you? We haven't made it past first base."

"Please stop talking about sex. You'll drive me mad."

"I'm trying to drag you down with me."

"You are a sadist."

"You must bring it out in me. I'll let you leave for work. Thank you for letting me do the research."

"I doubt you would listen if I told you not to."

She didn't reply, but he was right.

Around nine, she found her next suspect. Greg Tanner was thirty-nine years old and lived not too far from her in South Jordan—of course, in a million-dollar house. But the photo of him standing in front of his brand-new Mercedes caught her eye on his Facebook page. The car looked just like the one outside her condo earlier today! And more suspiciously, he worked at the same clinic her mom used to work at!

Justin said they were looking into the guest list now, but it would take them forever to vet everyone. One little drive and a quick peek. If she found anything suspicious, she'd let him know. She threw on sneakers and raced to the front door.

"Where are you going?" Lizzy looked up from the kitchen table where she was doing homework. Judith rolled her eyes. Lizzy would never understand.

"Taking a drive." She really couldn't stand how nosy her sister was.

"Any more news from the police?"

"Nope. They won't find shit," Judith snapped.

"I trust them to find Mom. You should too."

"They're cops, Lizzy. Always three steps behind."

"Don't give up yet!" Lizzy yelled as she slammed the door.

Judith sat in her car, deliberating. Was this a good idea? Yes, it was. The police sucked. And they had no idea what they were looking for.

It took her less than fifteen minutes to pull up to his house. The lights were on, and his dark Mercedes sat in the driveway.

She had promised Justin she wouldn't break into any houses. But did that mean she couldn't have a quick peek in the basement windows? Judith hurried along the side of the house, thinking all sorts of mad thoughts. What if Greg had been obsessed with her mom all these years and realized he had to take his chance when he found her sad and lonely at the wedding? If she fell in love with him, they wouldn't even call it an abduction after a while. He was attractive and more affluent than her dad. Given their shared interest in psychology, he probably thought he was the perfect catch.

She was now at the back of the house, and one of the basement windows was open. A light flickered on the far side of the room, and a scream pierced the darkness, followed by moaning. It wasn't a death scream; this was a sex scream. She couldn't tell whether it was a man or a woman. It could be a porno, but what if it was mom?

Judith deliberated, then jumped down into the window well for a better look. She saw nothing but a light underneath a closed door. Someone was in there. Was it her mom? She debated removing the screen and slipping in to check, but stopped and followed Justin's advice. She'd give him the license plate number and tell him what she found. He'd be pissed, but not after it turned out that she was right!

She crouched as she ran back along the side of the house, peeked in the back seat of his car, and spotted a woman's pair of heeled sandals. Were those her mom's? She snapped a shot of the license plate, the tire tread and the sandals. Scampering back to her car, she got in and shot off the photos to Justin with a message.

> I need you to check on this guy and follow his
> movements after the wedding. His name is Greg

Tanner. He is single. I hear screaming going on down in his basement right this second. I think it's a woman!

She hit send, wincing. *Please don't call. Please don't call.*

Her phone buzzed. He would be pissed, she knew it.

"Hello?" she squeaked.

"What the actual fuck? Where are you?"

"I didn't break in, Justin. There's no fence. I might have been back there looking for my cat. The window was open, so I hopped into the window well and took a peek. You would have done the same thing. Anyone would!"

"No, I would not do the same thing. Why can't you leave this to us? We will find this guy!"

"I have to be the one to find him!" she cried.

"I have gray hair. I've known you for less than a week, and I'm going gray."

"Can't you run a check? If something is off, you'd have reason to question him. Plus, this guy worked with my mom for years. He might have been obsessed with her. Saw her all sad at the wedding and wanted to rescue her! It has to be someone close and someone obsessed. Who else would take that kind of risk?"

"My God, what am I gonna do with you? You took the photos. Go home. I'll—"

"You'll what? Will you do anything?" she demanded.

There was a long pause until he said, "Did you look at his Facebook profile?"

"I saw a pic of his fancy new car, where he worked, and—"

"Then you obviously missed the part where he is gay."

"Gay?" she replied in amazement.

"Gay as in totally kissing another man."

"Oh." A long silence stretched between them.

"Go home. Now."

"I'm so embarrassed! Will you ever talk to me again?"

"I don't know. You're driving me nuts."

"Isn't that a good thing?"

"Not for me it isn't."

"Okay." A small sob escaped her. "I didn't mean to be a jackass, but nothing is happening. And my poor sweet mom is getting raped to death as we speak. She has never been happy. My dad made her miserable, then he dumped her. It's too much, Justin, to think about what she's going through. She doesn't deserve this!"

"I understand. You've lost your mind, and you're trying to cope. But Judith, you need to give up this investigating. Now. I have to go. I'm gonna text you in an hour, and you better text me back with a picture of you in your jammies, in your bed. Got it?"

"Okay. I will. Bye."

Judith hung up before he could say another word, devastated by her stupidity. She turned on her car and drove home. The tears wouldn't stop. Back at the condo, she opened her phone and texted her mom. Begging forgiveness, pleading with her to forget what a horrible daughter she was. She told her she loved her and wouldn't stop looking for her, then hit send. Her mom wouldn't read it, of course. But knowing that she sent it made her feel just a little better.

Chapter 25

Justin

After Judith hung up on him, Jones returned to the car with coffees and burritos from the gas station.

"What's up? Looks like something crawled up your ass."

"Judith's conducting her own investigation and it's fucking stressful."

"She's a handful. You better be careful, lover boy. I don't think you have what it takes to handle a hottie like her. She'll burn you."

"I'm already burning alive," he replied ambiguously.

"Tell her to contact Finley with any questions about the case. It's not like we know what's going on anyway."

"You're right. I need to get over this."

"You mean her?"

"I don't know what I mean."

"Judith needs a guy who will let her have her way. You, my friend, aren't that guy. You are way too controlling, Salviati. Just have a fling. Have a go at that hot body and call it good."

"No way. This is my only chance to get a girl like her."

"Be careful what you wish for. When someone is out of your league, it usually means you're not suited to each other."

"Well, Judith wants me, big time. I've never met a girl who wants me this bad. I don't want to pass up a chance like this. The lust is unreal."

Jones laughed. "The glories of youth."

An hour later, Justin texted her. About five minutes later, she sent a pic.

Her message read,

> Sorry, forgot the jammies.

Her hair was wet, and she was sitting on her bed, legs up and slightly apart, knees barely covering her breasts. He could almost make out between her legs. Jones glanced over and shook his head.

"You poor guy. You are at her mercy."

> Good enough for you?

Perfect.

> You wanna see more?

I'm at work. Can't handle it.

> I won't bother.

I don't want you to find this evil guy. He'll eat you for breakfast. Please trust me.

> I'm not used to trusting people.

Start with me, then.

A long pause. He watched the three dots wiggle for some time before she replied.

> Since you are so damn hot, I'll trust you.

I love the logic of that statement.

She sent him another pic of her lying on her back, blurring everything out below her neck just enough. He stared, trying to make out her naked body. This teasing was pure torture but he loved it.

> Hope that helps you sleep.

Then Messenger showed she was offline.

"She's toying with you, isn't she? Like my first wife. Be careful, my brown-eyed boy."

Justin laughed, ashamed of the turmoil she was putting his body through. He'd never had any serious relationships and treated most girls like friends. The one long-term girlfriend he had dumped him to marry her childhood sweetheart. Looking back, she was more of a gal pal. Justin had never lusted like this before, and at times wondered if he'd ever get laid again because he was too shy for the whole hookup scene. Judith was showing exactly how wrong he had been about himself. He really was one of those guys who would kill, die, and sell his soul for a woman. How could he play this in his favor? Win the girl when he kept pissing her off?

"What do I do? I feel like I'm chasing a feather."

"You need to see this as a fling, and then everything will make sense."

"That's easier said than done," Justin glowered.

"Not the way I see it. Sometimes people come into your life for a great fuck and that's it. Don't make it out to be more than it is."

"I want more than that, Jones."

"There's your problem. You want too much. You expect too much."

"Why can't I? Other people get what they want."

"True love is about as rare as an alien abduction. The rest is sex and tolerating each other's company."

"Sounds awful."

"You are romantic. These days we've done away with all that bullshit."

"I like the way I am," Justin replied stubbornly.

"That's fine. But you are a relic, like that car you drive. You don't belong in this century. Girls don't need a gentleman, and they don't want someone to chastise them for their stupid behavior. Let her do whatever she wants, and she'll reap the consequences."

"I wouldn't let my brothers do that."

"You ain't this girl's daddy. I'm just saying to back off and treat this like dessert before dinner. Damn, you don't even have to try. She's throwing herself into your bed. Go with it and have a little fun, then move on."

"I'm not that kind of person, and I never will be. I want something real. I want to make this into something real."

"You're precious. No wonder my wife is in love with you, and every girl down at the station, and every girl we meet on the job."

"That's not true." Justin's face reddened.

"It is. You are the sweet talk of the town."

"I don't wanna be."

"I won't lecture you anymore. You have to learn things the hard way, I guess."

No one would understand. He had never felt challenged like this before. Women were all blasé up to this point. Judith, he not only wanted her, he wanted to make her his. She was like every hot girl he lusted after in high school rolled into one. She would complete him, make him cool and popular, give him confidence, and damn, she would look so sexy in the passenger seat of his hot rod. He had to have her. Had to. And not as some fling. No. This girl was destined to be his better half. Now he had to make her crazy about him and never want to leave him.

Justin sighed and went back to staring at her blurry picture. He imagined a future where he got to see the rest of her and had all the right moves, like a bird of paradise, to capture her heart.

Chapter 26

Martha

Martha awoke around ten, which was the new normal after many midnight hours dedicated to having sex. She got dressed—if wearing lingerie counted—ate yogurt and did some yoga. When the door unlocked, she went downstairs, pulled out drawers and went through shelves and closets. She found a single photograph in the desk tucked into a pile of old letters.

Nicolas appeared to be about six. In the photo, there were two women, and one of them was holding him. A cage loomed behind them, and she made out the heads of two giraffes. The zoo. Who took the photo? Erik, she decided. On one of the rare weekends when he was in town.

Martha wandered around the living room, peering into drawers and rummaging through the closets, looking for memorabilia. Decided to go into Nicolas's room and stood outside his door until the lock disengaged. He wanted to let her in.

Wandering around his room, she pulled open the nightstand drawers, peered under the bed, and opened his closet. There were multiple sets of the same outfit, his server's apparel. The style worked for Nicolas; the starched white shirts set off his dark eyes and hair. Impulsively, she took a shirt and pulled it to her face. What was that cologne? It was divine.

In the bathroom, she went through the cabinet and found prescriptions for a mood stabilizer, an antipsychotic, as well as an antidepressant, next to a flask of Tom Ford Oud Wood. Under the sink, she found a whole array of size-enhancing pills and a prescription for Viagra. A doctor might prescribe something to offset the adverse side effects to his sexual performance that his prescriptions might induce. Lying back on his bed, she thought about her ridiculous dance and their two-hour-long romp. With the photo in hand, she left the room and went downstairs.

Martha hovered around the basement door for ten minutes. Stepping away for a quick drink of water, she heard the door click open, set the cup down, and ran to the door.

Erik was waiting for her anxiously and took her hands. It felt so natural to hug him. Martha didn't want him to let her go.

"How are you doing? Was last night bearable?"

Martha nodded. "He's crazy about me, Erik." She admitted.

"I still can't believe he abducted you, though. Even if he is head over heels in love. When he visits next time, I will demand that he release you. This is unacceptable."

"I have something to show you. Something I found. Do you recognize this?"

She handed him the photo. He grabbed a pair of reading glasses and studied the image.

"Why yes. This was a day at the zoo. I used Catrina's film camera and she gave me a copy of the photo. Feels like a lifetime ago."

"Who are the two women?"

"The one to the right is Marie, Nicolas's mother. The woman holding him is Catrina, his longtime nanny."

Martha nodded soberly.

"Why is she holding him? Nicolas has got to be at least six in this picture. Old enough to walk."

"Catrina was like that. She adored Nicolas. Carried him everywhere and pampered the hell out of him. It's probably why he became the spoiled brat he is today."

"I think she is the cause of his behavior, but not in the way you think."

"What do you mean?"

"Look at this photo, Erik. Study it! Look how she has her body turned away from his mother, possessively pressing Nicolas's head to her breast.

See how her hand is holding his privates. I'd bet a lot of money this woman had an inappropriate relationship with your son."

Erik blanched. "What!"

"How long did Nicolas have a nanny?"

"Until he no longer needed one. Ten or eleven, I believe."

"And from what age?"

"Four?" he answered weakly.

"My God. That's seven years. It's possible she started when he was young."

"How do you have that sort of relationship with a four-year-old?"

"Do you want to know?" she challenged.

"I can't believe it. I just can't."

"Who hired her?"

"Marie."

"Did she conduct a thorough background check?"

"She was a friend of her family's, so no."

"Erik, there is no reason for Nicolas to be like this unless he experienced abuse by a female figure. If it wasn't his mom, then it had to be this nanny."

"What does this mean?"

"Well, it explains why he tried to kill his mother. Perhaps he tried to tell her what Catrina was doing, but she ignored him."

"Anything a woman would do to a young boy isn't going to hurt them physically."

"There are plenty of ways to hurt a little boy. Stimulating him may cause pain, not pleasure. And the things she can make him do to her—it's disgusting to say the least. You don't think that destroying the boundaries and forcing intimacy on a young child doesn't screw them up?"

Erik shook his head and plopped on the couch.

"You're saying his behavior is my fault? I should have vetted the nanny."

"I'm not saying that. I'm only trying to understand why your son abducted a woman nearly old enough to be his mother. He's escalating, which is, of course, very concerning. Moreover, I doubt he has killed anyone, and he told me as much last night. I think he fantasizes about it quite a bit, but hasn't crossed the line. If he does, it will definitely be with me."

"I've met Catrina, and I have to say you bear a striking resemblance."

Martha looked at the photo, and he was right. Both were petite, had tan skin and brown curly hair. Sweet and wholesome.

"That might be the root of his obsession. He could be trying to replace her."

"When Nicolas visits next, I am going to confront him."

"Be careful. He will grow hostile and defensive. Would defend Catrina with his life. He wants to take back his power if he was forced to go along with something that hurt him. I see it all now. His pathology. I empathize with your boy."

"You are the best person I have ever met." Taking her in his arms, he kissed her head. "He abducts you, and all you can think is how to save him."

"It will set me free if I do. But we need to tread carefully. It's possible she did real damage. May have hurt him in ways that didn't leave scars. Threatened him if he ever told anyone. We don't want to send him spiraling into a psychotic break."

"Enough about Nicolas. Let's talk, you and me. I like you, Martha, and I want to know everything."

Erik's smile was dazzling. He was as gorgeous as his son, but with a sweetness, even a hint of sadness in his eyes. She wanted to kiss him, but that was absurd; she was currently screwing his son.

"I'm a recent divorcee. Have two lovely daughters."

"Names?" He was making them cappuccinos, and it smelled divine.

"Judith. She's a real beauty and hot-headed. A mix of Craig and me."

"Craig's the ex?"

"Yeah." She blushed, not knowing why.

"And Lizzy. So sweet and my one true support. I love both my girls."

"What about you?" He handed her a drink. "Who are you?"

"There's not a lot to me."

"I doubt that very much. What is your dream vacation?"

"Italy," she promptly replied.

"Why Italy?"

"The romance and history. The food. Everything. I love it all."

"I've been to Italy. Many times. I could give you the royal tour."

Martha realized. Oh, man. He wanted her. Was it the sexy lingerie? Was it that he hadn't had female companionship in months? Or was it something deeper? Something about her?

"I would love nothing better," she assured, and they held each other's eyes for a long time.

Martha told him about her career in counseling and how she had decided to return to school in hopes of becoming a teacher. She also shared Craig's failed businesses and success with his concrete company, primarily due to her involvement and networking. She even shared how she knew he never loved her and that they hooked up mainly because she helped him with his homework in college. She shed tears over feeling used and wasting so many years. Erik held her hand and listened. Martha felt like she could tell him anything.

"Life is one bumpy road. It sounds like things have been rough, but look at you. You are a success. You've raised two wonderful daughters, have a meaningful career, and are gorgeous. And still, half your life lies ahead of you. It sucks to look back and see what you've lost, but the only way is forward."

"But now I'm stuck here. And I have no idea how to escape this situation."

"I've messaged Nicolas repeatedly. I told him we needed to talk. He's ghosting me, which tells me he knows he's screwed up."

"Whatever is going on with him abducting me is a profound escalation."

"I agree. Nicolas showed all the signs of rehabilitation in the mental hospital, which is why they released him. I'm thinking my son knows how to manipulate the system."

"Well, he didn't manipulate me. Just took me by force. I think most people sense his emotional instability. I certainly did almost at once."

"What are you going to do? About him? Tonight?"

Martha rubbed her eyes and wished she could tell Erik what was happening. But she was so embarrassed. Sex with Nicolas was like some horrible legal drug that gave her an incredible high.

"Give him what he wants for now." Martha saw his jaw tense. He didn't like her reply.

"Guess I've always been a knight in shining armor type of guy. I hate the thought of what he's doing to you. I've barely slept since we met. Just lie in bed imagining you with him. It sucks. I want this to end. Now." Erik took her hand in his and kissed it. "I can't tell you what meeting you has done for me. I've been lonely for far longer than the last six months."

"An attractive guy like you could never be without prospects. I'm sure women line up to meet you."

Martha acknowledged with a hint of envy. Erik outdid her in every area—wealthy, successful and attractive. Who was she? A penniless divorcee with two kids and over fifty thousand dollars of new debt for a degree that might end up taking her nowhere.

"I didn't notice if they were. I've always set my sights too high. In my career, it has served me well. But in relationships, I'm a goddamn prude, and my standards are ridiculously high. I want a sweet, down-to-earth, motherly woman with a body that makes me crazy and a touch that makes me want to cuddle her forever. Martha," he pointed at her, "I've just described you."

"You've barely met me," she stammered.

"I have great instincts about people. I feel like I have searched the world for you, and in the most unlikely places, I've found you."

He reached over, cradled her jaw and kissed her, his lips triggering every muscle and nerve. Nicolas had kissed her, but this kiss was something different from just sex. This was passion with the possibility of real love. She pulled away nervously.

"What if he's watching?"

"Maybe he'll come downstairs and let me kick his ass."

"Erik, you are like, well, a man from my dreams. Once free of this situation, I'll throw myself at your feet if you still see me this way. I want you to know I want you as much as you seem to want me."

"You'd better get," he said solemnly, "before I drag you off to my bed. Seeing you like this." He gestured to her sexy apparel. "Telling me this. It's gonna keep me up tonight, that's for sure."

He flushed, and Martha wanted to throw her arms around him and kiss him down to the floor. But she was afraid of triggering a meltdown in Nicolas. He was obsessed with his idea of her, which meant she was worth far less than his fantasy.

"Okay," she agreed. "I'll leave, but I'll be back. I promise."

Martha turned and left the basement. Tears stung her eyes as she thought of all the countless nights she lay awake wishing for someone like Erik. She rushed back to her room and heard the door lock, reminding her that Nicolas was watching. He saw the kiss and their shared smiles. Surely, she would pay the price for her indiscretion.

Tanya Madsen

Chapter 27

Nicolas

Nicolas watched her with tears in his eyes. Martha sniffed his clothes! Lay in his bed! Went through all his things! She was as obsessed with him as he was with her! They were soulmates. He had never known such bliss in all his life. It was more than just her body and her willing servitude to his sexual preferences. It was her sweet, lovely soul. He buried his face in his hands and silently screamed with delight. How had he gotten so lucky? His whole body ached for her, although it had only been six hours since he last touched her.

How many more hours of work? This wedding reception was nearly over. But then there was a retirement party tonight. Maybe he should quit his job. He didn't need the money. He used it primarily as a tool to find the Replacement. Tons of older women in boring relationships attended weddings, retirement and anniversary parties. Usually, he would go home with them and spend the night making all their dreams come true. But he was always tired of them come morning because they were never the one. Not one of them was like Martha, who was practically a 42-year-old virgin.

He switched screens to snoop while Martha and his father talked. He was relieved they maintained a respectable distance, although he trusted Martha and didn't think she would cheat. If she did, then he'd have to kill them both and he didn't want that.

Martha was showing Erik something. He peered closer. It looked like a photo, and he racked his brain for what it might be. The only photo that came to mind was the one of him at the zoo as a kid. It was probably the only photo his shit father had ever taken of him. Then he thought of the person holding him. Catrina. And he let it go—all the tears. Let himself cry for the next ten minutes.

When he got home, Nicolas was especially tender with Martha. He kissed her as if they had been married for years. He was tired and had worked twelve hours. He considered leaving her alone tonight. He wasn't even sure he could perform after such an exhausting day.

Quietly, he dished up leftovers from an event, looking up at her occasionally to see if she was watching him.

"Long day?" Martha broke the silence.

"Yeah. Did you miss me?"

"Of course. But it was nice to have someone to talk to, so thanks for that."

"I watched you in my room today."

She looked chagrined, and his heart swelled.

"I hope you don't mind."

"I let you in, and no, I don't mind. You smelled my clothes, went through my things, checked out my cologne, and lay in my bed. I knew you wanted me, but seeing you do that confirmed my feelings. You made me so happy."

"I also found a picture of you as a child. You were darling. It looks like your nanny loved you, too," she probed.

Nicolas abruptly scraped his entire plate of food into the trash.

"I don't know about that. Things with her were up and down."

"What do you mean?"

"Guess I was a difficult kid to raise. She often had to punish me because I gave her a hard time."

"What sorts of punishments?" Martha dug in.

"Can we not talk about this? I don't want to think about Catrina, much less waste any words on her. Let's talk about us instead."

"What about us?"

"Martha, there's only us. Me and you, and the life I am planning for us to spend together."

"Nicolas, how? This is your dad's house. I have a family, and you have a whole life ahead of you."

"I don't want a whole life. I want one life—a life where I am finally loved. Let's go abroad. I'll work as a server in some high-end restaurant, and we'll spend our days on the beach somewhere. The nights we would spend in consummate pleasure."

"You poor guy! You're not living on planet Earth. How would it work out?"

"I would find a way. I've survived this far, and after finding you, I'll never give you up."

"I would miss my girls. They are everything to me."

"I want to be everything to you!" he screamed. "I just don't know how. How to make you love me the way I love you."

She just had to mention her girls, returning his mind to Judith. This was getting bad. He was starting to imagine Judith's face when having sex with Martha. He was seeing her everywhere and dreaming about her every night. Not only that, but he also wanted to talk to her and hear her voice. Touch her skin and kiss her. No. No! He had found the Replacement. The one who would save him. He had to hold it together!

"Love takes time. Like growing plants. Think of how long it takes a tree to grow."

"We don't have time," Nicolas sighed and collapsed onto the couch. He beckoned to her. "Come."

She seemed anxious tonight, and that worried him. When he took her, he figured it would take her some time to adjust. Maybe he should break down and buy her some regular clothes. But it was so sexy watching her like this—like a doll in a doll house where he could come home and play with her to his heart's content.

He touched her breasts and she responded with that shy gasp she always made. And his body responded, so he could perform after all. Her midnight blue lingerie was especially revealing; she looked like a goddess.

"Okay. You've convinced me. Let's get up to bed. I thought I was too tired, but I can never be too tired for you."

Once again, he sensed apprehension.

"What is it? You can't hide anything from me. I'm attuned to your feelings, so I can tell when they change."

"I hate being alone. I'm not used to spending this much time by myself."

"But I let you meet my dad," he protested. What more did she want?

"I'm still a prisoner. Locked in my room until you decide to let me out. It is, I don't know, depressing."

"I want to trust you."

"I can't leave the house. There are electric locks on all the windows and doors."

"I might be a bit controlling. I never thought I was possessive until I met you."

"I hate to tell you, Nicolas, but you are more than a bit controlling." She laughed and kissed him.

"You don't mind, right? This is who I am with you. Maybe not with someone else, but I have to be this way with you."

He pulled her into his arms and picked her up. She was so light and petite, just like her.

"You are sleeping with me tonight."

"Can we forgo the cuffs?"

Could he? Why couldn't she understand? It made his dick like three times bigger seeing her in them. And bigger was always better. It was all for her, it really was!

"We'll see. And I'll let you out tomorrow. You can make your own food like a normal person. Do whatever you want."

"That's noble of you."

She locked eyes with his. Her hazel eyes held a thousand mysteries, all of which he would somehow discover. But then her eyes morphed into Judith's piercing green orbs, and he was again lost in the tumult of his incomprehensible desire for her daughter. And he suddenly wanted everything from Judith instead. Everything. Imagined being inside her head and having such power over her that she couldn't want anything else but him. Thought about running away with her instead of Martha and loving her the way no man ever could. Helplessly, he let the force of his desires carry him away.

"Noble. I like that. I always wanted to be a prince."

"You certainly look like one."

This woman knew exactly what to say to get him going, and he wondered if Judith had the same talent. In the end, he had to use the cuffs to tease her mercilessly. Martha took it all in stride and gave him everything he wanted. Looking down at her, hoping to see the woman he was trying so hard to replace, all he could see was Judith. His mind, swirling with the millions of times they had made love across time and space since the world began.

Tuesday ~ Day 5

Chapter 28

Judith

Justin picked her up early in the evening in his restored electric-blue 1979 Chevy Camaro Z28. Judith was made speechless by his beautiful ride. She stood there and gawked.

"What?"

"This is the most beautiful car I've ever seen."

"It was my dad's. It took me years and far too much money to restore it."

"Justin, you are remarkable. What skill. You should be proud of yourself."

"Thank you. I'm happy you approve. Some girls are all about the fast and the furious. I'm old school."

"Old school. I love it."

"I didn't take you for a girl who would be into antiques."

"I never thought about what I liked, but now I know."

Judith stroked the glowing paint as he opened her door.

"Wow. Judith, you look incredible."

She loved that he looked so enchanted.

"Thanks."

Judith wore a short, gathered floral skirt paired with a fitted white t-shirt, which exposed the tiniest hint of cleavage, and a vintage 90s jean jacket. Short leather boots, her makeup was discreet, and her luscious waves were down. She was going for a natural country-girl vibe.

"Where are we going?" she asked excitedly.

"I hope you don't mind. I'm taking you home with me."

"Home?" she crowed with delight.

"I live with my mom and brothers. Is that too weird?"

"Not at all!" She laughed. "Now I'm not so ashamed about living with my mom."

"My mom really wants to meet you."

"I'm so flattered."

"I could move out, but I like taking care of them. I'm not ready to ditch them yet. Plus, I'm saving up to build a house. I already have the land."

"That's cool. I'd love to meet your family." This was serious if he already wanted her to meet his mom!

It was about an hour's drive. Justin lived down a country road out near Heber. They pulled up in front of a well-kept ranch-style home.

Justin escorted her inside, and his mother beamed. Tears came to Judith's eyes. She missed her mom so much!

"Judith, welcome to our home. I'm Nora."

"So nice to meet you." Judith smiled her pageant smile.

"We've heard all about what you've been through, and I wanna say I'm so sorry about your mother. I am praying the police will find her soon."

"Thank you," Judith said, swallowing her tears.

They sat at a table together and even said a blessing on the food, which she had only done a handful of times with her family. The meal was delicious. BBQ chicken, brown beans, evil white rolls, mixed salad, and some fluffy fruit salad—she wanted to shove the bowl into her purse and take it home; it was so good. Judith didn't think about the calories. She ate like a dainty pig, and Justin was pleased with her appetite, which thrilled her immensely.

After dinner, she talked to his mom while cleaning up. Nora was a stay-at-home mom but sold quilts online and had a YouTube channel. Judith thought that was cool.

Justin took her hand and said, "Let me give you the royal tour of my garage."

He led her out to a two-story barn-like structure and escorted her inside. An old, primed but unpainted car had its hood up, and tools were scattered everywhere. Judith zeroed in on the couch, backed him up, pushed him onto the sunken cushion and crawled on top of him.

"Whoa, what's this?"

"I think we've teased each other long enough, don't you think?" And she tore off her jacket.

Justin held her hands down.

"Not like this, Judith. Not in this dirty old garage. I've waited a long time to meet a girl like you. Never thought it would happen, actually. I'm so hung up on that fact alone. I don't need to go the distance just yet."

She couldn't hide her disappointment.

"What's the point of waiting? We're only torturing ourselves."

"The best things in life are worth waiting for."

"Like what? Getting old? Because that's what we're doing sitting here."

"How long does it take to rebuild a car or plant a garden? Those things are worth the wait. Let me, I don't know, experience this. Meeting you is like being hit with a meteor shower."

"Except one where you survive?"

"Barely. That first kiss. You are a vixen. And much too hot for me. I need to let this settle in."

"Justin, I have never wanted any guy like I want you. You've blown all your competition out of the water."

"When did you know?"

"When you handed me that wet wipe and then walked off, I realized you had the body of a Greek god, and it sealed the deal."

He laughed, pulled her to his chest, and kissed her head. She stared into his sparkling brown eyes.

"When did you know?" she echoed.

"When Jones shined the flashlight in your eyes, it was like someone hit me with a taser, but in a good way."

"I looked like a mess and immediately threw up!"

"All I remember was how I felt, and it was amazing."

"I can't believe I had the nerve to kiss you," she admitted.

"I can't either. I should have shoved you away. My bad." He brushed her hair back and stroked her cheek.

"I even confided about how I was a horrible daughter, and you didn't shun me."

"I can relate to that. The last time I saw my dad, I was mean, and then he died. I've never forgiven myself. When you said that, you straight-up hijacked my heart. I wanted to save you then and for the rest of your life."

She stroked his cheek in return, happier than she had ever been in her almost twenty years.

Finally, he said, "I wanna make out, but I decide when we call it quits."

"Which is when? You're ready to burst? I don't think you can handle just kissing me. I'm pretty good at this."

"You, my lady, have met your match. I have the willpower of a bull."

"Now you've got me thinking of other similarities you might have to a bull."

She grabbed the front of his jeans. He blushed furiously.

"You are so out of my league."

"I guess it's game on then. Let's see if I can drag you down from your high ideals."

He drew her face to his and pressed his mouth to hers, and she lost about thirty minutes of her life in blissful foreplay.

Judith pushed him. She did. Kept trying to put her hands down his pants, but he remained firm. Judith had never had anyone withhold anything from her. It was a strange new experience, like going on a starvation diet.

"Want me to tell you what I really wanna do?" she murmured between kisses.

"Hmm?"

"Find where you keep your handcuffs and cuff you to that pipe above your head."

"Then what?"

Judith proceeded to give him the finer details of what she'd like to do to his nether regions until he pushed her roughly onto her back and pinned her down.

"What have I gotten myself into?" he groaned.

"The best sex you will ever have," she confirmed. "Where are your high ideals now?"

His eyes were dilated, and he looked famished. It was better than an orgasm, getting this man to do what she wanted. He pulled off his t-shirt, revealing a chest so gorgeous that she gasped as she ran her hands over his rippling muscles and down his back, infused with lust.

"Justin."

"Hmm?"

"You are the hottest man I've ever touched. Your body is to die for."

In reply, he pulled off her t-shirt, and she was delighted. He stared down at her precisely the way he should. Crazy with desire.

"I guess we can play a little harder, but we're not going all the way." He replied breathlessly.

They petted ferociously until there was nothing but unquenchable hunger and no way to satisfy it. Judith was shocked when he abruptly stood, readjusted his jeans, and held his hand to her, flushed and shaking.

"You are insanely hot, and I want you more than I can express. But like I said, I want to enjoy every second. And rushing to the finish line is not my style."

"But I'm so horny now!" she cried in horror. "What can I do to push you over the edge?"

"Judith," he said sternly as he pulled her into his arms, "let this happen slowly. Not everything is a competition with a trophy at the end of the night."

Her body was calming down, and she threw her arms around his chest.

"Now that I've seen you half naked, I'm gonna be a wreck until I see the other half."

"I'm not the kind of guy to send a girl explicit pics."

"The ones you've sent so far have driven me crazy, that's for sure."

"I'm happy to know you're not into super trashy."

"I'm not. But you've pushed me too far. I wanna see everything," she demanded, "everything!"

"Give it some time. We'll get there."

"You are the weirdest guy I've ever met. My exes all had my panties off before they knew my last name."

"I don't intend to be another ex. I plan to figure you out. I can tell you don't like being bored, so I need to keep you guessing."

"Well, you're right. I do get bored. But never with you. You're not like any guy I've ever known. You might as well be an alien. The hottest alien on planet Earth. However, if you insist on rejecting my luscious body, there is at least one thing you can do."

"What?"

"Can you teach me some self-defense moves? Like real ones? Not the fluff they teach to girls online."

"Okay? May I ask why?" he asked, concerned. "You aren't breaking your promise to me, are you?"

"No," she lied. Of course, she was. She had no choice. She innocently replied. "After the other night, I've been scared. This would have never happened had my mom known how to defend herself."

"What I've learned is how to disarm someone who has a gun pointed at your head."

"Sounds great. Where can we practice?"

She stared around the oily floor, having second thoughts.

"I can think of a place."

It was dusk when he took her across a field to a flat grassy area.

"This technique is called Krav Maga." He grabbed her from behind in a bear hug. "I want you to drop your weight, like literally drop to the ground. This should throw your assailant off guard. Then take two of his fingers on the arm restraining you and bend them apart. Okay, let's practice."

Judith tried about ten times. She dropped her weight, and Justin lurched forward as she sank to the ground. They practiced, then combined the two. She dropped her weight, pulled, and attacked him. Soon, she was dropping like a stone every time.

"What if he has a gun? Won't he just shoot me? Should I try to get it away from him?"

"If you had three years of combat training, but you don't."

"Maybe I'd like to."

"A princess like you? I don't think you could handle combat training. It's for tough guys like me."

"Really now? You have no idea how hard I've had to work to be a beauty queen."

"Enlighten me."

"I have a brown belt in karate, four years of Taekwondo, and speak three languages. I'm proficient in Spanish, French and a little Japanese. I studied gymnastics and dance for years. Ran in three marathons, including one 24 K. I'm first-aid certified and a member of two non-profits where I volunteer. The rest of my time I spend on looking amazing."

"All this to win a trophy for being hot?" he asked incredulously.

"It's more than being hot. It's showing what women are capable of."

"Capable of? Why do you have to be capable? I mean, you're gorgeous. That's all that matters, right?"

Judith paused. Was Justin sexist? What should she say?

"I seriously hope you see more than just a hot girl standing here," she replied, frowning and folding her arms.

"No, I get it. Women wanna be equal to men. It's fine. I'm impressed. I used to practice MMA. Show me some of your moves."

And she did. She sparred with him. He brought out the tomboy in her, which hadn't happened—well, maybe never. Guys usually didn't like it when she got super competitive. She swept his legs out from under him after six tries. He pulled her down on top of him.

"Oh, now you want me after I kick your ass." She rolled her eyes.

"I think I will always want you."

"This field isn't much of an improvement from your garage."

"I haven't had enough of you yet."

They kissed until a full moon illuminated the dark sky.

Straddling his chest, Judith was delighted when he put his hands up her short skirt and traced along her thong. He moaned so loudly that she had to silence him with her mouth. And when he grazed between her legs, well, she had enough. She slid down and unzipped his jeans. Traced the outline of his dick with her mouth and reached in to pull it out. Frantically, he shoved her over and jumped to his feet. Reeling in place, tucking himself back in and buttoning his jeans, he mumbled.

"Time to get you home?"

Judith eyed him as if he had just tried to kill her. She stared at how aroused he was and decided Justin was insane. She sighed.

"I guess?"

Filled with disappointment, she let him pull her to her feet, and they headed for the car.

"Are you okay?"

He asked as he ushered her into her seat.

"Sure. I'm used to guys being different, is all."

"I'm not like the little assholes you've dated in the past, Judith."

She looked up at him, feeling the jealous edge in his voice.

"What do you mean?"

"I'm a good guy. A respectful guy. I'm not looking for quick hookups to score pussy."

"That's a relief." She flashed a smile as she glanced up at him.

"Is it?" He stared at her, his dark eyes throbbing with intensity.

There was something else. She wasn't sure what it was, but it felt like possessive desire. Her exes were never that committed. She had never been with a guy who was looking for anything long-term.

"Justin, I told you. I've never met a guy like you before."

"No, you haven't." And he shut her door.

The ride home was quiet. They drove with the windows rolled down, loving the freezing air blast as they headed into the valley. Judith thought she might float out the window and take off into the sky. He held her hand as he drove, and even though he deprived her of the hot sex, she was happy. Now she just had to find her mom, and life would be perfect.

At her door, he kissed her tenderly.

"Will I see you again?" Judith asked with a slight waver in her voice.

"You are never going to get rid of me now. Why so insecure?"

"With all my exes, things always got weird. They spent half the relationship messing with me. Filled with controlling mind games and kinks until they dumped me or I dumped them. They never loved me. I don't think anyone has ever loved me."

Justin pulled her into a hug.

"That's got to hurt. That's why it's so important that you believe me when I say I'm not here to score and then add you to my batting average. You deserve to feel respected."

"I'm sure I've never been respected," she admitted.

"Then let me be your first. Yes, you will see me again. This Thursday?"

"Sure. Still keeping dibs on the investigation? Are they tracking down car owners?"

"They are. I'll let you know of any new developments."

"Okay."

"Justin?"

He turned around and she stared at this man who was consuming all her dreams and transforming them into something real.

"I have never wanted anything as much as I want to be with you. Please don't give up on me. Even if I act like an idiot."

He digested what she said and replied.

"I can't let you go even if I wanted to. You're here now." He pointed to his heart. "You're here and you're not going anywhere."

Chapter 29

Justin

Justin whistled as he drove home. It had gone like a dream. Judith liked his car, she liked his mom and she even liked his garage! She was scary close to perfect. But he needed to push her away for now. He wanted more than crazy sex. He wanted her to want him for life. Playing hard to get might torture him in the short run, but by the time he consented, she would promise never to leave him. He had to make her desperate. Get her to chase him until she was ready to give him anything he asked for. Then he'd give in.

And this was fun. Teasing her, watching her foam at the mouth. The way she looked at him when he pulled off his t-shirt like she had never seen a real man before? Hot. No girl had ever wanted him like this. If only he could have recorded her in the garage to watch it on repeat. Pushing her away was as satisfying as making out with her. And that horrified expression on her face when he shoved her off him? Such a turn-on. He was probably the first guy who had ever rejected her. She was gonna go out of her mind to have him now.

Still, it took every shred of self-control he had not to take her in a frenzy on that couch, and even more to not let her go at him in the field. No girl had ever gone down on him, and now that Judith tried to, he was never going to stop thinking about it. He played the rest of that scenario out in his head. Her lips, then her hands and tongue on his bare skin. Shit. He needed to focus on the road. He felt like an idiot professing his high ideals when his dick was ready to burst through his pants. Who was he kidding?

A part of him did believe his bullshit. If she turned out to be the one, as in his lifelong partner, because he had no intention of ever divorcing like his parents did, he wanted a series of glorious memories leading up to their first time. He wanted it to be momentous. Set something up at a getaway. He was determined not to let it happen in either their childhood beds or in the back seat of his car. Although he did keep a blanket stashed back there in the unlikely event of getting laid. Not this girl. She was priceless. She was everything he had ever dreamed of.

Justin thought of touching her and got so aroused that he could barely concentrate on the road. This woman was wild and all in. Passionate and comfortable with her body and his. She was just what he needed. He tended to get caught up in his head and analyze everything to death, which worked great for taking down reports at work and fixing cars, but wasn't so helpful when trying to heat up a moment and stay there.

The time they spent kissing, though, he had no memory of time passing at all. Just one kiss after another. Stroking her breasts, her smooth bottom, and hearing her heavy breathing. Her kisses on his chest and neck. Wanting so badly to—was it too late to turn around and go back? Bang on the door, betray his principles and take her up against the wall? He never imagined he was capable of such lust! No one had ever aroused him like she did.

Somehow, he made it back to his house without turning around. His mom was still awake in the living room.

"Well?" He raised his eyebrows, awaiting the final verdict.

"She's a definite keeper, son. A real sweetheart, that one."

He rubbed his face and smiled in relief.

"But let me share my concerns."

"Okay?"

She sat him down next to her on the couch.

"Judith is a beautiful girl, but has a real emptiness. I think something happened to her when she was young that messed her up, but I can't be certain. I don't think she's ever felt loved by any guy. You'll have to give this girl more than a roll in the hay. She'll be needy and demanding at first. Take her a while to believe you'll stick around. Are you sure you're up for the challenge?"

"Why would she be afraid of that?"

"Honey, can't you see it in her eyes? She's desperately lonely."

"How can a girl that beautiful be lonely?"

"Her beauty is the reason she's lonely. Even her parents, I suspect, treated her like their trophy-winning prizefighter. Accolades for her looks, but that's it. She doesn't think she's got anything else to give. She's lost and doesn't know what she wants. But you know what she needs. I think she has what it takes to make you happy. Judith likes you and wants you to know it. She's besotted and stared at you with open lust all night. That kind of attraction doesn't come along every day. Trust me. You need the flames to keep the marriage bed on fire."

"Maybe." He thought of how hot she was with him in the garage. Yeah, she liked him.

"I just want you to realize what you're in for. She's insecure and will need a ton of reassurance."

"I told her we wouldn't have sex for a while yet. I don't want her to think that's all I want." He blushed when he told his mom this, and she smiled.

"You are such a prince, honey. But that's not the way to play it with this girl. Besides, she'll force you down to the floor if you don't give in. She's feisty. Playing hard to get is going to make her feel more insecure. I'd say you make plans to sweep this girl off her feet. You are, in my opinion, the perfect guy, and she knows it. She's a sensual person, and that's her love language. You won't know how much she loves you until you're sleeping with her, and she wants to show you how much she loves you. Don't push her away. Just be prepared."

"For what?"

"Teary eyes when you head off to work? Demanding extra attention, and if she doesn't get it, she'll go somewhere else. The need for constant reassurance that you love her? Tantrums if you're not spending enough time with her? Trust me, eventually she'll adapt to a life where she feels secure, but it will take time. Plus, she has no idea what she is doing with her life. She's lost and sad and needs someone like you, but doesn't feel worthy."

"She's worthy, alright. More than worthy."

"Then let it be your mission to make her see that."

"Thanks, Mom. I'm so glad you like her."

"Your brothers do too. Although they were both intimidated because she looked like a movie star."

"I need some sleep. I have a lot of catching up to do."

"Bet after meeting her, you haven't slept a wink?" She gave him a naughty look and shook her finger. "You buy yourself a couple of boxes of condoms because pretty soon you're going to need 'em."

Chapter 30

Martha

Martha woke in Nicolas's bed. There was another note.

I'll unlock all the doors at ten and let you hang out with my dad. But tonight, I have a special fantasy I want to make real with you. Be a good girl today. I'm still watching you!

Martha waited until the door clicked open, then rushed to her room to get ready. She showered and dressed carefully in lovely lavender lingerie, did her makeup and hair, and all the while butterflies danced in her stomach, like she was getting ready for a date. It was absurd.

To her astonishment, Erik stood in the living room, gazing out through the tall glass windows at miles of desert landscape. Dressed like he was on his way to work in a dark blue dress shirt and gray slacks. Damn, she wanted to take this man to bed. He turned and smiled as she descended the stairs.

"I'm a little overdressed," he joked.

"Erik, I love your style."

"Not as sexy as Nicolas, of course."

"Let's pretend we don't know who he is for a little while. Pretend it's just me coming to visit you."

"You look breathtaking, as I'm sure you know."

"I've never received compliments, so it's a pleasure to hear them."

Erik took her hand and led her to the couch. Martha was relieved that Nicolas had provided her with a somewhat modest pair of lace underwear. It was downright embarrassing not being able to cover your crotch.

She could smell his cologne from three feet away, and it was divine. Everything about him was. Maybe this was a bad idea. She wasn't sure she could be around him, not after having Nicolas awaken her dormant sexuality and satisfy her for the first time. Now she felt ravenous and wanted more and more, especially with Erik.

"Should we make lunch?" he asked as he walked into the kitchen. "I haven't been upstairs in months. It's absurd. I can't believe I've been such a pushover with my own son. It should be my middle name."

"Why do you say that?"

"In business, I'm hard and merciless, but in relationships, I'm mush. It's embarrassing. God shouldn't let attractive men also be born passive and weak."

"I don't think you're weak."

"I am, Martha. I'm a bleeding heart. Anyone who needs something from me doesn't have to push all that hard."

"I understand." And she gazed into his eyes, willing him to know how much she understood and didn't judge him. "Your house is so beautiful. Tell me about it."

Erik took her on a tour and explained the features, many of which he designed. He explained his reasoning behind the architecture and provided anecdotes on where he bought much of the furniture, mostly from high-end boutiques and a few pieces, like the dining set, from antique dealers. She told him she loved his taste and that he was seriously classy.

"I know a place in this house where there aren't any cameras. Do you want to try it?"

She knew exactly what he was suggesting. She shook her head eagerly.

Erik went into the kitchen pantry and she joined him a minute later. He grabbed her by the bottom, lifted her and placed her on a shelf. They kissed and explored each other's bodies hungrily.

"I haven't had sex in almost a year. Pathetic, right?"

"An ex-girlfriend?"

"Na. A business lunch. I drank too much, and the secretary took advantage of me."

Martha laughed.

"The last time for me, before Nicolas took me, was the night of my twentieth anniversary. It lasted about five minutes. Then, eight weeks later, Craig walked out on me. Two years later, here we are."

It was as if she were talking dirty. Her words had a delightful effect on him.

"Just knowing you are as sad and lonely as me is a huge turn-on. I'm the kind of guy who always loses his head over women, so as I've grown older, I try to avoid them as much as possible. It started with my first girlfriend at seventeen and never changed."

"And I married the first guy I slept with and tried to make it work for the next twenty years."

"Did you ever cheat?"

"I couldn't. I'm too shy."

"I love you, Martha. By the way, you look radiant in lavender."

"I thought you'd like it."

"We should leave the pantry now. If he's watching us, he'll grow suspicious."

"Erik, you have no idea the things I want to do with you."

He sank his lips into her neck and stroked her back. It was not only sexual but also heavenly. A massage while making love, like nothing she had ever experienced.

"I bet you're wonderful in bed," she whispered as she nibbled his ear.

"I'm no Nicolas," he replied sarcastically, "but ladies have never bitched about my sexual performance."

Martha kissed him and groaned as his hands wandered between her legs.

"I have a confession. I'm a pushover, too."

"Is it allowed for two pushovers to hook up?"

"There's no law against it."

"We have to get out of this small space. I can't take much more."

"Me neither. What were we doing?" She hopped down. "Oh yes, lunch."

Martha opened the door and helped Erik gather the ingredients to make pasta and a salad. They worked in harmony. She assembled the salad while he made the sauce and boiled the noodles. When it was ready, they sat next to each other at the table.

"Tell me about Nicolas's mother," Martha asked as she devoured her meal.

"I met Marie at a block party when I was twenty-one, and she was nineteen. I was in school and attended one of those events that I normally avoided. I guess she put her sights on me. Anyhow, I drank too much and while I wouldn't quite call it rape, I have never remembered having sex with her at all."

"You poor guy." Martha touched his hand, and he grasped hers.

"Three months later, she told me she was pregnant and because her family was religious, she wouldn't have an abortion. She kept it. Didn't even tell me when she went into labor. And I found out much later that she didn't list me as the father on the birth certificate, which hurt. I was busy with school and then an internship. Then, finally, my first job in the corporate world. When Nicolas was four, Marie hired a nanny on my dime. Catrina was an exchange student who had lived with her family during her teen years. She was friends with Marie and was just a year younger than her. Catrina was religious, like straight-up pious. That's why this is so hard to believe about her."

"Religion is often a haven for these types of predators," Martha declared.

"Catrina spoiled Nicolas when he was little, but got stricter as he grew up. He needed it to offset the spoiling he got from Marie when she cared to act like a mother. Marie made a part-time job out of dating. She would often take off on trips with boyfriends, leaving Nicolas with Catrina for weeks at a time. I saw him occasionally throughout his childhood, but it grew less and less as my business took off and required me to travel. It freaked me out to have a child. I never planned on having kids, and to see this boy who was a spitting image of myself at that age, but with the manners of a wild hyena, I found it terrifying."

"Bad behavior in a child is usually a cry for help."

"They should make everyone take Psychology 101 in school. I had no idea what was wrong with him. He was clingy and would hang on my pant leg when I went to leave. I feel so bad now. I was a selfish asshole which is why I'm in the situation you see me in now. I want to make it up to him, but I don't know how."

"That poor boy. What hell he must have endured."

"Have you confronted him about Catrina yet?"

"No. I plan to. I'm convinced this woman abused him and I want to help him face it."

"If it results in letting you and me go, it's worth it. Be careful. He worships her and talks about Catrina with reverence. As if she's a Catholic saint."

"That right there shows serious conditioning."

"I have to say, the more I think about it, the more I recall that you look a lot like Catrina, but ten times the beauty. Still the same petite build, olive skin and dark hair—the same, I don't know, virginal quality. If you are right about her, it may explain why he lost his shit and abducted you. Catrina up and left one day without even an explanation, apart from that Nicolas was getting too old."

"I'm sure he was. Hitting puberty is going to change a boy into a man overnight, which would be a major turn-off to a pedophile."

"Ugh. Thinking about it makes me nauseous. Are you done?"

Erik cleared their plates and cleaned up. Martha watched him, astonished at how much Nicolas shared mannerisms with his father without having been raised by him.

"Now what?"

"We can go cuddle on your couch."

"I want to do a lot more than cuddle." His dark eyes sparkled with a mix of hunger and tenderness.

"Me too."

Martha felt such love for this man. They had known each other for two days, yet she had shared more about herself and her internal struggles with him than with Craig. It was baffling. They talked for the rest of the afternoon. Martha had never connected with anyone quite like this. She hoped that Nicolas wasn't spying. With any luck, she could seduce him into thinking she was all his until she and Erik found a way out of this situation.

"When is your birthday?" He had his hand on her knee, even that light touch sent sparks through her.

"November."

"Me too!"

"Scorpio?" she asked wryly.

"Yep."

"We are the kings of sex according to the zodiac."

"Now that's funny."

"Maybe we just need the right partner." She suggested.

"Or Scorpios always need to stick together."

It was dark now. Nicolas would be home soon. Martha followed Erik down into his basement. At the threshold, he wrapped his arms around her.

"Martha, what can we do? This is hell."

"I know. Let me try to persuade him. He is so possessive of me, but if I am a surrogate for the woman who molested him, then I'm in real danger."

"Please be careful. Don't push him. He has proven he's crazy. I couldn't bear if anything happened to you."

"I'll be careful." She promised, then slipped upstairs and heard the locks engage behind her.

Martha had fallen asleep on the couch when Nicolas got home.

He woke her up with kisses on her thighs, and she bolted upright, terrified that he saw what was developing between her and Erik. To her amazement, he seemed utterly oblivious.

"Will you go out to the hot tub with me tonight? I have been obsessed with this fantasy all day and want to act it out."

"A soak sounds pretty good about now."

"Let's get to the hot tub. Now."

He stood eagerly and led her by the hand through a door off the kitchen. The moon shone through a glass atrium, and a large hot tub was in the center. He pulled off the top, turned on the jets and then stripped them both naked. He picked her up and shoved himself inside her, and by some miracle, he managed to walk up the steps into the steaming whirlpool without falling over. This guy might just have a bit of Greek god in him.

Sitting on the bench, he thrust. Martha stared into his eyes. They looked like oily pools of darkness, like a creature from a horror film. She tried not to shudder as she looked away, mesmerized by him. Nicolas had an aura like a black hole about to consume everything in his path.

"I'm close, Martha. This is what I need from you. Hold your breath. Please let me do this," he begged.

Then she realized what he wanted. She took a massive gulp of air just in time as he plunged her under the water. Standing with his hands on her hips, he shoved himself into her with a frenzy. Dragged back and forth through the hot bubbles, she ran out of air. The jerking movement deflated her lungs. She tried to push herself up to the surface, but he held her chest down. His face contorted in ecstasy as she opened her mouth and began to take in water. Furiously, she pushed to the surface. Highlighted by the moon, his eyes were euphoric as he watched her drown. He came violently and pulled her into his arms. Martha gasped for breath, spitting water out of her mouth and nose.

"I have wanted to try that for ages."

"You could have killed me," she whispered.

"That was the hottest fuck ever." He kissed her again and again.

"That was horrible."

"You didn't like it? I wanna do it again. Now that I know it works and that I won't kill you." He grinned, his dark hair falling in front of his eyes.

"I don't like pain, nor should you enjoy inflicting it. I thought you told me you had never tried to kill any of your girlfriends. What do you think this is?"

"It's not murder," he rationalized, "just a bit of foreplay."

"Too close to death for my liking."

"Trust me, I will never let anything happen to you. I can control this. Time it to perfection. But you need to give me this. I felt like Zeus standing over you, so hard that I could split you in two. And the bubbles coming out of your mouth, your hair all awry."

"Please. Not again," she begged, and Nicolas relented.

"Okay, I guess. But it was hot."

"Not for me. Something is wrong with you. You shouldn't like doing this."

He looked at her sadly as he slumped against the back of the hot tub.

"I know," he whispered, "I hate being this way. I have no control. I don't know what's wrong with me. I must fix something in here." He pointed to his head.

"Please let me help you figure this out," she entreated.

If they could trigger a memory, she could help him work through it. Then the moment he let her go, they could turn him over to the professionals for some serious therapy. Something had to give here. There had to be a way to free this twisted boy of his mental affliction and, in so doing, set her free.

Chapter 31

Nicolas

Nicolas didn't have to feel bad about nearly drowning Martha, but he did. So, he gave her a break, let her sleep in her room, and went to his own. He relived every second of his hot tub fantasy. It was too bad that none of the tubs in the house were big enough to accommodate them as he needed. This really needed to play out in a bathtub, and he didn't know why. It scared him that he was teetering on the edge and putting into practice the fantasies he had harbored for years. Something about Martha was setting him free.

He touched his penis and stared at it feeling downright proud of himself. Should have stopped to measure it. His size tonight had to be a record. It just had to be. Then he remembered all those times he was measured as a child and violently shut his eyes. No. Not now. Back to his perfect fantasy.

Martha underwater. Why was he so obsessed with this? What was wrong with him? Even he knew this kink was sick. Nicolas didn't want to be sick. He promised himself that when he left the mental hospital that he would learn how to be a functioning member of society. He hated being this way, but was at the mercy of unconscious forces outside his control.

Tomorrow would be a crazy day at work. Dina was giving him more and more shifts, which was annoying. Nicolas didn't want to work this much. He wanted to spend more time with Martha. It bothered him that he had caved into his desires to please her and allowed her to meet his dad. But he had zoomed in on his dad when he was around Martha. This was a delightful mindfuck. He was driving his dad insane. Part of him now wondered if part of his obsession with older women was to stick it to his dad. An "I can get the women you want" sort of thing. He was in competition with him. Had been so since he was a kid.

In the video footage, Nicolas caught the lust in his dad's eyes and gloated. Time to turn up the pressure and send his dear old dad footage of them having sex. It was so satisfying to imagine his dad's misery. Erik lusting after the object of his affection and giving the old bastard blue balls.

Of course, Martha was kind and sweet, laughing at all his jokes and letting him touch her leg, but no man had ever satisfied her body like he did. She was and always would be his. Still, this situation was unsustainable. He needed to track down Martha's passport, and then they could leave the country.

He considered Spain, fantasizing about moving there and running into Catrina with Martha on his arm. *Take that, you selfish bitch.* They needed a plan, but first, he needed to win her over so she would never try to leave him once the locks were gone.

It did bother him that Martha resented the handcuffs. His perfect woman would brandish her wrists with gladness and joy, understanding that to take her to his paradise, he required her to surrender all control. But she was so close to perfect that it made him a believer in God. Maybe he needed to pray. Ask for God's help in getting them safely to the other side of the planet, away from all distractions. No dad, no daughters, no career. Just him.

Thinking about Martha's daughters got him thinking of Judith—again. He tried to resist but failed. He pulled out his phone and stared at the pictures he had screenshotted. He couldn't stop thinking about her, like every ten minutes. He had a mission to carry out and didn't like having his body hijacked by unwanted desires.

Up to this point in his life, girls his age were intimidating, which forced him to act hostile and even mean. They made him feel insecure and sad because he doubted they would ever love him. The few guys he had hookups with made him anxious and even sadder because they could never be the Replacement.

He thought about what Martha said—that Judith never felt loved— and his heart throbbed with desire for her. He wanted her so badly that it was eclipsing his Replacement obsession. No. This wasn't allowed. He needed self-talk. Invoking The Secret. He had to get himself under control!

Plus, he had his seducing routine down to a science. Had never been seduced himself, had never been with a woman who called the shots and didn't know how he would handle that. Imagining Judith's hands on him, tearing off his clothes and touching his body, he was thrilled and terrified beyond belief.

Nicolas studied a pic of Judith up close. A promo shot of her from a few years ago. He stared at her blazing eyes for a long time and imagined again being a normal guy without his obsession with the Replacement and in a relationship with her. He wondered if she would wear the cuffs and let him drive her wild. Then he lay back thinking about her until he was so aroused that it was unreal. Usually, he would take care of a hard-on like this but he punished himself instead. Judith wasn't part of the plan. Stick to the goddamn plan.

Back to reality and Martha. Their great escape. If he succeeded in creating a life with her, then maybe this drowning fetish would vanish and he could get back to trying to be normal.

Maybe.

Tanya Madsen

Wednesday ~ Day 6

Chapter 32

Judith

Judith was tired when she awoke and hit the snooze. Last night, after their date, she stayed up doing research and found Lyle Summers. Invited by Lori, but her mom and dad knew him, too. She recalled the drama from about three years ago. Lyle lost a considerable bid, and her dad won. Her mom networked and used her connections to rope the contract into her dad's court for development on a huge business center. That's a lot of concrete. Her dad's business made a killing, and her family celebrated with a trip to Hawaii. Lyle never talked to her parents again.

Judith didn't remember seeing him at the wedding, but apparently, he attended. Maybe he took her mom as revenge for losing the bid?

She looked up his address. He lived in a neighborhood of estates. His house was huge, surrounded by empty land based on Google Maps. Single. No kids. Lived alone. But he could have a dungeon in his house where he held her sweet mom for all she knew. He lived way south in Utah County, so she would have to go tonight.

Judith had decided not to quit her job just yet. The sexy underwear and the gas out to Draper the other day left her with twenty bucks in her bank account. She had to cover the lunch rush at eleven, which wasn't too bad during the week unless there was a corporate event like today, which meant thirty disgusting businesspeople slurping down pasta and flirting with each other. It made her want to quit this second.

She unlocked her phone and saw that Justin had texted her five minutes ago!

Thinking of us last night.

A pic of his boxers with a delightful bulge. He was a tease! Not a dick pic. A thousand times hotter! Her mind ran all over the place. She had to match him. Time to pull out the biggest guns of all. She fired off her sexy boob shot and waited, nervous as hell. Ten seconds later.

> You vixen!
>
>> Brought those on yourself!
>
>> I won't be able to drag my eyes off these gorgeous babies for the rest of my life!
>
>>> Sounds like heaven to me. Serious about the rest of my life part?
>
>> What do you think?
>
>>> If I can't get my hands on you soon, I'm gonna lose my mind.

He wasn't texting back. Did she come on too strong? Scare him away?

Five minutes later.

>> Sorry. I had to take care of that hard-on. It was never gonna go away.
>
>>> Wanna see!
>
>> Came too fast.
>
>>> Bummer.
>
>> Next time?
>
>>> Yes!
>
>> You may very well be the sexiest woman alive.
>
>>> Hope you think so.
>
>> Want you. Bad.
>
>>> Want you even more. When I want something, I scream and throw a fit until I get it.
>
>> Love to see one of your tantrums. I'd give you a good spanking.
>
>>> Like to see you try!
>
>> Have to see you.
>
>>> Tomorrow night?
>
>> NOW.

A video call came through. It was Justin.

She plopped forward on her bed and answered.

"What? Wanna know what I'm wearing? It's nothing sexy. I sleep like a grandma covered in layers. I'm always cold."

"When you sleep with me, you won't need a stitch of clothes. My body temperature runs high."

"Sounds delightful."

"It is until mid-summer, then I'm miserable. I need to move to Alaska."

"Don't you dare."

"I wanted to tell you how much I enjoyed last night."

"I enjoyed it too, except for the part where you completely rejected me."

"Rejected you?"

"Never in my life have I had a guy push me off them, especially when I was about to go down on them. I guess there's a first time for everything."

"I'm sorry, Judith. I wasn't trying to reject you."

"Hmm. It sure felt like it. Are you not that into me? Do you think I'm a slut because I sexted you? And you prefer a good girl who will hug and kiss you like a sister and have sex with you twice a year on your birthday and Christmas? If that's what you want, move on. This is who I am. I like who I am, and the right guy will like me the way I am."

"Am I in danger of screwing this up?"

He sounded scared, which delighted her.

"Yes, you are," she said, although she didn't mean it. It was early days, and she hadn't even warmed up with her powers of seduction. She'd have him begging for it within the week.

"Judith, I didn't want you to think I was using you. You met me when I was working in a position of authority. For me to take advantage would make me a bad guy. I don't want to be that guy."

She loved him so much! What kind of guy even thought about such things?

"Justin, you are the best man I've ever met in my life. And of course, I want to respect your reservations. But you aren't forcing me to do anything." She lay back in her bed and stared into his dark eyes. "From the first moment, I wanted to tear your clothes off you, and I want to now more than ever. You aren't using me. Have you considered that we're just meant to be? And that's the reason for all this insane lust?"

"I'd like to think that. But I've never felt this way about anyone in my life. I didn't even think I could feel this way. So much desire that it feels like a bomb is gonna go off inside me."

"All it means is that you need to get laid. Sleep with me and you'll become the master of relaxation."

He laughed. "I'm never relaxed. Always fidgeting and thinking."

"We'll try again. Okay? Let's get naked and make each other happy, not hold out for some magical over-the-rainbow moment."

"You're right, of course. I was a jackass, pushing you off me like that. Trust me. It was the hardest thing I've ever done."

"Don't worry. It's good we called it quits. You were moaning loud enough to wake up your neighbor's neighbors."

"Was I now? What can I say?"

"You seriously want me?"

"That's already a given."

"What about the investigation? How's it going?"

"They are working through car owners. They go out to their homes, inspect their vehicles, and interview the owners if possible. We also checked the staff at the lodge, and none of them has a luxury car registered in their name. Guess they don't make enough to afford one."

"I've been tracking down people who have any negative connection to my mom. It might be someone with a grudge."

"If it's a grudge, she might already be dead."

"I don't think she is."

"Hang in there. We will find her. Detective work is all about patience. What are you planning today?"

Judith couldn't meet his eyes.

"Judith?"

"Nothing much. I'm just doing more Facebook stalking. I swear all these rich wedding guests are assholes. With all their trips to Italy and Mexico, I hate them all."

"Jealousy much?"

"It's not like that. They're so selfish. They disgust me. Not one of them supported my mom. They're practically evil. I used to want to be like them. Not anymore."

"What do you want now?" He sounded hopeful.

"I want a happy life. I want endless passion. To feel loved. Make a difference in the world. And I want a dog."

"A dog?" He laughed.

"Did I tell you your eyes remind me of Curry, the golden retriever we had when I was a kid? That's why I fell in love with you so fast. Those warm brown eyes."

"You are so sweet and adorable. Do you want me to take you to see my land? I can show you the blueprints I have for my house, too."

He sounded nervous, and Judith understood. This was the deep stuff. The layers you held out on. It was fine to gawk at each other's sexy body parts. That was fun and exciting. But sharing dreams was dangerous and even uncomfortable.

Judith couldn't stop her eyes from tearing up.

"Justin, I would like nothing better."

"Listen, I have a ton of chores and then some car maintenance to take care of. My beautiful ride thinks she's royalty. I can't wait to meet up tomorrow. Any ideas on what you wanna do?"

"Not anything that doesn't involve ripping your pants off. I'll have to pull my head out of the gutter and think hard on this one."

He laughed.

"You do that. I'm so happy to see your beautiful face. You take care."

After he hung up, Judith whispered, "I love you," and kissed her phone.

Judith went over her plan again and again. She would drive to Lyle's house, find an easy window to break into and sneak inside. Search the place, and if she didn't find her mom, she'd leave the way she came. No real harm done.

She went to work and hauled ass for five hours. Went home and freshened up. Lizzy was waiting in the hallway when she left the bathroom.

"You're dating the policeman?" She looked like she'd been crying.

"Justin and I went on a date."

"Have you already sexted him?"

Judith knew Lizzy was jealous of her and she endlessly judged her for being a slut. She didn't care.

"I did." She smiled with delight. "And he loved it. He called me a hot girl." Judith couldn't help but twirl like a ballerina.

"I hate you so much," Lizzy said after a pause, then went to her room and slammed the door.

In the living room, Judith felt the oppressive hate emanating from Lizzy's room. What? Did she have the hots for Justin, too? Probably. Every woman on the planet would.

At seven, she headed south. Lyle lived in an area with huge custom homes on three-acre lots. An hour and fifteen minutes later, she pulled over near his house. It was five hundred feet from the street, and no neighbors nearby. She got out and grabbed her screwdriver in case she needed to break a window. Then slipped up towards the house.

Judith wasn't sure if Lyle was their guy. Had no idea what car he drove, but he did have a motive. He hated her dad for good reason. He was single and didn't seem to have a life outside work. And he loved, not liked, every single pic of her mom posted online, which was creepy since he also hated her dad. Was that enough motive? She had no idea. But taking a quick peek around wouldn't hurt anything. There was no car parked, and all the lights were off. It could be in the garage, she wasn't sure.

The house had a full basement with large windows in the window wells. She jumped into one in the back, removed the screen, and the window slid open to her relief. This was easier than she imagined it would be. She hopped into the basement and pulled out her phone to use as a flashlight.

The room was empty. Quietly, she went to the door and slowly opened it. She peeked in and saw a pool table, bar, dartboards, and a huge flat-screen TV. This must be his man cave. Was it also his dungeon? She crept into the expansive room and started to open door after door. There were five doors in all. Three led to bedrooms, one to a bathroom, and one to a utility room. All empty. She sighed, wondering what she should do. Predators often kept their victims in basements. But maybe he had her chained up in his master bedroom. After thinking long and hard, she decided to go upstairs. The house was quiet and hopefully vacant.

Up the stairs, she now stood in a massive kitchen, and right around the corner were the stairs that headed up. She tiptoed into the living room, and suddenly a door opened. She stepped back to flee down the stairs as a man emerged from a study, dim light floating through the doorway.

"Who the hell are you?" he yelled.

Judith ran. Halfway down the stairs, he grabbed her by her long ponytail and dragged her back into the kitchen.

"Answer my question," he demanded as he pushed back his hair and tried to calm his breathing.

For an old guy, he was hot, she thought. Slim, tan and deep-set eyes. Her mom should have hooked up with him.

"Um, there's been a mistake. I'm sorry. Please, I'll just leave. I shouldn't have done this. I'm so sorry."

"Wait." He put his hand out. "I know you." He snapped his fingers and said, "The wedding. Last weekend. You were the bridesmaid."

He grinned now, probably reliving his experience of checking her out.

"Ah, yeah," Judith managed.

"What are you doing in my house?"

"Do you really wanna know?"

He folded his arms over his chest, his eyes flickering from her eyes to her boobs.

"I think I have a right to, don't you?"

"Lyle, right?"

"Uh huh."

"After the wedding last Friday, while my mom was driving home, our car broke down. My mom got out to fix it, and the next thing my sister and I knew, someone had abducted her. Right there on the side of the road. I am convinced it was someone from the wedding."

"And because I'm an unmarried man, you just assume it was me?"

"You weren't my first pick."

Judith hoped to reassure him. She was accusing him of something horrible. Nobody deserved this, except the actual kidnapper, of course.

"I didn't mean to be rude. I'm just desperate. The police have no leads. I'm just trying to help."

"Let me prove to you that I didn't take your mom, okay?"

He gestured for her to go upstairs. She started her ascent and noticed that he was gone. A minute later, he returned. He opened a door to a guest room, another office, a bathroom and a laundry room. Nothing. The last door opened to his bedroom. It was massive, as was the bed.

"Why don't you check the closet to be sure?" He suggested.

"You and my parents fought once, didn't you?"

"I lost a bid to your dad. It was no big deal."

"But you stopped talking to him."

"It wasn't over the bid. It was that he stole my girlfriend."

"Wait. You and Lori?"

"I should have been number four, not your dad," he sounded venomous.

Her estimation of Lyle fell through the floor—another stupid, pathetic Lori lover.

"The closet is right there," he gestured.

She opened the door and looked in—nothing apart from more men's clothes than she had ever seen in her life.

She closed the door and turned around. He had a gun pointed at her face.

"Take your clothes off and lie on the bed, sweetheart. You do this, and I won't call the cops on you. I think I deserve it after what you just put me through."

Judith put her arms up and walked towards the bed. What the hell was she going to do?

"I'm seventeen. If you call the cops, I'll say you solicited me for sex and took me here. Who are they going to believe?"

"You bitch!" In a rage, he came at her with his fist and punched her in the stomach.

Judith had never been punched. It felt like someone took a hand drill to her belly button. She screamed as he punched her again.

"You're a liar. I know you're not seventeen. And you broke into my house. So, my rules!" He punched her once more, this time knocking the air out of her lungs, and she collapsed backwards on the bed.

Lyle crawled on top of her. When he came close to her face and she could breathe again, she slammed her head into his. Lyle fell back off the bed, his nose bursting with blood. Judith leaped up and kicked him in the face. Flipped around and kicked him again. This time, he caught her foot and sent her flying.

"This is gonna be fun," Lyle swore and spit blood as he walked towards her, picked her up by her ponytail, and pinned her back to his chest, his arms holding her like a vise. He nestled his gun against her temple. Lyle was insane. Who wanted sex this bad?

"I should thank you for breaking in. You are letting me indulge in one of my long-time kinks, screwing a hottie at gunpoint. Seen it plenty of times online. Always wanted to act it out. Down on your knees. Now. We'll start there. Who knows where we'll take it? Bottom line? You owe me."

Judith took a deep breath and dropped like a stone, just like she practiced with Justin. His knees collapsed. She yanked his fingers apart, and he roared in pain, dropping the gun to cradle his throbbing hand. Judith flung herself to the floor, grabbing the pistol. She turned over on her back. He was coming at her. She pulled the trigger. Nothing. She pulled again and again. Lyle laughed as he dropped onto her chest.

"You didn't think I had it loaded, did you? I'm not an idiot. I guess I'm gonna have to settle for vanilla sex. You've got me so worked up, pretty girl. You are never gonna forget this."

He pressed her arms out and shoved her legs apart, kissed her, and nibbled at her breast through her t-shirt. When he let go of her wrist to unzip her jeans she slammed the butt of the gun against his temple. Dazed, he looked at her in shock. She hit him again on the back of the head as hard as possible. He moaned as he collapsed on top of her.

Screaming, Judith shoved him off. She took the gun and wiped off her prints, then threw it on the floor next to him. Raced down the stairs, unlocked the front door, and flew to her car. Squealed out onto the dark country road, sobbing so hard she could barely breathe. She could never do that again. He nearly raped her! Might have even killed her!

Judith cried all the way home. Justin texted her three times, and she ignored them all as she took a long, hot bath while stroking her throbbing belly. Crawling into bed, she sobbed some more.

She was insane. What was she doing? What had happened to her brain? Justin was right. She was a danger to herself and incredibly stupid. How would she hide this from him? If he found out, it would be over between them before it began. He was a keeper of the peace, loved order, rules and being the good guy. She didn't belong with him; she wasn't good enough for him. She was a psycho! Why did she pursue this? Investigating was a rush and she loved it, which was horrible and twisted. She was like some thrill-seeking criminal.

As she drifted off, she heard her phone buzz again. She texted Justin a bullshit reply, then put the pillow over her head and wished she could redo her entire life and be an entirely different person—someone who didn't harbor a perilous indefinable death wish.

Chapter 33

Justin

After talking to Judith, Justin threw himself into hard work. Mowed the lawn, cut down a dead tree and chopped it into firewood. Cleaned up his garage and organized his tools, the whole time his mind was raging. He was a goddamn fool like those kids in high school who went around bragging that they were saving themselves for marriage.

What if rejecting her resulted in turning her off for good? He went too far. Had the right idea, but he had to relent or she'd move on. It was time to make a comeback. Play his mind game while convincing her how serious he was. Justin did his laundry, cleaned his sheets, cleaned his room and even washed his windows. His mom gave him that knowing smile. Of course, he was trying to stay busy to prevent himself from driving down to the city and camping out on Judith's front step.

Around six, he lay down for a nap. His shift started at ten now that he was back to regular hours. He stared at Judith's photos until he was so aroused he couldn't see straight, then he got up and went for a run. Loved running in the dark and doing everything in the dark. Even liked working the graveyard shift. There was something magical about being awake when the world lay dormant. He completed a five-mile run in fifty minutes, elated that his hiatus from exercise hadn't affected his performance.

He got to work early and stopped to stare at the evidence board. They had so little to go on. So far, from what he heard, tracking down cars was proving pointless. Rich folks weren't the sort to kidnap their friend's wife. Annoyed by the insinuation, they weren't cooperative. Besides, this abduction screamed of mental illness or a crazy roadside killer. According to the staff, most guests didn't leave at all because they stayed at the lodge. The ones that did leave didn't head out until after midnight. Finley had requested footage from the night of the event, but there were no cameras in the car lot, and it was unlikely that the reception footage would prove useful.

Justin stared at the photo of Martha. Judith looked a lot like her. It was creepy to think that Judith might also attract this predator—one more reason he didn't want her to investigate this alone. Judith was fearless, but that was a bad thing in this world. Justin had read extensively about various criminal cases in school and at work, and knew how inscrutable people could be. If or when they caught this guy, he would take everyone down with him to survive.

Jones walked in.

"Ready, lover boy?"

"Yeah."

"Did you get laid last night or did you pussy out?"

"Can we not talk about my love life in public?"

"I see. You pussied out. Bet she's pissed."

Justin blushed furiously, and Jones chuckled.

"We love you around here. Don't take it to heart. And you're such a dear boy that I'm sure she'll forgive you. But be on your guard. The next time, she's gonna demand your handcuffs. That's what playing hard to get does to a person. Turns them wild."

"She won't do that, and I already realized I was stupid. We're all good."

"If you say so. But you should send her a message. You know what I mean. Show her what part of you is thinking of her." Jones grinned lasciviously.

"Pull your mind out of the gutter," Justin replied primly, following his partner to their patrol car.

Later during his shift, Justin texted Judith three times and tried calling her, but he received no response. What should he do? Was she okay? Did she do something stupid? It was a quiet weeknight, and Jones was streaming a rerun of Seinfeld. God, this was torture. He didn't want to live this way.

He wanted her to live with him, to know where she was at all times. Was he possessive? He never thought he was that sort of guy.

"What's going on, lover boy?" Jones murmured, distracted by his show.

"She's ghosting me."

"What? Come on. Not with your rock-hard bod. Even my wife drools over you."

"Then where is she?"

"Maybe she crashed out. Does she have a job?"

"She works as a server."

"If she served my table, I'd give her like a thirty percent tip."

Justin glared at him.

"Just giving your lady a compliment."

"I'm scared she's blowing me off."

"What are you gonna do?"

"I'd still like to follow my instincts despite what you say. Plan a getaway to celebrate our coming together the right way. I gotta play this in my favor, Jones. Make her crazy for me. She's had tons of boyfriends and is the kind of girl who gets bored. Trust me. I know what I'm doing."

Jones looked at him in horror.

"What is wrong with you, boy? Seize the moment. No wonder you're a twenty-four-year-old virgin."

"I'm not a fucking virgin, Jones," Justin muttered hotly.

"It's cool. No judgment. Realize some ladies, especially this particular lady, aren't into all that Victorian romance bullshit."

"I met her while on the job, which could be construed as abusing my position."

"Judith has every intention of abusing your position. Man, you don't stand a chance against her. I'd say you hand over your cuffs now. She's already stolen your heart, you might as well surrender your body too."

"Really think she's sleeping?"

"I'd say. She's had a rough week. Probably spends a lot of time crying when she's not trying to solve this case. Let her rest. You have your date with her tomorrow, right?"

Justin nodded.

"That's less than a day from now. Ogle those sexy pics she sent you and plan on how you're gonna make it up to her. Get down and dirty. I'm sure you have it in you. At least my wife thinks you do." Jones winked.

"Yeah, you're right."

Justin thought about this morning and how hard he had come in his hand while staring at her picture. He couldn't keep this up much longer. He had no idea that when he decided to play hard to get and push her off him on their first date, his unrequited urges would torture him every goddamn second. His body was cracking under the pressure. He had to up his game and get a commitment from this girl, or he was gonna lose his mind. In one week he had gone from level-headed and focused to lecherous and fucking obsessed.

He replayed their date in his head. The comment she made about his similarities to a bull was so sexy. The suggestion that she would cuff him to the pipe and suck him off made him dizzy with lust. He said he was glad she wasn't into super trashy, but he was secretly thrilled to discover that she had a dirty mind and a raunchy appetite. Justin promised himself that he would exercise some self-control but he pulled up the pic of her naked boobs anyway. Blew it up and stared, feeling the drool pooling around his tongue. Felt his dick start to swell. God almighty, she was so gorgeous. And she sent this to him! She was throwing herself at his feet! He wanted to take those beauties in his mouth and drive her wild.

He forced his phone into his pocket. This was torment in the literal sense. Judith had no idea what she unleashed when she kissed him. He was ashamed of this ravenous hunger. Now, he would have to reckon with the animal side of his nature when he convinced himself that he was some platonic prince who fought crime and saved all the maidens. Not tear their clothes off and go at it like beasts in the field. The thoughts she put in his head were perverse. He wanted to do things to her that he had never dreamed about before, which scared him—had to keep himself under control. Couldn't let this beast out. It would be unforgivable.

Justin didn't recognize himself anymore. He seethed at the online pics of her with her ex-boyfriends, consumed with jealousy when he had never been jealous before. He was possessive now. He wanted Judith with ferocious intensity and he used to talk shit about possessive guys. And finally, he felt complete. This scared him the most. Because he thought his simple life was enough. If he didn't score this girl and had to go back to life as it was before, he wasn't sure he'd survive.

Could he win her heart? Have her all to himself and finally be the guy with the hot girlfriend? He could barely comprehend how wonderful that would be. Throughout his teen years, he was a shy, hardworking boy whom girls overlooked. Hot girls blew him off like he was a dumb hick. As he grew older, Justin decided there wasn't a woman for him—at least not one he wanted this badly. He was happy for the most part with his family, his car and the occasional porno. Now there was Judith. And it wasn't just her incredible sex appeal. She was desperate for his approval. He had never met a girl who cared what he thought about her. Somehow, her need for his acceptance turned him on even more than her hot body. He loved being the good guy, and she definitely wanted a good guy.

His parents' divorce wrecked him. They were so happy when he was a kid. Dad would come home from deployment and he would hear their bed rocking like wild on the hardwood floor for days. He loved seeing his mom happy and his dad sure as hell made her happy. Then it all died, just like that. He promised himself a million times that he would never go through that.

No wonder he was terrified. It wasn't the commitment he was afraid of. It was the vulnerability.

Justin felt his phone buzz. Eagerly, pulled it out.

Sorry, I missed you. So tired. Had a rough, long
shift at work.

Adrenaline shot through his heart. Thank God. It was all back on. He pocketed his phone, put his hands behind his head, and started planning how to move things forward the next time they were together.

Chapter 34

Martha

Martha was falling into a rhythm. Around ten, she'd awaken, get dressed, slip downstairs, eat something, wait until the door opened and visit Erik.

After last night, Martha realized she needed to escape. She had to tell Erik what was happening between her and Nicolas, but she wasn't sure how. She finished her yogurt and peeled her butt from the kitchen stool. Nicolas kept the house warm, which was good since she had to walk around almost naked. The lock clicked open at eleven. She eagerly descended the stairs. Erik was standing in the kitchen, wearing only his boxers, staring at his iPad. She heard moaning and screaming in the video. It was her moaning and screaming.

She wanted to turn around and run away. Her face burned with embarrassment. What a little turd to send his dad a video of them! Nicolas was a horrible person.

"I'm a little confused, Martha. You told me Nicolas was violent and the sex was terrible. That's not what I'm seeing here. Other than the restraints, it seems like you're enjoying yourself. And my son isn't a liar. He knows how to please you."

He tried to sound lighthearted, but his voice had an edge. She knew what that edge was because she had heard it in her own voice many times. He was jealous. Martha wanted to die. She was falling in love with this man. How could she explain what was going on? Nicolas was using her as a proxy, and she played along because she had no choice.

"I'm sorry I lied." She had tears in her eyes as she took the iPad from his hands and turned off the video. "You were right. Nicolas is a Casanova. He seduces like you wouldn't believe."

"Why didn't you tell me?" He looked hurt and betrayed.

"It's so embarrassing! It's easier to say it's awful and violent. The truth is that Nicolas knew from the moment he met me that I was an unsatisfied, lonely woman. No man has ever wanted me, least of all my ex-husband, and I have never felt remotely desirable. Nicolas has awakened something in me. What he's doing to my body feels great, but forced pleasure is not my thing. He's just a boy, and I feel maternal towards him, making this situation unbelievably awkward."

This was a hundred times harder than anything she had ever done. Confessing to this man that part of her enjoyed what Nicolas did to her. Did she love him? No. Did she prefer him? Never. But she was playing the role he demanded. She had excelled at people-pleasing her entire life, and now this talent compromised her.

"Hmm." He looked at her as if trying to decide whether she was being honest with him.

"Please believe me. I don't want this. After last night." A sob escaped her. "I am in real danger. He took me into the hot tub and tried to drown me while we had sex. I don't think I'll live out the week."

"Good God." He pulled her into his arms and kissed her head.

"Why didn't you trust me? Did you think I was just flirting? I'm dead serious. I can never be frivolous about my feelings."

"I want to trust you. But this is your son. I'm at the mercy of an emotionally damaged boy on the verge of becoming a murderer. Erik, I'm convinced this is all a game he's playing with us. Setting us up and forcing me to walk around almost naked. He's tormenting you and using me to do it. Getting off on this scenario big time. Has such animosity for you, and this is just foreplay to him."

"He sends me this video just this morning. I think you're right."

"We're both completely at his mercy."

"The worst part is, even if we did manage to overpower him, we couldn't escape. Only he holds the code to open the front door. When I built this place, I never dreamed the locks would be used against me."

Martha felt his erection through his boxers, and she pressed her body closer.

"Seeing you in that footage, shit. You are so fucking sexy. I'm going to lose it here. I want you so bad. It's like I'm some male animal in a documentary and I wanna mark the desired female with my scent to keep him away," Erik confessed.

"Is there any way to cover up the camera?" she whispered.

"You mean in my bedroom?"

"I can't stop thinking about you."

"I could figure something out. Want to risk it?"

"Honestly, I have no idea. But I want you."

Erick stood back and sized her up.

"I'm not just flirting when I say I have never wanted a woman so bad in all my life."

"Because of him? Of what he's doing to me?"

"Because of you. If I had seen you at an airport, I would have overcome my shyness and asked for your number. If I had seen you at a restaurant, I might have even been super creepy and followed you home. Martha, you're perfect."

What was happening to her? All that Nicolas stirred up in her was climaxing, and she wanted to share this tsunami of passion with someone she truly desired. Not someone who objectified her and fantasized about killing her. A man with a pure heart who might love her. She held back, barely.

"Cover up the camera. Now."

"He might flip out. Maybe try to kill us both."

"I'm so hungry for you right now. I don't care."

He turned and rushed into his bedroom. A minute later, he was standing in his doorway completely naked, just like the first day they met. Martha threw caution to the wind and flew into his arms.

The afternoon and evening were the best of Martha's life. Erik was sublime, tender, erotic and incredibly passionate. Nothing pretentious existed between them. She knew exactly where to touch and how to arouse, and he did the same to her. They both had an insatiable desire to please each other. Martha didn't think such pleasure could exist or that such a man could exist. How did he manage to have the worst son alive? Nicolas had opened a door inside her and pulled her through. She would never return to the woman who felt unworthy of love.

After thoroughly exhausting each other, they lay tangled. Martha held her breath. This had to end. Somehow. She had to break free. She never wanted Nicolas to touch her again. How could she sleep with him again after this experience?

"I should go back upstairs," she sighed.

"Make sure to take a shower. If he smells me on you, I don't want to think about it."

"I can't bear to go along with this anymore. What if he figures it out?"

"With any luck, he won't. Listen, I know you must give in to his demands. I don't judge you at all for this. He's forcing you, and he knows it."

"Erik, we need to make a plan. We can't go on like this. He won't let us."

"For now, go along with his fantasy. It's just sex. You can survive this. If you survived twenty years with Craig, then you can survive this."

"If he sends you more footage of him and me, please believe it's an act?"

"Now that I've seen the real you, I know it's all an act. You must be so scared."

"I'm terrified."

"Go. But return tomorrow. I'm starting to feel like I can't live without you."

Martha kissed him soundly and left his room, her legs shaking as she ascended the stairs.

Chapter 35

Nicolas

After hours of back-to-back events, there was finally a lull in the dinner rush, so Nicolas hid in the bathroom stall, plopped down on the toilet seat, completely exhausted. Opened his app to check the surveillance cameras and spy on Martha. He looked through the different rooms in the house and didn't see Martha anywhere. Swishing through, his alarm was growing. Where the hell was she? He went to the basement and looked through the rooms. Not only did he not spot her, but he also didn't see his father anywhere. He scrolled back and forth. Then, he realized one of the screens was dark.

Something was covering the camera in his father's bedroom. Frantically, he thought about what this meant. She couldn't. She wouldn't! Would she? Would he?

Erik had abandoned him as a child, which is part of the reason he moved home and imprisoned the bastard in his own basement. He was a horrible dad and deserved far worse. But she was the Replacement, and the thought of her with his dad made him want to tear his eyes out. He had to leave. He had to catch them in the act! Nicolas shoved his phone in his pocket, left the stall, washed his hands and ran to find Dina.

"I've got to go. I'm so sorry. I have a family emergency." He cried as he rushed to his car.

The Mercedes roared to life, and he tore out of the parking lot. What would he do if his suspicions proved correct? Maybe it was nothing. They might be talking. He knew Martha was lonely, which is why he had let her visit his dad in the first place. Then he thought of his dad, who hadn't gotten laid in at least six months, and how he had sent him that video of him with Martha just this morning. It might have pushed him too far.

And then Martha. He had her walking around in the sexiest lingerie he could find. This was his fault. In his quest to torture his dad, he may have brought the house down on all of them.

He should have bought her a robe and told her to wear it when going downstairs. The thought of his dad inside her right now made him quiver with rage. What if they liked each other? What if they fell in love?

Nicolas felt like he was dying, so he turned the tables and imagined instead what it would be like to watch Martha die and fantasized about that all the way home.

By the time he reached the house, he had calmed down a bit. He was still angry but tried to keep it in perspective. Nicolas parked the car, opened the door, slammed it, stared at his reflection in the black-tinted window, and smiled. He was a perfect specimen of a man. No one could prefer some sweaty old dude over him. He would make this all go away.

Why did he keep getting everything wrong? He was so sure when he took her that it would work out. Positive that she was the one to love him. And last night in the hot tub, she was everything he had ever dreamed of. A compliant woman with the ability to satisfy him. And now he was supposed to give her up? To his dad?

He had to be the better lover. Try a new position, one that they hadn't tried yet. One that his father wouldn't even think of. Something better and braver. He could not lose this woman, least of all to the man he held responsible for his entire undoing.

He shuddered to think of what he would do if she chose Erik over him. It would never get that far. Nicolas had to win her back. He went into his room and downed half a bottle of vodka to calm his nerves. He was losing his mind here. Martha was genuine and sweet, and he knew that she loved him. So why was he not enough?

The walls of his carefully created fantasy were caving in. He tried so hard to survive. After his mom, after the mental institution, and after the college years, which were painful and miserable because he didn't have friends and didn't know how to make them. Girls his age scared him, which pushed him to go after women he was comfortable seducing. He never stopped thinking of her, his first love—the one who abandoned him and broke his heart.

Judith had screwed up his whole plan. She was not part of the plan, yet she had derailed everything. Five days straight of dreaming about her. Five days of obsession until he was so hungry for her that he didn't know what to do. Part of him didn't care if Martha had sex with his dad because maybe it was a sign that he was supposed to choose Judith instead. But no. He had to finish this. Retrieve the love and rekindle the devotion, even if it was pretend. It could still fix him and heal him. Only then could he be right in the head!

Nicolas believed Martha was sent to save him, and this is why he couldn't give her up. Sometimes, people exist to sacrifice themselves for you, the way he had existed for Catrina. He had to make Martha see what she was, and he knew she was so compassionate that she would surrender. There was still hope. He pushed the walls of his mind, cracking and leaking with trauma back into place, smoothed his lovely hair, went to her room to wait, and unlocked the basement door.

Chapter 36

Martha

Martha slipped through the door and headed upstairs. It was after dinner, and she wondered if Nicolas suspected anything. Soon, her fears were confirmed. Her heart nearly stopped when she found Nicolas sitting on the edge of her bed, arms folded.

"I give you freedom. I even let you meet that bastard living downstairs, and this is how you repay me?"

Martha thought her heart might explode in her chest. What did he see? He couldn't know they were having sex. Erik covered up the camera!

"When I realized what was going on down there—pun intended—I came home straightaway."

"But you let the door open! You let me meet him. You were toying with us, weren't you? Nicolas, you're sick!" she protested.

"I was trying to be nice, giving my lonely dad a bit of company and giving you someone to talk to while I was gone. That's it. No fucking allowed. Did I not make myself clear?"

"The human heart doesn't work that way," she cried.

"Why him? Why would you let his hairy hands on you like that when you have me at your beck and call?"

Martha couldn't answer. Tell him because you're a severely damaged boy. She could never be with someone who wanted to restrain or force her. His dad was the original model, and he was the defective clone.

"Stop. Alright? Just stop. I've fallen in love. It's done. I thank you from the bottom of my heart for abducting me so that I could meet Erik. This is the best thing that's ever happened to me. But now you need to do the right thing and let us go."

"The right thing?" He laughed. "The right thing for whom? You? Since when is this about you? I took you. You don't have a say. I took that away from you. You belong to me. Not him. Me!"

He was shaking, and his eyes darted erratically like he was about to lose his shit and kill her. She needed to disarm him so that he couldn't manage to hurt her.

"Go clean his stench off you. Then we'll talk. But trust me, you have a lot of making up to do, and don't think I'll ever let you near him again. You've broken my trust irrevocably."

"Just because I love Erik is no reflection of you. Let me go, then find a girl who is right for you. It's not me. I will never make you happy. I bring out something dark and twisted in you, and I am the last thing you need."

Martha showered quickly and dressed. She had to regain some of her power, which meant going straight to the heart of the issue. When she opened the door, Nicolas was sitting on her bed naked and fondling himself like an adolescent. He gazed up at her and held out his hand.

"Please. Let me have you. Please. Don't choose him."

She let him pull her into his arms and stared at his desperate countenance. Who did this to him? She had to make him face his past. Now. It was the only way to get free.

"Nicolas, can I be honest with you? I see you as a boy not much older than my children. You are like the son I never had. I have tried to figure out why you abducted me, and I think I know the answer. I understood what happened when I studied that photo of Catrina holding you. As if you were hers."

He stared past her. Tears formed in his eyes.

"No. We aren't going there."

"We have to. She's the reason you abducted me!"

"No. I don't wanna talk about it."

"I won't let it go. I realized my first night here that something was wrong with you."

"I'm fine. Nothing's wrong," he whispered.

"Bullshit. I found the photo, and I know the truth. And now I want to hear you say it. To my face. What she did."

"She loved me. She was only being affectionate!"

"Stop covering for her."

"Many people fall in love with kids," Nicolas protested. Martha sat next to him and took his hand.

"No, they don't. That photo shows a woman who acted as if she owned you. That's sick and wrong."

"My parents saw that photo a hundred times, and they never suspected. How can you?"

"I am trained to see the signs. And it's so obvious from your behavior. Your nanny molested you for years, didn't she? Tell me how it started. Tell me everything you remember! I can help you, my dear boy. Maybe I'm not supposed to be your lover. You were drawn to me because I can help you face your trauma."

He threw himself backwards, tears exploding. Pitiful, naked and crying, his whole body was shaking violently.

"I don't want to think about it," he begged.

"No one ever does! But remember that song from your childhood, *We're Going on a Bear Hunt?* The one that goes, 'You can't go over it, you can't go under it, you can't go around it, you gotta go through it!' That is what you must do now. Let me hold your hand, and we will walk through this together."

Nicolas pulled her to him, to her amazement. Martha lay with her ear to his chest, his hand clenched in hers. His heart was racing, and his body was in fight-or-flight mode.

"I'm sorry, I'm such an asshole. I hate my dad. I've hated him my whole life. He never wanted me. Then he abandoned me when I begged for rescue. He looked right through me and walked out the door, dooming me to hell. And I was stuck with those two bitches. My mom chased after every guy she met, and Catrina, well, she only had eyes for one tiny little dick. Mine." He sobbed in her arms. She pulled the comforter over his shaking form and took his face in her hands.

"What did she do to you?" Martha was crying alongside him.

"What didn't she do? Everything she could possibly imagine."

"Did she hurt you?"

"Everything hurt. Even when it didn't, it still did."

Martha understood what he meant by his cryptic statement. Nicolas never knew what to expect. Sometimes it tickled. Other times, it felt like torture.

"You tried to tell your mom, didn't you? And she didn't believe you?"

"Worse. She started taking me to doctor after doctor. Fed me tons of pills and tinctures for my so-called diseases. Found all these online remedies. I was her guinea pig. For years, I was sick and missed nearly all of junior high. And Catrina was always there."

"Wait. Your dad said Catrina took off when you were ten."

"See how little he knows about me or cares about me? That woman didn't leave until I was almost fourteen. She was besties with my mom. Tormented me and teased me up until the day she left. Nine years of my life, and she dumped me. Martha, I was so in love with her—obsessed with her! So proud that she loved me and wanted me. It made me feel better than all the boys at school, better than everyone! I would have died for her, and she left me. One day, she said I was too old. She didn't like my hairy dick. I swore I would shave and starve to be skinny. But no. She wasn't into men. She packed her bags, gave me a big fuck-you smile, and moved back to Spain."

"Did you ever tell any of your therapists about this?"

"I tried. They just went on about how all boys secretly want to fuck their mothers and it was a perfectly healthy fantasy. They put me on drugs, and I tried to kill myself again. I was pretty nuts back then and out of control. That's why they kept throwing me back in the hospital."

"Do you remember what you did to your mom? Tell me what happened."

Nicolas sighed. He was collapsing. The weight of these memories was too much. But Martha pushed because she needed to confirm that he wasn't yet a killer.

"That day, I gave her the pills she gave me. Some weird homeopathic bullshit. They made me puking sick, and she would force me to take them. Well, she drank her tea. Honest to God, I didn't realize she had fallen in the pool. I remember freezing when I found her, though—seeing my face in the water. Eventually, I snapped out of it and tried so hard to pull her out. I was a sickly, skinny-ass kid back then, and she had gotten quite fat. It probably did take me five minutes to get her out. Then I called 911. I tried to push the water out of her lungs. It was hopeless. The cops all thought I tried to kill her with those pills. But I thought they would make her puke, not fall into the swimming pool!"

"Oh, Nicolas. I'm so sorry." She stroked his face and chest to calm him, thinking about how it all played out. How the cops would have taken one look at this unstable boy and condemned him. How Erik would have believed the police report, and Nicolas would have been pushed to end his life—this poor guy. After a childhood of chronic abuse, then to have the system turn against him.

"Martha, something happened since we were in the hot tub last night. I don't know. It stirred up a bunch of stuff in my head and—"

He broke down into sobs. Martha held his head against her breast as he cried for a long time. She wondered if he had fallen asleep when, suddenly, she felt him go rigid, then sit up. He rubbed his eyes and shook his head wildly.

"Christ almighty, I remember."

She put her arm around his shoulder and held him to her.

"What do you remember?"

"It's like a light bulb has gone on upstairs."

She waited.

"You were right. It was a memory."

"Tell me," Martha whispered.

"She did try to drown me."

"Who?"

"Catrina."

"Where?"

"In the tub."

Trembling violently, Nicolas clung to her, and Martha held him tight.

"Either I didn't get her off good enough or my little boy penis wouldn't get hard. Sometimes it didn't, and I didn't know why. And she would punish me."

He was sobbing, gasping for air.

"It made her happy. To see me under the water until I passed out."

His weeping filled the silence for a whole minute as he relived the horrifying memory.

"Martha, I think I almost died. When I came to, she kissed me and hugged me, and then we had sex."

"How old were you?" Martha tried to hold in her tears so as not to antagonize his state of distress.

"Maybe eight?"

Martha let her sobs go loud and uninhibited, wrapped her arms around his neck, and said,

"You're safe now, Nicolas. You're safe now. No one will ever hurt you again."

"She spent years teaching me to be her lover. It was so difficult to get it right."

Martha tried to block this image. It made her want to vomit.

"But she promised that if I did, I would be like the Greek gods and could have any woman I wanted when I grew up."

"Oh, Nicolas!"

"All I wanted was her. I wanted to make her scream because she begged me to make her scream. So that's why I need the screaming."

"What happened to you is horrible, illegal and sick beyond words."

"We had a party when my body changed and I could finally have legit sex. The first time she sucked me off and I came, I thought it was the best day of my life."

"You poor, sweet boy. What an evil bitch."

"Then things got crazy, and I became obsessed. She showed me how to use the cuffs on her. She'd beg me and scream like a banshee, and I would go crazy to please her. Not only that, but she'd excuse absences to keep me home from school, and we'd go at it all day. I thought we were gonna get married when I got old enough. But nope. One day, she was done with me."

"How could she do that to you? You were a child. An innocent child!"

"But it wasn't just sex. Catrina loved me. She shared every secret she ever had with me. She was possessive of me and didn't want me to have any friends, so I was a loner and a weirdo—the way she wanted me to be. I gave her every second of my life and every inch of my heart. I let her hurt me in a million ways. She was often cruel and even vicious. It was a nonstop roller coaster of making her happy, giving her orgasms and comforting her when she cried. Her brother had done the same thing to her, see. We were bonded together by what she did to me."

"That's no excuse. She was an evil predator. I hope you can see that."

He nodded without listening. Nicolas was slipping away into his mind. Frantically, she comforted him as best as she knew how. He collapsed and pulled her with him. Then rolled over and lay on top of her, still as death, but his heart was racing.

"It's like a movie going on inside my head. I remember so much like a dam has broken. What should I do?"

"Let it wash through you. I'm right here. I'm not going anywhere. You are going through this, and you are not alone."

After a while, he said, "I'm drawn to older women because I'm trying to replace her?"

"Yes."

"And sometimes I have the urge to drown them because she tried to drown me?"

"Yes."

Martha knew that the best therapist was oneself, which was the whole point of therapy, teaching someone how to analyze themselves.

"And I need to be the best lover on the planet because she made me this way?"

"Yes."

"And I'm so obsessed with my size because she used to measure my penis every month. I don't know why, since she hated me the moment I started looking like a man. I'm a mess. No wonder you'd rather be with my dad than me."

Martha saw his Casanova facade slip away, revealing a broken boy with no self-worth. He tried so hard to make women love him using the only skills he had, sex skills. But he didn't love himself and had no idea what love was. It was heartbreaking.

"Nicolas, you are deliciously handsome and an incredible lover. But you need someone who engages your good qualities, not someone who triggers your trauma. I do belong in your life. You do need a mother, and you do need friends. Dear boy, you got your wires all crossed by what happened to you. I promise, you can work through this, and someday you will be loved."

"The day Catrina walked out, I swore to get her back. All these years, it was the only thing I had to live for. When I realized it could never happen, I decided to replace her with a better version of her. That's you, Martha. You are the Replacement."

Martha wept into the comforter. She had triggered an emotional apocalypse in this boy. He really believed that abducting her would solve all his problems. Nicolas needed serious help. She feared he was going to spiral out of control now that he had lost her. She had no idea what to say or do.

"Let's just sleep, okay? You need to rest. Let your mind heal from remembering these horrible memories."

"Don't leave me. I feel like I've been dipped into a fire pit. I'm sore and blistered all inside myself. I want—"

"I'll stay with you, my boy. You are not alone."

Her empathy ran so deep that if she could stop or mitigate his suffering in any way, she would. Nicolas slept, but he tossed and turned, reliving the nightmares of his childhood. Martha held him like the baby he once was. Slowly, he calmed, and finally she closed her eyes and joined him.

233

Thursday ~ Day 7

Chapter 37

Judith

Judith woke up feeling the worst pain ever. Her stomach was on fire. Her head pounded. She could never tell Justin what happened last night. He would flip his shit.

Once again, she was mistaken. This was awful. Who took her? Who? Why couldn't she find her mom? She was convinced it was up to her. The cops weren't going to find anything. It wasn't their fault. This abductor was too smart for them. But not for her.

It was already after ten. She unlocked her phone and saw nothing yet. No pics. Hmm. Thought about sending another pic, but after blowing Justin away with her boob shot yesterday, everything else would seem anticlimactic. She couldn't talk to him yet because she had to pull it together. Overcome her traumatizing evening. Plus, she'd see him tonight.

Last night was terrifying. She could never do that again. She almost got herself killed! Which made her realize what she needed to do today. It was time to buy a gun.

Judith dressed in all black, then took her credit card from her jewelry box and headed out. She searched for gun stores and finally decided on one, then drove off. Thankfully, she was able to get the gun out of his hand last night, but what a close call! She thought of her mom with a gun to her head right now and wanted to scream bloody murder.

Three guys approached her in the store to ask if she needed help. As usual, they were all drooling. She was sick of getting attention. Why couldn't people treat her as normal? She wasn't dressed up or even wearing makeup. What the hell?

"I'm here to buy a gun," she declared.

The older of the dudes was the one who won out, and she followed him over to the counter.

"What are you looking for?"

"Oh, you know. A pistol, I guess. For protection. Just show me what you got."

He spent the next hour showing her gun after gun until she found one she liked. He ran a background check, then rang it all up for her with a ton of extra magazines. She abruptly said she had to go when he started to flirt with her.

Judith sat in her car, staring at the gun. Justin would have to show her how to use it. She didn't understand a word the salesclerk said about any of it.

After the gun purchase, she went home and gave herself a mani-pedi. Her stomach was bruising badly. Nothing she could do about that. She doubted Justin would cave in and sleep with her, but she could always hope. Part of her was scared that he thought she was a skank. She had come onto him hard, and the sexting made her seem desperate. Who was she kidding? She was desperate! Justin was the nicest guy she had ever met. If he slipped through her fingers, she would never forgive herself. Of course, she was throwing herself in front of him like a used car salesman. She'd sell her soul if it meant he'd like her. Why was she so needy?

Judith thought about this while she waited for her toenails to dry. She had never been this aggressive with any guy. Usually, guys manipulated her and coerced her to sleep with them, and sadly, she was an easy conquest. Now she met the first guy who wanted to respect her. She hoped his pushing her off him wasn't a sign of mind games. She couldn't handle it when guys did the takeaway and withheld love and attention to make her act desperate and trashy, because it worked like a charm. Judith thought of his puppy dog eyes and how he helped her to the car after barfing the night they met. Justin was like Superman. She wanted to be his Lois Lane and could do nothing about it now.

She was desperate because her life sucked. Stuck here with no money, grades not good enough for college, she'd have to start all over at community college, which would suck. No opportunities, no way to gain skills for a better job. Other than becoming a stripper, she didn't see a way ahead. And the thought of strangers ogling her all night made her nauseous.

How did Justin become a police officer? He must have done well in high school to attend college. She wasn't like her mom, who was brilliant and even got a scholarship, or like smarty-pants Lizzy. No. Instead, she was pretty. Pretty got you nowhere. Everyone was pretty these days with their AI filters. Pretty was bullshit.

Judith wished she could take back the last seven years of her life and do them over. Not wasting all her time on the beauty pageant circuit, but making plans to help her as an adult. Her parents never did a damn thing to prepare her for real life. Which was part of the reason she was so angry.

She was ready. Justin would arrive in an hour. She thought about what to wear and then put on the same old clothes. All the goods were ready and waiting under these rags. Justin only had to seize his chance; what he'd find underneath would make all his dreams come true.

Chapter 38

Justin

When Justin pulled up, Judith was waiting outside. She wore black jeans, a nicely fitted black t-shirt, and was carrying a backpack. Now that he knew what she looked like naked on top, he couldn't stop staring at her chest. She was gonna think he was a pervert.

What was she planning? Judith got in and kissed him soundly. She licked all around the rim of his lips with her tongue, and his dick went from zero to sixty in three seconds. How would he handle a night in public, feeling like this around her?

"I need something from you. Once you do it, then we can get on with the rest of our night."

"Okay?"

She opened her backpack and pulled out a brand-new gun.

"I need you to teach me how to use this."

He stared in horror. What was she planning? Why did she buy herself a gun?

"Judith, what the hell?"

"I'm just being like all other Americans. It's not a big deal. I need to learn how to use it. I don't even know how to put the bullets in."

"Didn't the salesclerk show you?"

"He tried, but was too busy staring at my chest and kept stopping mid-sentence, so I didn't understand what he was saying."

"You poor girl."

"That's right. It's called living in a man's world. Justin, please. I don't intend on killing anyone."

"Or hunting anyone down?"

He was concerned. Had she found a lead she was keeping from him? Goddamn it. She said she couldn't lie to him! What was going on here?

"There's a shooting range nearby. I Googled it. We can spend an hour or so there, then grab some food. We'll end up back at my place." She looked at him suggestively. "I have a special place for us," she reassured, "it's not a dirty old garage. If I don't see the rest of your hot bod tonight, they'll have to drag me off to the loony bin. I can't stop thinking about having sex with you, and it's to the point of crisis. Justin, while I appreciate your high ideals and realize you don't want me to feel taken advantage of, I will be forced to take advantage of you. You don't want that."

"Maybe I do." He squirmed as she slid onto his lap, squeezing between him and the steering wheel.

"What's this?" She grabbed his crotch and stroked him until his legs turned to jelly. "And this?" She put his hand between her legs. "I am so ready for you. You're an idiot to pass this up."

"Jesus Christ, Judith." His cheeks flooded with embarrassment as a couple walked by his car and smirked at them.

"Please give in to me. You will never be the same. I will never be the same!" She crushed her body up against his and, eye to eye, said, "Crawl down off your high horse and have sex with me. That's what I want, and I'm not asking. I'm begging."

Judith kissed him so hard that he thought he might burst out of his clothes. His mom was right. She wouldn't take no for an answer. How the hell was he gonna keep playing hard to get with this girl?

He groaned. "Should we take care of the gun lesson first?"

She slid off his lap. "Thank you. Thank you!"

He started the car with shaking fingers, hoping his body would calm down. He had never felt so hot and bothered in all his life.

By the time they pulled into the shooting range, Justin was fit to be seen in public again. Once inside, he showed her the basics. She had chosen a Smith and Wesson Shield .380, a great starter gun that was easy to learn.

Justin showed her how to operate the slide and load the magazine. Then he took her into the shooting range and positioned her body. He told her where to point, how to point and how to shoot. Judith was a natural. He couldn't take any credit for this.

After thirty minutes, he gave her a thumbs-up and she followed him out.

"You, Missy, are a born marksman."

She glowed.

"Really? I'm so happy. I love being good at things."

"I am concerned about why you bought this. And don't tell me it's because you're scared."

"It's because of the dream I had. Someone was gonna kill my mom and I was the only one who could stop them. I know it's going to be me."

"I won't let that happen."

"You won't have a choice. Something the pastor said to my mom at the wedding. He told her a darkness was coming and to remember that she had a daughter to die for. At the time, I thought he was just a weird old man. Now I believe he saw something. The future even. And he knew that it would be her daughter who'd save her."

Justin digested this as they sat in the car. The sun was low in the sky, and they still hadn't decided where to eat. He didn't believe in anything mystical, but it was strange for a pastor to say something like that.

"He was trying to console her after marrying her ex to a new woman."

"He was warning her. More importantly, he was warning me."

"What does this mean? You're going to take on the man who abducted your mom? You'll be dead before you pull out your gun." He protested.

How could he make her see how dangerous this was? Justin wished with everything he had that he could control this woman. She was nuts and she was driving him nuts. He was not the kind of guy who could handle intense emotions like passion or rage. He needed to stick with the lighter side of the heart and had done so successfully in his life so far. He feared he was making a big mistake by falling for this woman. First, she turned him into a caveman with a massive lust-filled hard-on for her. Now she threatened to turn him into a controlling, obsessive freak. Not the person he wanted to be, for sure.

"You don't understand. Fine. Let's grab dinner and go to a park."

"A park?"

"Don't you like birds?"

"You know I do."

"I thought we'd go to the aviary."

This woman was an angel wrapped in the sexiest body a man could wish for.

"Sounds perfect."

After munching on burgers and fries and sucking down cokes, they went to the aviary. Justin got his nerd on and taught her about birds—owls, eagles, vultures and parakeets. They spent forever watching the birds of paradise, and Justin pulled up a video to show Judith their mating rituals. She laughed heartily and snuggled up against his chest as she watched, his arms around her, his lips to her ear. He felt so happy to be real with her and reveal his vulnerable side.

They walked around until closing time, then left. Strolling around the park hand in hand, Justin asked.

"Do you miss your dad?"

"For a while, I did. And I blamed the divorce on my mom, even though he was the one who cheated and left her. Like I told you, I've been a horrible daughter."

"Do you miss him now?"

"Nope. I told him I hoped he and Lori would get eaten by piranhas in Brazil. I kinda meant it too."

He laughed. "That's harsh."

"He was rude to me on the phone and doesn't care what happens to my mom, so he deserves it."

"I have a feeling that we will find your mom, Judith. And I think you will break this case. I've never seen anyone so obsessed."

"I think so too. I do have something to confess," she sighed, "because I can't keep a thing from you and it drives me crazy, but there it is."

Oh, dear lord. Here we go.

"I did stalk a potential suspect. Last night I broke into his house and he caught me."

"Judith!" He turned her around and shook her. "What did I say?"

"It's fine! He was an old friend of my parents. They fell out. I thought he was doing it as some revenge plot. No. He was still pissed at them. But he thought it was sweet that I took things so far. Gave me a tour of his super awesome house. Although—"

"What?" He glared.

He was furious at her and had no idea what to do about it. Why the hell didn't she listen to him? This was like having an untrained puppy running around shitting all over the house. She didn't listen to a goddamn thing he said!

"When we got to his bedroom, he demanded I have sex with him and wouldn't call the police on me if I did. I had to hit him over the head and run like hell. Oh, Justin! You were right! It is dangerous to break into people's houses. I promise. I'll never do it again."

She had her body pressed up to him in a plea for forgiveness. He wanted to shake her silly. Instead, he folded her in his arms and let her cry.

"Judith, you're gonna be the death of me. I can't believe it. You are scarier than any cop I've ever met. You could work for the CIA."

"Really? I used that self-defense move you taught me, and it totally worked. I felt like such a badass." She smiled through her tears.

"Let's take you home and let me digest this. Hit him over the head. With what?"

"His gun?"

"Oh my God, he had a gun!"

"Not after I took it from him. Remember, I know karate?"

"I need to lock you up and hide the key, even from myself!"

"Don't worry. He won't call the cops. I lied and said I was seventeen and if he calls them, I'll tell them he solicited me for sex, brought me to his house and threatened to rape me. Let's see who they'll believe."

Justin placed her in the front seat and squatted in front of her. She was still crying.

"It was traumatic. I thought I was gonna die."

"You are going to drive me insane. I want to protect you. That's my life's work as a cop. Keeping the peace and putting the bad guys away. I can't handle this. You have gotta stop looking for this guy or you'll get yourself killed."

She threw her arms around him. "If I don't rescue my mom, I think I will kill myself. You don't understand how crazy this makes me." She was sobbing now. He held her for a long time until her sobs receded.

"It's alright. I'm here." He comforted her, trying to think of what he should do. Judith was impossible, but he wanted her so badly that a full-out battle was underway between his head and his heart.

"Please stay with me tonight. I'll even obey your high ideals, and we won't have sex. Just hold me tonight?"

What could he say? Of course, he was keeping her in his arms. And if he could figure out how, he would take her home and never let her out of his sight again.

"You know I will."

They drove in silence. He parked. Judith led him briskly into her condo, into what must be her mom's room. She sat on the bed, leaned back on her elbows, and said,

"Okay, Mister Hot Cop. Show me."

"What?"

She smiled coyly.

"Everything. Strip. I wanna see everything."

"I thought I told you we were gonna wait."

"Give me a sneak preview, then."

Justin felt shy and awkward. But something else too. This sexy woman had supercharged his ego, and he could feel it swelling inside him now. Confidence, he didn't know he had seized him by the hair, and like a marionette, he began to move. Justin made a performance out of pulling off his t-shirt. He tossed it at her, she caught it and giggled. For the first time in his life, he felt the reward for all his hard work at the gym. A beauty queen, an actual beauty queen, wanted to eat him alive. Judith ogled his muscled chest and six pack, and he grinned, self-conscious and thrilled at the same time. This must be what strippers felt when guys went crazy over them. All this sexual power. What was he to do with it?

"Pants too," she whispered, licking her lips.

He bent over and removed his shoes. Then, slowly pulling down the zipper, he let his jeans drop to his feet. His exhibition had caused an immediate erection, and he posed to make it even more prominent. Not that he planned on fucking her, but he was happy to be rock hard if only to watch her drool over him. Her eyes were glued to his dick. He never felt so sexy in his life. God, she was going to tackle him to the floor like his mom warned him. Would he give in or tease her harder?

"Justin, get your ass over here."

Judith eagerly stripped off her jeans and then stood, pulling her t-shirt over her head. He gasped in horror. Her stomach was covered in dark purple bruises.

"What the hell?" he cried out.

"That asshole got a few hits in too." Judith frowned.

Justin got down on his knees and kissed her belly softly as she winced and moaned. But they were moans of pain. He wanted this guy's address to go beat the shit out of him.

"This looks painful. Think you need an X-ray?"

"It's just a couple of bruises."

"You should report him."

"He held a gun to my head and forced me down on the bed. But I started it by breaking into his house."

"Any judge would throw the book at that bastard. Attempted rape and aggravated assault? Someone like that needs to go down."

"I can't face a trial. I was stupid. He wasn't our guy. When I went to shoot him, the gun wasn't even loaded. It's all so embarrassing. I'm sorry I got beaten up. This hurts worse than it did last night. I was hoping to go at it until morning."

"I'm never gonna sleep tonight," he admitted. Now that he had touched her, he had no idea how he would survive lying next to her almost naked. Especially since he wasn't planning on having sex. This was going to be hell.

"One sec. I need painkillers and the lube."

He watched her leave the room, his eyes glued to her rounded ass. How had he gotten this lucky? Soon she was back, crawling into his arms.

"You wanna go home? I'm not sure I can sleep next to you after all."

"It's fine, Judith. We'll cuddle tonight. That's it."

"Justin, I can't cuddle next to a dick that hard. After that strip tease? I'm so fucking horny. You're driving me crazy, and we haven't even started. Even if you won't have sex with me, there are other things we can do. The question is, what are your limits?"

"I already told you. I wanna make it special. You know, go somewhere nice."

She sighed heavily.

"You just said yesterday, you were ready to give in."

"I changed my mind."

"What about oral? That's not sex, right?"

She purred as she pushed him onto his back and stroked his lower belly, arousing every nerve.

Jesus, God. Yes, oh yes. His mind exploded with all the fantasies he'd indulged in since their date. She tickled his groin, and he trembled in frustration. Shit. It was hell playing hard to get. But at the same time, no. Time to delay the gratification, no matter how badly he wanted to surrender. He had to hold out a bit longer. Make her chase him harder. Force her to her knees in fervent hero worship. Get her so desperate for him that she would be praying at his feet for a wedding ring by the time he finally caved in.

"Let's wait on that, too." He forced himself to say.

"Okay, I guess. But you have no idea how much you are missing out. How about this?"

"What?"

He was terrified of the evil urges throbbing through his body. Horrified by the violence erupting from somewhere deep inside him, threatening to explode like a volcano. He wanted to flip Judith over and fuck her so hard his mom could hear her screams up in Heber. Erotic, violent images, each more depraved than the last, invaded his mind. What was this woman doing to him?

"Touch each other until we crash out. The rule is hands only. We'll save our love-making extravaganza for your special plan. So, you get to keep your high ideals. Can you at least give me that?"

It was time to relent. Give her a taste of what was to come. Just a taste. This was good. Keeping her on a short leash would invariably drive her wild. And when he finally let her have him, she would rip his clothes off like a begging whore and let him twist her around his finger. He couldn't wait. What was he to do with this vicious lust, though? He was a good guy.

A good guy! Not some disgusting sex offender. But something about Judith. Something about this seductive, vain, hot girl unleashed a vile, predatory aggression he had never felt before. He was so hard that he didn't think he'd last a minute. Not after months and months of no pussy. Not after only ever having vanilla sex with shy, boring country girls. He was going to lose his mind here. Fuck this.

"Fine."

Judith crawled on top of him, sat up and removed her bra. He took her gorgeous breasts in his large hands, and they fit perfectly. He pulled her down to his mouth, like he had fantasized endlessly about since yesterday. Thank God, she couldn't tell this was a first for him because he had never been with a girl like her. He was in fantasy land now and couldn't rely on his limited sexual experiences to guide him. Writhing against him, moaning, this woman was too goddamn sexy. He couldn't take much more of this and still string her along. So he shocked her by pushing her away. Tucking his hands behind his head and invoking the willpower of a bull, he let her attack him.

Judith tore open his boxers, took him in a tight fist, and whispered all the things she would do to him when he finally let her, igniting his imagination, and it began to spin. Once she had her hands on him, he watched her unravel completely. Drooling with lust over his sexy body and huge dick. He was the hottest man alive. She wanted to suck him off so bad. Begged to let her ride him. Begged. Please. She was so wet, throbbing, dying for sex. Please. She tortured him with her dirty mouth as her hands teased him beyond endurance.

Stroking with increasing pressure and speed, she drove him to thrust like mad, groan and curse as he shot off in her hand. Wave after wave of ecstasy vibrated through him as she whispered that she couldn't wait until he hit the finish line between her lips. Holy shit. In a mere five minutes, Judith transcended every sexual experience he ever had. And that was only the beginning.

Justin couldn't believe how creative she was at steering him into crazy eights that rocked him to the core. She made his hard-ons roar like a V10 engine, and he let her think she controlled the speed.

Lord, this was fun. A power struggle he was guaranteed to win. He had no idea this was his kink. Playing hard to get was an aphrodisiac, as she tried every ploy to break him and failed. He closed his eyes and let his imagination run wild as she aroused him again and again. At one point, she grabbed his hands, trapped them under his ass and slid his dick in her mouth. She sucked so hard he felt an orgasm instantly detonate throughout his body, his mind convulsing from a scenario so spicy he could barely contain himself.

Take her by surprise, drag her by the hair, smack her pretty face, rip her panties into shreds, spank her perfect ass, squeeze her Barbie tits, hold her down into a pillow, fuck her doggy style, feel her climax from the pain, smother her screams of ecstasy, come in a rage of frenzied lust.

Justin wanted to act out a rape scenario in the sexiest way possible. And in his mind, he did. Groaning and shuddering violently, fighting for control, he pushed her away as he climaxed in his fantasy and erupted for the third time.

"Hands only, remember?" he mumbled incoherently.

"How can you reject me?" she cried.

He held her shoulders; her face loomed inches above his dick. She was trying to lick the cum off like a ravenous animal. Jesus fucking Christ. He wanted to pound a hole in this woman like a porn star.

"I'd give you anything, Justin. Tell me how you want it and it's yours."

"I already told you. I wanna show some respect." He lied.

"I don't need respect. I just need you," she pleaded.

"No sex until I say." He shoved her over, conflicted and tortured.

He had to come to terms with himself here. His good guy image was sort of bullshit. Right now, the last thing he wanted to do was respect Judith. She was corrupting him. Changing him. He was the luckiest man alive because Judith was more than just a hot girl; she was a whore. A real, bona fide whore destined to make all his darkest fantasies come true.

He knew she would be hot in bed, but this was the fiery pits of hell hot. Now he had to make this woman crazy for him; rejecting her was the only way. Once she was all his, the real fun would begin.

"Fine. We'll do it your way then."

She plopped onto her back, and he watched in satisfaction as she reconciled herself to his will. Spread her legs, put his hand in her panties, guiding his inexperienced fingers, and with her help, he had her climaxing within minutes. She came so hard, and he imagined it was in part because of his cruel sex game. Now the hot girl was chasing him, and he was the one rejecting her. He would never get enough of teasing this vixen. And he was shocked at himself for holding out for his special consummation plan, which he'd dangle like a carrot until she danced to his tune.

He had done it. Figured Judith out inside a week. He knew exactly how to push her buttons. He was The Man. The apex bird of paradise with all the right moves. He would lure this female to move in with him, manipulate her to marry him and stay with him forever. This was perfect. She was perfect. Finally, they wrapped up like a pretzel, and Justin enjoyed the best sleep of his entire life.

Chapter 39

Martha

Nicolas slept in late. When Martha nudged him awake, he looked up at her through bleary eyes and collapsed.

"I'm still alive. I wish I weren't. I have the worst hangover."

"I'm very concerned for you, Nicolas. What you unrepressed last night could have repercussions."

"Like what?" he mumbled, burying his head in the comforter.

"I'm not sure. But I think we need to talk our way through this."

"I don't wanna talk."

"How are you feeling?"

"Angry."

"About what?"

"At my father. The asshole left me with Catrina."

"I mentioned to your dad what I suspected. He was horrified. He cares about you."

"I don't believe that for a second. If I did, I wouldn't have made him a prisoner in his own house."

"Let's talk about Catrina. Tell me about your relationship."

"She was a peach, let me tell you. And now I know why I wanted to drown you, thanks to your mad therapy skills. Now I remember everything, as if it were a horror film. She held me down in the tub and said if I told anyone about us, she'd kill me just like that. Once, I passed out, and she had to resuscitate me. I awoke choking and barfing up water. I remember her laughing and thinking it was cute. Cute. That bitch."

"Why didn't you tell anyone? That woman should be put behind bars for the rest of her human life!"

"I did! I told Mom!"

"She never told your dad. If she had, he would have moved heaven and earth to save you."

"Of course she didn't. Mom said I was crazy and that finding good help was difficult. Thought I was bitching because Catrina was strict. She promised she would talk to her about being kinder to me."

"What happened?"

"She wasn't kinder, that's for sure."

"When exactly did Catrina begin to hurt you?"

"I know my exact age because she talked of the first time that she went down on me with extreme fondness. I was in a relationship with Catrina from four to thirteen."

"Where was your mom when all this happened? Did she ever walk in and catch any of this? It's hard to believe a woman could get away with this for nine years!"

"Nope. She was off sleeping with every guy in town. Left me all alone with Catrina throughout my childhood. Mom didn't give a shit about me. Then, dad never visited, even though I sent him emails begging to let me come live with him as soon as I learned how. He never answered them. Some of it was great, you know. Catrina would play with me for hours like I was a little doll, twisting and turning as she liked. But when it came time to get her off, I wasn't such a pro. And she punished me quite a bit. She'd tie me up for hours. Sometimes in the middle of the night. You can't imagine how insane it was. I would be so tired at school the next day. It was endless."

"That explains your kink with bondage and dressing me up in a dollhouse."

"I guess so."

"I'm so sorry. You should never have had to endure any of that. I can see what it has done to you, and it's tragic."

Martha stroked his back, feeling tremendous sorrow and concern for this heartbroken boy. She recognized the signs of reliving trauma. Nicolas was hungover and depressed. He needed more care than she could currently give him. Now she was no longer Catrina's replacement. She was Martha. The therapist who had broken his fantasy by falling in love with his dad. It was only a matter of time before Nicolas lashed out with violence.

"I wanted her to love me. I just wanted someone to love me!"

"My dear boy, she wasn't capable of love."

"Over the years, though, I've come to realize, what did she do? Turn me into the best lover the world has ever known? That's what they all say. Every single woman I've ever slept with. What Catrina did to me turned me into a sex god. I have joined the Greek pantheon, like she said. Although it hurt and messed me up, it also made me into who I am."

"Nicolas, she stole your innocence. She abused you and took advantage of you. She made you powerless—"

"Now I do the same thing to others and they thank me for it!"

"This isn't going to work. It's too late to go back now. You have seen the horror of her actions with your own eyes. Connecting the dots, now it makes sense why you have these urges. You are simply reliving your trauma."

"Maybe. But it feels great."

"Right now. But eventually, it will feel like an obsession you can't control. And what will that make you? Do you want to become a murderer? Because that's the path you are heading down."

"Perhaps I don't care. Or it will be a fetish like me and you in the hot tub. I controlled it then, and it was unbelievable."

"Of course it was. Reliving trauma is about as close to a near-death experience as you can get. But it's dangerous and unhealthy."

"I'm not the one almost dying now. It's them. It's you." He corrected.

"Don't take responsibility for this. You need to place the blame where it belongs."

"It's too late. She's already made me this way. I can't change now," he protested.

"You must let me find you help. What you do here—coercing women and forcing them to want you—is so wrong. What you did to me is criminal. You'll be lost for good unless you can regain control of yourself."

"These women, they're not kids like I was. I'm not forcing them."

"You're not forcing them? You abducted me! What is wrong with you? I have children and a career. A life! You can't do that!"

"A life? You call what you have a life? You should have seen yourself at that wedding, Martha. It was the most pathetic thing I've ever witnessed. You deserve for me to take you and treat you like a goddess."

"By abducting me, forcing me?" Martha cried. "You are out of your mind."

Nicolas flushed deep red, jumped up and screamed, "Fuck you, Martha. Fuck you!"

Martha watched helplessly as Nicolas raced out of her room, slamming the door behind him. What would he do now? Damn it. She should have kept her mouth shut.

Chapter 40

Nicolas

Nicolas couldn't stop shaking. Refused to consider Martha's accusations. He loved her and she loved him! And he asked for her consent first! He thought of how Martha had pushed his buttons last night, pulling out these awful memories. Probably thanks to all that vodka. It was spectacular. He felt liberated, like he was on fire. But he was also enormously depressed at the same time, like he wanted to jump off a ten-story building.

He quickly dressed, then went downstairs and unlocked the door to the basement. For some paranoid reason, he took his dad's loaded pistol from the gun safe with him. If Erik had fallen in love with Martha, he might try to fight him and help her escape. That sure wasn't going to happen.

Erik walked into the living room in his boxers, towel-drying his wet hair. Nicolas looked at his father's hard body and mentally kicked himself for letting the old bastard keep his exercise equipment down here. No wonder she slept with him. He looked incredible for a guy his age.

"What the hell, Nicolas?" Erik was using his dad voice.

That wouldn't work now. He was immune. Immune!

"You know why I'm down here, right?" Nicolas wanted to shoot him in the gut so bad. His fingers trembled on the trigger.

"Put the gun down, son. Let's work this out. I'm not the enemy here."

"You are! You took her from me!" Nicolas couldn't stop tears from forming in his eyes.

"You are the one who took her! From her life, her children. Who are you? How are you even related to me? I hate to admit this, but you belong behind bars."

"Is that so?" Nicolas laughed. "I love how you are so anxious to be rid of me. I'm stiff competition. Martha would be perfectly content with me if it weren't for you."

Erik rubbed his face and put up his hands.

"When you told me you had girlfriends moving in, I was anxious because I knew you were messed up in the head, but I could never have imagined this. Wow. You are outdoing yourself."

"Dad, I don't care what you think. I just need you to help me win Martha back."

"I'm not going to do anything to hurt that sweet lady. You are a monster, and I'll do everything possible to protect her from you."

"Oh, so that's it? You're in love now? After one single afternoon?"

"The best of my life so far, and yes, I am in love," he admitted, "how could I not be with a woman like her?"

"I am too! Finally, I find someone perfect for me, and you have to go and take her?"

"Nicolas, you're not what Martha needs."

He was going to die for using his dad voice, take a bullet in the brain if he didn't stop. Right. Now. Nicolas couldn't take it anymore.

"I am totally what she wants!" he shrieked.

Erik sighed in defeat. "I don't want to fight someone who has a gun pointed at my head. What sort of help do you need?"

"Tell her you don't want her. Just give her back to me!"

"Nicolas?"

"What?"

He was changing the subject. Goddamn him!

"Martha told me what she suspected about Catrina. Is it true?"

"What do you think?"

"Yes?"

"You are so selfish. You never cared. Not even for a second."

"Son," Erik said, putting his hands up in surrender. "Let's sit. I was never there for you, I admit. I didn't think something like that could happen to us. We were rich. The rich don't get screwed around."

"Is that how you justify feeding me to the wolves?"

"Why in God's name did you never tell me?"

"Where were you? Off in Europe somewhere and visited maybe three times a year. I won't let you apologize for this. Besides, like I told Martha, it's not so bad. Sure, Catrina abused me, but she also made me into a god. I couldn't possibly have such mad skills if it weren't for her."

"I don't think getting molested by your nanny constitutes mad sex skills, son."

"It was more than sex. I loved her. She taught me to love with the insane devotion I now feel for Martha. Most humans never experience such a depth of emotion."

"This depth is bizarre and obsessive. It's not what Martha or any woman needs or wants. It's part of a sickness, one that requires professional help to overcome. Please listen to Martha. She believes we can find you excellent care. She has connections, and I have the money. I will do whatever it takes to help you. I promise."

"Promises. Promises." Nicolas laughed. "I don't believe you, Dad. If I let you go, you'll bring down the sky on my head, like you did when Mom got hurt. I know it was you who got me institutionalized. I won't ever make the mistake of trusting you again. Honestly, I wish I had just killed you when I moved back here. Taken everything and let you rot in the desert."

"I'm sure you do." Erik dismissed his threat, which enraged Nicolas to the point of madness. "Thanks for being honest with me about Catrina. Whatever you say, you're wrong. Hurting a child is a sin and a universal crime. I blame her for turning you into this animal."

"If I'm an animal, it's your fault. Not hers. I came from you."

"Take some responsibility for your actions!" Erik shouted.

Nicolas jumped in surprise, pulling the trigger. The gunshot rang throughout the basement as it hit the microwave, blowing a hole through the glass door. Shit. He had never pulled the trigger before. That was loud. Nicolas backed up to the door. Erik was pleading with him, hands outstretched.

"Don't hurt her. If there is any good left in you, spare it for her. Martha is an angel."

"She is. Martha is my angel," Nicolas snarled. He shut the basement door and ensured it locked, then headed back upstairs to heaven, where his angel awaited his return.

Nicolas slumped to the steps. His heart was still raging after pulling the trigger. He felt like he might have a panic attack. He had experienced them repeatedly in the mental hospital and had no desire to relive those days.

What should he do? He thought of the beautiful woman upstairs and the monster downstairs who tried to steal her from him. Should he off his dad right now? Get rid of the competition? But Martha would never forgive him. Why did this happen? He was such a fool! He thought they might become friends and harbored fantasies of bringing Martha home to Thanksgiving dinners, secretly shoving it in his dad's face that he found a woman his age who chose Nicolas and only Nicolas. Somehow, when she gave him that look and touched his arm at the wedding reception, he honestly believed she was the Replacement.

His breakdown had shoved Judith out of his mind for the moment, so that was a relief. His obsession had reached epic proportions right before he discovered Martha's affair. At work yesterday, he was planning to stalk her again. But now she seemed like an impossible dream and needed to stay in his dreams for good. He would never be normal. Martha would never love him enough to heal his broken heart because she loved someone else. Everything was lost and ruined.

Suddenly, the weight of a thousand tears fell on his shoulders. He wanted to go back to sleep. Part of his mind was stuck in his memory from last night. It was so vivid. And the same as all the fantasies he had over the years. Martha called them flashbacks, and now he realized they were—his face underwater in the huge claw-foot tub and Catrina's manicured nails on top of his skinny white chest. Why did Catrina do it? She must have been terrified that he would tell on her, probably as terrified as he felt right now at the thought of getting caught for what he did to Martha. She must have loved him so much to scare him. So afraid of losing him.

Nicolas held on to that thought like a life raft. It was so much better than all the other thoughts—she dumped him, never cared for him, he was never enough for her, never good enough at pleasing her. All he ever wanted was to find a woman who would love him, who he could make happy, who would never leave him. What was so wrong with that?

He slowly climbed the stairs. What the hell to do? He tried touching his dick, no response. This was depression. The kind he suffered for years. He needed sex. Maybe in the hot tub, maybe not.

He opened the door and found Martha sleeping. Tears were still wet on her cheeks. They weren't tears for him. They were tears for HIM. His dad needed to die. That was all there was to it. Even if it took him down, too, and sent him to prison, just knowing they could never be together was enough to keep him holding on.

He lifted her into his arms and carried her into his bed. He locked his door and went into the bathroom. The erectile dysfunction was back, so he took Viagra. Hopefully, he'd have an erection that would last the rest of the day. See how she liked that. Then he returned to the bed and wrapped his arms around her. How she stayed asleep, he didn't know. He wanted to rouse her and make her please him. But he also felt terrible for scaring her. She looked at him now like he was a psycho. He wanted loving looks, tender touches, and genuine cries for his body to press into hers. He wanted her to be as obsessed with him as he was with her. But it was hopeless. He would never have that. He lay his head next to her sleeping face, and he cried.

Somehow, he slept. When he awoke, Martha was lying beside him, eyes open, stroking his face.

"Are you doing all right? Any nightmares?"

"No nightmares. It's because you are next to me. You're like some sort of ward."

"I'm not Nicolas. I'm a normal woman."

"Not to me."

"We need to talk about what happens next."

"I don't wanna talk. I want to go to heaven with you and stay there." He kissed her until she pulled away.

"You are showing all the signs of severe PTSD. We need to get you help. You might suffer a mental breakdown. I don't want to see that happen. I found anti-psychotics in your bathroom cupboard. Have you been taking them?"

"Not since you arrived. You are my medicine now." He pulled her on top of him.

"That's dangerous. You must take them. Are you on any antidepressants as well?"

"I hate anything interfering with my sexual performance. And you can't force me to take my meds. They destroy my hard-ons. I hate it. Even with the Viagra. You wouldn't like what they do to me."

"Right now, I care more about your mental state than your sex life. Please go take your meds. I'll wait here."

"No." He shook his head. "I said no. I don't need them. I have you!" He shoved her over and crawled on top of her.

"Please listen to me!"

"I see what I've done wrong. I've been too demanding. I've only tried to please myself, but never thought of what you might want. Tell me, Martha. I'll do anything. Any kink, any position, I'll try them all as long as it's with you."

"Nicolas, you're a sex addict. You use sex as a way of not dealing with your problems. I don't want to enable you."

"What? Just because I think of sex constantly and have made it my life's work to be the best at it?" he replied sarcastically, "of course I'm an addict. How do you think I got so good?"

Martha sighed. It was written on her face; she didn't want him anymore. His dad had ruined everything, down to his ability to please the woman who mattered the most.

"That's it. I'm going to kill him. Go down there, bury a bullet in his head, and pull the footage for you to watch. I can't handle this. He's stolen you from me. This can't happen." He shoved her over, and she pulled his arms, dragging him back down to the bed.

"No!" she begged and covered his face in kisses. "Don't touch him! It's patricide! It's evil. Please, I'll stay here. I'll do whatever you want. I'm not an obsessive person, so you'll have to forgive me. But I am compassionate and have true, unrelenting compassion for you, Nicolas!"

She was crying. Those tears were only half for him, but half was better than nothing. He laid the gun on the nightstand and shoved her over.

"I left the cuffs in your room."

"I don't need the cuffs. I'll keep my hands above my head." Her face shone with tears.

"It's not the same." He reminded her as he pulled off his pants.

"I will scream and beg however you want, just no cuffs. Give me this one thing."

"I did just promise to go with your kinks. Guess I have to bend on something. Let's return to the basics. I'm gonna make you come five times and get you so crazy you won't remember your name. Then it will be my turn."

Many hours later, the sun had set, and they hadn't left the bedroom. To his horror, Nicolas was too depressed to perform, even with Viagra. He couldn't get it up and didn't even have his prescriptions to blame it on. He was miserable and heartbroken. The one thing he was good at was gone. He wanted to die.

Martha lay next to him, stroking his chest, comforting him, and looking at him with those teary eyes until his heart might burst.

"You want to be with him, don't you? Especially now that I can't even fuck you," he mumbled.

"Nicolas, I care about you, and I want to see you get help. We don't need the sex. Please believe me."

He searched for any signs of discontent. How could he eradicate his dad from her mind forever? He sighed. There was no way. He was starving, and they had to eat.

"I'll grab us food if you want to wait here. And a bottle of wine. We need something to celebrate."

Filled with sadness, he jumped off the bed and stumbled downstairs. He was going to lose her, he knew it. Because he was incapable of making anyone love him.

Listlessly, he pulled cheese, crackers and various antipasti to prepare a dish. He went to his dad's wine cabinet, selected a burgundy and then took the whole thing upstairs.

In bed, they ate ravenously, and Nicolas alone finished the bottle of wine within minutes.

"I wish I could read your mind. I would give anything to know if you are still thinking of him."

"Of whom?" She stared blankly, and he smiled with relief. Now they were getting somewhere.

"I visited my dad today. I wanted to kill him, but I couldn't bring myself to do it," he confessed.

"This means that you are still a good person." She reached out to stroke his face, and for one moment, he saw the utter panic in her eyes.

The entire day was a waste. His whole life, for that matter! She was pretending. She was pretending! His heart began to pound. He began to shake. Martha laid him back and put a pillow under his head. She stroked his bare belly and kissed his face. But it was all pretend. The way Catrina pretended the last time, after she was already disgusted with him, but too afraid to say it. She had regarded him with those same fearful, deer-in-the-headlights eyes. He had lost Martha. It was all over. He had to end this. End him. He had failed, and failing meant being alone for the rest of his life. When he woke up, the first thing he would do was kill everyone, including himself.

Friday ~ Day 8

Chapter 41

Justin

Justin awoke with the urge to worship the sex goddess lying next to him. Last night was the best night of his life so far, and it was just a taste of what lay ahead. Energized and filled with peace, he wondered how long he had to wait before suggesting they live together. He got up and went to find the bathroom. It was after eleven, and he was shocked to have slept for nine hours. He ran into Lizzy in the kitchen.

"Hey, mister policeman. Nice to see you again." She gazed at him starry-eyed and giggled like a kid. Justin nodded uncomfortably.

"Good morning, Lizzy. Are you doing alright?"

"Not really. I'm glad you're here, though. Judith has been acting nuts."

"I know."

"I've been what?" Judith entered the room wearing her bra and panties.

Lizzy took one look at her and screamed. "Judith? What happened to you?"

She ran to her sister's side and touched her bruised stomach.

"Judith has been stalking guests since the wedding. She's convinced the abductor was there and followed you home." Justin gave Judith a chastising look, which she ignored.

Lizzy was incredulous. "Why?"

"Because it has to be someone obsessed with her, I know it!"

"Who would be that obsessed?"

"That's what I've been trying to figure out. Someone put their sights on Mom. Then they decided to abduct her, and I am gonna find out who."

"Um, there is something. I just thought of it. It's probably nothing, but you might be right." Lizzy looked scared, which made Justin's stomach drop. She had seen something. She knew something, and they may have missed out on a crucial lead because he hadn't questioned her thoroughly enough. Shit.

"What do you mean?" Judith muttered as she swallowed ibuprofen.

"Remember that server who waited on our table? He was seriously checking Mom out. And remember how she forgot her purse? Well, it was he who handed it to her. I saw him like two inches away from her face, Judith. And they talked for like five minutes."

"I didn't see this." Judith sounded skeptical.

"You were in a bad mood as usual. Which means you were stuck on yourself."

Lizzy looked at Justin, and he sensed she was trying to warn him about Judith as if he didn't already know that she was an impulsive hothead. He rolled his eyes.

"I guess," Judith muttered.

"I thought they were just flirting. Mom's gorgeous, so it's only natural."

"That server was young. Hardly older than me. And he served tons of tables."

"Still, he had a crazy gleam in his eyes. Like he wanted to devour mom."

Judith stared at Lizzy for a long time. "I'm starting to remember now. He was gorgeous, like your typical fuck boy—vain and sexy. But yeah, I see what you mean. Creepy too. Did he touch her?"

"He stroked her arm. Oh my God. I just remembered. Mom kissed him on the cheek!"

"Are you serious?" Justin cried.

"Mom wouldn't lead someone on. She's not like that." Judith said defensively.

"But she was acting weird. Remember when she came out to find us and we thought she was drunk? Maybe she was happy that someone was flirting with her."

"Or was she being nice, and he read into it? It wouldn't be the first time."

"Dad's friends were all assholes and completely shunned mom. Perhaps he's got some savior complex. He saw mom all sad and wanted to help her."

"You should have told the police!" Judith's eyes were accusing.

"I was a zombie that night when Justin took my statement, and you know why." Lizzy stared at him as if he were Jesus and she were his Mary Magdalene. "Plus, I figured they would interview everyone at the lodge. I only remembered it when you said it was someone from the wedding. You should have talked to me this week instead of blowing me off like you always do."

Judith glared at Lizzy, and Justin felt the temperature rise. These sisters did not like each other.

"It can't be a staff member. We checked. None of them owns a luxury car like the one used to take your mom," Justin interjected.

Judith shook her head. "That doesn't mean anything. I used to drive my dad's Porsche, even though I didn't own it. He might have just borrowed it."

Of course. They should have considered that. But that would have taken more interviews, and Finley wasn't even convinced they were looking for someone from the wedding.

"It looked like a bit of harmless flirting. I have no proof it was him," Lizzy insisted, "I feel bad now, like it's my fault. I didn't think about it. He's just a server. Why would he abduct Mom?"

"I can't believe this! It's been a whole week. We should have figured this out sooner." Judith put her head between her hands and screamed.

Justin returned from the bedroom, pulling on his shoes.

"Justin?" Judith followed him as he grabbed his wallet and car keys.

"This might be our break. An obsessive server? Who cares if the car angle doesn't fit? I've got to tell Finley about it. Now."

He kissed Judith at the door and said, "I promise. I will call if we find anything."

As he started his car, Justin pulled out his phone and called station dispatch.

"Put me through to Detective Finley. His private phone."

Twenty seconds later, he answered. "Finley here."

"Detective Finley, it's Officer Salviati."

"Hey, Salviati. Calling for another update? I hear you're dating the daughter. Is that kosher?"

"Listen, I was just talking to the younger daughter, Lizzy. She says she noticed a server at the wedding reception hitting on their mom. He handed Martha her purse when she forgot it, and she kissed him. None of the staff members owns a high-end ride. But the catering company wasn't a part of the staff. And Judith reminded me they could have borrowed the car from someone else."

Finley paused. "Where are you?"

"Down in Salt Lake."

"About an hour away. Okay. We need to track this server down. I'll head to the station. You are welcome to join me since you nailed down the lead."

"Thank you, sir."

Justin hung up and gunned his engine. This was a bitching Camaro. He would make it to the station in forty.

He made it in forty-five and headed to Finley's office. Finley finished a call and hung up the phone.

"What do we have?"

"I feel like a jackass. Sure, we interviewed the staff at the lodge, but we should've tracked down the catering staff." Finley looked stressed as hell.

"Okay. What did you find?"

"I spoke with the owner of Lazique Catering. Name is Dina. She knew exactly who we were talking about. His name is Nicolas Winters and he's only twenty-five years old. Thinks he's a Casanova. Has quite a reputation for womanizing older ladies. He tends to leave work early when he scores, and that night, he asked to leave early. Dina said that he left in a hurry during his shift on Wednesday afternoon, claiming a family emergency, and hasn't shown up to work since. She had never observed what car he drove, but asked around, and someone said they saw him pull up in a Mercedes that night."

"We have an address?"

"He has an apartment on Fort Union Drive. We're sending officers down in the valley to check it out."

"A far commute, isn't it?"

"Sir, you'll want to see this." Another officer handed Finley a piece of paper.

"Ah, the background check." He scanned the paper, then stared at Salviati.

"A police report from nine years ago. Officers responded to a 911 call made by Nicolas Winters. His mother fell into the swimming pool. When they got there, she was unconscious. Nicolas said he found her that way and pulled her out. Upon further investigation, they found drugs in her tea. Tried to bring 2nd-degree attempted homicide charges against him, but it never even went to court. He attempted suicide, was institutionalized, and the charges against him were eventually dropped. Moreover, over the past nine months, several women have filed complaints that he tried to coerce them into coming home with him, but they didn't press charges. And I can see why. Look at him."

Finley handed him a picture of the driver's license. Nicolas Winters was gorgeous, with a radiant smile and cutie-boy features. Justin wasn't into men, but he recognized when he was looking at a hot one. This guy could get away with anything. Justin felt his gut tighten. He wanted to be the one to arrest this pervert.

"He couldn't be holding Martha in his apartment."

"Let's confirm that. The warrant should come through at any time. I guess we sit by the phone and wait."

Justin sent Judith a text.

> Found him. Nicolas Winters. Institutionalized at sixteen for attempted matricide. Only twenty-five.

> My God! I wish I were with you!

> Stay home. Keep you posted.

Around three in the afternoon, Finley got a call. He put it on speakerphone.

"This is Detective Finley."

"Detective, we've conducted a search of Nicolas Winter's apartment. There is no one here. The place is vacant. It looks like no one has lived here in months."

Finley sighed. "So nothing? You found nothing?"

"One thing. A receipt. For a purchase at a nearby sex shop. Four hundred dollars for lingerie, made just last Saturday."

"That's creepy." Justin shuddered. This was definitely their guy.

"Send someone to visit this shop and interview the owner. Verify it was him and ask if he said anything. You know the drill."

"Sure thing, detective."

Once he hung up, Finley said, "We need to search for other addresses to which he might be connected or any family members in the area."

"It makes no sense that he lives in Salt Lake. And what about the car?"

"Let me wrap my mind around this. We have vetted all the car owners in a thirty-mile radius that met our criteria, meaning luxury cars running a specific tire, and found no leads."

"Yep."

"No prints on the hair comb. The shoe print fits the sort of shoes a server would wear."

"Okay."

"We've found no family members living in the state. Mom is in a home for disabled adults in Utah County. There's no father listed on his birth certificate. We haven't found any connection to a father, at least not so far. No grandparents are alive. No social media under his legal name. No cell phone records connected to his legal name."

"He's borrowing someone's car," Justin stated. "So where did he get the fancy wheels?"

"We are missing something."

"I agree. A whole lot of something. And going from hookups to abduction, that's a leap."

"His boss has got to know more. I've tried calling her again and again. Goes to voicemail. She doesn't have a physical address either. Probably has an event tonight since it's the weekend, but I have no idea where." Finley rubbed his face. "I'm going to get burned on this case big time. Judith was right. It was someone from the fucking wedding."

"Listen, there was hardly any evidence to suggest an abduction, much less involvement by some rich snob from the wedding. Let it go."

"Easier said than done. I've never worked on an abduction case before. This is a small town. Shit like that happens down in the valley, not here. I honestly didn't think we were dealing with an abduction. I haven't known what to think."

Justin didn't know what to say. A server carrying out a high-risk abduction on a low-risk victim in front of two witnesses was extremely far-fetched. You'd have to be nuts to try something like that.

"We need to track down this guy. I can help if you'd like." Justin offered. "My shift doesn't start for a few hours, and I'm gonna go out of my mind until we find him."

"Sure. Dig deep." Finely nodded. "You're smart, and I hear good things about you around here. Keep it up."

"Thanks. I plan to. What am I going to tell Judith?"

"You like the daughter?"

Justin wasn't sure how to answer.

"I guess that's my answer then," he chuckled, "tell her we put an APB out on Nicolas Winters. We have someone staked outside his apartment. It's all we can do until we track down the owner of his fancy ride."

Justin nodded and headed back to his computer. He was starting to feel the way Judith did, obsessed with finding this perpetrator. Justin hated Nicolas the moment he saw his gorgeous face. He preyed on vulnerable women, and Justin hoped they would find him tonight. But first, he needed to track Nicolas down. All he could think of was how disappointed Judith would be when she discovered how little they had so far.

Chapter 42

Martha

When Martha awoke, Nicolas wasn't next to her. It was early afternoon, which made sense. They were up all night dealing with Nicolas's fits. A dam had truly broken, and the past was flooding the murky waters of his fractured mind. Memory after memory rose from the depths like rusty sunken treasures stirred up by meeting and abducting her. She felt horribly responsible. Since facing his trauma, he was a critical life risk and Martha was deeply concerned. Nicolas wasn't going to make it. He needed help. Now.

His bathroom door was closed. Martha checked the handle. Locked.

"Nicolas?"

She pounded.

"Nicolas?"

She screamed. Nothing.

She had to break down this door. Thankfully, the bathroom doors had regular handles. She could remove the handle and then the lock. She searched for something to work as a screwdriver until she found a manicure kit in the nightstand drawer. Using a nail file, she undid the screws, pulled the lock apart and pushed the door open.

Nicolas was lying next to the toilet, semi-conscious. A bottle of pills lay strewn on the floor next to an empty bottle of vodka.

"Oh God, you stupid boy."

Martha knelt over him, opened his mouth, and shoved her fingers down his throat as far as possible, then held his face over the toilet. Within moments, he was vomiting.

"Get it all out, Nicolas. This is not how you end things."

He threw up until he collapsed against the tub.

"Just let me die," he pleaded, his voice hoarse and weary.

"No way. You need to go to the hospital."

"Fuck that. Never again."

"It's the only way!"

"They can't help me! I've tried their help. No. There's only one way out for me."

Helplessly, Martha thought about what to do.

"We need your father up here."

"I don't want him near me. He stole you from me!"

"He can help you. Please let us help you!"

"You want to go to him, fine! Go!"

He grabbed his phone and pushed a button to unlock the doors. "There! All the inside doors are open. Go fuck him to your heart's content and let me die!"

"Let me help you!" she screamed.

"I can hear you all in my head—you and my dad. And I saw your face last night. You're pretending! You all want me dead. Like Catrina did. No one loves me. Just let me die!"

Martha looked at him, terrified. She realized she had made a huge mistake by encouraging Nicolas to recover these memories. He was in a psychotic break. Seeing things, hearing things and believing things that weren't real. He wanted to kill himself, and he might even kill them all. This was an emergency. She had to go for help. Now. She turned to leave, and Nicolas cried out.

"No. Wait." The doors clicked shut. He stumbled forward and fell into her arms. "Don't leave me. Not like she left me."

Catrina. That bitch. Martha hated being the surrogate for that awful woman. She led him to the bed and lay him down.

"We need to have you checked out at the hospital."

"I want to be free. Inside here. I'm so mixed up. It's like bombs are going off inside my head. Will you help me? Please?" He hit his head against his hands until she pulled him into her arms and restrained his hands to his sides. "It's all replaying over and over. All those years with Catrina, her holding me underwater, you and Dad together, trying to save Mom in the pool, then being stuck in the mental hospital. My whole life, I've been alive for one reason: to give people what they want to take. What about me? Why can't I take what I want?"

"What you want to take isn't what you need. I know I keep saying it, but you need professional help."

"It doesn't work the way it says it will on paper. When I went to the hospital, I thought it was the answer, too, but it only made things worse. The only thing that has made me feel better is finding you."

Martha held this sobbing guy in her arms. She stroked his back and tried to calm him. Many facilities indeed failed to meet standards. State hospitals were often the worst. But presently, Nicolas needed to be committed for his protection.

A few minutes later, he dried his face and held her gaze.

"I saw it in your eyes last night. You're terrified of me. I don't know what I did. Maybe I got too mad at you for fucking Erik the Great. I can't bear to see you look at me like I'm a monster." He kissed her and pushed her back onto the bed.

Martha shoved him off her and sat up.

"I am not scared of you, Nicolas. I'm scared for you! I have seen people lose their minds to trauma. Slide into catatonic states where they never find the strength to leave. You are past your limit. No one is safe now. Until you receive treatment, you are a danger to everyone, especially yourself. What will it take to make you see that?"

"I can't get it out of my head. You wanna lock me up so you can be with my dad. You want an easy escape, and I won't give it to you. It's not fair. I did all the hard work by saving you. Why should he reap the rewards?"

"Does it matter anymore? Do you want to end up dead? You're so young. You have your whole life ahead of you. Would you forgo emergency care if you were hit by a bus? Of course not. Your mind has cracked open like an egg, and what has poured out is poisoning every part of you."

"I'm so glad you love me." Nicolas threw his arms around her and buried her in kisses. He reeked of vomit and shook uncontrollably. The alcohol was still in his system.

"Why did you take me? What did you think it would accomplish?" Martha asked softly.

"I thought if I could find someone to replace Catrina—someone who looked like her, reminded me of her, but wasn't horrible like her—it would heal my broken heart. All I ever wanted was to find a woman who would love me, who I could make happy, who would never leave me. I thought you were that woman, Martha. You look so much like Catrina, but you aren't cruel like her. I know we can be happy together."

"Dear, sweet boy. You need to calm down." She stroked his face.

"I need to go down on you," he murmured, "it's the only thing that will make me feel better."

"Let's get you in the shower, then get you dressed." She tried instead.

"Only if you will go with me," he pleaded.

Martha nodded in consent and guided him to the bathroom, filled with discouragement. She stripped them both, pulled him into the shower, and scrubbed away the vomit like he was her child. Shampooed his lovely hair and rinsed it thoroughly. He was such a beautiful man. It was soul-crushing to see him in this comatose state. Then she led him out of the shower and towel-dried him. Automatically, he put on deodorant and cologne, pulled out an electric razor and shaved, looking past his reflection in the mirror.

She pulled on her lingerie. When he finished, she helped him dress. Eyes glazed over, he was lost inside his head, and she couldn't bring him back. It was devastating.

Nicolas was showing her how feeble her skills were. She couldn't help him or herself. Nothing in all her education prepared her for this. Anything she did would either enable him or incite him. What horrific damage Catrina had done. Martha wondered how he had made it to twenty-five years old without someone reporting him for inappropriate conduct. Or maybe he cracked due to meeting and abducting her. Martha realized how badly she was failing him, and without immediate intervention, she feared the consequences would be swift and harsh.

Tanya Madsen

Chapter 43

Judith

Judith paced back and forth until five in the afternoon. It had been six hours since Justin left. She spent forever online searching for anything about Nicolas Winters. No social media. No dating profiles. It's like he didn't exist. Didn't seem to have even gone to high school. Justin finally texted her to say they'd found nothing at his apartment.

She called him right back.

"Seriously, nothing?"

"I'm sorry. I've searched for hours. I can't find a thing about this guy. He has no family here. Mom has been in a home for adults with disabilities since he nearly killed her. He was institutionalized on and off for a year. We've requested medical records to determine next of kin but are waiting to hear back from the hospital. When he got out, it looks like he attended Berkeley."

"How could he afford that? Someone must be bankrolling him."

"Good point. I'll mention it to Finley. But figuring out who paid his tuition will take days. Listen, we have an APB out, and someone is watching his place. If he sneezes, we'll hear him."

"Okay."

"Are you okay? Is your stomach doing any better? I hope last night didn't agitate you."

"Last night was heaven on earth, and you know it. My stomach is doing a little better."

"You know what I'd like to do? Take you somewhere secluded. Strip naked, sit in a hot tub and get our game on—"

"Really?"

"I'll do some searching tonight. Make reservations. I've got a ton of vacation time. I haven't used any in over a year."

"Justin, I think you're the one. The guy I dreamed about as a little girl before life messed me up."

"What do you mean?"

"Ah, it's nothing."

"No. Tell me."

"Um, I lost my virginity young. Like really young. To the father of another contestant."

"Oh, Judith. I'm so sorry."

"For years, I blamed my mom. She was friends with this guy and his wife. They attended a lot of the same competitions as we did. He flirted with my mom, too. He was a real dirtbag. But now I realize that he flirted to make her feel comfortable so he could have access to me. It made me so mad. Mom would be having drinks with his wife at the pool. Then he'd corner me somewhere and—it was awful. I think that's why I've hated her for years. It's unfair, I know."

"I'm glad you told me."

"I guess what I'm saying is that if I act like a psycho, it's because I'm secretly a mess. I mean, tons of girls who went into acting, music or pageants went through the same thing. For a long time, I thought it was normal. But after my encounter with Lyle the other night, it brought it all back."

"Judith, I won't let anyone hurt you ever again."

"You really are my Captain America."

"Jones told me to be careful with you since you might see me as a superhero, but after we found your mom, you'd just dump me."

"No wonder you've been pushing me away."

"I don't want to get hurt. I'm not the kind of guy to give my heart away. I couldn't survive a painful breakup like my parents went through."

"Neither could I."

"I'm working an early shift tonight and it's about to start. You take care and I'll come down tomorrow after I wake up."

"Okay. And Justin?"

"Yes?"

"I love you."

"I love you too."

They had said the magic words to each other. Judith hung up and lay back on the couch, lightheaded with joy.

It was after six p.m. when Judith decided she had to do something. She dressed in black jeans, a black tank top and a leather jacket with a massive pocket to hide her gun. She looked in the mirror and smiled at the sexy badass. She pulled on her black shit-kicker boots, grabbed her backpack filled with ammo and called for Lizzy.

"Come with me."

"Where are we going?"

"To find this guy."

Lizzy looked horrified.

"Justin said to stay here!"

"The cops were unsuccessful, just like I figured."

"What can we do that they haven't?" Lizzy pulled on her shoes and a hoodie.

"We can go talk to his boss. Something's not adding up here."

Judith got into the driver's seat of her mom's car and plugged in her phone. She wanted it fully charged in case of an emergency.

"We're heading back to the lodge?"

"Yep. I called and confirmed that the same catering company is working there tonight. Best to start at the beginning."

On the freeway, Lizzy said, "Why did you have to take Justin?"

"What do you mean?"

"Couldn't you tell I liked him?" Lizzy asked petulantly. "It was love at first sight! That's why I couldn't give a statement. He's like—"

"Captain America?" Judith smiled.

"Yes." Lizzy put her head against the glass and sighed.

"Lizzy, Justin and I. This is it, sis. He's the one I've been looking for. He's my honey."

"You're such a bitch. You can get anyone. You just take anything you want."

"Um, no. But Justin is the man I've been looking for my whole life."

"Have you already had sex?"

"Not yet. He says he wants to respect me and make our first time special."

"I hope he finds out what a whoring bitch you are," Lizzy said venomously.

"Wow. Some sister you are." Judith wasn't surprised. Lizzy had always hated her.

They drove in uncomfortable silence. It had started to rain, and the air was freezing. By the time they arrived in Heber, the rain had turned to snow, and the drive took twice as long this time. With weekend traffic and a quick stop for gas, it was eight by the time they made it to the lodge.

An event was in full swing. Judith parked off to the side of the road. They walked up the steep hill to the lodge together, then went through the entrance they had used only a week earlier.

Judith entered the kitchen. Servers were everywhere. Judith asked for someone to point her to whoever was in charge. They directed her to a big gal with gorgeous dreadlocks.

"Dina?" Judith shouted over the commotion.

She looked up and nodded her head. "Who's asking?"

"We were here last Friday. Our mom went missing that night. We need to talk about Nicolas Winters."

Dina handed the bowl of sauce she was stirring to someone and said, "Follow me."

She escorted Judith and Lizzy into a quieter room.

"I already told the police everything I know."

"That night, was Nicolas acting weird?"

"Now that you mention it, he was. He asked to leave early to follow a hookup home. It wasn't the first time. Nicolas is a womanizer. A successful one too."

"I'm sure my mom blew him off. She's not into casual hookups," Judith replied, "you have absolutely no idea where he lives?"

"No. But it can't be too far from here. I've often called him to work at this venue on short notice. He was always here in under thirty minutes."

"See, the cops say he lives down in the valley."

"There's no way," Dina confirmed. "Wait a minute." She snapped her fingers, trying to flick a light on in her head. "When he started working for me, I asked him where he lived. He said he was staying at his dad's castle for a few weeks. When I asked him what he meant by that, he said his dad was some living-off-the-grid guru. Like a contractor or something."

"Wait. The police said he has no father listed on his birth certificate."

"I'm just telling you what he told me."

"Thanks. If he does show up—"

"I know the drill. Call the cops."

"Do you happen to have a photo of Nicolas?"

"We took a group photo for my website around Christmas. Yep. What's your number?"

Judith gave it to her. When it came through, she blew up the photo and stared at it for a long time. Nicolas was gorgeous, and he was her type—that slim build and deep-set eyes. There was something familiar about him. How had she not noticed him at the wedding?

"Thanks. Wow. He is hot."

"I always thought Nicolas came off a bit psycho."

"I guess he tried to murder his mom."

"Lord, I need to start running background checks."

"Thanks again." Judith waved, and they rushed back to the car.

Judith searched online with the car idling and the heater at full blast.

"Help me, Lizzy. We're looking for any off-the-grid mansions here in northern Utah."

After about fifteen minutes, Judith snarled in rage.

"Dammit! Nothing!"

"We could drive around and look for mansions."

"A waste of time. Let's search for off-the-grid building contractors in the state."

Five minutes later, Lizzy said, "I found one. His name is Erik Stanley. Here's his pic."

Judith compared Nicolas's picture on her phone to Erik's picture on Lizzy's.

"Oh my God." Impulsively, Judith threw her arms around her sister and they hugged wildly. "We need his address."

They both searched and found multiple addresses under his name. But after mapping them, they found one residence close to the lodge.

Judith called Justin. No answer. She called Detective Finley. Voicemail. She screamed with rage and sent Justin a text.

Call Me. I FOUND HIM.

She added Erik Stanley's address.

"Let's go."

"Judith. No. Let's wait for the police."

"Mom might die any second. She might already be dead. We are going there. Now."

Judith put the car in drive, turned around and headed back to the main road, where navigation showed the house was only twenty-five minutes away. She tried to keep under the speed limit. The last thing she wanted was a speeding ticket right now.

They drove in silence.

"What are you going to do when we get there?" Lizzy sounded terrified.

"I'm going to knock on the door, and when he answers, I will scream at him to give us our mother. He's a dumb guy about my age. How scary can he be?" Judith said with more conviction than she felt.

"You'll get us both killed!"

"No. Because you will call the police, but they can't arrive first. If this guy has already tried to kill his mom, he'll flip out and kill our mom when the cops show up."

"What if Mom is already dead? Then he'll kill you too, and it will all be a big waste! Call Justin again."

Judith sighed and called again. Still no answer.

They pulled onto a desolate paved road and turned onto a dirt road, one after another. She didn't see a house for miles. The dirt roads slowed them down, which was enormously frustrating.

They turned onto an even rougher dirt road and drove a mile until they reached a majestic custom home covered in massive windows. It had a huge front door. A dark Mercedes was parked on the side—the same car she had seen parked outside her condo earlier in the week.

Judith's heart was racing. What was she doing? Lizzy was right! She needed to wait for the police to arrive.

"Here, I am going to call you. You need to call the police station dispatch on the other line and ask them to connect you with Officer Salviati. Say it's an emergency and you need to speak with him directly. Tell Justin where we are, then add him to our call. I'll keep my phone on in my pocket so you can hear everything."

Lizzy threw her arms around Judith. "You are so brave, it's scary!"

"I need to make it up to Mom. I've been a royal bitch to her, and now I'll make things right by saving her from this asshole."

"You don't have to do this!"

"But I want to do this. I need to save Mom." She kissed Lizzy and said, "Call. Now."

Pistol cocked and ready, Judith slipped her phone in her deep jacket pocket and walked towards the front door.

Chapter 44

Martha

For the rest of the afternoon and evening, Martha begged to see Erik. Nicolas refused. He went from being hysterical and hypersexual to lying in a comatose state. He had unraveled completely. Martha tried every relaxation technique she could think of to calm him. He was lying on his side, picking at the comforter. Desolate and crushed. She couldn't bear to see him like this, knowing it was her fault. Now it was dark. She was starving and scared.

"Nicolas?"

"Huh?" He was in the throes of a depressive slump.

She stood on the side of the bed and pleaded with him.

"Please let me out. Let me go to your father. I promise I won't touch him, but I need to see him. If you love me, you'll do this for me."

He looked up and stared at her face for a long time.

"First, tell me and be honest. Why am I not enough?"

His eyes were empty as if all life had poured out of him. He looked dead. Martha thought hard about what to say. Should she be honest? Would that wreck him?

"When I met you at the reception, I immediately lusted after you. When you abducted me and I woke up naked and saw you, part of me was thrilled beyond belief. I'm ashamed to say I have never felt so alive as I have with you."

His lips trembled. Tears formed once again.

"All my life, I have been a people pleaser. It locked me in a miserable relationship for twenty years and caused problems for me in my career."

"That's what I love about you. You'll do anything to please me. You're perfect!"

"You have to understand. I didn't plan for this to happen. But your dad, he and I are a lot alike. Both pushovers, he would say. This makes us soulmates in a way. I have never felt so understood as I have with him. It's exhilarating. So while you take me to erotic places I've never been, he has brought me home. I'm at home with him, comforted and comfortable."

His eyes glittered with jealousy.

"It's not the sex that won you over. It's him, which is worse. I can compete with another lover, but I can't compete with another man." He squeezed his eyes shut and shook his head miserably. "I completely messed this up myself. I should never have let you two meet. Now it's ruined. I ruined everything."

"Nicolas, having sex with you has been the most intense experience of my life. But I need more than five orgasms before breakfast. I need love. How can you say you love me when you also try to drown me? You don't love me, my boy. You don't know how to love. You have never felt loved, so you don't know what it looks or feels like. It's so heartbreaking, and I swear to God, I'll get you the help you need so that someday you'll feel loved! But the way you are going about this, it will all end in tears."

"Maybe I can get over my kink. I don't know. You don't even want to try with me. I see it now. You two are in love. It happened in seconds. And I am on the outside looking in. Leave me be. I have to decide what to do. I have a big decision to make." Nicolas took his phone and unlocked the doors. "Go. He's yours. You can have him. I can't bear to look at your face right now." Then he turned to his pillow and hid from her.

Martha sat there wondering if she should leave. She had to. She had to take this chance. Darting towards the door, she looked back and saw him staring after her. His aura was black and deadly. They had to get the hell out of here and take this kid to a hospital before he killed them all.

Martha burst into Erik's bedroom. It had only been two days since she had last seen him, but it seemed like an eternity.

"Erik!"

He jumped out of bed and raced to her. Kissing her, holding her.

"My God. I was so scared. I kept messaging him, but he wouldn't reply. I was terrified that he hurt you!"

"No. Thank God. And we haven't had sex since you and I. I'm so relieved."

"Then why haven't you come down?"

"We have a serious problem. Nicolas recovered a memory of Catrina trying to drown him two nights ago, which explains his drowning fantasies. He has since spiraled into a psychotic break. I found him locked in the bathroom this morning, overdosing on pills and vodka. He's been erratic all day; he's seriously out of control. He needs a hospital. We aren't safe!"

Erik paced back and forth. "Let me pull on some pants and we'll figure this out."

"We must convince him to open that goddamn door! He says he won't go back to the mental hospital, but he needs emergency treatment. I have contacts. I'll find him the best care in the country. That is, if you're willing to pay for it."

"Pay to help the man who abducted the love of my life? This is hard, Martha. Part of me thinks he's not worth redeeming."

"He's your son. And you abandoned him to a life of hell. You need to take responsibility for your neglect and help that boy! If you could only comprehend what he's suffered."

"You're right. It's not about the money. It's about my feelings for you."

"I hate to say it, but we would have never met if it weren't for him abducting me, so there's that."

"Let's go find him and try to talk sense into him. Although I'll be worthless, he hates me."

"Just a sec. I think I hear him." Martha slipped out of the room as Erik pulled on clothes. Nicolas stood in the basement entrance, looking like a broken little boy.

"Nicolas!" Martha ran to him and pulled him into her arms.

His eyes were brimming with pain, like bottomless pits. He grabbed her by the shoulders and flipped her around. To her horror, Nicolas pressed a blade up against her neck.

She screamed. Erik came running into the living room.

"Nicolas! Let her go! Now!" he bellowed.

Nicolas tossed a pair of handcuffs on the floor in front of Erik.

"Cuff yourself to the island towel rack. There. Or she's dead."

Martha registered the terror in Erik's eyes as he knelt on the floor and obeyed.

"Nicolas, please. We love you. I love you! Don't do this!"

"You love him more. Like you said, no one has ever loved me. I'm gonna do what I should have done when I found out about you two. First, I'll kill you, then him, and finally myself. I don't wanna live without love anymore."

"I know I've been a terrible dad, but you coming to live with me was my path to redemption. Let's not end it like this. Okay? Just let us go."

"And watch you two run off into the sunset? Together? While I'm left behind. Again? All alone? Abandoned? Fuck you! I told you I was vindictive. I tried to talk myself out of this. Tried to let it go. It was one single fuck. It's not cheating, right? But I can't forgive you, and I'll never forget." His spittle ran along her ear. His whole body radiated with agony, as if he were burning alive.

"Son, what can I do to make you put down that knife?"

"Not a goddamn thing," Nicolas said coldly, "even if you gave her up, which you wouldn't, she doesn't want me now. Not like she wants you. Martha, you have ripped out my heart, and now you get to see what a heartless man is really like."

"Nicolas, I'll stay with you. I love you!"

"Not in the way I love you." It came out as a whine. "Plus, I screwed up too much. I stole you. I saw how sweet and caring you were and how you looked like Catrina, and I couldn't help it. Didn't care that I was breaking the law. I thought the incredible sex would win you over in a day and make you love me, and maybe for once, I would feel loved. I bet on the roulette table and once again I lost."

"What you have gone through is enough to decimate the strongest man. Dealing with trauma is dangerous, and I'm sorry I encouraged you. I promise, if you let us help you, I have contacts. I will find you the best hospital in the nation. In the world! It won't be like the last time. I promise!"

"It doesn't matter. Not after what happened to mom and not after what I did to you. They'll send me to prison."

"You drugged and nearly killed your mother! What was everyone supposed to think?"

"That I was telling the truth and she was shoving pills down my throat, left and right? I tried to tell her about Catrina, but she didn't listen? None of that matters now anyway. I've made up my mind. If I can't have you, Martha, then no one can."

With that, he backed up and pulled a bucket of water into the room. Set it down with one hand and knelt while dragging her down with him. She screamed and fought. He held her in a vise-like grip, threw the knife and a bottle of pills at Erik's feet.

"Take your pick. Drug overdose or slit your wrists. I'll take last pick. But she's gotta go this way because I'm gonna make you watch her die like you watched me die."

"Nicolas, I can assure you that I did not make your abuse happen, nor did I want it to happen."

"But you did nothing to prevent it. So you are just as guilty."

Nicolas positioned his body until she was under him, and he scooted them over to the bucket. Martha watched Erik strain against the handcuff to kick over the bucket. It was barely out of reach. He looked tortured.

"Stop this, Nicolas. I swear to God, I'll give you everything. I'll sell the business and give you all I own. Please don't hurt her!"

Martha felt the tears running down Nicolas's face and dripping onto her cheek. His whole body was shaking as he sobbed. He had her hands pinned behind her back with one hand and the other hand on top of her head.

"Goodbye, my one and only. I believe there is a life after death and we will meet again. Soon. In our own private universe. It sucks that this must end in tragedy. I wanted us to save each other. I guess this is how it's got to be done."

She screamed again.

"Stop. Nicolas. Please! Remember us in bed? Remember how good it was? Do you want to give that up? I will stay with you. Forever! Anything you say, I will do!"

"You can't do the one thing I need. You can't take back falling in love with my dad."

With that, he plunged her head into the bucket. The water was warm, and she tried to hold her breath. Nicolas pushed her head down and pressed it to the bottom. She tried so hard for as long as she could, shuddering beneath Nicolas's trembling body. Echoes persisted. Erik—screaming, crying and begging. The loud, relentless banging of someone at the door upstairs. The door!

Oh, God. Hold on, Martha. Help has arrived. You can make it.

Then she couldn't hold her breath any longer. Her mouth sputtered open, and water flooded in. She gasped, choked, and shook uncontrollably, and then—nothing.

Chapter 45

Justin

Justin was finishing taking a statement on a vandalism case. Some old dude claimed kids vandalized his four-wheeler and siphoned gas. There were a couple of scratches on the paint, and it was out of gas. But Justin thought he saw kids running through his yard and decided to fabricate the story to spice up his weekend—typical hicks.

A call came over the radio.

"Dispatch to Salviati."

"Salviati here."

"I have a Lizzy Monroe on the line. Says she's trying to reach you. Says it's a life-or-death emergency and she will only talk to you. Can I put the call through?"

An icy hand gripped Justin's heart as he raced to his patrol car. He pulled his phone out of the holder and saw that he had missed two calls from Judith.

He read her text, *Call me. I FOUND HIM,* saw the mapped address sent thirty minutes ago, and nearly fainted.

"Yes. Put her through."

After a pause, a girl answered.

"Justin?" She sounded terrified.

"Lizzy? Where are you?"

"We are here! We found his father and his house. We tried to call you and sent you the address. Judith took a gun and went to knock on the door. She said to call you and then add you to a three-way call. She has her phone in her pocket so that we will hear everything."

"Lizzy, add me to the call. Okay?" Then he screamed into the chilly night air. "What the hell, Judith? Are you insane?"

"I'm going to hang up and connect you to our call now," Lizzy said, and the line went dead.

Justin bellowed out the door.

"Jones! We have to go! Judith found our perp and is walking into his house with a gun right now! I'm texting you the address. We have a possible homicide ongoing. NOW!"

His phone was ringing. With trembling fingers, he answered, and with a clarity that boiled through him like acid rain, a man with a husky soft voice spoke.

"What the hell are you doing here?"

Justin heard Judith pause. She was breathing heavily.

"I'm the daughter of the woman you abducted last week. Martha. Take me to her or I'll blow your head off!"

The sound of clapping hands.

"Of course, I remember you. I haven't been able to get you out of my head. You're the daughter, all rage and discontent. How lovely to finally meet."

"Take me to my mother, Nicolas!" Judith screamed again, and Justin heard boots crunching on gravel.

In a fake British accent, he mocked her.

"I'm all astonishment. Brains and beauty. How ever did you find me?"

"Let me see my mother!" she growled and pulled the trigger. A series of shots exploded, and Justin sensed that Judith was terrified.

"My lady, you have my heart falling out of my chest. I knew you were beautiful, but you are breathtaking up close. Did you dress up for me because you are fucking sexy in that getup."

"Listen, stupid fuck boy, take me to my mother. Now!"

"A fuck boy, huh? You're enchanting. I've never had a woman hit on me while holding a gun to my head."

"I'm not here to flirt, asshole. Let me in!"

"Fine. But know this. Once you pass through this door, you're mine. Thanks to Martha's betrayal, there's an open vacancy, so your timing is perfect."

Justin slammed his fist into the dashboard.

"Goddamn it, Judith!"

Jones, who was now listening, eyes filled with the horror that Justin felt, turned on the flashing lights and tore out of the driveway.

"This place is out in the middle of nowhere! Miles from anything on all dirt roads and over thirty minutes away!" Jones yelled to no one in particular.

"Sure, whatever. Lead the way," Judith snapped, and a heavy door slammed shut.

Justin had his volume all the way up. The police radio was loud and interfering, and he wanted to turn it off. Jones contacted Finley, who was also on his way. Judith had gone in with a gun to the perp's head. Justin hoped this wouldn't come back on her, playing vigilante like this. She was so stupid. How could she do this? How!

The click of a man's dress shoes on hardwood was unmistakable, then it stopped.

"I have to admit, I wanna drag you to the floor and eat you out like your life depends on it, right this second. You are an absolute feast. I want you so bad it's infectious."

Jones put his hand on Justin's shoulder.

"Doing alright, buddy? Hang in there. We'll catch him."

Judith snorted, "Is that what you did to my mom? Took her and gave her the best sex of her life because you're so insecure you can't fuck girls your own age? I have met so many guys like you. They all think they are the hottest pieces of shit walking the planet. You're not special. You're just another little dick. Now. Take me to my mother!" she screamed.

"You don't know me," he warned, his voice venomous, "I am special. I was trained to be!"

"What, like some prostitute to the king?" She laughed. "Do you live your life in a porno? Who the fuck even are you?"

"No, Judith, you're goading him. Stop goading him!" Justin pleaded into the phone, willing his voice inside her head. Judith was a complete idiot. How could he love someone so foolish and fearless?

"I hate guys like you. Think their good looks will take them anywhere. Where is she? Is she alive? Did you hurt her?!"

"Good looks? I'm flattered you noticed."

"Take me to her now, or I'll just kill you and find her myself!"

Gunshots echoed through what sounded like a huge open room.

"Would you stop shooting that thing at me?!" Nicolas demanded, "I hate guns!"

"Not a chance!"

"You wanna play then? Fine!"

The swish of movement, a loud grunt, and then a crack reverberated through his heart as Judith cried out in pain. Tussling, more grunting, heavy breathing, and good God, sloppy kisses.

"This is better," Nicolas chirped, "much better. You have me at your mercy. I've never felt so out of control in all my life."

Silence fell like a hammer as Justin gripped the phone tighter. What was he doing to her?

"Poor Judith. I had to kiss it better. And this has to go."

Something metal hit the wall and clattered to the floor.

"My dick's too big to need to play with your gun. I would love to show you—my dick. Let's play with that instead. Martha says I'm a sex addict.

She's right. There's only one way to get good at something, and I am the best of the best."

Jones put his hand over Justin's phone.

"We don't have to listen to this, Salviati. Take it off speaker. This is too much for anyone."

Justin shoved his hand away.

"I can handle it. Judith is strong and regardless of what he does to her, she'll pull through."

But his voice wavered despite his brave face.

Scuffling across the floor, sounding very close to the phone, Nicolas whispered,

"You are no match for me. I can seduce any woman I want. And right now, I want you."

Nicolas silenced her with kisses. Justin could hear his hands roaming all over his girl. Then Judith moaned. Not a pain moan. The other kind. The hairs on Justin's arms rose as a thousand volts of jealousy electrified him. He couldn't wait to wring this fucker's neck.

"You are a wild cat version of your mom. I've dreamed about you every night since I first saw you. I can't believe I'm on top of you right now."

"Keep dreaming. And get your goddamn hand off my pussy."

"I'll keep dreaming forever of everything I'm gonna do with you. I told you when you stepped through that door, you were mine. I've never felt such an instantaneous, insane desire. I mean, I knew I wanted you when I saw you at the wedding, and from my obsessing over you ever since, but you weren't part of the plan. I don't know what's happening here but my dick is going crazy. And after two days of nonstop limp-dick it's a fucking miracle."

Her shriek echoed through the room like some Viking shield maiden inciting a war raid. Judith spat, probably straight into his eye, a thud, then a groan of pain that sounded like she kneed him in the groin.

"Goddamn it!" he screeched.

Jones chuckled nervously, "this little lady's something else. What did they feed her growing up? Bear testicles?"

"You haven't seen nothing yet!" She smacked him again and again—more sounds of struggle and then more smacks.

"You really want to fight me, don't you?" Nicolas barked.

Justin heard the sound of screams and smacks as they fought back and forth, followed by a thud as his hand turned into a fist, and she cried out in pain. She immediately returned the favor.

"Fuck, that hurt. You are vicious. I love it. You know, I checked you out online. Wow. A beauty queen. I pledge my fealty."

"Get the fuck off me," she growled.

"Oh, Judith, I can think of a hundred different things I want to do, but getting off you is not one of them. I thought only a forty-plus could get me going, but you, my dear, are a game changer. I'll have you know that despite your abuse, I'm still delightfully ready to romp. I wanna drag you upstairs right now, but I am a gentleman and prefer to let my women have a say."

"You're no gentleman. I am not your woman. And I can feel your dick against my thigh. It's the size of a twig!"

"You won't think that once I'm inside you. Here, what about now? Take those words back."

Never in his life had Justin felt such rage. He wanted to reach through the phone and——

"You wouldn't even be able to find your way in with that tiny thing. What, are you related to leprechauns? I didn't think a dick could be that small!"

"You're lying! Why are you fucking with me?"

Sounds of struggle arose in a war of fists, grunting and cursing, until Judith let out an ear-curdling scream.

"Oh my God! That hurt!"

"Jones, what the hell can I do? What is he doing to her? Why is she goading him like this? Is she crazy? Who does this?" Justin rubbed his face ferociously as Jones patted his shoulder.

"I'm so sorry, man. This psycho won't win. He won't. Your sweetheart found him and led us straight to him."

"That's what you get for talking shit about my penis," Nicolas chastised.

"You sadistic bastard. You are so dead." Judith's voice trembled precariously.

"Sadistic? Two minutes around you, you have me reincarnating as the Marquis de Sade. What are you, a witch?"

"I am going to murder you!"

"Make yourself at home. You interrupted the bath I was having with your mom in a bucket. After fucking my dad, she practically begged me to! But I don't know—in the end, I couldn't. I just couldn't. I let her go and now I don't know what to do. Then you show up like some sexy force of nature. Now I have three people to kill or, I don't know, I don't know!"

"You worthless piece of shit. Remove yourself from my chest and take me to her now, or when it comes time to kill you, I'll rip your testicles off with my bare teeth!" she threatened.

"She's insane, your girl. Is she this way with you?" Jones yelled.

Justin couldn't answer. He was stunned, made speechless by Judith's bravado. He couldn't be this stupidly brave in a million years.

"Now you've got me thinking of your mouth on me with those blowjob lips. Come on. You know you wanna."

"You'd have to chain me to a mountain and starve me to death first," she snarled.

"I love how you think, and restraints do get me off. But fine. You won't be any fun until I give in to your demands. I can see that you are just as spoiled as me and I've finally met my match. Maybe you can bring her back.

I was an idiot, I admit. It was so much easier in all my fantasies. Here, take my hand."

Justin heard Judith gasp in pain as Nicolas pulled her to her feet. A door opened.

"Come with me, Belladonna. That will be my name for you, now and forever. It means beautiful lady, but also refers to a deadly form of nightshade. A perfect description of you, I think."

"I don't care what you call me. After tonight, I hope to see you dragged away in a straitjacket."

"I'm no stranger to those awful things, I admit. But then you'd miss out on the best sex of your life. You don't want that. Belladonna? After you."

"Salviati, almost there," Jones said harshly. "Then we're going to nail his ass to the wall. Hear me? And if we take a headshot, it'll be you who saves the day. I promise."

Thirty minutes might as well be thirty years.

Justin whispered into the phone.

"You doing okay, Lizzy?"

"My sister is insane," she said tonelessly.

"I agree," Justin muttered, "I totally agree."

Chapter 46

Judith

What Judith found in that basement would haunt her for the rest of her life. Her mother was lying unconscious next to a bucket now drained of all its contents, but it was clear this monster had tried to drown her in front of—Judith saw a man. It was Erik, the father in the online picture, handcuffed to a towel rack on the side of the kitchen island.

"Please check if she's breathing!"

Judith dropped to her knees and lay her mom on her back, feeling her neck for a pulse. She was alive.

Her first-aid training which had seemed like pointless bullshit to win a trophy at the time came flooding back. She looked at her mom and noticed what she was wearing.

Nicolas was now lounging over the arm of a nearby sofa in mock fascination.

"Lingerie? You pervert." She glared at him.

"Do you want me to blush? Martha is a doll, and I've made her feel sexier than she's ever felt in her life. She loved every second of her awakening. I adore her in red. Compliments her olive skin."

Judith wanted to murder this snide, smirking man who did this to her good, sweet, loving mom. Tears blurred her vision as she bent over and listened for her breathing. Nothing. *Please, Mom*, she prayed. *Let me save you.* Erik asked.

"Can you feel a pulse?"

"Yes. But she's not breathing."

"No chest compressions. She's in respiratory arrest and needs immediate ventilation. Give her one ventilation every five seconds. Each one should last about a second and make the chest rise. Got it?"

Grateful for Erik's CPR recap, Judith nodded.

"I do." Judith pinched her mom's nose, put her mouth over hers and breathed.

Nicolas clapped his hands.

"Gorgeous and useful. I love it! Such a hallmark moment. Please bring her back. I admit I was rash, and I'm sorry, Dad. I lost my shit and I feel awful."

"Nicolas, you need to step down and let us go," Erik growled.

"Dad, I am in charge around here. Haven't you figured that out yet? So shut up and be the pushover. That's right. Martha told me all about your soulmate bullshit."

Judith kept at it, pleading inside her head as she counted to five and breathed for one. Counted to five and breathed for one.

"Please save her. I love her. She's the best thing that's ever happened to me." Erik confessed.

"I can't handle this. I found her! I saved her! You make me so angry!" Nicolas shrieked as he ran upstairs.

Judith focused on what to do next—one breath after another. Nothing else mattered. She thought of a lifetime of memories with this woman. She understood now why her mom was so sad. Craig broke her when she was a little older than Judith was now, then kept her around for comfort and nostalgia. She understood why her mom couldn't let him go for so long. She wasn't weak. Mom knew Craig was nothing without her.

It was Mom who built his business and made him look good in public. Mom, who trained him for negotiations, landed their biggest investor by becoming friends with the wife. She was an expert at diplomacy and communication. She had invested in Craig, and he turned out to be a bad investment. She held on to Craig in the vain hope of a return that never came. In the end, she lost everything.

This was hopeless. She had been at this for at least a minute. Judith stopped and screamed until her lungs burned.

"Don't give up! Keep going! We have to keep trying!" Erik begged.

Somehow, Judith returned her hands to her mother's face and began again. One. Two. Three. Four. Five. Then one. And then. Another multitude of seconds passed. And then. Oh my God. Finally, her mother jerked violently, a spasm coursed through her body, and she coughed. Coughed! And she choked and coughed, vomited and vomited some more, and finally breathed.

Judith gathered her mom to her chest and hugged her so hard she might smother her. She kissed her wet hair and clammy forehead.

"Mom, oh Mom. Thank God."

She sat back as her mom looked around, rubbing her eyes in disbelief.

"Judith?" she whispered.

"I found you, Mom. I've been searching from day one. No one else could find you, so I did it myself."

Her mom shook uncontrollably. Judith raced to the couch, grabbed a blanket, and wrapped it around her. Her mom replied, every bit a shrink.

"Nicolas was abused throughout his entire childhood by his nanny and mother. From my observations, he exhibits the signs of borderline personality disorder. Excessive mood swings, love-and-sex addiction, extremely poor impulse control, anger issues and a tendency to fight, a crippling fear of abandonment, risky behavior, suicidal ideation—all of it. Moreover, he suffers from clinical depression. He's off his meds and has lost all control. He's in a psychotic break and is in critical need of treatment."

Judith felt her mom's compassion wash through her, and she pushed it away.

"I don't care what he suffers from. When I'm done with him, he will get his head full of lead. Where does he keep the key for those?"

Judith pointed to the cuff on Erik's wrist.

"On his person?" Erik presumed.

"Guess I'm gonna have to kill him then," Judith snapped.

Her mom crawled across the floor and into Erik's arms. He held her with his free arm and kissed her face.

"I'm so sorry. I couldn't do a goddamn thing. He stopped, though. Nicolas had a complete meltdown when he realized what he was doing and was unable to go through with it. Pulled you out, turned you over, and kissed you like a maniac to wake you up. Then he rushed upstairs to see who was at the door. He loves you, Martha, even if it's insane and obsessive."

"I know. We need to save Nicolas from himself." She sounded so weak.

"Judith, if you hadn't shown up when you did—thank you!"

Erik was crying as her mom kissed him passionately on his mouth and all over his face. They shook as they held each other as if they had both nearly drowned together.

Judith hid her smile. What the hell? Her mom was lying in the arms of a man who would die for her, for the first time in her life. He wasn't bad-looking. After all, he was Nicolas's dad, and he hadn't checked out the heroic daughter once, so her opinion of him was rising.

Judith stood and paced the room.

"Is there a way out of this house?"

"No. The lock opens with an app or a code."

"I guess we just wait." Judith plopped on the couch.

"For what?" Martha asked weakly.

"I purposely let Nicolas take me inside. I needed to save you, Mom. Remember what the pastor said? I wanted to be a daughter to die for."

"Oh, Judith!" she cried through chattering teeth.

"Lizzy's outside. Called the cops. Justin's on his way. They'll be here soon."

"Who's Justin?" Erik asked.

Judith pulled out her phone.

"Justin? How far away are you?" she asked under her breath. There was major static on the line. He was talking, but she couldn't hear him. Judith stepped out into the hallway to get a better signal.

"Can you hear me?"

"Yes. Where are you in the house? There's a lot of interference."

She could hear him now, but it was still breaking up.

"In the basement."

"We are twenty to thirty minutes away. I am so pissed at you right now," he growled, and Judith felt his fury through the line.

"I'm sorry! I tried to call you! I had to!"

"No, you did not. Playing vigilante is against the law. I told you and told you. Leave it to us! You're gonna die. I can't handle this. Jones?"

There was fumbling on the line.

"Judith, this is Officer Jones. Listen. Do exactly as I say. You need to treat this like an active shooter event. Shut the basement door. If you can, barricade it, then hide. Now."

"Where?"

"He's gonna kill you. Why didn't you wait?" Justin yelled.

"Don't worry. I can take him!" Judith shouted with more confidence than she felt.

"Take him? Are you insane? He's got your gun. Beat the shit out of you and plans to rape you. He's psycho!"

"My mom is okay, but she's shivering. What do I do?"

"Sounds like she's in shock. You need to raise her temperature. But first, shut that door and barricade it," Jones reiterated calmly.

Judith returned to the living room, slammed the door shut, and looked around for something to use as a barricade.

"There's nothing here. I can't barricade the door!"

"A couch. A shelf. Find something!" Justin demanded, the line breaking up again.

"I have to help my mom first."

Judith heard Justin screaming on the phone as she slipped it back in her pocket.

"She needs a heating pad. Where?" Judith asked frantically.

"Grab the first aid kit under the sink. It holds emergency hand warmers. And blankets are in my room." Erik was busy rubbing her arms with his free hand. "Crawl between my legs and I'll warm you." He told her mom who did so, then he crossed his legs over her.

Judith gathered the first-aid kit and another blanket from the bedroom. Her heart was racing from her encounter with Nicolas. Why did she goad him like that? When he kissed her, his hunger triggered something, and she felt it exploding in her now.

Returning to the living room, she heard the door click open and Nicolas entered. His black eyes were exploding like oil geysers rising in never-ending smoke.

"You brought her back to me, Belladonna? Oh my God! Thank you!"

He was staring in astonishment at Martha cuddling between Erik's legs.

"Nicolas, it's time to surrender. You've proven you can't go through with it. You're not a murderer. It's time to take the next step and get you help."

Her mom was using her therapist voice. So that's how she played this, as his shrink. Smart mom. Helping him uncover the root of his issues. Nicolas stared down at her mom in agony. Judith understood how it all happened. He had taken her mom out of some uncontrollable response to his trauma, and she played along because she was a people pleaser. Then somehow, she met his father, and genuine love and passion took hold.

Nicolas didn't have a chance. He lost her, and now he would have his revenge. The ruined child, the rotten man who never had a woman love him, now had to endure seeing his father steal away the object of his affection. He was seriously crazy.

Nicolas was clutching his hair, pacing in a circle, ready to ignite.

"Please, Nicolas," her mom begged. "Let me help you! Don't let things end this way!"

He held out his hand like an infant grasping for its pacifier.

"Choose me! Make my dream come true. That's why I did this. For you! To save you from your shitty life. I saved you!"

"You did! You've changed me. Forever!" Her mom sounded so genuine. "Now it's my turn to save you."

She stood shakily to her feet. Her teeth were chattering, and her skin was still blue. Judith had no idea how she was able to stand. Erik tried to pull her back with his free hand.

"Martha, don't move any closer."

"It's okay. I trust him. He won't hurt me."

Nicolas bent down, picked up a knife Judith hadn't noticed lying on the floor, and pointed it at her.

"Stay back," he threatened as he reached for her mom. "Martha, take my hand. We'll leave. Shut the door on these two and run away. It's not too late for us."

"You need to let them go."

"Not her."

"She's my daughter!"

He brandished the knife at Judith.

"You barge your way into my house at gunpoint, insult my penis size and threaten to murder me. I can't believe I ever had the hots for you!"

"I'm not done with you yet, psycho." Judith put her hands up like a boxer.

"Think your little fists can stop me?" He hopped wildly, and Judith backed into a shelf.

Martha screamed, "Nicolas, just stop! You're out of control. I won't tell the police or press charges for what you've done. Okay? What more do you want?"

"If you no longer love me, I've lost everything. I can't bear to lose you again."

"I do love you, but you're not losing me again. You've only known me for a week. I'm not Catrina. Your nanny is gone. You need to move on and let her go. You don't need her! A woman who only took from you and never gave. Let Catrina go. Now." She took another step, hands out. "Take my hand and we will leave this Catrina obsession for good. Ready?"

"I just wanted her to love me! Why didn't she love me? Why did she abandon me?" He was shaking and crying like nothing Judith had ever seen.

"She was a child molester, and she used you for sex. She tortured and manipulated your mind and body. She made you suffer, and she kept you in bondage for nine years. A person like that isn't capable of real love."

"When will I be loved? I've tried so hard to find anyone who will love me, but it's impossible!"

"You poor sweet guy. I'm sorry you have suffered so much. You will be loved, I promise."

"Please, Martha. Love me instead!"

"I can't be your lover, my boy. I am in love with your father, which means I might end up being your stepmother. Let me fill that role."

"I need a mom, I do. But everything is ruined. I'm gonna be all alone again and permanently fucked in the head if you abandon me."

"Everything isn't ruined. Life is a series of ups and downs. We'll get through this! Tonight, you killed her, okay? Say it."

"I killed her."

"She's gone."

"She's gone," he echoed.

"She has no more power over you."

"She has no more power over me."

"You're taking your love back."

"I'm taking my love back."

"Now it's yours and you are free!"

"It's mine and I am free," he recited.

"You have now freed yourself. Taken your memories of that horrible woman and drowned them the way she tried to drown you. She is dead. You have snuffed the life out of her. You are free now. Free to find someone who will love you. She's out there waiting for you, I promise. Your heart will guide you to her."

"But it doesn't change anything right now in this room. You betrayed me, he abandoned me, and that beauty queen is here to destroy me. You're all against me!"

"We aren't."

"I am. You took my mom, and you deserve to die!" Judith yelled.

"Judith," Her mom pleaded, "let me help him. No more violence."

Nicolas turned to Judith and said, "You make me feel crazier than I already am. I don't know whether I want to kiss you or murder you. It's a toss-up."

"I know which I'd prefer," Judith replied sweetly as she dazzled him with her pageant smile, and he responded like she was his celebrity crush. Judith wrapped her fingers around his hand, gripping the knife, and twisted it down. He looked at her in shock and confusion, then retaliated in a tug of war. Judith stared and Nicolas stared. An instant bond was forged as their eyes locked. Something was communicating in an ancient tongue, something powerful, reaching across lifetimes and pulling her into his current, twisting her toward familiar trade winds of memory and instinct. A flash of inspiration illuminated his soul, and oh my God. She knew this man. Deeply. Intimately. Eternally.

Suddenly, her mom's hands were on her wrist as all three fought for the knife.

"Stop it. I'll put it down! Let go of my hand, Belladonna!" Nicolas shrieked.

"Don't hurt her, Nicolas!" Her mom shoved him back. Instinctively, he retaliated. There was a flash of red as she wedged her body in front of Judith, and then an explosion of red as he plunged the knife into her and she collapsed to the floor.

Chapter 47

Judith

Now, everyone was screaming—Judith, Erik and Nicolas. Nicolas dropped the knife and stared down at the bleeding woman, then butchered Judith with his eyes.

"No!" Nicolas looked enraged beyond all comprehension. "That was an accident. I was going to put it down. Why did you fight me for it? You did this!" He lunged forward and grabbed Judith by the hair.

"Nicolas. Let me treat her wound. There are bandages. She may still survive. Help me! Put pressure on her wound." Judith begged. He collapsed to the floor, cursing, but did what she said. He staunched the wound with his hands as Judith ripped open the first-aid kit.

"Quick," Erik yelled. "Grab that Israeli bandage. Wrap the wound tight. Now!"

Judith tore it out of the package and placed gauze under his fingers.

"Keep applying pressure," she instructed Nicolas as she unfurled the bandage and pulled it around the wound, engaging the pressure applicator.

"Done? You are coming with me." Nicolas muttered as he stood on shaky legs, grabbed Judith by the ponytail, and she cursed herself for not tucking it up into a hat. Dragging her, he slammed the basement door shut and hauled her up the stairs. In the living room, he released her, bent over in agony, buried his face in his hands and raged in pain. Judith took her chance and rushed for her gun beside the wall.

"No, you don't!"

Nicolas threw himself on top of her. They crashed to the floor. Judith twisted him onto his back and climbed on his chest, punching him with every ounce of hatred she had. His nose burst with blood. His eyes bruised the color of grapes. And still, she couldn't stop. All the rage she had nurtured throughout her life came rising to the moment. She gave it everything she had as she beat the shit out of this beautiful man.

Until he reached past her flying fists, grabbed her throat in a choke hold and rolled over, slamming her on the floor beside him, wrestler style, and leapt to his feet. Snatched a fistful of her long hair and began to drag her. In a mere second lull, she pulled out of his grasp, devastated by the chunk of her lovely locks now caught between his sticky, bloody fingers.

Springing from a back bend in a move she had practiced a million times in gymnastics, she planted her feet, circled, gathering momentum, and kicked him in his chest, her boot heel crunching against his ribs. Nicolas went flying backwards onto the glass coffee table. It shattered beneath him. She flew at him like a banshee out of hell.

"I'm gonna rip you apart!"

Lying in the shards of glass, he cowered in terror, shielding his body as she stomped on him with her boots. The glass crunched amid his furious grunts and she kicked him until breathless. Judith withdrew in amazement as he leapt to his feet like a ghoul incapable of death.

Nicolas rushed her. She timed it perfectly, threw her head forward, and slammed into his mouth.

"Ouch!" he wailed.

Judith sank to her knees, crouching, moving her legs like a fan blade. She swept his feet out from under him, dropping him like a sack of potatoes. Rolling apart, legs sprawled, Judith went in for the kill. She kicked him so hard in the groin that his face went sheet white and he gasped for breath. He turned to his side, protecting himself with shaking hands. Kicking him again and again, Judith screamed with fury. His fingers took the damage until he stopped moving.

Turning wildly, looking for something to knock him unconscious with, she heard a sound. Swiveled. Holy shit, this guy was unbeatable.

She punched him in the face as he came at her. He smacked her head again and again until she heard her neck crack. Threw another fist at his jaw, and he grabbed it. They pummeled each other in hand-to-hand combat until she hooked his ankles with her boot and shoved him backwards. He fell to the ground, hitting his head hard. Judith fell on him, straddling his chest once again. With both hands around his neck, she choked him until his body went still.

Judith let go, took his face in her hands and gazed down at him, her heart throbbing. Something about Nicolas made her feel unhinged. She wanted to kiss him again. Tear off his clothes. Grab his twig and make history. Shaking, she forced herself to crawl off him. She stood and went to pull out her phone to tell Justin they needed an EMT for her mom. Heard a sound. No way. Smirking, he lunged.

"Psyched you out, didn't I? Payback time."

Seizing her by the throat, he carried her, feet dragging on the floor, choking and gasping, and slammed her up against the floor-to-ceiling window.

"I was going to give you the royal treatment. Make you want me more than you want to breathe. Now? Fuck that shit."

Nicolas shoved her to the floor. From his waistband, he procured a gun. It wasn't her gun. What the fuck? From his pocket, he pulled out a pair of handcuffs. What the double fuck?

"Take your clothes off and put these on."

He tossed the handcuffs at her feet. Overcome with exertion, eyes crazed, Judith had the horrifying realization that she had done this. Quenched his rage, riled him up, called him out, and now, like a wild cat, he was ready to devour his kill.

"Over my dead body. I'm not putting your handcuffs on," she spat.

"I'm not asking. You have stolen the thing I wanted more than anything. Martha's love. So quid pro quo. You get to take her place. I'm gonna make you mine right now."

"Stole her? You just stabbed her, you psycho!"

"It was an accident! She was my salvation."

"You don't deserve to be saved."

"She loved me!"

"You don't deserve to be loved!"

"You're gonna eat those words because I am gonna make you love me."

He shot the gun above his head into the ceiling and made her jump. She tucked her phone into her front jeans pocket. When her coat and tank top were lying on the floor, he eyed her hungrily.

"Come on, Belladonna. Take it all off."

"Why?" She glared at him with a look of pure hatred.

"Do I have to say it? You don't get that you're mine now? Take it off!"

"I'm not yours, you misogynist pig! Plan for a fight to the death!"

Judith watched Nicolas stare at a mirror on the wall. He was despicably gorgeous; his sex appeal was astonishing, like an incubus.

"You have ruined my beautiful face. Fucking ruined it!"

"Boo-hoo. You vain asshole," she screamed.

Nicolas pointed at the mirror and shot it again and again. The sound of glass shattering was deafening as he stared down at her and aimed.

"I have this gun pointed at your head," he insisted through clenched teeth, "I have to process my rage. I can't keep it bottled up like this. It's just not healthy. And I'm in major pain right now. Because of you!" He fired again, blowing a hole in the kitchen cupboards. Judith threw her arms around his legs, shoving him backwards and slamming his head into the corner of an end table.

"Goddamn it!" Nicolas moaned and rolled back and forth in pain. "I hate you!"

"Not as much as I hate you!" she proclaimed, scrambling on hands and knees for his gun. Grabbed it. Pointed it at his face. Sitting up, he taunted her.

"Go ahead, Belladonna. Shoot me."

Judith aimed. Fired. Nothing. What, again!

"Shit!" She threw the gun at him, and it hit his forehead as he laughed.

"I counted the bullets. I'm a genius that way. It's empty. The way my cock is going to feel in less than two minutes."

Nicolas grabbed his handcuffs and scooted in front of her. She raked him across the face with her nails and punched him in the chest as he shoved her backward, then crawled on top of her. All at once, the mood changed and the air crackled with kinky foreplay vibes instead of rape and murder vibes.

To her shock and confusion, Judith began to giggle uncontrollably. Was it the stress from fighting? She felt entirely out of control as he pinned her hips down, and she no longer saw a dangerous lunatic, but a guy who was crazy about her and had no idea how to express that. He smiled.

"What?"

"It's silly, but I'm getting flashbacks of grade school."

"You did this in school?"

"I fought with boys but was usually the one on top."

"I'd let you be on top all day long."

"Then it would be you in the cuffs. Don't think you'd like that."

"If you were on top of me, I most definitely would."

She continued to giggle and tried to resist as he reached behind and undid her bra, then tossed it over his shoulder.

"Fuck me, you are gorgeous."

Nicolas stared at her boobs as if he had just been struck by lightning. Then he pinned one arm above her head at a time and snapped the cuffs on her wrists. He held her down and kissed her sloppily, and she responded. They weren't fighting anymore. What the hell happened? This had evolved into a sexual dalliance with the force of a tsunami. She had to keep pretending to fight, at least. Justin could not think she wanted this guy for a second.

"Get ready for the hottest fuck ever, Belladonna. You're gonna love it."

Yanking her up by the cuffs, he dragged her over to a teak wood dining table, kicked the chair aside, and shoved her forward on her stomach. Crippled with panic but thrilled with excitement, Judith fought like a wildcat, but his arms were so strong and he crushed her body against his. With one hand, he pulled down her jeans and panties to mid-thigh and spread her legs apart. Pressed up against her, she felt his erection, amazed that he could have one after she just bludgeoned his dick.

"Nicolas, stop!" Judith pleaded, although her body really didn't want him to stop.

"I've never gone crazy like this. What have you done to me?"

"You said you were a gentleman!"

"I am. I was!"

"Just don't. I surrender!"

"You surrender to me?"

"Yes!" she screamed.

"Perfect. Now let me seduce you, my sweet."

Nicolas sounded so pleased with himself. Justin was going to flip out.

"We need to take this upstairs."

Nicolas murmured as he planted kisses along her neck, stroking her back and side boobs, fondling her butt until her body vibrated with chills, every nerve on fire. His hands made their way down between her legs. She quivered and moaned as he explored again, then again, until his body relaxed.

"My God, you don't need seducing. You're as horny as I am."

"Nope," she denied.

"Oh yeah. Super wet. Soft. I'm gonna come in my pants touching you like this."

"I was like that before I got here," she countered. Justin could not hear this.

"If I went down on you right now, I'd get you off in seconds."

"It's the fighting. It's not you." She tried to sound convincing.

"It most definitely is me. You can't fake me out. I know a woman's pussy like the back of my hand."

He rolled her onto her back, his eyes blazing with a ravenous hunger like she had never seen before, and his mouth formed an exuberant grin. Arms propped on either side of her head, burying her in his heat and driving her with his racing heart. Two seconds ago, he was gonna rape her. Now he was all charm and sweetness.

"Wow. We're both getting off on our lovers' quarrel. I thought it was just me."

"It's, uh, it's not like that," she stammered under her breath.

"I think you know it is. Your body betrays you. You want me as bad as I want you. I can't believe it." He stared at her up and down. "What is happening right now?" A light dawned in his eyes. "Something. Is. Happening."

Arms up, hands clenching his hair, shaking his head in amazement, he leaned down. "Oh my God." Crushing her breasts, his chest to hers. "Oh my God!" Sweeping her hair away from her neck, he said into her ear. "I've been such a silly boy. It was never Martha. She just led the way. I was always meant to find you. It's why I was so drawn to you from that first moment. You weren't part of the plan, but you were the whole purpose behind the plan. I'm so happy. I'm so happy!"

He stared into her eyes, and again, she felt that connection. Time stood still. She could hear his thoughts exploding and feel his living, breathing body. A keening from centuries past echoed in her head. She knew him from other times and places and always would. What was going on here?

In the present, remorse burned through her. Fighting like this with Nicolas was hot, and she had no idea why. She made a terrible mistake. Thought she was tough. Could take this crazy bastard on, fill his head with bullets and save the day. But the moment she entered his realm and got up close and personal with this man, her body completely turned against her.

Nicolas whooped and loudly kissed her everywhere.

"Belladonna,"

Kiss.

"We're gonna have the hottest,"

Kiss, kiss.

"Fuck,"

Kiss.

"Ever!"

Long kiss.

"Better than the hot tub,"

Kiss, kiss.

"Better than anything!"

Judith whimpered as he devoured her, his hands and mouth crawling all over her like a fiend. No guy had ever gone at her in such a frenzy as this. It had to be their fight. It meant nothing!

"Young like me, so beautiful, and what vicious rage! In a total-war death match, I find my soul mate! Belladonna, I've been searching for you my whole life."

Starry-eyed, love-struck, Nicolas maneuvered her to the edge of the table, his mouth back to riding her like a bee on nectar, pollinating her with his passion.

"We need to celebrate." He declared between kisses.

"This doesn't count as a party?"

"You came to kick my ass and now we're fucking. Yeah, this counts."

"I came to kill you, actually."

"My evil Belladonna."

"You're the one who did this to me. Made me evil."

"It's only the start of what I'm gonna do."

"You'd better move fast then."

"If I don't get inside you right this second, I'm gonna go insane." He panted.

"I think you're way past insane."

Judith couldn't take it anymore. She yanked Nicolas down by his bloody shirt and covered his lips with hers, her arms behind his neck. Lips and tongues, they kissed like two snakes trying to eat each other. Nicolas was crazy, but she couldn't control this.

Mouths entangled, he moaned as he lifted her hips to him in frustration and yearning, his hands shaking and his body quaking with urgency. He tore down her pants and she heard the clatter of her phone fall out of her front pocket onto the hardwood floor.

"What's this?" Nicolas stopped, knelt and scooped up the phone. "Are you recording this?" His tone was aghast. "You're on a call? Right now?" He hit speakerphone and said after a pause, "Hello?"

Mortified, Judith heard Justin's voice as he pulled her back to reality. He sounded furious and part of that fury was directed at her.

"Listen here, you crazy bastard. You get your hands off her right now. Let Judith go or I swear to God, we'll come in guns blazing and take you the fuck down."

"Was that the cops? Did you call the cops before you even got here? Fuck!" He slammed his fist down on the table, stared at her phone, disconnected the call and put it in his pocket.

"Well, now I have the hardest boner in my life, thanks to you. And I don't get to play out a classic father-to-son showdown of which Shakespeare would be proud, thanks to you again! You're coming with me."

He pulled her into his arms and kissed her ferociously. She pulled up her jeans then he grabbed her cuffed hands.

"We have to run."

In his other hand, he picked up a black bag off the floor and dragged her to the front door, where he entered the code. He pulled her behind him into the night air. Her breasts tingled in the cold breeze. He shoved her in front of him over to his car where he opened the passenger door.

"Get in. We have unfinished business—lots of it. A lifetime of it. I am never going to let you go now. I can't believe I finally found you."

Oh God, she hadn't expected this. She thought the police would have gotten here quicker. She lowered herself into the Mercedes, searching for any moment of weakness but she was at his mercy. He crawled in on top of her, kissed her hard on the mouth, and continued kissing her as he held her arms above her head, laid them over the headrest, and cuffed her to a pair of handcuffs hanging off the metal extender bars.

"That fight was the hottest experience of my life. I'm so worked up, I don't think I'll ever come down. You have set me on fire, Belladonna. I'm burning alive."

"Handcuffs in your car? You're sick."

"I always keep cuffs handy for when a lady wants my special treatment on the road. You'd be surprised at how many do."

Judith felt a surge of jealousy for all those ladies who had his special treatment and didn't know why. This must be her kind of kink. She felt horribly ashamed of herself as he took her face in his hands and stared into her eyes.

"I am so in love with you." He whispered between kisses, then sat back and ogled her bare breasts. "Straight out of my hottest fantasies." He kissed her again, got out, slammed her door, opened the back door, tossed his bag in and raced to the driver's side and got in. Nicolas engaged the ignition, jumped into gear, and tore off through the rocks and desert brush, swerving until he was back on the road. Pressing the pedal to the floor, the Mercedes burst into lightning speed.

"The escape is now in progress," Nicolas replied like a news reporter. "He's got his sexy soulmate, his daddy's cash and nothing is gonna stop him now."

Justin was dead right. He warned her that this guy would eat her for breakfast. She hadn't realized what that meant—just kept pushing it. Because why? Was she crazy? Stupid? No. It was because she had a death wish. Part of her wanted to risk her life like this, and part of her was enjoying it. She was one messed-up chic.

She shouldn't have tried to save her mom, had such a high opinion of herself—cocky and deluded. Now her mom might be dead from trying to protect her, and she was his new obsession. And for some reason, to her horror, she wanted Nicolas with everything she had.

Judith was so confused. She had already chosen Justin. What was happening to her? Lying her throbbing face against the cold glass, she drifted away. Flying after her soul in a futile attempt to regain her sanity, which somehow Nicolas had stolen from her in their total-war death match.

Chapter 48

Justin

When Justin heard those words, *I know a woman's pussy like the back of my hand,* he knew he had one purpose in life. It was to destroy Nicolas Winters.

Once Judith went downstairs, the call nearly dropped. He couldn't hear anything, which was hugely frustrating. He sat there, clenching the phone, imagining what it would feel like when he got his hands on that fuck boy who dared touch his girl. He would have blood on them tonight, that was for sure.

There was a violent commotion, and he ascertained that Nicolas had gone to attack Judith, but her mom intervened and was injured instead. And then his heart took a deep dive. Consumed with dread as Nicolas dragged Judith up the stairs. Amazed as she kicked the living shit out of him. Then Nicolas managed to turn the tables. As he went to rape her, Justin listened as Nicolas went at her in a frenzy, and she responded. In the silence, he heard her moans of pleasure. Justin had never burned with rage like this. Was going to have a heart attack. He needed to chill the fuck out.

Less than ten minutes away, the bastard found the phone. Justin replied in the only way he could, with murderous, justifiable rage. And screwed everything up because now they were probably long gone.

Please still be there. Please still be there!

They were flying down a dirt road, driving at seventy miles an hour. A large house loomed up ahead. They screeched to a stop, and Justin raced out of the car.

Lizzy was standing outside her car door. When she saw him, she rushed over and threw her arms around him, trembling.

"He took her, Justin. He took her in his car. She was half naked and so scared—"

Shaking like a leaf, Lizzy tried kissing him, but he wasn't having any of that. Justin roared with anger. He wanted to beat a hole in the ground. He had to listen to that piece of shit hurt and defile his girl, then pledge his love to her! And now he had escaped, and she was with him, and they needed to track him and take him down and—

"Ten minutes ago. You have to find her! I got his license plate."

Lizzy finally let go and handed it to Justin, who nodded his thanks and handed it to Jones.

Three minutes later, the EMTs arrived. The police used a battering ram to knock down the massive front door and then did the same thing to the basement door.

Martha lay in a pool of blood but was conscious. Her skimpy outfit made Justin automatically cover her with the blanket, but the EMTs pulled it off and proceeded to prepare her for transport. The man shackled to the towel rack spoke.

"Is Judith okay?"

"He took her," Justin growled.

"She saved her mom's life. Got the bandage out of the first-aid kit and wrapped it around her. Nicolas helped. This whole thing is a horrible accident. My son needs treatment. When you catch him, please go gentle." He pleaded.

"Not a chance," Justin swore. Ran upstairs and raced to his patrol car.

"Jones!" he yelled for his partner to follow. "We need to go. Come on!"

This time, Justin took the wheel.

"Which direction do you think he'll head?" asked Jones.

"I don't know. South maybe? His best chance to escape isn't back down the canyon into the valley, where a million cops are waiting. Through Heber and then to Duchesne, he'll either head for Colorado or connect back to the I-15 and go south. That's what I would do."

"He's driving a fast car."

"But there are more of us, and I plan to hunt this animal to the ends of the earth."

Jones coordinated the manhunt over the radio and told Finley they were in pursuit. Then they tore off down the dirt road. A medevac unit arrived to extract Martha. Every cop within two counties would soon be on the lookout for the Mercedes.

Justin felt a sense of relief. They would find him. And Judith was safer now that Nicolas was stuck behind the steering wheel. He couldn't punch her, rape her or shoot her while otherwise engaged. He focused on the road, and with lights flashing, he drove.

By the time they got to Heber, Justin was second-guessing. The cops hadn't seen a thing. How? Did Nicolas vanish into thin air? Change cars? Where was he?

"Maybe he didn't come this way. Everyone is looking for him. I doubt we'll find him driving aimlessly, though. We need to stay within our jurisdiction, Salviati."

Justin shook his head stubbornly.

"No. We head to Duchesne. He has her, Jones, and he has to be heading south. I'm gonna be the one to find her, and I'm gonna rip him apart for what he did to her."

"I support you one hundred percent. But I have a bad feeling. If we get locked in a car chase, this crazy bastard's gonna take the easy way out to keep her. Drive them both over a cliff."

They cut their way through the darkness, like a beacon illuminating the desert. Justin couldn't think of what he had heard Judith endure, but he was unable to stop thinking about it either. Judith was a warrior like Boadicea. Her pain ran through his veins, as did a deep fury at her for disobeying his direct order. How could he forgive her for this? A war waged between his desire for her and his resentment of her, and he stood helplessly caught in the middle.

He wished he could take back that night and interview Lizzy more closely. Ask the right questions. But she had been so traumatized, mute and incapable of providing them with any information, and he only had eyes for Judith. If only they had found Nicolas sooner. How had Judith even discovered the dad? She was brilliant.

Twenty minutes outside Duchesne County, a call came through on the radio.

"We've got eyes on the Mercedes you're all looking for. Passing through Duchesne now. Want us to pursue?"

"We're almost there. Follow, but keep your distance. No sirens. We'll call the sheriff in Carbon County and ask him to have his boys head him off at the other end of Highway 191. He's boxed in with nowhere to hide. That canyon becomes treacherous up top, and we don't want to run him off the road. This guy is batshit crazy and may try to end in a suicide-by-cop scenario. We can't have that." He turned to Justin, who nodded in agreement. "He's carrying precious cargo." Jones finished with the radio and said to Justin, "Got him."

Chapter 49

Judith

Judith woke to a delightful tingling sensation. Nicolas was stroking her nipple, sending delicious shudders vibrating through her, and smiling like they were lovers heading to Vegas.

"Belladonna, I've never touched a girl as hot as you before. It makes me wanna stop somewhere and worship your body. You aren't happy hanging like that. I'll take you down soon. But seeing you cuffed like this has given me a massive hard-on. Sorta like the one I had the moment I laid eyes on you, and exactly what I need after that bullshit back at the house. You were seriously trying to kill me, and you almost did. Which is so fucking sexy and I don't know why."

She stared as he masturbated. He was certainly bigger than a twig. When she told him he was the size of a twig, she had no idea why. She wanted to mess with him for some bizarre reason. Filled with a host of carnal thoughts, she finally tore her eyes away. The cops were right behind them. Justin would never stop looking for her. They would save her. They had to.

Judith gazed out the dark window, trying to figure out where they were. Nicolas veered dangerously, weaving along the curb at ninety miles an hour, shuddering as he came all over the steering wheel. He caught her staring and grinned. It was the hottest thing to watch his hand in action, and she felt extremely aroused by his reckless sexuality.

How was she attracted to this pervert? Nicolas had a death wish as deep as hers, and that struck a chord in her. He was a crazy sex fiend like her, too—both unstable, beautiful, insecure thrill seekers who were desperate for love. The similarities were terrifying. They might be soulmates of a sort, she considered—not the good kind, though.

"Where are we going?" she whispered.

"Almost to Duchesne now." He tucked himself in. "I saw that look in your eyes. You can't deny it. I'm no twig, right? That's what you're thinking, and I'm feeling your vibes. You want me, I can tell. Don't worry. I'll let you go at me with a vengeance as soon as we find a hotel. But I wanna know why. Is watching me jerk off your kink? I wanna know everything about you, Belladonna. Indulge my obsession. Please."

"Why Duchesne?"

Was she that easy to read? She hoped it was wishful thinking on his part, not that he had figured her out.

"Trying to decide. I have a bag full of cash in the back seat and my dad's passport. His picture is old, and I'm practically his clone. Maybe head to Mexico. But you need a passport, which would take time that we don't have. Don't worry. I'll think of something. Always do. I have to say, I got a little carried away back at the house. You've done something to me. I've never felt unhinged like this in my entire life. I've spent all these years trying to replace Catrina. Suddenly, that's all gone, and I feel liberated. Anyhow, I hope you'll let me make it up to you. I can't wait to explore your body. It's a compelling challenge to satisfy a doll like you. And that would have scared the shit out of me even a few hours ago. Meeting you has somehow rewired my brain."

"I doubt I'm your type. I'm pretty aggressive in bed."

"You, my sweet, are a femme fatale, and I am a homme fatale. We are apex seducers. A perfect match."

"When you went to rape me, I thought you were the devil himself."

"The devil is just a god, like me." He laughed. "And don't deny it. You want me as bad as I want you."

Judith couldn't argue. It was true.

"I don't know what is happening," she confessed.

"I do. It's called love at first sight, and it's what I've been going out of my mind to discover for years. I'd better stay free long enough to find a hotel so we can celebrate, you vixen."

That's what Justin called her—a vixen. Thinking of Justin filled her with remorse.

"I've finally turned a corner. Martha healed me tonight. I'm over my Catrina obsession. Poof, just like that. It's a miracle! And I think we have a real chance together. I only ever dreamed a girl my age could want me like this. I'm flattered, excited and head over heels, my love." He pinched her cheek.

It was so unfair. All of it. Why did her dad have to cheat, then remarry, then force them to the wedding, which forced Nicolas to meet her mom, which forced her to find her mom, resulting in this lurid encounter? Judith couldn't help her smart mouth.

"That cop on the phone? He's my boyfriend. I call him my Captain America because he's one of the good guys. He's going to hunt you down and rip you into pieces."

"Awesome. I hate cops. It explains why he was so pissy with me. You're having the time of your life seducing that poor sucker, aren't you?"

"It is fun. He's so naïve. It's sweet," she admitted.

"Bet he's panting with jealousy after hearing us go at it on the dining table. Haha. I'm stealing you right from under his nose! And clever Belladonna! In a phone call with the cops. Now they have tons of evidence against me. Even that mouth of yours is a turn-on. Do I wanna smack it or kiss it? I'm a bit conflicted, so watch out. But I enjoy conflict, don't you?"

Nicolas snickered, but a twinge of fear flickered in his eyes, giving her a thrill of satisfaction.

In Duchesne, the streets were dark and quiet, with not a car in sight. Nicolas pulled over and took out her phone.

"Give me your password," he demanded.

She paused. What did he want with her phone?

"I'm waiting."

"Fine. 033003."

"Your birthday?"

"Yep."

"An Aries, huh? I'm an Aquarius. Fire and air, I can feel it."

"I'd love to burn you to the ground."

"I'll only add fuel to your flames. We're super-hot shit."

Nicolas stared at a Google map.

"I hate decisions. You pick. Arizona or Colorado?"

"Arizona?"

There was more traffic going south than east.

"Sounds like a plan, boss. Oh, a scenic drive through Indian Canyon. Perfect for a picnic. Forget the hotel. My dick and your pussy can hook up. Like I told you, I'm a sex addict. This will be such a treat. I'll make up for all that pain from our lovers' quarrel. You need a pick-me-up and so do I."

They weaved down residential streets until they were on a two-way highway climbing through a desert landscape up a canyon.

"You must understand. I didn't ask to be this way. I was made this way. I need to pleasure someone every single day because I've been doing so since I was a kid. The right woman will understand this about me. All I've ever wanted was to find my one and only. I thought it was Martha. Why she threw me over for my dad, I'll never understand."

"Because you can't comprehend love. You can't create it because you're a narcissist, and you can't feel it because you're damaged beyond repair." Judith couldn't stop the mean words from rolling out.

"I think you're right. I can't comprehend love because I've never had any. I guess I need to learn how to live without wanting it so badly. That's so hard. There are over seven billion people in the world, half of them women, and I can't find a single one to love me?"

His admonition struck home, and it hurt. Judith had never met a guy who admitted that they wanted to be loved. They wanted sex and more sex. Nicolas was seriously weird.

"You know, I can't think of a word in the English language to describe you. Your ruthless obsession, your sex addiction, and your depraved quest for love. Is my mom right? Is it all due to being abused by your nanny?"

"What do you think?" he replied softly.

"I call bullshit. I was abused. Lost my virginity at thirteen. Raped on and off for an entire year by a hairy old man with a disgustingly fat belly. I'm not crazy."

"I finally see the light. I wondered why I was so drawn to you. That must be it, then, our soul connection. We both have a trauma bond from our childhoods. But you're not crazy like me because at least you were loved by Martha. No one has ever loved me."

"We don't have a connection," she whispered.

"But we do, and you know it."

They did, and it scared her. Nicolas was her worst nightmare, a reflection of her. And never in her life had she wanted a man like this. She wanted Nicolas even more than Justin, which threatened her perfect fantasy of being saved by the good guy. Judith drank in this beautiful man—slim body, deep-set eyes, a tremulous mouth, sensual fingers gripping the steering wheel, a mesmerizing dark aura, and a heartbreaking soul energy—sucked away, filled with acute desire. She had to get away from him. Now.

They drove in silence until Nicolas spoke, his voice filled with emotion.

"You think I'm a psychopath. I can't explain it. When I saw Martha, I knew she was the one who would heal me." He wiped a tear away. "All I ever wanted was a woman who would love me, who I could make happy, and who would never leave me the way Catrina did."

"You can't force someone to love you." Judith grimaced as pang after pang of sympathy resonated with him.

"You don't understand. You were always loved. I have never been loved, not even for a second. It's so easy to say that you can't force someone. But what if it's like a hunger so powerful you can't control it, and it controls you instead? I keep hoping that if I can satisfy a woman enough, she'll love me. But so far, it hasn't happened. I don't get it. I'm like a Greek god. I turn women into goddesses. I'm a supreme lover. I should be in the Guinness Book of World Records."

Nicolas was a deluded mess. Judith wished he would shut the hell up. This was worse than getting her ass kicked. Hearing him pour out his feelings like this made her care about him. It was a violation of her heart. Her poor mom. Manipulated by his bullshit plus she was a bleeding heart for crazy people. It made sense why she tried to save Nicolas to the end.

"Do you think you could love me? I mean, Martha loves my dad now. But you're young, and we have this crazy connection. I know we are hot for one another. I've never experienced such fiery passion from any woman. It's always me generating the sparks. Do you think we can at least try? Here, let me go down on you. Show you my mad skills. If you like, then we really can run away together."

Nicolas sounded so forlorn that Judith was speechless with sorrow. He echoed the desperation she felt for Justin. She didn't want Nicolas to know how badly she wanted him. Couldn't admit it and refused to give in. She had already chosen Justin. She chose the good guy!

"You stabbed my mom and were going to stab me. I'll never love you!"

"It was a stupid accident. What the hell came over me? When you walked in, I lost my mind! Listen, the police were probably almost there. Martha might be okay. I see now. She wasn't the one for me. Maybe she was supposed to be with my dad, and I just warmed her up. She had never felt desired and had no idea how sexy she was until I showed her. I was meant to find you instead."

"What you have is called love addiction. It's not healthy." Judith heard her mom talk about it once and had the chronic need to convince herself that Nicolas was a freak.

"I'm a sex addict and a love addict? I don't know, it sounds like I'm the perfect boyfriend!"

Judith saw a bird of paradise perched before her with impressive moves, convinced he could woo any female. He was mesmerizing. And like a bird, he flapped his beautiful wings, flew over while stopping the car in the middle of the road and kissed her long and hard.

Chapter 50

Judith

"You have my heart racing. I don't know if it was all our foreplay back at the house, but I'm so horny it's unreal." Nicolas beamed.

"You are out of your mind. I nearly murdered you. And I would have succeeded if you hadn't pulled out your gun."

"And I would have forced myself on you, something I swore I would never do, until I discovered how hot you were for me. We had a sexy first encounter, didn't we?"

Judith said nothing. There was no reasoning with this psycho. How could he transfer his obsession with her mom onto her in less than five minutes?

"I loved it when you said you would rip off my testicles with your teeth. The thought of your mouth on me drives me wild. Your rage is hot. I've never felt like this before. You, Belladonna, are dangerous, and I want it."

"I am more than dangerous. I'm deadly." She glared at him, and he laughed.

"You have me so worked up now. We were so close to the finish line on the dining table. We need a replay right this second. I know you think I'm crazy, but this is who I am. And if I don't take this chance with you, I'll never forgive myself." His eyes glittered, and he licked his lips. His lust crashed into her like a tidal wave. He was an addict, and now she was his new drug of choice. "I'm gonna make you come so hard you'll forget your Captain America boyfriend and love me instead. I am insatiable when a woman is taken. The challenge brings out the best in me. I'm a class-A homewrecker, let me tell you. I've seduced so many women and ruined it for their men. Showed them what they're missing out on. No one can match me in bed."

"There's more to love than just sex, you jackass."

"Maybe, maybe not. All I know is I have a fan club of women who beg me to come home. I'm a regular heartbreaker. I don't care about any of them, of course. Always searching for my one and only. Looks like we are near the peak. Bet these are campsites on this turnoff. No one knows we're out this way. This place is desolate. It's perfect."

Nicolas slowed, pulled onto a dirt road, and took it around a bend until he was satisfied. He turned off the car, got out, shut his door and went to the passenger's side. He opened her door, adjusted her chair until she was nearly prone, and slid it back. Arms above her head, breasts exposed, she felt like a maiden lying on a sacrificial table about to be ravished. This scenario was fucking hot.

"I've done this so many times. Feels like I should be getting paid for it."

He wedged himself down in front of her and tugged at her jeans.

"Na. These things have got to come off. Sorry, but I gotta strip you bare."

Nicolas pulled her jeans and panties down to her boots, removed her boots, and threw the pile out the open door. Then he rested his chin on her thighs and looked up at her like some cherubic angel in a Renaissance painting.

"Will you let me?"

Judith stared at his bruised face, his eyes pleading. She could barely comprehend what was happening. Nicolas wanted to seduce her instead of getting to safety. He looked desperate for love and terrifyingly sad. She had to escape Nicolas at once. He was like the devil, seducing her psychologically and sexually, and she couldn't take it. Why did she kiss him? Why couldn't she control herself? She wanted Justin! Nicolas was—what was he? She hated him! Why did she feel connected to him in some incomprehensible way?

She had an idea to free herself of the cuffs. Fake him out. Make him think he couldn't get her off. Guys usually sucked at this anyway. His failure would drive him nuts, and she would use that to get him to release her. Then she'd run away. Somehow. If she didn't try, she might not have another chance. What if the cops couldn't find her? Drove right by this turnoff and missed her entirely. What if he did drag her all the way to Mexico? He said she was his now, and part of her felt like she already was.

And maybe a tiny part of her was curious. How good in bed was this fuck boy? She wanted Justin, but he would never do anything like this. Cuffs and seduction? She wondered if he even planned on having sex with her at all. Shoving her off him drove her wild, though, and now all that pent-up lust was screaming for release. So yeah, there was no way in hell she could pass this up.

"Fine. Show me what you've got."

Nicolas looked like a kid on Christmas morning. He wriggled with delight.

"I've never tried to seduce a girl my age, especially one like you. I'm terrified. What if you don't like me? Let me warm you up first."

Her heart was in overdrive as he crawled on top of her, dick hard up against her belly.

"How is it you're hard again so soon?"

"I haven't been able to get it up after my psychotic break. Meeting you has restored me, and I'm stuck in high gear. You must have magical powers."

"I have to admit. You're so fucking sexy. Are you even real?"

"That's what women always say. But coming from you, it's the highest honor ever."

Blood mixed with his musky cologne, his hot, sweet breath, Nicolas was mythical, with pheromones that were out of this world. He really could be a Greek god. Once again, she had no idea how she missed him at the wedding.

"That love bite. I'm sorry. Not my style at all. But our fight ignited a fatal attraction, you know what I mean? Like Wuthering Heights or something."

Stroking and kissing her, he said, "God, your skin. Like a baby, your skin is so soft."

Chills vibrated through her as he tenderly nibbled at her earlobes. Like a vampire, he exposed her neck and sank those amorous lips to her skin. Soft, wet hickies ignited bursts of pleasure until her body was simmering with heat. Sensual hands roamed her breasts, circling and squeezing, and he groaned as he touched her. He kissed down the center of her chest, lifted a round, firm breast in his hand. She watched him lick her nipple with a languorous tongue until it eagerly blossomed. Then he sucked with just enough pressure to send her body back to the delirium he had her in on the dining table. With each pulse of his mouth, she lost her mind a little more. Back and forth, he teased her breasts with subtle urgency. Then, with hands cradling her bottom, he rubbed his hard groin in tantalizing circles against hers. Eyes locked with hers, he smiled with satisfaction. He knew he had her at his mercy, and she was loving it. She arched her back, strained against the cuffs, gasping with pleasure.

"You're like an incubus."

"I'm your sex demon, huh? I can tell you love the cuffs. You're my dream girl, Belladonna. Down to the penny."

She did love the cuffs. This was definitely her kink. And Nicolas had skills off the charts. She shouldn't have said yes. Had no idea he was this good. Had no idea any guy could be this good. No wonder Nicolas had a fan club. Her plan was going to fail miserably. His hands and mouth were everywhere, arousing every square inch of her body. She spread her thighs in anticipation, shocked at how easily she responded to him.

"Perfect timing for kicking my ass. You are in estrus."

"Or maybe it's just you."

She moaned as he sucked her nipples harder, slid a finger up inside her and found her sweet spot, massaging it with ungodly precision. Didn't even need to paw around. Knew right where it was. What the hell?

"Thank you. I'd love to think so. You are upping my game, big time. And I'm now addicted to your perfect breasts. I could play with these beauts forever."

"Where did you learn to do this? I've been with tons of guys. Is there like a book of sex secrets you found hidden in a library?"

"Tons of guys? What a challenge. I'm gonna blow them all away. And you're so cute. Na. My child-molesting nanny showed me the ropes. Sad, huh?"

"I'm in pain from the cuffs so you won't take me all the way, but you're close, that's for sure."

"I beg to differ. I think you're in real danger here. I can see your tough-girl shell cracking. I did this to your mom, and she came so hard. Said she hadn't had an orgasm in years. I more than made it up to her. I love making women happy. Being the one guy giving them what they secretly want. That's me."

Judith remembered Justin's mouth on her breasts last night and swallowed a choir of longing. Justin was everything she wanted. This was cheating and the way her body responded was definitely cheating. The thought filled her with agony. If she survived this, Justin was never going to touch her again unless she lied her ass off. Going after Nicolas on her own was more than stupid. It was criminally insane.

"Nicolas, just do it." Her voice trembled as she tilted her hips in invitation. Nicolas was intoxicating—his body, his passion, his crazy inhibition. She'd have to figure out how to lie about it later.

"You want to feel my twig up inside you? So do I. You're making me so happy. I'm really close, too close. But you gotta come first. I have a reputation to maintain."

"I'm not gonna come."

She promised, halfheartedly. A few guys had tried this on her but they all sucked, and she was forced to fake an orgasm so they didn't feel like shit. She had never climaxed from oral sex, and hoped to God this time she wouldn't either.

"We'll see," he replied in a sing-song voice, "I love the challenge you're giving me but I will win."

Nicolas got on the floor and shoved her legs apart, his hair tickling her thighs as he examined her. This was hell. What was she thinking? How was she gonna fake not having an orgasm? He was too good. She was an idiot!

"Belladonna, have you any idea how hot you are? The sweetest pussy ever. Yum, yum."

Bracing herself, she felt a burst of chilly air as he spread her open, followed by the warmth of his mouth. When he began to stroke her love bud in perfect circles with his tongue, she knew she was fucked. He teased her to the edge of madness, then held her there until she was trembling in his hands. Rubbing, sucking, licking. Massaging her sweet spot. Her body had been raging with lust since they met and this incubus was the best of the best. She froze her body to the swirling mass of sensation and clenched her lips to stop from crying out in ecstasy. One chance to make him think he failed. He was so obsessed with being the best lover, he couldn't take the defeat.

Vigorously, he rushed her to the top of the world, then shot her off to a galaxy far away. She came so unbelievably hard she nearly fainted as euphoria exploded through her, over and over. Never in her life had she climaxed like this. She let her breath out slowly and pushed her body out of her mind as she spasmed uncontrollably from a full-body orgasm. He was licking her nipples and fingering her throbbing vagina in a frenzy. Getting her off seriously turned him on. She wanted him to fuck her so bad she had to bite her tongue from begging for it.

"I won. You just came so hard."

"No," she whimpered. Burning alive in the afterglow, she wanted more and more.

No. She didn't. She wanted Justin. Even though he rejected her. His sexy strip tease, soulful brown eyes, noble kisses and high ideals. He was her man, not this crazy sex demon.

"Why are you lying to me? I felt your orgasm on my tongue for like a minute. I just got you off so hard. I won, Belladonna."

Eye-to-eye, he pressed his forehead against hers. Judith stared into his hungry orbs and couldn't stop herself from replying like a sassy slut.

"You think that's good? I can give you a blow job that will make you lose your mind."

She sucked his mouth to hers and he went wild. Bumping and grinding, ready to burst through his pants, and now she couldn't stop from crying out.

"Come on, you crazy fuck boy. Do it already."

"Oh Lordy. I'm a believer. I don't have to make you into a goddess. You already are." He scooped her bottom in his hands, dry humping her in torturous thrusts, hard and fast.

"For fuck's sake. Pull down your goddamn pants," she cried.

"Fuck, oh fuck. Oh—" He collapsed, moaning and shuddering. She felt the wetness through his pants and rubbed against him as he spasmed, prolonging his orgasm.

"Fuck! I'm so dizzy. I've never come prematurely like that. That was insane. I've never felt this unhinged with anyone. I've always been, I don't know, premeditated. Mechanical."

"You are one horny Casanova," she said breathlessly.

"It's because of you. I've never met a woman who makes me feel this way. I couldn't even wait long enough to pull down my pants. I'm fucking out of bounds. This is all so new. I thought I had all the sex games figured down to a science. What have you done to me? Please admit it. I made you come, right?"

"Sorry. But nope." She lied again, unconvincingly, wishing now that she hadn't thought to trick him. Wishing everything were different. "You will never get me off hanging like this."

"I know I won, girl of my dreams, and you just want to torment me, but whatever. We need to make this real. Let's take it to the back seat and let you have your turn. We can only go for a few minutes, then we have to skedaddle." Between kisses, he said, "I curse you, Belladonna. I'm casting a love spell on you. I'm making you mine forever."

Judith felt his will ensnaring her heart, her soul climaxing with desire. He had her. She was his now. His fateful declaration penetrated her to the core. In response, she drew his lips to hers, breathing fire into his icy regions until he lifted her to his heaven and carried her away.

Chapter 51

Judith

Nicolas uncuffed her from the headrest. She moaned in relief as her arms fell forward. He gathered her to him, sinking his body into hers and kissing her neck. Her legs wrapped around his hips, and they fit perfectly. Her arms locked around his neck, never wanting to let go. She stared into those dreamy dark eyes and felt drunk off her ass with desire.

How the hell had she managed to meet two guys in one week who filled her with this kind of lust? Nicolas was a shot of pure adrenaline, like drinking three Red Bulls straight, and Justin was like a warm cappuccino. The caffeine hit you slower, but tasted just as good. Still, she loved caffeine either way.

"I could commit to you for the rest of my life, Belladonna. I have slept with so many women, but nothing comes close to this. I've always been the one in control, seducing them. Followed all the steps to getting a woman off like the good soldier Catrina taught me to be. But you are seducing me, and you're not even trying! I've never been seduced! It's so wonderful. I've been afraid for so long, but I'm not afraid anymore. Please run away with me. Choose me. Our bodies fit like puzzle pieces. Can't you feel this? The chemistry between us? Isn't it amazing?"

He was right. They were compatible. Maybe even more so than her and Justin. But he was also wrong. Because she had already decided to give her heart to Justin, so this was impossible.

"You screwed it all up, Nicolas. You took my mom. Now you're a wanted man. Because of you, I met that cop, Justin. He was the one who responded to our 911 call when she went missing. He and I. Well, it's not perfect because he won't sleep with me yet, which sucks."

"What do you mean?"

"Justin's a good guy. Says he wants to respect me and doesn't want me to feel used, but I've never had anyone reject me before."

"He sounds like a loser playing hard-to-get to make you chase him. For some assholes, it's the only way they could ever get a girl like you. You've known him for only one week? Fuck him. Choose me."

"It's too late. You set into motion all of these events."

"It's not too late. It can't be. This is fate."

"Then why didn't we meet at the reception?"

"Because I'm a mess. I wish I could go back to the reception and ask you out. I was so hot for you that night. If I were a normal guy, I would have chased you instead of your mom." He looked so sad. "I can't bear to think I've lost you forever because of one dumb mistake. Honestly, though, I had to take Martha. I'm only with you because she somehow freed me from my Catrina obsession. Why is life such a twisted game of fate?"

He sighed and sat up, pulling her onto his lap. Kissed her again and again, and she couldn't resist. Arms around each other, they made out until he lay her head against his chest and held her tight. Finally, he got out of the car, pulled her into his arms, and clung to her like they were in *Gone with the Wind,* the Rhett and Scarlett vibes roiling between them. Their lust reminded her of swimming in the ocean and how the tide pulled you down, no matter how hard you kicked to the surface. The air was freezing, and a dusting of snow lay on the ground. He stood back and ogled her greedily.

"This may be the hottest date I've ever been on. You, deliciously naked and shivering in the snow like some wood nymph. I wish I could record this and watch it over and over. In fact."

He pulled out her phone and took a picture.

"Perfect."

Nicolas looked so innocent, a sweet guy. His untucked bloodied white shirt, unzipped slacks, tousled hair, and even with his battered face, he was gorgeous. He opened the back door with one hand and tossed the black bag outside on the ground while holding her cuffs with the other.

Should she? If she got in that back seat with him, it would be over with Justin. Was it worth it? To lose her one chance with a good guy like Justin forever? Something was happening between Nicolas and her—magical, mystical, and even spiritual. But it wasn't real. Things like this didn't happen in real life. Soulmates were fiction.

Judith waited for his hold to slacken. She yanked her hands free in that split second, catching Nicolas off guard. He lunged for her, but she scampered into the trees.

"Seriously? We're playing hide-and-seek now. You are full of surprises." She heard him step cautiously towards the tree line. With a voice so compelling, he pleaded, "you're naked, Belladonna. You don't need to do this. Is it the cuffs? I'll take them off if you promise to run away with me. I can see us on a beach in Mexico now. Me, stroking your beautiful skin. You will never want for pleasure, and you will discover what a prince I am. I will listen to you endlessly and satisfy your every desire. I have never been a boyfriend and have waited my whole life to be loved. But I know my heart. Let me be your lover, your best friend and your valiant protector."

Judith imagined what it would be like to run away with Nicolas and live like what? Vagabonds? Her mind was overwrought with memories. Or were they fantasies? Hand in hand racing along a sandy shore, running through a forest, jumping into a river, lying next to a fire in the woods, fingers entwined holding a newborn baby, planting a garden, counting the stars, fucking and living and loving—it went on and on. They were all visions of her and Nicolas, from other times and places. Judith had no idea what was happening to her. Fear and confusion—such tremendous sadness and fear. A never-ending, unbroken circle of fate.

"I can hear what you're thinking," he whispered, getting closer, "about the epic sex and the legendary fights we'll have—the erotic future of us. I am too. This is it. The reason I was supposed to take Martha. To find you. We are soulmates. Please don't reject this. I know you feel the same as me. There is something broken in each of us, victims who learned how to tear the world down to survive. I can feel your pain and rage. It more than gets me off. It satisfies me. And I have never in my whole life felt satisfied."

Judith raised her cuffed hands in anticipation. Nicolas stopped, listening, just around the tree—so close. She heard his breathing, inhaled his scent and fought against her animal instincts, which begged her body to surrender. She needed to get back to the safety of her hero as soon as possible.

Justin and the night they met burned like a beacon guiding her out of this madness. The noble cop she wanted so badly, and that something he had that she craved—his approval. She thought of every encounter since. How he didn't want her to feel used and rebuffed her, although she tried so hard to seduce him. How naïve and precious he was. A man with a virgin heart, hers for the taking. How unworthy she felt to be with him. He was like the father she lost—disapproving and treating her like a child—and she wanted to make him love her and never leave her.

Perhaps she did belong with Nicolas. She was a desperate slut like him who had sexted anyone and spread her legs far too often, and she hated that girl behind the beautiful mask. Justin was the first guy who made her think she could be someone different.

Nicolas took another step. His back was to her now. This was her one chance. She had to make her final decision. She had to choose the man she loved, the life she desired, and the woman she wanted to become. Right. This. Second.

Judith sprung. She leaped into the air and threw her arms over his head, squeezing the cuffs against his neck like a garrote, she pulled with the strength of the entire Greek pantheon. She heaved up and wrapped her legs around his waist. Nicolas grasped at his neck, choking and stumbling back towards the car as she squeezed. He fell to his knees, gasping and wheezing. She strained with all her might, screaming with exertion. The veins in his forehead bulged, and his tongue lolled out of his mouth. His skin turned blue. It was a fitting retaliation for him trying to drown her mother. After the longest minute of her entire life, Nicolas collapsed beneath her. She fell to the ground beside him, shoved him onto his back and felt for a pulse. He was still alive.

Judith sat there staring at him, enchanted. She was crying with loss and she couldn't understand why. She loved him, which made no sense because she wanted Justin! Nicolas was so tragic, sad, beautiful and irresistible. Leaning forward, she kissed him until he stirred beneath her lips. She pushed up his shirt and ran her hand over his warm chest. Couldn't stop herself from fondling his groin. He grew hard beneath her fingertips, and it felt so good. She pulled his dick out, held it upright, comparing him to Justin. Nicolas was fucking perfect.

No. Stop. She couldn't pull away, but she had to. Now. Judith fought the urge to mount him and ride him awake. Imagined the euphoria in his eyes if she did. Even half dead, he had power over her. She had to get away from him before she lost her mind. He was inside her head now. How had it happened so quickly? He was a crazy, bad person, yet he was her missing piece. But no. HELL NO.

Judith whispered in his ear,

"I could ride you forever, you gorgeous fuck boy. Let you cuff me, have me and love me, but I refuse to be that girl. Goodbye, Nicolas."

She jumped to her feet. Staring down at his broken face, illuminating his shattered spirit, she realized Nicolas never had a chance. He was a ruined person, like a tomato that had gone rotten on the vine. Her heart throbbed with longing and sorrow. What was the world supposed to do with such people?

Rushing to the car, she climbed in, turned it on and locked the doors. Then she backed up, deliberating. She couldn't decide. Leaving Nicolas would tear her heart in two. Already, she was hemorrhaging from their separation. She lay her head against the steering wheel and cried for the painful loss of letting go.

Chapter 52

Judith

Judith was frozen with indecision because she didn't want to leave Nicolas. If she did, the cops would find him. He would go to prison. This tragic guy would be locked up for life. It was unbearable. But should she sacrifice herself to help him get free? Lose everything else as a result?

Fate shoved her towards Nicolas, the same way it did with Justin. Why? How could life be so cruel? She couldn't have two men! Especially not these two. The hero and the villain? Never. She had to choose!

Judith nearly jumped out of her skin when Nicolas screamed for her to open the door, begging her not to leave him, and pounded against the passenger window. He was going to break the glass. Take her back. Make her his. Oh God, oh God. She wanted to so bad. Let him in and let him have her. Already compromised, her encounter with him was tearing her soul in two.

Instead, she rammed the car in reverse, squealed as she backed up, and then tore off down the pitch-black dirt road. Out on the highway, hands shaking, she considered what to do.

Judith turned left to head back towards Duchesne. Less than a minute later, police lights flashed ahead. She turned on her hazards. Pulled over. So did they. Their door opened. So did hers. She saw Justin stand. Leave his car. Rush towards her. She stepped out on shaking feet and fell headlong into his arms. He carried her to the seat of his car. They couldn't stop kissing. She was unable to stop trembling. Someone gave her a jacket, and Justin pulled it on her after he removed her cuffs. She couldn't form sentences. She never wanted him to let go of her again. Between kisses, he chastised her.

"You should have waited, Judith. You shouldn't have gone in there."

"But I needed to save my mom!"

"We would have saved her. You're impossible. You went up against a maniac, and I had to listen as he almost—I couldn't reach you in time."

Furious, barely controlled, Justin had problems controlling his anger, she realized.

"I'm so sorry. You're right. I was an idiot."

"Where is he? We had a unit following, but they somehow lost you. Went halfway through the canyon, then circled back. We thought we had him boxed in. Did he pull off the road?"

"Nicolas is at a turn-off on the right side," she confessed, wondering if she should have lied to buy him some time. "But don't leave me," she begged, clinging to him like a life raft in the stormy sea of this fated night.

"How did you escape him?"

"I can't tell you. I'm so ashamed!"

"I'm gonna imagine the absolute worst then."

Justin was shaking with rage. She took his face in her hands, trying to calm him. He was about to explode, and she didn't want to see that.

"I can't tell you, Justin. I just can't."

"You said you couldn't lie to me."

"You don't want to know."

"Well, you're fucking naked, so I think I already know."

Of course, he would assume the worst. He sounded so disappointed in her, so she relented.

"Okay. I'll tell you, but please don't hate me. I let him seduce me to get free. Once free, I strangled him with my cuffs until he passed out. Say you'll forgive me!"

She watched Justin's face change. His eyes went black with hatred, and his jaw tensed as her superhero slid to the dark side. Her arrogance had caused this. She had taken Nicolas on and, by doing so, brought this on herself.

"Did he fuck you?" he demanded.

Did dry humping count as sex? She was going to go with a no on this one.

"No. No. He didn't. You can't imagine what he's like. He's persuasive like the devil himself. He cuffed me to the headrest and went down on me for like a minute," Judith cried. She would never *ever* let him know the whole truth.

"Did he get you off?"

Why couldn't she lie to this guy!

"Yes," she confessed in a tiny voice.

"He got you off in one fucking minute?"

She should have kept her mouth shut. She crushed herself against his chest.

"The fight got me hot and bothered. I don't know why."

"You guys were out there for a while. At least fifteen minutes ahead of us. One minute? No way. I'm not buying it. What really went on between you two?"

His eyes bore into her. They weren't even boyfriend and girlfriend yet! How was he already this possessive? What could she say to win him back? Somehow, Justin knew something had developed between her and Nicolas, and all the lying in the world wouldn't cover it up.

"He was making me run away with him. He's in love with me now and wouldn't take no for an answer. It seemed like the only way to get free. I wasn't sure if you were coming!"

Her jacket had fallen open as she sat on his lap, naked except for her socks. His eyes roved all over her body as he kissed the swell of her breasts and her bruised neck, jealousy raging like an angry bull about to trample everything in its path.

"On the phone at the house after the fight, it sounded like a fucking porno. What was he doing to you?"

Judith flushed with embarrassment. She couldn't tell him! Justin looked away. Furious.

"And why did you surrender? You made him think you were begging for it."

"Justin, please. I don't know what that was. Things got out of hand, and I'm not sure why. It was just the fighting. I went crazy, and so did he. It means nothing. Nothing!"

"So you enjoyed him kicking your ass then trying to rape you?"

"I don't know what happened," Judith protested. She tried to catch his eye, and when he looked at her, she saw a violent hunger swirling in those dark eyes.

"I am so pissed at you. I warned you about going up against this guy. I told you he would eat you for breakfast, and you didn't listen. You're so fucking impossible to control."

Pain washed through her. She was going to lose him after sacrificing Nicolas and nearly killing him. The thought was unbearable.

"Justin, I tried to murder Nicolas. Doesn't that mean anything?"

"That's not your job, Judith. That's my job."

He shoved her off his lap and went to let Jones know of Nicolas's whereabouts.

Judith laid her head back and tried not to cry. She made a mistake. Now Justin would never forgive her. She thought of how she sacrificed Nicolas to get back to Justin. She better have made the right choice. Otherwise, she would be haunted forever. What if Nicolas was her soulmate? Could that be possible? Did such things exist? How could fate be this cruel?

Justin returned. He stood in front of her, eyes still angry.

"It's gonna take me a minute to calm down. I really wanted to take down that fucker. You can't imagine what it felt like for me to hear him beat you up, threaten to rape you, nearly fuck you, put his hands all over you, claim you as his then swear his love for you. He's a fucking maniac that needs to be put away for life."

"Justin, don't hate me. I never dreamed this would happen."

"You need to look in my eyes and swear you didn't enjoy it, or else we're done."

Of course, she did. That was the hottest hookup ever. Judith couldn't lie to Justin, and she could never tell him the truth. He closed his eyes in frustration at her long pause. She had to think fast or lose her hot hero cop before she even had a chance to make it work. Justin was the ultimate prize, and she had to have him.

Judith took the risk and kissed him with every bit of lust lingering from her encounter with Nicolas. She wrapped her body around his, pressing close. Stroked between his legs to make sure and felt his instant response. She cast her spell and it worked. He pulled away, flushed and aroused. Satisfied, Judith smiled. She had this boy wrapped around her finger.

"Sorry. You don't need me to be a clingy asshole right now. Even if we did catch up to him, I was afraid he'd go ape shit and take you both over the edge of a cliff. I doubt he would ever let you go. You are smart, Judith, and courageous, using his weakness against him."

"Nicolas is gone now, and he's never coming back. I'm gonna leave it up to you to erase that memory of him, okay?"

She wanted so badly to believe Justin could free her, but Nicolas had already cursed her with his love spell. Still, she consoled him, looked into his eyes, and convinced him she wanted him above all others because she desperately wanted to be the good girl who captured the good guy.

"I am gonna do more than erase that memory. I'm gonna create a million more," he stammered, trying to regain control of himself.

Finally, Justin's face returned to its noble expression.

"I may be your Captain America, but you are my Wonder Woman. I would have loved to see you with your cuffs around his neck, like a whip. You're remarkable. I need you to show us where you left him so we can secure the perimeter. We don't want him to slip through. Can you handle this? If you must see him again?"

"If you are there with me, I can do anything."

They headed back up the dark canyon road, and Judith took them to the spot. Sure enough, Nicolas was gone, along with the black bag.

"How did I fail? I choked him forever!" Judith stared at the empty place on the ground as relief burned through her. Nicolas escaped. Maybe he would make it to Mexico. She thought of how she kissed and touched his inert body like a pervert, then whispered in his ear. She was a horrible person and deserved to get cancer. Justin could never know how sick she was.

Judith found her jeans, panties, boots, and got dressed, then zipped up the jacket. The clothes made her feel less vulnerable.

"Killing someone is hard. It proves you are a good person. Don't worry. We'll have a dozen officers searching this area within an hour. He can't have gone far."

"In the car, I started to feel empathy for Nicolas. He got inside my head, Justin. I'll never be free of him now. It's horrible. It was easier when I hated his guts."

"I'll break you free of him. He's a devil, and you're an angel. This is the way it is in this line of work. Every person who commits a crime has a valid reason for doing so. They usually aren't doing it because they planned to. Nicolas clearly has mental issues and lost control. I love you for having compassion. Even though I certainly don't."

Jones coordinated the search party and left Justin to hold Judith in his arms. He had forgiven her, or so it seemed. They couldn't stop kissing, and now cops were showing up, and Judith was afraid Justin might be embarrassed. He didn't care, and she loved him for it.

"I feel like someone drilled a hole in my heart tonight. Listening to what you went through in that house. I hope you understand. I guess I'm a possessive guy. I never want you out of my sight again. Especially while he's still on the loose. He pledged his undying love. He'll try to come for you, and when he does, I'll be waiting. I want you to move in with me tonight so I can take care of you, protect you, and know you are safe every day from now on. And then I hope to spend the rest of our lives erasing that bastard and this nightmare from existence. So will you? Move in with me?" he asked expectantly.

Justin wanted her to move in with him after only one week? Tears sprang to her eyes. This is what she wanted, wasn't it? A whole new life with someone who loved her? Was this love? She pictured Nicolas lying unconscious in the snow and felt the tears for him roll down her face. She was pretty sure that psycho had stolen her heart, and she had no idea what to do about it.

"Yes, Justin. I will."

He sighed with relief and pumped the air.

"I thought it would take months to convince you. I'm so fucking relieved. This was the worst night of my life. But you're safe now. Just promise never to do anything like this again."

"Justin, please forgive me for what I put you through tonight. I swear I'll make it up to you."

"You may have to say that a few more times," he murmured fiercely.

And she would. She'd say it one hundred times if it meant he would love her.

But something deep inside her had awakened. Nicolas had satisfied her body and soul in a way she had never experienced before. He wrecked her with that exquisite orgasm, and lying to him about it wrecked her even further. Their death match and fated encounter were beyond the scope of her imagination. She couldn't stop thinking about him and was afraid she never would. Her mind raged with the obsession he imposed on her. To her horror, after getting her ass chewed out by Justin, she regretted not running away with him.

Judith was convinced she had made the right choice with Justin. So why did her heart feel broken? Nicolas was a criminal, and he didn't deserve her love. She would fight this, beat this, and force her heart into the shape she wanted it to take.

Justin was talking to her. She needed to pull it together and stuff this experience somewhere down deep.

"I have some good news."

"What?"

"Your mom was conscious when I left. They took her to the hospital by medevac. Erik let Jones know that it looks promising. You prevented massive blood loss by getting her bandaged so quickly. They'll keep us updated."

Judith fell against his chest and she sobbed for joy.

Chapter 53

Nicolas

Nicolas stood there freezing, his heart like a precious gem torn from an iceberg as Belladonna drove away. This was unthinkable. It couldn't be happening. His whole life led to this point: finding her. He saw it all with exceptional clarity. It started with Catrina abandoning him. His obsession to replace her grew as he got older, which ultimately led him to Martha, who, like a complete psychopath, he abducted and tried to seduce, only to lose her to his fucking dad. Then came the apex moment—the daughter arrived to rescue her mom from his clutches and then slipped through his grasp.

Madly, he thought of what to do. It was pitch black, and the ground was dusted with snow. He unlocked her phone and looked at the photo of her he had taken only minutes before. She was naked and so stunningly gorgeous that he had no words to describe how she made him feel. He wanted to sit and stare, work a little magic on himself, and fantasize a new ending from the one he was currently forced to endure. But he also had to get the hell out of here. So, he turned on the phone flashlight instead and started down the trail.

Why had Belladonna done this? Nicolas was convinced he had given her the best orgasm of her life, and she lied through her teeth. Why? Of course. She tricked him. Knew he would uncuff her and take her to the back seat. She used his lust against him, and it worked. Brilliant. Like some hot CIA spy. It made him want her more.

Belladonna was his soulmate, and now she was inside him, her sassy cynicism echoing in his head, calling him a jackass, a narcissist and telling him that he was damaged beyond repair. Her eyes on him when he jerked off—the raging lust in those blazing eyes. Kicking his ass, then getting him so aroused that he went insane.

Oh my God. He was cursed. She was a witch; she had to be. No woman had ever made him feel this way. Her straightforward manner. She would never tolerate bullshit. She was a dream come true.

Tears froze on his face as he thought about her cradled in his arms beneath him after he dry-humped her like some perverted maniac. Where had all his smooth Casanova moves gone? He went at her like a fifteen-year-old just graduating from wet dreams, like an idiot. When she stared into his eyes, her cuffed hands linked around his neck, that moment lasted forever. They were a perfect fit. He couldn't live without her.

Nicolas had always been reckless and uncontrollable, especially when it came to sex. He'd fuck anyone at any time. Now he felt her pulling his heartstrings together, binding him into some version of normalcy and making sense of his madness. She was like Martha, but better because she was the one he was meant to find.

He hadn't taken his pills for over a week, and he could tell. Plus, Martha was right, he was undergoing a psychotic break from those horrid memories of Catrina trying to drown him. He was a fucking mess, and he had a mental illness that made him obsessed with finding someone to love him, but he knew—HE KNEW—he was right about this. He and Belladonna belonged together.

To his astonishment, he nearly walked headlong into a camper with a car parked beside it. He padded closer and, to his even greater astonishment, saw that the keys were lying in the cup holder and the door was unlocked. It was an old car from the nineties, which you might expect to find in the sticks. He opened the door quietly and crawled into the front seat, placing his bag of cash on the passenger seat.

He started the car and drove away with the lights off. A light flickered on in the camper, but he steadied his nerves and kept his eyes peeled for a way through the rough terrain.

It had been less than twenty minutes since she tried to kill him. His throat was on fire, and his neck throbbed with pain. Why did she do it? Why did she try to kill him and then abandon him? And when he lay there, slowly gaining consciousness, he felt her hands arousing him. Heard the sexy words she whispered. Belladonna was his missing piece.

The heat and desire that rolled off her still vibrated through him. He was sure he had never been with a woman who responded so easily to his touch. She looked drunk on desire and loved being in the cuffs. She wanted to scream with ecstasy so badly that she was biting her tongue. Why didn't she? Why did she resist him? He even put forth an excellent argument for why they belonged together. He nearly convinced her! It couldn't be because of that fucking cop, could it?

Nicolas refused to let this happen. He was a survivor. He had to fight harder for what he wanted than most people, and he was fine with it. There was no way this was over. He would have Belladonna's love if it were the last thing he did.

Driving with his lights off, he sped off down the main highway. He had to reach the border before they put out a nationwide search. Hoped to God he could pull this off and make it into Mexico using his dad's passport. This car was nothing like the Mercedes, which sucked, but pedal to the metal, he made it through the canyon in less than thirty minutes and hauled ass towards Price. From there, he returned to the I-15 and set the cruise control at eighty-five. He had a full tank of gas. Probably would only need to gas up once with this tiny junker.

He stopped once, grabbed four Red Bulls to keep himself awake and refueled. He hadn't seen a single cop, so he felt confident about his getaway. This sucked, though. He was leaving everything and everyone behind. Not the way he wanted things to go. Around ten in the morning, he arrived at the border and joined the line to drive through. They checked his passport and car registration. Thank God no one reported the car stolen yet. They didn't say a word. Home free.

He studied a Google map, trying to formulate a game plan. He had some money, so he should be fine for now. But where should he head? Mexico City? He stared at the map, feeling even more lost than on his first day at Berkeley. After being a shut-in kid who was sick all the time and missed more school than not, to living in a mental hospital, then suddenly thrust into the world, college was brutal. But this. He didn't speak Spanish and had no idea how to survive on his own—had never done so. This would be harder still.

Nicolas decided on Cabo San Lucas. It was touristy, so there would likely be plenty of server jobs. Once he chose, he set his destination on her phone and headed west towards the coast. A day later, leaning against his car, staring at the Pacific Ocean, and scrolling through her phone, he was delighted to find tons of nude photos and sex videos. This girl was hotter than every woman he'd ever slept with combined. It was insane how much he wanted her. Like a disease, but one that he was happy to have contracted. These should keep him sustained until his hands were on her delicious body once again.

Nicolas furiously thought about how in the hell to contact her. He had to contact her and establish a link. There was only one option. He researched which high school she attended, created a fake Facebook account as a classmate, and sent her a friend request. To his astonishment, she accepted right away. He got to work. He was going to stalk the fuck out of this girl and learn how she ticked from the inside out. Time for more self-talk. Time to invoke The Secret like he never had before. He needed the help of the entire universe if he even stood a chance at winning his soulmate's heart.

For the first time in his life, Nicolas felt happy. His Catrina obsession drained him. Chasing older women kept him imprisoned, forcing him to re-traumatize himself as he struggled to recreate that dynamic. Somehow, Saint Martha broke the cycle. She helped to free his heart, which instantly found a new home where it belonged forever, with Belladonna. He closed his eyes and let the tears roll down his face. There was a reason he survived the suicide attempts and the nightmare years of child abuse. There was a reason he lost Martha to his dad. And soon, Belladonna would know he had her to thank for restoring his quest for love.

Chapter 54

Martha

Nicolas was a catalyst. He brought them together and then nearly destroyed them. A tsunami of obsession and unquenchable longing, he sought to crawl out of his personal hell by rebuffing the trauma imposed on him. He was everything to despise and so easy to hate. But out of his madness, two lonely people were fused into one. That is how Martha saw things now. She would never stop loving Nicolas and hoped he would escape to build a life worth living for himself.

Martha gave her official statement to the police. Said she had left her girls in the car and willingly went with Nicolas. Yes, he followed her and seduced her, but she couldn't resist. This lie was easy because the night he took her, he asked her first, and a huge part of her wanted to up and leave her lonely life and run away with that beautiful boy. She explained how she met Erik, who lived in the basement, and swiftly formed a relationship. Didn't mention the drowning at all and begged Erik to tell Judith not to either. When they asked about the empty bucket, she played dumb. Martha explained that everything, including the lingerie and Erik being handcuffed as well as the knife, was all part of a sex game. This made her blush furiously, and she felt ridiculous. She would never do such a thing in real life, and she knew the police doubted she would either.

Martha convinced Erik to go on record saying that the knife incident was purely accidental, that Nicolas never meant to harm her. As for what went on between Nicolas and Judith once he took her, she could only guess. There was fire between those two as they fought over the knife. Whatever hatred they initially felt towards each other would quickly morph into a sexual encounter the moment they were alone, of that she was sure.

Nicolas had shown extreme interest in Judith from the beginning, and Judith showed all the signs of heated attraction when she goaded him into a rage in her feisty, flirtatious manner. She wondered what Judith wasn't saying about their encounter in the canyon. Martha could tell she harbored a secret and imagined that if Nicolas seduced her, she would never admit it to Justin or another living soul.

Lying was her gift to that broken young man. The police looked at her skeptically, and her story didn't add up. But she had to. Nicolas would never see the light of day again if he were arrested. The system didn't make exceptions for those suffering from emotional conditions, and they looked at the term "psychotic break" as a cop-out provided by the defense and the bleeding-heart mental health community. Prison would kill that boy for sure. She couldn't have that on her conscience.

Nicolas's life was heartbreaking, and she had experienced his trauma with him the night he remembered Catrina's attempts to drown him. She couldn't put him through any more suffering. Law enforcement would likely bring charges against Nicolas for Judith's abduction. It didn't look good that Judith was found stark naked in the canyon, but the rape kit came back negative. Who knew? Maybe the boy would get off scot-free. She could only hope. If it ever went to court, she'd speak in his defense.

She was healing well from her surgery and was due to leave the hospital today. Erik had begged her to move in with him. He barely left her side for the last week. Slept on the couch in the corner and only retreated when the nurses kicked him out of the hospital. Martha thought of everything they had gone through and marveled that she had found the man of her dreams.

"I was going to wait to give you this, but I can't."

Erik procured a small box and opened it. Martha gasped. It was a beautiful ring with a splendid opal surrounded by diamonds. It had to be worth at least five thousand dollars.

"If marriage is too big a word, I won't say it. Take it as a token of my affection."

Martha took his face and pressed her cheek to his.

"I would be honored to be your wife."

"I feel so guilty knowing it was my flesh and blood that nearly killed you. Twice. I created him."

"Erik, you conceived him. Life created him. Life can and often is a brutal force that strips us of our dignity and sanity. For Nicolas, life has been a soul-crushing nightmare, and he strove to break free from it by pulling others down with him. I forgive him for this, and I hope you will too."

"Well, Saint Martha, I would be honored to have and to hold till death do us part with you. If you can handle sharing a life with this old pushover."

"You, dear sweet man, are the stuff my dreams are made of. I will be yours forever."

"Everything is set. You'll be in your new home by nightfall."

"Thank you."

He kissed her until someone was at the door, clearing their throat. Martha looked up. It was Craig. The two men sized each other up, and Martha saw Craig's feathers flare. He would always consider her his, even though he threw her away like trash.

"Let me pull the car around." Erik didn't acknowledge Craig as he left the room.

"It looks like you hit the jackpot. Gorgeous and rich too." Craig said nastily.

"Did you want something?"

"You went missing due to my wedding. I guess I feel responsible."

Craig sat down. To Martha's shock, tears glistened in his eyes.

"What I did, leaving you and the girls, was unforgivable. I want you to know I realize that. It was impossible to say no to Lori. I was never good enough for you, Martha. I know that now. And I'm sorry about inviting you to my wedding. Forcing you to lose me all over like that. It was a dick move."

She nodded mutely, overcome with emotion.

"Anyhow, I don't know what happened or why you took off with that server. You must have been out of your mind with grief. But I get it. I might have done the same thing just to forget. I suppose it all worked out for you. Thank God you survived."

"Thanks to our fearless daughter," Martha managed. She was so embarrassed. Covering for Nicolas's crime was going to mar her reputation for life.

"Judith is something else."

"You met Justin?"

"She adores him, doesn't she? Never took my baby girl for hooking up with a cop."

"I know. He's such a good guy. She calls him her hero. It's sweet. I'm so happy for her."

"Life is crazy. Well, Lori is waiting in the car. I just wanted to wish you well and tell you I'm jealous, but I'll get over it. If anyone deserves to be loved the right way, it's you."

"Thank you, Craig. Best of luck to you."

Craig nodded, kissed her on the cheek, and left.

The nurse gathered Martha's things and moved her into a wheelchair. Martha could walk, but decided to keep her feet up and let the world take care of her for a change.

Although Nicolas missed her heart when he stabbed her, he punctured it permanently over that fateful week. She went too deep into the jungles of his trauma, thinking she might conduct a field study and nothing more. Instead, she went native, trying to unravel his mystery. In her futile attempt to save him, part of her was now lost somewhere in his soul, and it made no sense. But that was what trauma did. It stole parts of you and twisted them into every sort of heartbreak imaginable.

She thought of that broken man who had succumbed to his compulsion to abduct her and endured an ache so deep she feared she might never recover. It wasn't true love and felt more like pure agony, like unrequited love, but dark and incomprehensible. He absorbed her pain, and she absorbed his. Nicolas might never break free from his psychological bondage. But she believed that when he plunged that knife into her, it took something from him. Something, hopefully, he would never get back.

The nurse whisked her down the hall. Erik whisked her away in the car. The next thing she knew, she was standing in the living room of a gorgeous custom home. Erik put his arms around her and kissed her neck.

"Martha, welcome to your new life."

Martha turned and embraced this wonderful new beginning with the sweetest man ever to live, silently thanking the darkness for leading her into the light.

About the Author

Tanya Madsen has a BA in English and a passion for emotional drama. When she's not working her day job as a technical writer, she writes novels, plays computer games, cuddles with her fur babies, or relaxes in the mountains. She lives in Northern Utah with her husband and four grown children.

http://www.tanyamadsen.com